GUARDING EVELYN

What Reviewers Say About Erin Zak's Work

The Other Women

"This book is like a love letter to anyone with a broken heart. Erin Zak is telling you that you will get through it, and if someone breaks your heart, they were never worthy in the first place."—*Les Rêveur*

The Road Home

"Zak writes interesting, unusual and unique circumstances in which the leading ladies meet but their chemistry is so awesome right off the bat that you are rooting for them all along. …This is a wonderfully immersive read and highly recommended."—*Best Lesfic Reviews*

"Lila and Gwen have chemistry for days. They also have quick witty banter that keeps you on your toes. I love this angsty drama, it is just an amazing read. I could gush over this one for days, but I am just going to say don't deny yourself this one."—*Romantic Reader Blog*

Beautiful Accidents

"The main characters had so much chemistry I felt like I was right there with them observing every interaction. The attraction was so well written from their first meeting. The writing was engaging and well paced."—Melina Bickard, Librarian (Waterloo Library, London UK)

"*Beautiful Accidents* is an intriguing and exciting romance with real depth, and I really appreciated how romance is reframed as enrichment rather than sacrifice. Stevie and Bernadette never give up any aspects of their real identities to be together; Zak has created a pair of characters that are definitely going to stick with me."—*Beyond the Words*

"This book kept me engaged from beginning to end. I enjoyed the chemistry between Stevie and Bernadette."—Maggie Shullick, Librarian, Lorain and Cuyahoga County (Ohio)

"[T]his lesbian age gap romance book is [Zak's] best to date. This is an easy one to recommend to romance fans who like a lot of chemistry and some angst."—*Lez Review Books*

"[I]f you want big dramatic feelings, Zak is the way to go."—Colleen Corgel, Librarian, Queens Borough Public Library

"This book made my heart ache from the start. When Stevie sees Bernadette for the first time, her breath catches. Mine did too. The way Erin Zak describes reactions, both physical and mental, pulled me in absolutely. It's both wonderful and painful. It's what I'm looking for in romances. It's the best feeling."—*Jude in the Stars*

"Zak takes her time with the characters in developing them as individuals and allowing the relationship time to develop. ...This is a bit more of a mature romance in that there is unquestionably a connection but both characters recognize that with their lives at major turning points...that HEA isn't easy and compromising for the other person holds the danger of regret. There's drama, but not overblown—it's real, messy and complicated with difficult decisions that have to be made."—*C-Spot Reviews*

Create a Life to Love

"Erin Zak does unexpected attraction and sexual awakening late in life really, really well."—*Reviewer@large*

"*Create A Life To Love* is a soulful story of how love can conquer all. I laughed, cried (sobbed) and got butterflies more than once, and did you see the cover art? Fantastic."—*Les Rêveur*

"This is officially one of my favorite books of all time."—Maggie Shullick, Librarian, Lorain and Cuyahoga County (Ohio)

Breaking Down Her Walls

"If I could describe this book in one word it would be this: annnngggssstt. …If angst is your thing, this a great book for you." —Colleen Corgel, Librarian, Queens Public Library

"*Breaking Down Her Walls* had me completely spun. One minute I'm thinking that it's such a sweet romance, the next I found it sexy as hell then by the end, I had it as an all-encompassing love story that I just adored."—*Les Rêveur*

"I loved the attraction between the two main characters and the opposites attract part of the story. The setting was amazing. …I look forward to reading more from this author."—Kat Adams, Bookseller (QBD Books, Australia)

"This is a charming contemporary romance set on a cattle ranch near the Colorado Mountains. …This is a slow burn romance, but the chemistry is obvious and strong almost from the beginning. *Breaking Down her Walls* made me feel good…"—*Rainbow Reflections*

"If you like contemporary romances, ice queens, ranchers, or age gap pairings, you'll want to pick up *Breaking Down Her Walls*." —*Lesbian Review*

Falling Into Her

"*Falling Into Her* by Erin Zak is an age gap, toaster oven romance that I really enjoyed. The romance has a nice burn that's slow without being too slow. And while I'm glad that lesfic isn't all coming out stories anymore, I enjoyed this particular one because it shows how it can happen in a person's 40s."—*Lesbian Review*

Visit us at www.boldstrokesbooks.com

By the Author

Falling into Her

Breaking Down Her Walls

Create a Life to Love

Beautiful Accidents

Closed Door Policy (Novella in Hot Ice)

The Road Home

The Other Women

Guarding Evelyn

GUARDING EVELYN

Lauren,

Thank you for everything.
You are amazing. Head up!

– ♡ – [signature]

by

Erin Zak

BOLD
STROKES
BOOKS

2021

GUARDING EVELYN

ISBN 13: 978-1-63555-841-8

This Trade Paperback Original Is Published By
Bold Strokes Books, Inc.
P.O. Box 249
Valley Falls, NY 12185

First Edition: March 2021

CREDITS
Editor: Barbara Ann Wright
Production Design: Susan Ramundo
Cover Design By Tammy Seidick

Acknowledgments

Whelp. This one, you guys. Damn. This one *almost* killed me. And I only mean because writing during a pandemic, trying to find creativity during quarantine, working with characters who had no idea what I was going through mentally, was absolutely awful. I know there are people out there who have suffered through a lot worse, but damn, this was not fun. Ten out of ten, would not recommend.

That being said, I finished it! And I wouldn't have without my amazing editor's help. Barbara, without you, I wouldn't be even more afraid of spiders and I would have never laughed at all while doing my first editing read-through of this. It's been a long road. That's for sure. Thank you so much for not giving up on me. Even though I would have never questioned it if you would have.

Thank you so much to Radclyffe, Sandy, and the entire BSB team. It's so amazing to work with you all. I am blessed. Truly.

To Gail, who saw every up and down this writing journey took me on—THANK YOU. Seriously. I don't know what I would do without you.

And last, but never least, thank you to anyone who picks this book up. I sincerely hope it doesn't disappoint you. And I hope you enjoy the ride.

PROLOGUE

"Madame President, are you always on edge now?" Alden Ryan bites her cheek to stop from showing too much of herself.

Jennifer Simmons, America's first female president, pours iced tea into two slim clear glasses. She's slender, with shoulder-length blond hair and blue eyes, the picture of small-town USA. She is an intimidating woman, though, and as the first in a long history of men, has gone through her share of turmoil. The latest has caused the entire administration to take a breath and examine things they wouldn't otherwise examine. Including and especially, her relationship with Alden.

"Sometimes, Alden, yes." She looks over her shoulder. Her blue eyes are piercing. "Are you?"

Alden's right canine begins to penetrate the soft, wet skin of her cheek. She wants to lie. She wants to be the picture of strength and courage the Secret Service is supposed to stand for. She wants to say proudly that she is not scared, nor will she ever be. But she can't bring herself to lie to the woman she's grown so close to over the years of her first term. She breathes out as she nods.

"Do you regret it?" President Simmons glides across the Oval Office and hands her a glass of iced tea.

Alden breaks eye contact and looks at the way the president grips the glass, and she wonders if she'll ever get over the honorable, yet harsh experience of fulfilling an oath. The oath to take a bullet if needed. She didn't hesitate in the moment. She did everything she was supposed to do. Except being in that moment to begin with. But is getting shot supposed to ruin everything inside her? Including a spleen and three ribs?

She finally looks back into the president's blue eyes and stands straighter. "I will never regret it, Madame President."

The president smiles her perfect smile, places a hand on Alden's right bicep, and squeezes. "I don't regret it, either." She turns, motions to the sofa, and sits in one fluid motion. "Please. Sit with me."

Alden does as instructed, unbuttoning her black suit jacket before cautiously sitting on the soft cushion. She's still healing, still sore in more ways than one, and movement causes a lot of discomfort. The pain isn't the only discomfort, though, as the president sips her tea.

"I think you know what I want to speak with you about."

Alden holds her breath.

"I spoke with Director Stevens. He and I are on the same page, but I asked if I could speak with you."

She rolls her lips together and closes her eyes. She can't bear to look at the president. At Jennifer. She knows what's coming.

"We've agreed you should take leave to…heal."

Alden doesn't respond. She keeps her eyes closed.

"Director Stevens has reported you've been very distant. Removed. And I know why but…"

Alden keeps her eyes clamped, closing the route for the shame that has been backed up for miles. "I'm so sorry." She opens her eyes, forces a brave face, and smiles. "I'm trying. I really am. But getting past this"—she motions between them—"has been so much harder than I anticipated." She tries to be as convincing as possible because it has been very difficult. But *so much harder than she anticipated* is really just code for *the toughest hill she has ever climbed in her entire life.*

"I understand. I do. But things are tense right now, and I need to know everyone is on their A game."

"President Simmons—"

"Alden, please. You know this isn't what I want." Her voice is whisper-soft, and Alden swears there is a sadness that Jennifer wouldn't let just anyone see.

Her breath snags. She opens her mouth, but no sound escapes.

"You taking that bullet for me..." Her eyes, *Jennifer's beautiful eyes*, fill with tears and blink rapidly as she reaches for a Kleenex to dab at the wetness. She's just a woman now. A lovely woman with the most intense eyes, and seeing her get so emotional that honest-to-God tears form in her eyes is an event Alden never thought she'd have to experience.

"Madame President, please don't let me go."

In an instant, President Simmons's expression changes, and the fragile facade is replaced with the determined demeanor of the formidable woman who won the presidency by a landslide. "You need to heal. Physically. Emotionally. Mentally. And quite frankly, so do I." She raises her glass to her lips, and Alden sees the tremor in her hand. This decision is not easy, and protesting is not only *not* an option but is also incredibly disrespectful, so Alden forces herself to swallow the disappointment, the sadness, *and* the anger. When the president sets her glass on the coffee table, she stands. Alden stands as well and takes her extended hand. "Thank you for...for...*everything*."

Alden's healing injuries aren't where the sincerity in the president's voice hits her. She feels it in her heart as it squeezes and closes in on itself. "Thank you, Madame President." Her voice comes out as a whisper, and when the president squeezes her hand before promptly letting go, Alden knows that healing emotionally will be the hardest thing she's ever had to do.

CHAPTER ONE

Two days later, Alden stands in front of her parents' Wrigleyville townhome with a sense of dread hanging over her like a raincloud. She's thirty-four. She isn't supposed to be moving back in with her parents. This was not part of her plan. Not now. Not ever. So this whole thing, the idea of having to move back home to Chicago with her family, is quite suffocating. Sure, she has more than enough money to rent something on her own, but the stress that accompanies that makes her want to curl into the fetal position. Regardless of her ma and pops's overbearing tendencies, it's easier to move in with family rather than try to do this on her own. They mean well, but she can practically hear her ma asking her if she is planning on making her bed today or her pops shouting at her when she tells him for the hundredth time that she really is a democrat.

A small part of her hopes for relief. Relief at not having a stressful job anymore. Relief that she has no one to report to. Relief that she can finally find a little peace inside her very not-peaceful brain.

"Well, are ya just gonna stand there?" Her parents' neighbor Ricky is standing a few paces away, cane in hand. He looks awful, but his presence is calming for some reason.

"Zigzag," she says, calling him by the nickname he's used for as long as she can remember. He's not a stranger to anyone on the block. He makes sure of it. The best part is, his gravelly voice makes her smile for the first time since getting off the plane at Midway.

"I heard the only way to get in a house these days is to go *inside* the house."

She squeezes his shoulder when he approaches, and he smiles haggardly, showing off coffee-stained teeth. "Is that so?"

He laughs, clears his throat, and plants the end of his cane firmly into the ground. "You know," he starts, his voice much softer now. "I heard what happened."

The pain in Alden's abdomen radiates. It doesn't hurt often, but when it does, it reminds her of how small and insignificant she is ninety-nine percent of the time. "Yeah," she says over a sharp breath. "Not fun."

"I admire you. Your courage. Don't sell yourself short."

Alden is not a crier. She never has been. But lately? She can't seem to hold back any sort of emotion, including tears, which happen more frequently and without warning. Her sudden lack of an emotional gauge isn't annoying so much as it's hard to handle. "How're the Cubbies doing?" She doesn't want to let this old man see her cry. Especially since he admires her. Zigzag admiring her. She thought she'd never see the day. She vividly remembers getting yelled at for riding her bike through his yard.

His gray eyes twinkle. "They're good this year. Better than last and David Ross is back."

"Oh yeah. I heard about that. Manager. How fun."

"It's gonna be a great season. Heading into May over five hundred."

"That's my boys in blue."

Ricky begins to hobble away, his cane thumping onto the sidewalk. "Come listen to a game one day," he shouts over his shoulder. "I know you'll need to get away from your parents."

Alden laughs, low and deep. "You know me so well."

"Maybe you're the good luck we need."

"Gotta be better than a goat, eh?" Alden shouts, and Ricky holds his cane in the air, mimicking a cheering position.

She glances back at the house. After one deep breath, then another, she rolls her suitcase to the steps leading to the front door. With each step, another memory slams into her: her first skinned knee, spraining an ankle playing basketball at the park, getting her shoelace caught in the chain of her bike. She loves her parents more than anything. But not having to report to them on an hourly basis has been amazing. She lived with them throughout college, throughout her tiny stint at the Chicago Police Department, and then lit out and hoped she would never have to go back. If only her mental state was a little better, she wouldn't have to go back on that promise to herself.

"You can do this," she says as she unlocks and pushes the heavy wooden door open.

The smell of her ma's perfume, her pops's aftershave, Bounce fabric softener, every scent she grew up with, envelops her. *Home.* She can also smell pierogis. Her ma makes them every single time she comes home for a visit. Except she's not home for a visit. She's not home for just a few days.

She's home for the foreseeable future.

Her stomach flips at the cruel sting of reality.

She props her suitcase by the table in the entryway and maneuvers through the cramped hallway. "Ma? Pops?" She listens, then moves toward the back of the house and the kitchen.

"Oh, Aldie." Her ma swings her tiny body around and bounds across the kitchen. Alden has been told since she was five how much she resembles her ma. Same sharp features, same green eyes. The only difference is their hair. She inherited her pops's blond. Ma is sixty-five and still moves like a teenager. Her salt and pepper hair is cut short, but she has pushed her bangs back with a purple headband. She's already getting a tan from putzing around in their small backyard, planting her garden. Seeing her smile moves something inside Alden's chest. She wonders if this will be the moment she finally breaks down. Her ma wraps her arms around Alden and holds her close. She pulls away and places her warm hands on Alden's cheeks. "Are you okay? How are you holding up?"

"Ugh, Ma, I'm fine, okay?"

"Like hell you're fine," comes her pops's booming voice. He enters from the backyard, and she can hear AM 670, with Pat Hughes, the Cubs announcer calling the game as the screen door slams shut behind him. Pops is a large man with no sense of fashion whatsoever. His plaid button-down does not match the black shorts, and he's wearing socks with slippers. As hilarious as he looks, retirement also looks really good on him. "Get your skinny ass over here and give me a hug. You've had us worried sick."

Alden smiles as she takes two strides and hugs him. "Pops, I'm fine, I promise."

He chuckles and smacks her back lightly with his large, heavy hand. "Who'd have thunk you were going to have to take a bullet for the president?" Everything he's doing—holding her, his large hand thumping her back, even the smell of his aftershave—is hitting her way harder than she expected. "Maybe you can regale us with how it went down?"

"Yeah, probably not." She sighs. "It's a lot of top-secret details I'm not supposed to let civilians in on," Alden says with a chuckle laced with far too much sorrow than she's comfortable showing. If she couldn't let Ricky see her cry and didn't lose it when her ma hugged her, there's no way she's going to let her hard-ass dad see her cry. No way in hell.

"Well, you're home now, Aldie." Her ma gently touches her shoulder. "And I'm making pierogis, and we have stuffed cabbage, too."

She can't help but smile. On a normal day, she could really take a pass on stuffed cabbage. Her ma knows this, but for some reason, she is looking forward to it. Coming home has its disadvantages, but free food is definitely not one of them. And all she has to do is ask for cookies, and her ma will have a freshly baked pile of chocolate chip deliciousness in front of her. She doesn't have it as bad as her anxious brain is trying to tell her. If she can just settle down, relax, and find a place inside herself to hide all of these godforsaken feelings, maybe she can get back to the White House one day.

It's a pipe dream. But no one ever said a word about dreams being a bad thing.

Chapter Two

Things are weirder than usual at home.

Ma has upped her overbearing game, which is one-hundred-percent out of worry, even if she won't admit that's the case. But it's obvious. Glaringly so. As endearing as worrying can be, it can be equally as aggravating.

"Do you want a sandwich?"

I can make a freaking sandwich myself.

"Do you need me to do your laundry?"

You haven't done my laundry since I turned sixteen. Why would you start again now?

"Didn't you have a different shirt on an hour ago? Or do you enjoy me doing your laundry?"

You don't need to do my laundry, Ma.

"Want to go to Mariano's with me?"

I want some peace and quiet, so no. But I'll take some of that awesome fresh salsa they make.

"Don't lift those boxes, Alden, you're going to hurt yourself."

I'm a grown woman. I can lift a freaking box.

"I ironed your sheets."

For Pete's sake, why would you iron sheets? Of all the ridiculous things to do.

The constant hovering and fussing causes Alden to be on edge way more than normal. Her parents have always been super involved in her life, especially growing up. When she left for the Secret Service, they backed off a lot, which Alden loved. She could finally breathe.

But the last week or so has been off the charts. She loves them to death, but lately, they're both too much.

Even Pops doesn't know what to do with himself. He asks about a zillion questions and hangs out for none of the answers. "You still in pain? I bet that bullet really did a number on ya, huh? Damn, the time I got shot was so painful. You better be showing that scar off, okay? That's what it's there for. To show you were doing your job." And then he turns and walks out. Doesn't matter what room they're in. Unless it's the kitchen. In that case, he grabs a bag of pretzels and *then* leaves.

Thankfully, Ma hosts a book club on Thursday nights. A few ladies who attend have been in Alden's life since she was a child. There's Ruth Dean, Tina Doolin, and Millie Masters, each of them nurses who worked together in the emergency room at Cook County Hospital, where they saw their fair share of rough times and leaned on one another to get through it all. There are also a couple new ladies who were brought into the fold right before Ma retired. They're a loud, rambunctious group, and Alden is surprised they get any discussion about books done at all.

When Alden comes bounding down the steps so she can go for an evening run, they're seated around the living room coffee table, wine in hand, laughing about a patient who, "had a pair of pliers stuck up his anus."

Apparently, they really *don't* get any discussion about books done.

"No! His anus?"

"Right up it. We kept asking how it happened, and he kept saying—"

"I fell on them," Ruth, Tina, and Ma say in unison. They descend into laughter, including the younger nurses.

"Things don't happen like that anymore."

"Oh no, they come in with dildos stuck in their anus now."

"They came in with dildos up their butts then, too, y'know. We just didn't gossip about it as much." Ruth sips her wine after she raises her eyebrows in mock judgment.

"We were just gossiping about each other's sex lives."

Ruth and Tina shout, "Hear, hear," and Ma laughs and laughs. They should be discussing *Where the Crawdads Sing*.

"Aldie, honey, come say hello before you take off into the night."

Alden, her hand on the doorknob, rolls her eyes and swings around. "Ma," she says softly and shakes her head. "You're in the middle of a very lively conversation. I didn't want to interrupt."

"Oh my word, is that Alden?"

Alden laughs. "Hello, everyone." She waves in a sweeping motion. "Miss Ruth, how are you?" She leans down to hug Ruth Dean. She's aged well. "And Miss Tina, you look great."

"Well, hello there, brat." Tina smacks Alden on the rear end and laughs. "I can't believe you. All grown-up."

Ruth smiles as she places a hand on Alden's face. "We remember you coming into the emergency room with your papa to visit when we were working. Hard to believe that was thirty years ago."

"Almost thirty-one," Ma says with a chuckle before she sips her wine. "Okay, you're free to go."

Alden pushes through the gaggle of ladies and makes it out the door without having to stop again. The minute her shoes hit the street, she takes off toward Wrigley Field. It's a gorgeous spring evening in the city. There's a game going on tonight, but she doesn't care. She loves the hustle and bustle when there's a game. The sights, the sounds, the scents, the people. She missed every single thing about Chicago. Even the bitter cold.

But summer in Chicago is by far her favorite time of the year. The days getting longer and the weather getting warmer is exactly what she needs to get her through the depression pumping through her veins. She would never tell a soul she's feeling this way. She isn't even sure what *this way* is. Things are different. Not light, *heavy*. Not complete, *missing*. And something foreign exists inside her, and it's not the shrapnel they couldn't remove.

Or maybe it is?

Either way, running helps. Doesn't it always? Running from her past. Running from her problems. Running from her parents. Running from her gunshot wound. Running from her depression.

Her feet hitting the pavement, the *thud thud thudding* of her Adidas as she speeds up, the blood coursing, her knees aching the familiar torn meniscus ache. Every other sensation is better than explaining what is really going on.

Because how does she explain what is really going on when she doesn't know? She could wager a guess and would probably be correct, but it can't be that easy. Can it? Talking about it would help. At least that's what she's been told a thousand times. But who would she talk to?

She could tell her pops. He's a retired cop. He'd know and understand. But then he'd look at her like the weakling she is. He'd finally see the truth.

She could tell her ma. She's seen gunshot wound after gunshot wound from working overnight shifts in the emergency room. She understands intimately what a body looks like when a bullet rips through the flesh, nicks an internal organ, leaves the person completely debilitated, physically but also mentally.

Or...

She can keep it bottled up because that's *super* healthy. And she's all about healthy.

As Alden turns onto Addison from Magnolia Street, the ballpark comes into view. The lights are on, and it's sure to be a great game between the Cubs and the Astros. She's itching to get to a game, even if it means going with Ricky. Pops is a diehard fan, but he hasn't been to the stadium since his father died. "Too many memories," he says, then quickly changes the subject.

She waits patiently for the light to turn green, jogging behind a group of girls who are decked out in Cubs gear, who have most definitely been drinking. Are they even old enough? She chuckles at the memory of her first time getting drunk at a game.

There are so many memories. So many good times. So many horrible times. But more importantly, there are so many things she was almost taken from. One gunshot and *bam*.

It could have ended so much differently.

When she arrives in front of the field, she stops, pulls her earbuds out, and stares at the giant sign.

Wrigley Field, Home of Chicago Cubs.

She's home. *Finally*. And as much as she might be struggling, it is really fucking good to have these city streets back under her feet.

❖

Alden's run is one of the best she's had since being back at home. She is invigorated as she strips and jumps into the shower afterward. Her ma is still going strong with her friends, and her pops is across the street with Zigzag, so she can escape to go hang out with her own friends.

Freshly dressed in her most comfortable skinny jeans, a Cubs sweatshirt, and a pair of checkerboard Vans, she pushes through the crowded, after-game sidewalks. She's eager to see familiar faces whose first thoughts of her don't include the Secret Service and gunshot wounds.

"Alden Ryan."

She smiles at the sound of her name being shouted from the second floor bar at the Butcher's Tap. She waves. "Rawlings."

"Get yer fine ass up here right now."

She laughs as she takes the rest of the distance to the entrance as quickly as possible, maneuvers through the busy bottom floor, and flies up the stairs. She sees her friends, and they cheer when she makes her way toward them.

"For she's a jolly good fella," they sing at the top of their lungs, and all Alden can do is grin.

"You guys are the worst," she says as she throws her arms around her best friend Melissa Rawlings. Her thick, curly, dark hair is shorter than it was the last time they saw each other. It's brushing her shoulders, and when Alden buries her head into it, it smells of expensive hair products and spa treatments, just like normal. Mel has been in her life since college, and they feel as close as two people can be. Years of working at the same police station made it impossible not to get close. Mel knows everything about her without needing to ask, which is what Alden needs in her life, especially now. Someone who understands her. Doesn't push her. Sympathizes with the weight of her sorrow without needing to talk about it. Mel is a force to be reckoned with, too. She's hilarious, kind, and loyal, almost to a fault.

Alden pulls away and puts her hands on Mel's round cheeks. "Oh my God, I missed you, Mel."

"Alden," she says while crying. "I missed you so fucking much."

"I feel like I've been gone for years."

"You have been gone for years," Serena Chan says with a laugh. "You left five years ago."

"Holy shit, you're right. It's been five years. How the hell does time fly so fast?"

Mel drapes an arm around Alden's shoulder and squeezes. "This is the first time we've been together since we graduated."

"No way. *Really?*"

"Yes way," Tobias says while nodding vigorously, a sly smile displayed. *Tobias fucking Markham and his classic good looks has to be here to witness my stunning defeat.* The only thing she wants to do is ask who the hell invited him. The most bizarre part of their relationship is that he's been in her life longer than anyone else still in her circle. High School. College. The Academy. And now. A friend. And a constant adversary. "Every time we get together, it's like, two or three of us. Never the original four."

Alden leans her head against Mel's shoulder. "We have to remedy that now that I'm home for a while." Adjusting to life outside the Secret Service has been as hard as she assumed it'd be. Going from having a purpose, a command, for every single move, to not even needing to move if she doesn't want to, has been a major shock to her system. Not completely in a bad way, which she is so thankful for. But in a way that has her questioning herself and her self-awareness, which has never been an issue for her. Her ability to know every set of eyes in the room was on her was part of her charm.

And now?

Now she wants to hide her face, crawl under the table, and hide from whatever judgmental opinions are being mentally hurled toward her.

Tobias leans forward, propping his elbows on the table, both fists wedged under his chin, and sighs. Alden has always been leery of how gorgeous he is. It's hard to trust people who care more about their looks than about the people around them. Shaggy blond hair, blue eyes, muscles for days. Even beard scruff looks good on him. The department would never allow scruff before. She wonders where he's working now, but she doesn't want to ask because if there's one thing Tobias loves doing aside from shooting a gun, it's talking about himself. "So how are you? How's everything going? How's not working?"

Serena smacks him on the arm. "Seriously? We agreed not to ask."

"It's completely okay," Alden says while laughing. "I can talk about it." The internal groan is deafening.

"We know, but we figured you didn't want to." Mel lifts a glass of red wine but before she drinks, adds, "We know how much you love talking about your feelings."

"Yeah, well, fuck you jerks for knowing me so well." They laugh. Alden's Goose Island 312 is delivered and slid expertly across the table by the server. She grabs it and takes a long pull of the wheat ale and hopes the subject will change, but as she waits, no one says a word. She sighs, sets the bottle on the table, and focuses. Not on her friends, no. On the bottle. On the tiny tear in the paper around the neck of the brown glass. Mel nudges her. "What?" She starts to rip the paper more.

"You okay?"

"Me?" She laughs. "I'm fine." She shrugs, still focused on the paper, on the smoothness of the glass. "Hanging in there, I guess." Tobias clears his throat, and the noise irritates her almost before she hears it. Her inability to deal with his condescending sounds isn't unanticipated. How they didn't kill each other during their time together at the academy remains a mystery to this day. It doesn't matter how many times they've buried the hatchet; their competition remains consistent. Neck and neck in everything. And oh, he was so jealous when she was selected for the Secret Service. He left the Chicago police force within days of the news, which struck her as odd, and stopped talking to her for most of the time she was gone. The break from him was a much-needed respite. "Tobias," she says softly. "I really don't need to hear it from you."

"Whoa, whoa," he says as he reaches across the round table. "I get everything you're going through. I would never. Okay? I promise."

She hesitates as she observes his outstretched hand. Taking this olive branch seems risky, but she also doesn't have the mental capacity to continue to be angry about inconsequential things from her past. She studies him, and for the first time in forever, she sees something in his eyes that looks a hell of a lot like kindness. She relents, and when he squeezes, she makes a promise to work on letting go of her inability to trust him. Well, not just him, but everyone in her life. Especially now during these bleak days of her life.

Alden isn't stupid. Being shot was always a possibility. It was a part of the job she signed up for without question. But she never anticipated the anxiety, the fear, the depression that came with the territory, including taking a bullet for the president. And she never thought any of that would lead to a leave of absence. A *forced* leave of absence. The words still hang in her mind like streamers that made it through a really great party, although just barely. A token of the fun she had. But a reminder of the mess she still needs to clean up.

Serena clears her throat, and Alden looks at her dark eyes and flawless complexion. She's the picture of beauty, and she hasn't changed much since they'd worked together at the police department. Maybe she's gotten even more striking, if that's possible. Her hair is so long, so black, and so wavy. She keeps it pulled back usually, but tonight, it's flowing freely. She looks good. Happy. And a part of Alden deep, deep, *deep* inside, tastes the tang of envy as it rears its ugly head. *She* wants to look good and happy again. Is it possible?

God, I hope so.

"Chief Anderson wanted me to say hey and invite you to come in if you want." Serena smiles a smile that is so genuine, Alden senses it in her sternum. "Y'know, to like, see everyone or whatever. She was super happy to hear you were back in town."

"Oh, Chief. How's she doing? I heard things were looking really good under her."

Serena shrugs. "I mean, it's Chicago. One day it's good. The next it's horrifying."

"So about the same as when I left?"

"We're getting shot at left and right—" Serena's abrupt stop is accentuated by Mel's movement under the table and the sound of a *thump*. "I mean, things are good."

"You guys." Alden half laughs, half huffs. "I can handle talking about this stuff. I promise."

"Just not yourself?" Mel's question is soft, not accusatory.

"I'll talk about myself one day. Just…" She pauses, considering whether or not to down her entire beer to take the edge off this conversation. "Just not today. Okay? Can we drink, and let me forget a little about everything? I'm living with my parents again. My entire life has changed. It's insanely different than it was a month ago. I need to drink."

Tobias raises his Old Style. "To drinking."

"Thank you." Alden eyes him, and he smiles.

"Let's fucking get drunk," Serena says as she signals for the server. "We need some shots."

Mel's eyes go huge. "Please, God, do not get those fucking Rocky Mountain Bear Fucker shots again. Those are the devil."

Alden laughs at the flashback of them, three sheets to the wind at a Korean karaoke bar, doing shots and singing at the top of their lungs. "I don't know. Maybe now is the perfect time for that."

"Fuck," Mel says under her breath. "I better text Patrick and let him know I won't be home tonight."

As their laughter dies down, the elephant-size weight on Alden's chest moves ever so slightly. The weight is still there, still as present as possible, but it budged, which it hasn't done since everything happened. Sometimes, it's so hard to breathe, to think, to do anything with the ever-present elephant that it's easier to do nothing at all. But she cannot continue that way. She needs to get moving. She needs to start talking. Because this person she has become is not who she wants to be. Or even who she is capable of being. And if she's annoying herself, she can't imagine how bad she must be annoying everyone around her. Accepting reality means coming to grips with everything. Her successes and her failures. Her misses and her hits. But more importantly? She needs to remember that this too shall pass. And she needs this night with her friends, Rocky Mountain Bear Fuckers be damned.

CHAPTER THREE

"Hey!"

Alden doesn't open her eyes when she hears the booming voice. She is lounging on the chaise in the backyard of her childhood home, appreciating that the hangover she's nursed for two solid days, courtesy of her unrelenting friends, decided to finally take a hike. And she's enjoying a few rare minutes of alone time. She loves her parents, but Jesus, they love to talk. And talk. And talk. And as much as she used to be a talker, these days, the only thing she wants is silence. Well, silence coupled with her *Chill the Fuck Out* playlist. It'd be lovely if chilling out was as easy as some of the songs on the playlist make it seem.

"Hey, Ryan. You gonna answer me?"

Alden finally opens her eyes, pushes her sunglasses up, and glances over her shoulder at the chain link fence where Tobias is standing. "What the hell do you want? I'm trying to get some sun." The weather is beautiful, with not a single cloud in the sky. It's not normal for springtime in Chicago. She's trying to soak up as much of it as she can. "I am not going out again. I am too old to drink like that anymore."

"Is that any way to treat your oldest friend?"

Alden rolls her eyes as she repositions her sunglasses, leans back, and waves. "Yes. And the gate is unlocked." She hears the squeak of the hinges and the *crunch, crunch, crunch* of the grass as he walks over. She can hear two sets of feet, though, so she shields her eyes from the sun and looks up. "What is going on?"

He chuckles, hands on his hips. "I don't remember you being this bitchy before."

"Well, your memory was never the greatest."

"Seriously, Alden." He sighs, swiping his aviator sunglasses from his face. She irritated him, and she's not sure if she's happy about it or equally irritated. "I didn't come here to annoy you. It's a work thing. Can you at least not embarrass me?"

"Fine." She stands at attention, and smiles. "Alden Ryan, sir, reporting for duty."

Tobias fidgets with his sunglasses. Her condescension has thrown *him* this time, and it's fun. "You're an ass, you know that?"

"Yes," she says with a grin.

"Look, Alden, this is Connor Glass."

She crosses her arms and eyes the older man accompanying him. He's impeccably dressed in a navy, three-piece suit and is holding a fedora that matches his suit perfectly. "Am I supposed to know—"

"Evelyn Glass's father." Tobias shakes his head when Alden doesn't respond with anything other than a blank stare. "Jesus, Alden, have you been living under a rock?"

Alden's chest tightens as she clenches her fists and plants a foot. "Ex*cuse* me?" Tobias fucking Markham knows where she's been living. And it wasn't under a fucking rock. She has never been able to handle insults well but especially not his. Some people can shrug comments like his off and move on. Not Alden. She has a short fuse and when pushed, she snaps very easily. And she loathes that part of herself. Fortunately, training helped her to control it. Losing her shit wasn't an option in the Secret Service. But now, with no one to report to, no boss to control her, no president to respectfully fear, her fuse seems even shorter. And it is one of the many things she's starting to hate about this pod person who has moved into her body.

Tobias takes a small step back, always able to read her. "I just meant..." He sighs. "You know what I meant." He rubs his eyes with the heels of his palms. "Listen, it's Evelyn *Glass*. She's a huge Hollywood star, and she has been cast in a hit show that's filming on-site in Chicago."

"Good for her."

"Alden, seriously?" Tobias waves. His stress level must be off the charts because he's normally so much more composed. "Y'know what? Never mind." He looks at Connor Glass and shrugs. "I misjudged this one. I'm sorry. Let's go."

Connor Glass sidesteps Tobias, though, and reaches to Alden. "Look, Miss, Tobias told me you were possibly interested in some work. I don't mean to bug you. I…uh…I'm in a bind, and you'd really be helping me out." He isn't nervous, per se, but there's something behind his dark eyes that begins to defrost Alden's cold demeanor. "She's my daughter. Evelyn. And she…"

"She needs protection." Tobias folds his arms across his chest. "This is what I do now. It's why I left the force. I find people protection."

Alden narrows her eyes. "You mean bodyguards?"

"Yes." Tobias shifts his stance. It's the first time he's ever looked uncomfortable in the entire time she's known him.

"And you can't find someone else?"

He shakes his head.

"You see," Connor Glass begins before he places the fedora on his head. "I need this person to be able to handle her. Evelyn is…" A small smile tugs at the corner of his mouth. "She's an intimidating woman."

"You mean she's hard to control."

"I didn't say that." He shrugs again. "She's just tough. And I think a woman will be good for her."

His statement is very interesting, and Alden's curiosity is piqued. Only slightly, but still. She sighs. "I don't know if I'm ready to start working again."

Tobias looks to the ground as if he's gathering his words for a debate, then looks at Alden. She prepares herself for whatever argument he's gathered. "You need this, Alden. You need to have a purpose again. I know you're struggling, but this could be exactly what you need."

She swallows. Damn, that was good.

"Miss?" Connor Glass clears his throat. "Would you at least come meet her?" He slips his hand into the breast pocket in his jacket and pulls out a business card. She eyes the completely black paper with white lettering:

Connor Glass
312-345-8900

The card sort of throws her. There's no business name, no address. This whole meeting is starting to seem more and more clandestine, and she wonders what she's about to get herself into. Alden slips it into the back pocket of her ratty jean shorts. "Okay. I'll come meet her." She notices the relief on Tobias's face. What is his deal? Why does this mean so much to him? "But if it doesn't go well…"

"It will go well." Tobias rubs the back of his neck. "I promise. Connor? Hand over the dossier."

Connor Glass looks at Tobias, then back at Alden. He hands over a large envelope, the clasp securely fastened, the sides almost splitting open. "A brief history, if you will," he explains and tilts his head in the direction of the envelope.

"So you know what you'll be getting into." Tobias gives her a pleading look before they turn to leave. Neither says a word to the other. It seems strange, as does the look on Connor Glass's face. He didn't seem convinced that this first meeting with Evelyn Glass would go well. And he should know, considering she's his daughter. The knot in Alden's stomach starts to tighten. This isn't a good idea. She can feel it. She has a sixth sense about these things. Part of what made her amazing at her job was her ability to know when things were going to be dicey. Regardless of that instinct, she somehow seems to always be in the wrong place at the right time. Normally, she has been able to use that to her advantage.

Until she took a bullet for the president.

Her life certainly took a turn after that happened.

"Mel, it seemed really weird."

"Listen," Mel says as she sets her coffee on the counter in Alden's parents' kitchen. "Tobias has been doing this for quite some time. I don't think you should worry too much."

"Personal bodyguards, though? I don't know. It seems... sketchy."

"Come on. It's Tobias. You've known him most of your life. He's not going to get you into something he doesn't think you can handle." Mel takes a drink, then scrunches her face. "I mean, right?"

"Oh my God, you don't trust him, either. I knew it." They both laugh. "This is going to go horribly. I can seriously feel it in my bones."

"You and that damn sixth sense."

"I swear, it's never been wrong." Alden takes a bite from one of her ma's cookies. She's been using her ma's inability to say no to her sweet tooth. Things could be a hell of a lot worse. "I googled this actress last night."

"No offense, but how do you not know who she is?"

Alden huffs. "Oh, I don't know? Maybe because I've been neck deep in politics for a while now? When you're protecting politicians, especially the president, you don't watch a lot of television that isn't the news."

"Think you'll ever not bring that up?" Mel laughs as she swipes a cookie. "The president." She mimics Alden's tone perfectly.

"You're not nice," Alden says with a laugh as she flips Mel off, middle finger to the sky. An easy silence falls between them, and Alden flashes to the endless photos she scrolled through and the articles upon articles she read about Evelyn Glass. "She's very famous."

Mel chuckles as she chews, her curly hair bouncing. "Uh, yeah."

"And very, um, yeah."

"Um, yeah, what?"

"I was just going to say, she's not bad looking."

Mel scoffs.

"What?"

"Not bad looking?"

"I mean, I wouldn't kick her out of bed for eating crackers."

"You are too much." Mel shakes her head. "She's gorgeous. And you are going to want to take the job after you see her in person. She's even prettier."

"How would you know?"

"The last time Patrick and I went to dinner at RPM, she was there. Some guy on her arm. Patrick wanted to get a picture with her, but I wouldn't let him. I hate that. Bothering celebrities when they're trying to do normal, everyday things…"

Alden has stopped listening and is starting to freak out. Celebrities and normal, everyday things and being shot and having to carry a weapon again, and the idea of this new job is starting to feel heavier and heavier.

Mel must be able to see it because she puts a hand on Alden's arm and calmly asks, "Hey, Alden, are you okay?"

She continues to stare at the crumbs on the plate, the chocolate chips, the walnuts. "I don't think I want to do this, Mel. I don't think I'm ready."

"Oh, honey." She smooths her hand over Alden's forearm. "You're going to be okay. You know that, right?"

Alden sighs. "It doesn't feel like it some days."

"Do you want me to come with you tomorrow?"

"God, no." She laughs. "I just…"

"It's okay to be nervous."

Mel is right. It is okay to be nervous. But it's not okay to be on edge. She needs to find a way to pull herself back. The bullet left a scar that will never go away. She just hopes one day, she can find a way to not constantly judge herself because of it.

CHAPTER FOUR

When Alden arrives at the address Connor Glass texted her, she is speechless. Winnetka is home to some pretty affluent people and has its fair share of fancy rich homes, but the sheer size of the mansion Evelyn Glass chose is startling. It's absolutely gorgeous, on Sheridan Road, on what looks to be at least an acre. That amount of property is not cheap, especially since it butts against the beach of Lake Michigan.

After she rings the doorbell, she pushes the sleeves of her lightweight white button-down up to her biceps and tries to calm herself. She didn't want to dress up. This isn't the type of interview where she wants to impress because she's not even sure she wants the job. And dressing up would have made her nervous, and she doesn't want to be nervous. After all, it's equal parts them interviewing her and her doing the same to them.

Either way, the size of the front door is causing her to tense up. She used to be in the Oval Office every single day, though. *It's fine. You're fine.* She hopes it's not obvious she's forcing herself to go through with this. Having a job to focus on is not a bad thing. After all, she wants to get out of her parents' house and find a sense of normalcy again. But if she's not comfortable, she's going to bail. She'd already made that decision before she shifted her father's Oldsmobile into drive.

After a few seconds of waiting, the door opens, and a young boy holding a tattered copy of a *Thor* comic book is standing there, a worn baseball cap pulled down on his head. "You lost?"

"Uh, I don't think so." She steps back to check out the address then hears the boy start to giggle. "I'm pretty sure this is the correct address."

"You must be the bodyguard," he says, a grin on his thin pink lips.

Alden lets out a laugh as she pushes her long hair over her shoulder. She shoves her hands into her front jean pockets so she will quit fidgeting. "And why would you think that?"

"I'm thirteen. I have ears. And eyes. I'm Ethan. Evelyn's my mom." He holds his hand out, brown eyes staring into hers. "It's nice to meet you."

Alden smiles back, unable to stop herself, and shakes his hand. "Hi, Ethan. I'm Alden. Alden Ryan." She's normally very reserved around children. Partly because kids frighten her, and also because she's not used to them. She grew up as an only child with two cousins. She never had to share any sort of spotlight with a kid. She never wanted to have kids. The idea of raising one is not something she ever wanted. Most of the time, she wondered if her DNA just wasn't imbued with the maternal instinct.

"I know your name," he says. "My mom and her crew are through here. They're doing their read through for the next episode. Follow me."

The entryway is even more beautiful than the outside. A grand staircase, white marble floors, an intricate chandelier. She turns. "Do I need to take my boots off?" Her question comes out as a whisper.

Ethan laughs, motions to his Nike-clad feet, and shrugs. "Nah, it's fine." He waves at her to follow him, then stops. "Let me warn you, though. My mom, she um"—he pauses and leans closer—"she can be a little, um, hard to read. So...don't be surprised if, ya know, she..."

"Hates me?"

"Yeah," he answers. "You get used to it." He is a cute kid, even with the gap in his front teeth. "Come on." She follows him down a well-lit hallway and through two ornate French doors. The natural light from the numerous windows is lovely. Her senses are on high alert, taking in everything: the number of steps from the front door to where they're standing, the amount of noise their steps make as they walk the now hardwood floors, the smell of whatever is being prepared in the kitchen, which she slows and admires. The island in the center is as big as a queen-size mattress. There are stools lined up on the outside, and a giant vase of fresh flowers resides on the center of the white marble countertop. There is an industrial stove and cooktop on the left-hand side, and on the back wall, beneath a large bay window facing the lake, is the most beautiful, stainless steel farmhouse sink she has ever seen. Everything about this kitchen makes her want to start cooking. Since being home, the one thing she has vowed to do is get back to her roots, start making meals again, even if most of them are of the Polish variety. She used to love being in the kitchen with her grandma or ma on those rare nights her ma had off from the hospital. Alden stayed so busy in the Secret Service that most of her meals were eaten on the run. Or microwavable and hardly delicious.

"*Psst.*"

Alden jerks to attention and picks up the pace. "Sorry, that kitchen is something else."

He chuckles. "Yeah, Mom loves to cook, so her main request when she was looking for this house was it had to have a huge kitchen. We need to go through here." He pushes open a door to a massive room with an office-like feel. There's a long conference table surrounded by comfortable desk chairs, and opposite that is a massive space that resembles a photo shoot studio with lights on stands and large reflective umbrellas. Whatever this room was before, it has been transformed into a place where Evelyn must spend most of her time. The pictures on the walls, large and small, are mostly of Evelyn, either scantily clad or dressed in ridiculous costumes. It's jarring seeing so much of a woman who Alden knew nothing about twenty-four hours ago, and it takes her a couple seconds to find her bearings.

Twelve or so people are busy mingling, laughing, and talking toward the back. They all *look* like television stars, if a television star has a look, which Alden assumes they do. And it hits her that this must be Evelyn Glass's entourage. How often these people will be around, she has no idea, but she hopes she isn't roped into protecting them all.

"Ms. Ryan." She hears Connor before she sees him squeeze between two larger men near the center of the room. He's rushing across the room, a smile on his face she hasn't seen from him yet. He must be really excited she decided to do this. When he's finally in front of her, he breathes deep and slaps his large hands on her arms. "I'm so glad you changed your mind."

He clears his throat, and that must be Ethan's cue to leave. His eyes move quickly from hers to Connor's and back. She nods at him before he disappears through the door. "This is quite the house."

"Ah, yes, Evelyn refused to relocate to Chicago unless she found the perfect place. She originally wanted to find a condo downtown, but once she saw this estate, she knew this was it. This is her second season on the show, but she has been promised more. And since they're filming in the city for the foreseeable future..." He pauses, a forlorn expression on his wrinkled face. "Anyway, I think she really nailed it with this one. It's dramatic and beautiful."

"It suits her." Alden smiles, wondering if the small prod went undetected. When he glances at her, she motions to the people. "Who are they?"

"Robert Jackson," Connor starts, pointing at a dark-haired man dressed in black leather pants, a black button-down, and a black vest. "Her publicist. He's a live wire."

"Great."

"The rest are costars."

"All men?"

"Mm-hmm. She's the leading lady this season. Possibly next, depending on ratings. They killed off the last leading lady because she wasn't bringing in the numbers like they'd experienced the few seasons before. There are rumblings of another woman costar being brought in this season. But we'll see." His expression turns from informative to sad. "Whatever happens, though, I'd like to not see Evelyn killed off in any form."

Jesus. *In any form?* What has she been thrown into? "Obviously." She swallows as she stares across the room. Robert Jackson is walking toward them. Well, not really walking so much as strutting. He's holding a tumbler of dark liquor at eleven a.m. What the hell kind of publicist is he?

"This is the famous bodyguard?" Robert drinks, then points at Alden. "Look here, little lady—"

"Please don't call me little lady." Alden makes sure to remain calm.

"Oh, well, my apologies." He rolls his eyes, and Alden forces herself to not react. "I'm not really a fan of this whole arrangement Connor set up. Evelyn Glass is a *star*, you see. She's going to continue to be a *star*, and to stifle that by having a bodyguard telling her what to do and always around is utter bullshit."

"Thank you for your opinion." This guy is a complete asshole. She already hates him. Luckily, she is well versed in handling men who behave like this. Kill them with kindness. Well, as much kindness as possible.

"Don't step out of line here. I can get rid of you quicker than he hired you." Robert takes a step into Alden's personal space and glances at her lips, then back up to her eyes.

"Good Lord, Robert," Connor finally interjects. "Leave the bodyguard alone."

Alden glares, watching as he retreats, turns, and walks toward the crowd. The group starts to disperse when Evelyn Glass emerges from the center, laughing, smiling, and looking as if she just walked off the cover of *Cosmopolitan*.

Their eyes meet from across the expanse, and just like that, the air seems to be pulled from the room. The people fade away like remnants of smoke, leaving only her and Evelyn standing there.

To say that Evelyn is stunning is an understatement.

The pictures do her no justice. Her dark brown hair and light brown skin are even more radiant in person. After an extensive Google search, Alden is an expert in her background—a Puerto Rican mother and Italian roots from Connor—and filmography, which Alden, of course, started to rent on iTunes. She's probably more of an expert than that asshat of a publicist. And now here Evelyn stands. Dressed to the nines. Black heels, black slacks, a flowy pale-pink blouse. Her hair is pulled back, exposing her neck, and Alden shakes her head to stop staring. Evelyn is vibrating her senses. She's seen beauty in her life. And she's seen powerful beauty, but this?

"Wow." She breathes the word, then snaps her jaw closed, clenching her teeth. She hopes Connor didn't hear.

"Uh, Evelyn," Connor semi-shouts, waving her over.

Evelyn pauses, irritation displayed all over her striking features and lifts her chin as if whatever is going to happen next is absolutely beneath her. She glides over, the sound of her heels a sharp staccato on the dark hardwood floor. She looks Alden up and down slowly, deliberately. "Yes?" she asks, poised, perfect, regal.

"This is—"

"The *bodyguard*." Robert is right behind Evelyn, his arms are crossed, his demeanor smug.

Evelyn's eyes are now on Alden's. She has a giant lump taking up residence in her throat. Why is the very sight of this actress making her feel trivial? She worked for and protected the most powerful woman in the entire world and never felt as unsure of herself as she does right this second. "Hi." Her greeting comes out too soft, with as much confidence as a gnat. She wants to roll her eyes at herself but refrains.

Evelyn takes a couple steps closer. "Can we get you something to drink, Ms...."

"Ryan. Her name is Alden Ryan," Connor says. He readjusts his stance and unbuttons the button on his suit jacket.

"Alden Ryan."

The way her name rolls off Evelyn's tongue is almost too much for her to handle. It instantly transports her back to high school when she realized for the first time that she liked women more than men, and it's making her heartbeat falter.

"That's an interesting name." Evelyn's left eyebrow arches. *Holy fuck, she's hot.* Her voice is bold, dark, smooth. Just the way Alden likes her coffee, liquor, *anything*, really. "And you don't *look* like a bodyguard."

Alden licks her very parched lips. "What were you expecting?" Evelyn Glass may be the most attractive woman Alden has ever seen, but she reminds herself that there is no way in hell she is going to let anyone intimidate her. If being around intimidating and powerful women for the past three years has taught her anything, it's never to show her trepidation.

After folding her arms, taking a slight step back, and tilting her head, Evelyn narrows her eyes, then throws a glance over her shoulder to a man standing by one of the entryways with his hands in his pockets. "I was expecting someone like my costar, Sam. You know, big, brooding, a *man*."

"Evelyn—" Connor starts.

Evelyn holds up a hand and displays a very fake smile. "Daddy, I'm old enough to make the decisions here. Thank you, but I don't think this is necessary."

"Not this time, Evelyn," Connor says. "I'm making this decision."

"No, *Connor*," Evelyn says, this time more forceful and more spoiled-brat like. "This isn't *that* big of a deal."

"She's right, *Connor*. It's not a big deal. It was only a tiny hiccup." Robert chuckles before loudly answering his cell phone, shouting some obscenities into the device before scurrying away.

"What hiccup?" Alden asks, looking at Connor for an answer.

"Nothing," Evelyn answers way too quickly.

Alden shoots a look at Evelyn and then glares at Connor. "What hiccup is he talking about?"

"Nothing," Connor says as he exhales. "Just some unwanted attention."

"Listen." Evelyn's voice is an octave higher than it had been a minute earlier. Not to mention a decibel higher, as well. The entire room stands still, everyone turning toward her. "I am not willing to do this." She waves at Alden as if signaling to her entire being. "There's no way to have a bodyguard without him inserting himself into every aspect of my life. So thanks, but no thanks. Daddy, please see this"— her eyebrow arches again—"woman out."

"No need. I'll see myself out." Alden heads out the door, making sure to close it with force. "What a piece of work," she whispers before pulling in a deep breath and gathering the remaining shards of her dignity. She has never been treated like that before, and she's had to arrest some real winners in her past.

As she scurries through the house, she of course takes a wrong turn and only realizes she's lost when she notices a large sliding glass door in the living room. It's open, and Ethan is sitting on the patio. She looks around as if an exit sign will miraculously appear. After taking a deep breath, she walks through the living area, then out the door. The warm air hits her, and she takes another deep breath. The patio leads onto a rather large lawn. Stretching out into the distance like an ocean is Lake Michigan. The view is breathtaking. Almost as breathtaking as Evelyn Glass.

Ethan chuckles. "You lost?"

"I'm ashamed to admit it, but yes." Hands on her hips, she shakes her head as she looks at her boots. "She threw me for a loop."

"Already on her good side, huh?"

Alden lets out a small laugh as she sits next to him. "Not necessarily. I don't think this is the right job for me."

He looks out toward the lake. "Yeah, I figured," he says with a sigh.

"Oh, you did, hmm?" She pushes playfully on his shoulder.

"Yeah, I did. You can't handle her."

"Look, Ethan…" She pauses. "I know what you're doing."

"You do?"

"Oh, yeah. Reverse psychology doesn't typically work on me. I can handle her. I just…" She sighs. "What am I supposed to do here?"

"You're asking a thirteen-year-old you barely know for advice?" He laughs. "You really are lost, aren't you?"

She shakes her head, looking at the ground, her hair falling over her shoulders, shielding the emotions she isn't supposed to show. "I don't need the drama," she says softly. "Tell your grandfather that if your mom changes her mind, give me a call, okay?" She stands and takes off in the direction of the front door, hoping no one stops her. She isn't sure what she was thinking, but this was not what she expected, and it's certainly not what she needs. When she's safely inside the Oldsmobile, she lets out a breath and drives away, leaving this shit show in her past.

Mug to her nose, Alden breathes in the aroma of freshly brewed coffee. "I've missed Intelligentsia so much." Eyes closed, she takes a sip, letting the notes of chocolate and citrus and a hint of apple coat her taste buds. Coffee is her weakness. Especially good coffee. Some people reach for a good wine to unwind. Not her. Something about the dark, delicious brew calms her. And this cup of coffee with Mel is no exception. The meeting with Evelyn was haunting her every thought, and she needed to get out of her head. She groans after swallowing. "Oh God, I swear, this coffee is better than sex."

Mel, who is drinking an iced vanilla latte with an extra shot of judgment on her face, scoffs. "How long has it been for you if a cup of fucking coffee is better than coming?"

"I didn't say that. An orgasm is one thing, but the whole act of sex? The emotions and the staring into each other's eyes and… ugh." She flashes back to the last time. Short blond hair and blue eyes and accidentally ripping a lapel, and the memory makes her stomach churn. "It's been a while." She lies because the truth, and the consequence of the truth, is too much.

"Shut up."

She shrugs.

"Like, what? A couple months?"

She shrugs again. "Years." Another lie. Will lying always be easier than the truth? Probably.

"I refuse to believe that."

"Maybe a couple random times after that." *They were far from random.* "But I haven't been in a relationship since then."

"Okay, that's better. I was starting to worry about you and your libido." Mel sets her cup down and leans forward. "Your strongest relationship cannot be the one you have with coffee."

"It'll never break my heart, though, so really? I feel like I'm much smarter than you realize."

"Wait for the day you accidentally get a cup of decaf. You'll be crushed."

Alden laughs. "The ultimate betrayal, hmm?" She drinks again. She isn't sure when her love affair with coffee started, but it really is her strongest, and probably her longest, relationship. Maybe it was the endless nights she had to stay up studying in the police academy. Or maybe it was the long hours patrolling the Chicago streets. Or maybe it was when she was on duty overnight, protecting the president. Either way, it's the one vice she refuses to give up.

Silence falls between them as they enjoy their drinks. The Intelligentsia Café near Millennium Park is, like always, a revolving door of customers. A steady flow of people come and go. A few students study in the brightly lit window seats. Businessmen and women rush in, dressed to impress, ordering espressos and cappuccinos to go. The constant flow is reassuring for some weird reason. The idea that life continues even when hers seems so stuck is calming, even if slightly frustrating.

There's a Maggie Rogers's song on the radio overhead. "Fallingwater." And the lyrics resonate inside the walls of her chest like an echo against rock in a canyon. She needs to get her shit together and figured out because being like this forever isn't an option. At least not an option she feels good about.

"She's really a bitch, hmm?"

Mel's question shakes Alden out of her reverie. She makes eye contact, swallows, and gathers her thoughts. "You mean Evelyn Glass?"

"I certainly don't mean the president."

Alden hasn't said much about President Simmons since being back. Actually, she never spoke much about her even when in her service. Talking about those years seems to defeat the purpose of healing. So much happened in such a short span. Three years out of the thirty-four she's been alive. Yet they impacted her in ways she didn't even realize at the time. But she didn't think she'd ever have to take a break.

Her thoughts pause, and pain centers itself in the middle of her sternum. She amends her statement. She certainly didn't think she'd ever be *forced* to take a break from the Secret Service to recover.

Recover.

Protecting people is her passion. And now the very thought of it causes her to cringe, causes her skin to crawl, causes her heartbeat to race. She cannot handle the thought of *what if she had failed.* Even though she didn't fail. And she wouldn't. She breathes in and lets it out slowly through her nose. "She was most definitely not super friendly."

"And you really don't want to take the job? To see what happens?"

"No, I really don't." And once again, she's lying. She sort of wants to take the job because her parents are driving her nuts, and making that kind of money would be amazing right now. The job wouldn't be forever, according to the dossier. Her mind flashes to Evelyn's eyes, to the dark storms raging in them, and a chill races through her body. The fear of failing those eyes is holding her back, absorbing her like a sponge absorbs liquid.

"Um." Mel shifts in her seat and sits up straighter. She's on high alert.

"What's up?" Alden looks to the front door. "Oh Jesus," she says as her eyes land on Connor Glass. He starts toward them, determination fueling his black patent leathers. "What the hell are you doing here? How did you even know where I was?"

He licks his lips when he stops, hands firmly on his hips. He squares his shoulders, chin held high. "I think you should reconsider."

"Connor—"

He holds his hand up. "She's...she needs someone like you. Someone who can handle her."

"You didn't answer my question."

His smirk is perfectly timed. "Which question?"

"How did you find me?"

He pulls out a chair and sits, his hands balled into fists in his lap. "I'm very resourceful."

"Seriously," Mel says with a laugh. She shakes her head. "Answer the question."

He sighs. "I went to your house, and your mother, who is a very nice woman, by the way, way nicer than you, said you were here." He shrugs.

"Reason number four hundred and fifty of why I need to move out," Alden says, followed by a groan.

"Look," he starts and when he unclenches his fists, he's shaking. "I don't get scared about things. I'm a big guy." He puffs his chest. "But I'm nervous about everything going on these days with Evelyn. From her divorce to the publicity with this show and now—"

"Have Tobias find you someone else. A man. Someone who looks like a bodyguard."

He sighs. "I don't want a man. I want *you*."

Alden leans forward, completely bewildered. "Why is this so important that you tracked me down?"

"I know I should have called first. I need to have a conversation with just the two of us." He glances at Mel. "The three of us."

Mel smiles. "Don't worry. I'm a vault."

"Good to know."

"I am so confused right now."

Mel chuckles. "Alden doesn't handle surprises very well."

His face falls. "I don't want to bother you. I feel very strongly about this. And I don't want to keep going round after round with Evelyn. What I say goes this time. And she's going to like it or..."

"Or what?"

"I don't know. Go to bed without dinner?"

Alden laughs, as does Mel. "I mean, that sounds *very* menacing."

"Please, reconsider." He stands, pushes his chair in, and places a hand on Alden's shoulder. "Once you get there and settle into the apartment upstairs, you'll feel a lot better."

"Whoa." Alden's ears perk. She glances at Mel, whose eyes have gone wide. "Apartment?"

"Yes, I want you to stay on site." He rakes fingers through salt and pepper hair. "You think about it, okay? You have my number." And just like that, he turns and takes his leave.

"Well, well, well." Mel's iced coffee is gone, but the ice has melted enough to get a few extra sips. She slurps, then sets the cup on the table with force. "An apartment, hmm? Seems like someone is going to change her mind and use this opportunity to her advantage."

"No, that's not it at all."

"Oh puh-lease. You should have seen your face when he said apartment." She rolls her eyes. "You have got to stop wallowing. You know the only way to heal is to get back out there and fucking heal. You think I want to keep seeing you playing this whole 'woe is me' routine?"

"Whoa."

"No, no *whoa*. I am being serious, Alden." Mel gathers her bag, cup of half-melted ice, and stands. "You've got to figure this out." She sighs. "I'm running late for an appointment. Call me later."

Alden has no words as she watches Mel leave. Taking a job right now would go against everything she's trying to do while being home. It would halt the relaxing. But maybe Mel is right because the only solid thought Alden can form is how she's even annoying herself. And that simply cannot continue.

CHAPTER FIVE

There have been a couple times in Alden's life where she held on to regret. The first was in high school. Senior class prank was to, somehow, sneak a car into the building. The stunt could be done, and the entire class listened to her. The perks of not being a wallflower, apparently, and they got the job done and also got suspended for a day. Oh, and it was her father's squad car.

They should have picked something less conspicuous.

The other time was when she allowed things to go too far with the most powerful woman in the free world. Saying no to the president didn't seem like an option, though, and Alden wanted it just as badly as Jennifer Simmons did.

The memory, even a year later, makes her stomach churn.

A wave of nausea wafts over her as she pulls down the driveway to Evelyn's mansion, where she is going to relent and take the position. Not because of Evelyn, no, but because of Connor, who pulled on her heartstrings just enough by offering an apartment.

And because Mel's response to the whole thing was exactly what she thought it'd be, and now she can add letting her best friend down to the list of regrets.

She parks off to the side. There is no gate, no intercom to buzz in, no guard to check in with, and for someone with some "unwanted attention," all of those things will need to be remedied.

"Alden."

She perks up after hearing Connor Glass's booming voice. He's walking toward her, his tie blowing over his shoulder. "Well, let's see what happens now," she whispers before she plasters a fake smile on her face.

"Alden," he says again. He's huffing a little, his larger body clearly not in the best of shape. "Woo," he puffs. "It's hot for May, isn't it?"

It's not hot at all. She was freezing before she left her parents' house, which is why she's wearing a jean jacket over her mustard colored top. She smooths her hands over her hips, wiping sweaty palms on her dark skinny jeans because even though the temperature only reads sixty-five, she's sweating now, too. "Yeah, I guess it is," she answers before shaking his hand.

"Thank you so much for reconsidering." He straightens his tie, then runs a hand over his hair. Is it possible it's longer now? She only met him four days ago. "I had a long talk with Robert. And with Evelyn. This is the route we want to go."

Alden wants to ask a million questions about what transpired but she has no idea where to start.

A smile is on his lips when he leans closer. "I'm the one paying Robert. You have problems with him, you come to me, okay?"

"Robert's not the one I'm worried about, Connor. Things seemed a little tense with Ms. Glass." Alden shifts, folds her arms across her chest. "It's sort of hard to protect someone who doesn't want protection. Or at the very least, doesn't understand why protection is necessary."

Connor sighs. "I know."

"Well, that's going to be a problem, more so than Robert. He's inconsequential, but Evelyn? She's the reason I'm here."

"Well, the reason you're here runs a little deeper than some random crazed fans."

The new information causes her to take a step back. "Oh?"

He claps, clearly wanting to change the subject. "Anyway, I'm so glad you decided to come back. I'll explain everything. I promise."

She studies the deep wrinkles around his eyes, the way his forehead creases when he's clearly uncomfortable. "And you're sure Evelyn is on board? I am not about to go down this road if it's going to cause a horrible accident." She hopes the look on her face conveys the meaning of her sentence.

"I have spoken with her," he says. "Let me just say, she is going to cooperate. She may not understand why yet, but she will. I can assure you."

Alden isn't convinced. At all. "We have a lot to talk about."

He rubs his hand over his neatly maintained salt and pepper beard. "Alden, listen. I know what this looks like."

"Do you?"

"I do."

"I don't think you do." She shrugs. "Like I already said, you cannot force someone to want protection. So two things must happen before we go any further." She starts toward the front door. "One, and probably the most important, I need to know everything. Every single thing that led up to her needing protection and every single thing moving forward. Every event. Every outing. Every autograph session. Every dinner. Every date." His eyebrows rise. "And yes, I mean literal dates. I won't go with them, but I must know about it. Okay?"

"You don't need to worry about dating—"

"Connor, I am serious."

He clears his throat, his entire demeanor changing. "Okay, I get it." He takes a deep breath, then releases. "And the second thing?"

"Evelyn has to listen to me."

"Good luck with that." He laughs, then must notice she is not finding it funny at all. He clears his throat again. "It won't be a problem."

"I know it seems like I'm being a dictator, but you have to understand what protecting someone means." She stops outside the front door on the brick steps. "If I am left in the dark, bad things could happen. People could get hurt." She makes herself stop explaining when the unfortunate familiarity of guilt rises to the surface. *What the fuck, Alden?* She mentally slaps herself, pulls a quick breath in, and stops making intense eye contact. She takes a swipe at her nose and pulls her shoulders back. "Just so we're both on the same page."

His pause for one, two, three beats does not go unnoticed. She realizes he saw her falter and wants to smack herself. *Emotions and guns do not mix well*, she remembers from her first Secret Service trainer. *Don't show them, and do not let people see them.* She likes to live in that buttoned-up way. Until recently.

"Are you going to get me up to speed?" She straightens her jacket and makes eye contact again. The expression on his face is thankfully not one of regret over hiring a fucking basket case. He seems more concerned than anything; even his wrinkles hold concern, and that concern cannot go any further than this doorstep. "Connor, let's go, please."

He simply nods before he opens the door, and she follows him inside and up the grand staircase.

When they arrive at a closed door, Connor glances over his shoulder before he opens it. "She hasn't been sleeping in here."

He pushes the dark oak door open very slow. Evelyn's bedroom. Vaulted ceilings, exposed wooden beams, a fireplace, a gigantic bed, a seating area. *It's a lot.* Too much, in fact, but aside from the fact that it's bigger than any apartment Alden has ever rented, the room is at least trying to feel cozy. The decorations are soft, elegant, easy on the eyes, words that could also be used to describe Evelyn. Creams, sandy browns, black accents, pops of yellow here and there. A picture collage hangs over the king-size bed. There is also a massive black and white photograph over the fireplace. A woman stands in a field of flowers, back to the camera, face tilted to the heavens. There's something about the photograph that calls to Alden. The flowers, the wide-open space, it's calming.

Connor stands at the foot of the bed. "We found a letter right there." He motions to the duvet.

"Excuse me?" Alden's spine stiffens.

"Someone broke in and left the note right there. Middle of the bed. I have it. Evelyn found it and hasn't been able to sleep in here since."

She turns slowly, taking in the windows. She unlocks and slides them open. They're very heavy. No beep of an alarm. "Why the hell wouldn't you tell me this to begin with?" She hopes her stare is making him feel smaller than his six-foot-two frame.

"I'm telling you *now.*" He blinks rapidly. "Do you think this has been easy for us? For her? You have to understand what a private person she is. Just because she's been in the spotlight nonstop the last few years doesn't mean she deals well with it."

Alden can't help but scoff. She understands all too well what he's saying. The constant desire to be liked, needed, feel important, but attention can't happen behind closed doors where it's safe and sound. "Look—"

"No, you need to listen to me." His words come out in a hushed whisper. He takes three large, fast steps and puts his hand on the crook of her arm, moving her so she's facing him. "This is big. Someone got into this house. Someone..." He stops, his eyes and tears now the problem. A sense of relief washes over her that she's not the only person unable to keep their shit together. "I think it's the same person that..." Again, he pauses, gathering words or courage, she isn't sure. "Two weeks ago, at the *Entertainment Weekly* event in LA, a basket of presents arrived, and thank God Evelyn wasn't anywhere near her dressing room because one of the gifts was an explosive."

"Connor, what the fuck?"

"I know. I *know*." He turns and sits on the bench at the end of the bed, elbows propped on his knees, head bent, heels of his hands on his forehead. He's stressed and for good reason. This entire situation has gone from zero to sixty in the blink of an eye. "We didn't tell Evelyn about the explosive."

"Did you tell the police?"

Connor shakes his head.

"Why not?"

"Robert thought it would be unwise, so he covered it up. It didn't go off, and he disposed of it. He told her we had to move her dressing room because of an electrical problem. I disagreed, but he's very convincing. And Evelyn hates being thrown off her game."

"That's the dumbest thing I've ever heard of in my entire life." She can feel her mouth hanging open in shock at the pure stupidity. "I thought you said Robert listens to you? Because it sounds like he's the one calling the shots. And they aren't good shots. They're ignorant shots."

"Robert has been a, um, thorn in my side for quite some time. He has Evelyn convinced that he's her best option for another shot at fame. And unfortunately, I can't seem to make her see he's not. He listens to me but..."

Alden kneels in front of him. "Robert has to listen to me or he needs to go. Period."

"I know."

"And Evelyn is going to be thrown off her game permanently if she gets killed by some overzealous asshole."

He nods, head still in his hands. "She's my daughter. My only child." He looks up, his eyes red. "I just want her to be okay. She loves doing this. She loves acting. She always has. This is her passion, and asking her to stop because she has crazed fans seems like jumping the gun."

"Let's take this one day at a time. First things first. I need total control of security."

"Do whatever you need to do. Money is no object."

"Good to hear because I plan on spending a decent amount, okay? Please show me the rest of the house." She follows him into the hallway. Her mind is racing. This job went from nice and easy, working with an uptight jerk, to dangerous and mysterious, working with a clueless celebrity. The worst part is, Evelyn will probably not get on board easily. Which means the only way to convince her is for something scary to happen. And Alden one-hundred-percent hopes that's not the route they have to take.

Chapter Six

Ma, I gotta talk to you about something." Alden sits at the kitchen table and pushes the stack of bills her ma is working on to the side.

"Yes, let's talk about what we're making for dinner."

"No, Ma, it's important."

"And dinner isn't important?" She looks over the top of red-framed bifocals.

"I took a job."

"You what?" She slides her glasses from her face and sets them on the table. "Aldie, that's...Wait. Does your father know?"

"Yes, I told him already. He said I had to tell you."

Ma is smiling, but it fades quickly. "What else?"

"It's sort of, um..." She scrunches her face. Why is she so nervous to say she's moving out again?

"Spit it out."

"Geez. Fine." She bites her lip. "It requires me to move out."

Ma pulls her shoulders back and crosses her arms. "I don't like the sound of that. At all."

"I understand. But the job requires me to be on-site."

"Yeah, that seems sketchy."

"Ma, come on."

"I'm sorry, but you came running home with this sadness coursing through you and injured, to boot, and now you're just ready to take a job and move back out?" She laughs. "I don't think so."

"Seriously?" Alden can't fight back the urge to laugh, too. "Ha. You're nuts."

"I'm nuts?"

"Yes."

"No, sorry." Ma slides her bifocals back on and rests them at the end of her nose. She smiles. "You're not leaving yet. You *just* moved back in."

"I mean, it was two suitcases and a couple boxes. Sort of sad for someone who hasn't lived here for quite some time."

"Just means you don't like clutter." Ma stands and moves around the kitchen, grabbing pots and pans. "I guess I should be the one making dinner tonight. Since you seem to be leaving again."

"Ma, come on." Alden moves to where her ma is standing by the stove. "I know you're nervous about what happened to me. I mean, you've been even more overbearing than normal since I've been home."

"Me? Overbearing?"

"Oh, Ma. It's not a bad thing. I just need to move past what happened and be okay again."

"I don't like the sound of this." Her eyes are displaying more sadness than her voice ever could. "When do you leave?"

Alden pulls in a breath through clenched teeth. "Um…tomorrow."

"Oh, Alden."

"I'm really sorry. I know it's sudden, and I've been going back and forth in my head. Should I do this? Should I not? And ultimately, I know it's for the best. It's not that I don't want to stay here anymore. I just…I love you, and you know that."

"I know." Ma's voice is whisper soft as she pulls her glasses from her face again. She's crying but in true Ma fashion, she hates letting anyone see, so she lays a hand over her eyes. That little eccentricity was passed down to Alden, so she understands. Crying in their house has always been considered weak. And neither of them is weak.

"Ma, look at me." Alden places her hands on her ma's shoulders and bends so she can look into her eyes when she moves her hand. "I love you so much, and you've been so helpful. You and Pops both. But you know I need to do this."

Ma takes a shaky breath before she shrugs the hands from her shoulder. "Okay. So your last night here. What would you like? I can make beef stroganoff or sausage and sauerkraut or…Oh, I'll pull out some pierogis, and we can fry those up. And I really think—"

"Ma." Alden stops her frantic movements. "I promise. I'll be okay."

"Honey," Ma says with more force than Alden knew she had. "Do you not remember that you were *shot*? Your father and I had to hear about it from another agent. We had to hope you'd pull out of it. And now you come home, and you're...you haven't been the same since it happened."

"Pops says the only way to get better is to get back out there."

"Your father is an idiot," Ma says with a tear-filled laugh.

She laughs along. "He really is."

"What are you two laughing about in here?" Pops steps into the kitchen from the back porch and points at them. "It better not be me. I ain't no butt of a joke. Ya hear?"

Alden and her ma continue to laugh, and he winks before he goes back out. "Okay, can I at least help cook?" Alden smiles, waiting for the answer when her ma turns around and hugs her. Hugs from her parents are always something she's looked forward to. There's something about that unconditional love that shows through.

"Grab that chuck steak from the fridge. And the mushrooms. Let's do a little stroganoff."

Alden does as she's asked, grabbing the ingredients to make one of her ma's signature dishes. That conversation went over exactly as she suspected it would. Pops would be fine with it, and Ma would hate it. As much as Pops was the rule maker when she was a kid, Ma is the one who scares Alden the most. Not in a mean way but because Alden hates disappointing her. She hates knowing her ma does nothing but worry about her. And the worries escalated when she got shot.

But now that breaking the news to Ma is out of the way, Alden feels a little lighter. She hopes when she moves out this time, it will be for good, but she hoped it would be into her own place. The idea of moving into Evelyn Glass's house seems like a cop-out, and it's nerve-racking to think she could see Evelyn at any moment of the day, but "an on-site bodyguard" is in the contract. It's the only way to be immersed in protecting her. She's so tense about the whole thing. The nerves feel good, though, like before she had to do her shooting test. She knew she would pass, but knowing she can be the best is always a little nerve-racking.

And she can be the best again. She wants Evelyn to think she's the best, as well. She shouldn't be having those thoughts already. Unfortunately, there's something about Evelyn's icy display that makes Alden want to figure her out. When she does figure her out, and she is sure she will, she prays she doesn't like her any more than she should.

The likelihood of that is so slim. And she knows it. But she also knows the only way to beat it is to chase those thoughts from her mind right now.

❖

Ethan answers the door again when she arrives at the mansion with her two suitcases. "Are you the son or the butler?"

He laughs the same giggle he did when she first met him. "Not much to do around here but answer the door. Come with me, and I'll show you to your room."

She opted to not bring the rest of her belongings, mainly because who knows how long this set-up is going to last? She is fully aware this is temporary and is very happy about that.

After Ethan leads her up the main staircase and past his room—"Y'know, just in case you need anything"—he leads her up another flight of stairs into what he calls the "attic apartment." He opens the door and they climb the small staircase to a room. As soon as she sees the space, she falls in love with it. The natural light, as in the rest of the house, is perfect. The walls are slanted on the right side of the long room, and there are three large skylights. Ethan eagerly shows her the bells and whistles, which includes an iPad with remote control features to open each skylight to create a cross breeze.

"I used to come up here to read," he says after he sets the iPad on a small coffee table in front of a taupe couch. There are navy accent pillows at each end. A beautiful floral rug is one of the highlights. The end of the apartment closest to the entrance is complete with a small refrigerator, sink, and microwave. Alden moves to where the bed is situated along the far end. There are two more windows and a door that leads onto a small veranda, where two chairs sit facing Lake Michigan. She sighs as she pictures herself watching the sunset. The lake is a beautiful sea-green today and aside from the water being choppy, the view is one of the most calming features of the room.

"Well, feel free to visit whenever you'd like," she hears herself say. It shocks her, this willingness to get close to Ethan, but there's something about him. He seems like he has the lay of the land, which not only includes knowing the house but also his mother and her moods, something that will take Alden a while to be well versed in.

"I don't know if my mom would like that. She already had a talk with me concerning you. I'm supposed to help you remain professional or something like that." He rolls his eyes, hands jammed into the pockets of his cargo shorts. "I mean, whatever. I think you're okay so far."

Alden fights the urge to push him on what else was said. She's already struggling between wanting to know for professional reasons and personal reasons. Other than maybe a shred of respect, which she will never get, she isn't exactly sure what she expects from Evelyn. Time will tell, but until then, she'll keep Ethan on her good side. "Well, I'm glad you're forming your own opinions, but don't get into trouble with your mom. I can handle myself."

His dark eyes sparkle when he smiles. "Oh, I know." He turns to leave but looks over his shoulder. "Oh, and dinner is at seven if you want to join us. I don't know if Mom told you that or not."

"Thank you, Ethan, for the invitation, but I will fend for myself for meals."

"Well, maybe one day?"

Alden chuckles. "Sure, maybe one day."

"Okay, well, if you need anything, let me know." He bounds out the door and down the steps, singing a Taylor Swift song. Alden shakes her head. *What an interesting kid.*

Alden pulls her baseball cap down a bit as she makes her way around the perimeter of the residence. She called in a favor with Serena and was emailed a copy of the land survey. She wants to know exactly where the property starts and ends. She also wants to see any breaks in the fencing. She already made a call to a security company to get everything outfitted at the house.

The fence is old and rickety on the far side of the lot. It's seen a lot of wear and tear for such a lovely home. She makes a note to get the fence company out here so she can get more options that are safer than wrought iron. She also isn't sure if there's an HOA or rules that need to be followed.

Securing the White House was a piece of cake compared to this.

As she gets to the seawall, she jumps onto the next platform, then again, and again until she's on the sand. She takes a deep breath as she stares across the water. Living here wouldn't be half-bad if she wasn't so worried about the person she's protecting. She's only seen Evelyn once, and it was not a pleasant meeting. As far as first impressions go, Evelyn Glass is one hell of a piece of work. Alden isn't shocked by this. She's had run-ins with her fair share of jerks. Especially in politics. She can handle most people. Not just because she was trained how to in the academy, but also because she's just good with different types. She is reserved by nature, but she understands the human psyche, and she has an underlying desire to calm people when they're upset, help them when they're in need, soothe them when they're injured, and protect them from harm. That ability to be a well-rounded protector while still remaining professional was always one of her greatest talents.

Until recently…when everything fell apart.

She picks up a flat rock from the beach. She flings it into the water, skipping it expertly. "Move on, Alden," she whispers. "It's time."

She turns, and her eyes land on Evelyn walking down the wooden steps to the water. She looks up and sees Alden at almost the same time. She stops, gripping the railing before she continues. When she gets to the bottom, she walks, determination in her steps, toward Alden. "This is how it's going to be? You're just going to *be* places?"

Alden tilts her head, confused. "No, that's not how it's going to be. I am going to *be* places with you, typically. I'm just surveying the property—"

"Oh, okay, great. So you'll be lurking every time I turn around. Wonderful." She rolls her eyes and pulls a black shawl tighter around her shoulders. The light breeze coming off the lake is chilly, and she has goose bumps on her light brown forearms.

GUARDING EVELYN

"A lot of important people have bodyguards, Ms. Glass."

Evelyn scoffs. "All it does is make people think I can't handle myself." Alden smirks but tries to recover. Unfortunately, Evelyn seems to see it. "Oh, I see. You are one of those people."

"I can assure you, I have never once thought that."

Evelyn turns to the water, pulls a deep breath in, and holds it for what seems like forever. Her profile is as striking as staring at her head on. She has perfect skin, highlighted now by the late-afternoon sun.

"You know, my father is the only reason you're here." Evelyn's eyes slide closed, and Alden wonders if she is even wearing makeup. She looks fresh, clean, and so gorgeous that it's making it hard to form a coherent thought. "You can thank him for liking you so much." She turns, eyes now open and boring holes into Alden. "For whatever reason, he seems to think you're who I need."

The thought that she could be who Evelyn Glass needs causes her palms to go sweaty. She tries to wet her dry mouth. It's no use. She's useless. What kind of a person loses themselves within minutes of being hired to *not lose themselves*? That's essentially what being a bodyguard means, and Alden can't even keep her shit together for more than two minutes. Hopefully, Evelyn's crass attitude and inability to be a nice person helps Alden hold on to herself. "Ms. Glass?"

"What?"

"I promise you, you will not regret this decision." Alden lets herself smile, albeit a small one, and finishes with, "You would have way more regrets if you didn't hire me."

"I hope you're right, Ms. Ryan." Evelyn purses her dark pink lips, bites the bottom one, then releases before she turns and stares into Alden's eyes. Their height difference is more apparent now since they're on a level playing field: Alden wearing boots and Evelyn wearing flat sandals. Alden has to admit, it gives her a little more courage because she's taller and bigger, and maybe sheer size will be enough of an indicator that she's good at her job. "Because I have little use for people who give me regrets." And with that, she stalks away, climbing the stairs two at a time, leaving a bewildered, yet annoyed Alden standing there frozen, wondering what the hell she has gotten herself into.

CHAPTER SEVEN

I need this hedge line cut back." Alden motions to the shrubs and foliage lining both sides of the property. "And these trees elevated. I want the canopy around the entire property raised to twelve feet and thinned. And this dune grass needs to be cut back, as well." She walks up the driveway, pointing along the way. "These ornamental shrubs, too. Seriously, every inch of this landscaping needs to be manicured, not just for aesthetics, but because you can easily hide a body there if someone wanted to. Nothing can obstruct the view of the driveway." She glances back at the landscaper. "Got it?"

After he confirms, she moves over to Joe, her security guru, and his assistant. "As far as locking this place down," she starts, and Joe's assistant begins scribbling away on a notepad. "We need to make sure it is as top-notch and as high tech as possible. I want HD security cameras, and I want access to them twenty-four-seven. I want the gate to be the best of the best, and I want a top-of-the-line intercom." Alden stops and looks down the driveway. "Joe, what do you think about a couple cameras facing up and down the road?"

"I think that's a great idea. What about a motion activated light?"

"Yes. I like where your head's at. Can you give me a timeline for installation?"

"Well, you're requesting a complete overhaul, so really, I'm thinking three weeks for everything, soup to nuts, if we really hustle. But we can work around the clock if you want us to, Alden. I mean, anything for you." He adjusts his raggedy ball cap. "I'm giving you my cost on everything, too."

"Oh, don't worry. Cost is not an object. I want to make sure everything is completely secure. I also want to resecure the house. New panels, new codes, the whole thing. I'd also like cameras installed around the house. Inside, too, in certain areas."

"And you mentioned being able to control the system remotely. Everything can be hooked to an app on your phone."

"Perfect." She motions to Joe and his assistant to follow. "Let's check out the back area."

❖

When the contractors leave, Alden does another perimeter sweep. She's beginning to like the solitude of her walks around the property. The grounds are really beautiful, and now that she has blazed some new trails, it's easier to get around. She's eager for the security system to be in place, but she trusts Joe and in the next week or so, things should be up and running.

Once near the water, she watches from about thirty paces as Ethan works with a younger woman and a paddleboard. "Okay, so you can take off from the shore because you're so light, but you can also paddle out on your belly."

Ethan mounts the board on his stomach. They're both wearing wet suits and life jackets. "Like this?" he asks, and the dark-haired woman shakes her head.

"Exactly. And then you paddle with your hands. Then you carefully get up. I'll show you once we're in the water."

"Can we go in now?"

"Sure, just let me get you out there."

Ethan gets up, then notices Alden. He shouts her name, waving, so she jogs over. "Hey. You gotta meet Stella." He looks at the dark-haired woman. "Stella, this is Alden. The new bodyguard."

"Oh, so you're the one Mom is up in arms about?"

"Guilty," Alden says with a laugh. "Did you just say Mom?"

"Guilty," Stella says, also while laughing. "I'm Evelyn's oldest."

"Yeah, Mom had her when she was super young."

Very interesting. Definitely not something uncovered in her hours of Google searches. "I had no idea she had another kid."

"I'm the black sheep of the family." Stella smiles. "Short hair, hippie, surfer chick, and I have no job. I'm one-hundred-percent not what Mom would want publicized. I mean, I exist, but I try not to cause trouble."

Hearing her say it like that breaks Alden's heart a little. "Either way, it's really nice to meet you."

"Ha, thanks." She pushes her shaggy hair away from her face. "Feel free to come with us. We have another board."

"Thanks, but I'll stay safe on the shore for now. You two go. Good luck getting up, Ethan."

As the two carry their boards into the water, she hears Stella say, "Ooo someone has a crush on the bodyguard."

He splashes her and protests. It's playful and fun, and it makes Alden long for a connection like that with someone. Being an only child has its advantages, but loneliness is definitely one of the disadvantages. Sadly, loneliness is one of the only reasons she took the position.

Well, that and dark hair, dark eyes, and the most amazing lips she has ever seen in her entire life.

One of the only things Alden looks forward to are her early morning runs. She hated running in the morning when she was in training. The constant strain it put on her barely warmed-up knees was awful, and she couldn't stand the sound of her feet hitting the pavement. The *thump, thump, thump* was like the ticking of a clock. Too exact, too stable. She needed things that pushed her, made her want to be better, and running reminded her of problems she'd never outrun.

But now?

Now running reminds her she's alive. She survived the bullet. She survived.

She needs to be reminded that she took that bullet for a reason. And irresponsibility isn't the reason.

Well, maybe a small part, but it was mostly love, and telling people is not an option. She can't tell a soul that she'd fallen in love with President Jennifer Simmons.

Alden's steady stride is what she focuses on now as she heads north on the beach, sand kicking up with every step.

The feelings between them were mutual. Or maybe they weren't? *Who knows anymore?* A single woman leading the country was out of the ordinary, and when Jennifer Simmons wanted a female Secret Service officer in her protection detail, it was just as out of the ordinary.

And she was so smart, well-spoken, intense…everything Alden wanted in a leader, but when it dawned on her that they were also the things she wanted in a romantic partner? She knew she was sunk, so she worked at keeping the longing in her heart under control. She remained professional. She had to. It was her duty to not only the country, but to President Simmons.

But then she had to be charming.

And she had to be captivating.

And dammit, she had to be so fucking sexy.

Alden stops and bends over to catch her breath. She's been running for the past thirty minutes at almost a sprint. Thinking about Jennifer Simmons is doing nothing good for her, except to remind her how stupid she was for letting things get out of control.

Now here she is, embarking on another mission with a woman who's smart, well-spoken, intense. The only thing she can hope for is that Evelyn never makes the turn to charming, captivating, and fucking sexy.

She turns and starts back toward the house. Her pace is slower, but she's still getting ready to pass another runner. Alden recognizes the small frame. It's Evelyn, who stops almost instantly.

"Come on," Alden says as she stops to run in place. She motions with her arm. "Run with me. I can push you."

"No way." Evelyn waves her off.

"Afraid I'm faster?"

Evelyn shakes her head dramatically and after an evil laugh says, "Oh, you wish." She takes off like a shot, her legs working hard, stretching into a decent runner's stride.

Alden catches up with ease. "Not bad, not bad at all." She's barely breathing hard, but she is enjoying the company far more than the actual exercise.

"This isn't fast for me. I was just giving you a fighting chance."

"Go for it, lady. Show me what you got." Alden starts to run faster, picking up the pace little by little, and much to her surprise, Evelyn continues to keep up. They're neck and neck, getting closer and closer to the beach behind the house. They're both pushing each other, Alden pulling ahead only to be taken over by Evelyn. *She's got stamina, I'll give her that.*

As they get to the house, Alden slows and lets Evelyn pull ahead. She watches her legs, her ass, her lean torso covered with a spandex top, showing off her curves. It's a shame, really, that Alden will never be able to see more of her. Because, damn, Evelyn Glass has an amazing figure.

Evelyn stops first, raising her arms and folding them above her head. She's breathing hard, much harder than Alden, but she looks like she might have enjoyed herself.

"Thanks for the run," Alden says when she gets closer.

"You call that a run?" Evelyn rolls her eyes. "Leisurely stroll is more like it."

"Oh, I'm sorry." Alden scoffs. "I mean, I was shot in the stomach six months ago. I'm sorry I couldn't run faster to push you harder." She sees the words "shot" and "six months ago" slam into Evelyn, and she wants to pull them back, but it's too late. The damage has been done. Alden takes off running in the opposite direction.

This time, instead of running with Evelyn, she's running away from her and the intense fear of letting anything more about herself slip out into the void.

CHAPTER EIGHT

M s. Ryan?"

Alden stands from her kneeling position next to the rear of the black Land Rover. She's been doing explosive sweeps and brake line checks every single morning and evening. One can never be too sure, and since the gate won't be installed until the end of the week, she needs to stay extra vigilant.

A young woman with very short blond hair waits by the hood. She's dressed sharply in a black button-down with a black vest and straight-legged jeans.

"Can I help you?"

"Yes, I, um, Mr. Glass told me to find you."

"He did, did he?"

"Yes, ma'am. I'm Talon."

Alden smiles. "Talon?"

"Yes, ma'am. I'm the, um, the driver. I have been, um..." She pauses and clears the apparent nerves from her throat. "I've been driving for Ms. Glass for a while now."

Alden wipes her hands on a rag. Connor had mentioned the driver, but for some reason, Alden assumed it was a man. She wants to kick herself. She should never assume those things; she used to get so bent out of shape when people assumed she was a man before meeting her. She leans against the back door, crossing her right leg over her left, and sizes Talon up. She's tall, lanky, but seems sturdy at the same time. She's attractive, with sharp features and a small lip

ERIN ZAK

piercing. Definitely not something that would be allowed if she were hired from a driving service. "How long is a while?"

"Three years. She hired me in LA." Talon shifts, outwardly uncomfortable. She is put together and professional, but she's nervous, and Alden can see it from a mile away.

"And what did you do before this?"

Talon pulls her shoulders back, stands a little straighter, and lifts her chin. "Not much. But I needed a job. And um…" A blush fills her cheeks. "I am friends with Stella."

It's Alden's turn to nod. "Friends, hmm?"

Talon's small smile gives her away. "If it's okay with you, I'd like to keep this job. I really enjoy it. I've never had a ticket. And I'm really good at parallel parking."

"Oh yeah? That's definitely a skill to have here in Chicago." She tosses the rag onto the work bench in the garage, walks around Talon to the passenger door, and hops in before she adds, "Show me what you got." She slips on the aviator frames hooked over the neck of her black T-shirt, then pats the driver's seat.

Talon's eyes go wide. "N…now?"

Alden can be intimidating when she wants to be, but right now, she offers a small smile. "Unless you have somewhere else you need to be? Don't worry. I don't bite."

Talon shakes her head and visibly gulps.

"Okay, then, hop in. Let's go for a ride."

Talon climbs in, buckling her seat belt before she starts the engine. The cabin of the SUV now smells like cologne, and even though Alden doesn't miss the smell of a man, she has to confess, it smells pretty nice on Talon.

"There's an empty parking lot at the high school. Go there."

Talon shifts into drive and starts off. She's driving very safely, checking her blind spots, making sure she's not speeding, using her turn signals, everything she should be doing if taking a driving test. But this isn't a normal test. This is a test to see how Talon handles pressure. So far, she's handling things just fine, but what happens if things get dicey? It's in those situations that a chauffeur becomes a driver, and a situation might come up where *Driving Miss Daisy* is not the speed they'll want to travel at.

• 70 •

Talon comes to a stop in the parking lot. She puts the SUV in park and takes a deep breath. Alden smiles. "You okay?" When Talon doesn't speak right away, she adds, "You realize I'm not going to fire you, right?

Talon's head snaps toward her. "You're not?" The look of relief on her sharp features is almost laughable. "Oh thank God." She lets out a ragged breath. "I thought for sure you were going to can me."

"No." Alden laughs. "But I am going to show you some things that will help if things were to go...awry."

"Awry? You mean, like, a bad situation?"

"Yes. That's exactly what I mean." Alden makes eye contact and holds it for one beat, two, before she continues with, "I want you to listen very carefully. This lot is long and wide and a perfect place to accelerate and work on sharp turns at a high speed."

Talon visibly gulps again.

"It's okay. I know how to do this. I've trained other agents. Believe me. I can train you."

"Okay." Her voice comes out as a whisper. She shifts into drive and accelerates slowly.

"Faster."

Talon presses the gas so they're going around forty miles per hour. She keeps looking at the speedometer.

"Keep your eyes on the road." Alden keeps her voice soft. "You never know what might run out in front of you.

"Ms. Ryan—"

"Alden," she corrects.

"Okay, um, I have never driven this car this fast. If Ms. Glass knew about this..."

Alden chuckles. "She won't. Don't worry. Now speed up."

"I'm already going fifty."

"Take it to seventy."

"Alden..."

"It's straight for days. Don't worry...too much." Alden smiles from the rush of going this fast. "Good, good. Now, hit the brakes, and take this corner as safely as you can while still maintaining a good speed."

Talon does as she's told. Every direction she's given, she completes with shocking skill. Alden is thoroughly impressed, especially after she performs the next turn, a one-eighty, almost flawlessly. Alden does have to lean over and help pull the wheel, but that's normal on a first attempt. She's pleased, though.

After they've driven the length of the parking lot ten or eleven times, executed a few flying turns, and even maneuvered through invisible cones, Alden directs them back to the house. "You realize, most police officers don't drive like this even after being on the force for years?"

Talon laughs as they turn onto the driveway. She shakes her head. "I can't say I wasn't insanely nervous the entire time."

"Well, you already know how the vehicle handles, so that helped."

"God, if Ms. Glass ever finds out…"

"Don't worry. She will one day when she's in the back seat, and you save us from an out-of-control situation."

"Holy cow." Talon breathes out as they pull up to the large garage off to the side of the house. "Is that really why you're here?"

"Pretty much." She shrugs. "But look, this won't work if you don't have my back. Can I trust you?"

"Yeah, I mean, absolutely." Talon climbs out and meets her at the front. "I am loyal to a fault, so if you need anything, please ask."

"You interested in learning how to shoot a gun?" She places her hand on the hood and leans into it. "I could always use backup."

Talon's visible gulp, which happens for the third time today, is going to be a great indicator of when she's not ready for something.

"Look, we'll discuss it, okay?"

"Okay, Ms. Ryan."

"Alden. Please."

Talon smiles as she holds out her hand. "Thanks for the lessons."

"Thank you," Alden says as they shake. Just as she turns to leave, she notices something out of the corner of her eye. "Did you see that?" She can barely make it out, but it looks like someone's in the bushes. "Hurry and get inside, lock the door." Alden smacks the hood of the car when Talon stands there with a blank stare on her face. "Now."

Alden draws her weapon as she runs in the direction of the movement. She pulls to an abrupt stop when she gets close, takes a few careful steps, and before she can act, the person is taking off in the opposite direction through the still-overgrown brush. "Hey," she shouts, taking off. She hurdles a fallen tree expertly and then slides on her thigh underneath some brush. She pops up and looks around.

It's silent.

Nothing but the sounds of seagulls.

She bends over, picks up a stone and throws it, causing some birds to chatter and flap their wings.

"Fuck," she whispers, hitting her thigh. She wipes at the sweat on her forehead with the back of her forearm before making her way back to the gate.

When she gets to the house, Evelyn is standing outside talking to Talon, who rushes over. "What happened? Are you okay?"

Alden holsters her gun and adjusts her sunglasses. "Yeah, I'm okay. I'm just happy that brush will be cut back, and the fence will be replaced tomorrow."

"Ms. Ryan," Evelyn says as she approaches.

Alden's stomach drops. She turns, and as well as being completely taken aback by how gorgeous Evelyn looks, she can barely find her voice. "Yes?" she finally manages. She's so thankful for her sunglasses; she can take in every single square inch of Evelyn in her black pencil skirt and low-cut red top. Alden's pulse is racing, and she isn't sure if it's from running after an assailant or from looking at Evelyn Glass in that outfit.

"Are you quite finished running through the bushes while waving a gun around? I swear to God, if the neighbors see you..."

Alden rolls her eyes. She's had it up to here with this attitude. For someone who was supposed to be onboard with everything, she certainly is not. "Oh, I'm so sorry for doing what I was hired to do."

That one must sting because Evelyn pulls up short, as if the comment quite literally stopped her in her tracks. She doesn't speak for a few seconds. It feels like a lifetime before she finally says, "Ms. Ryan, tonight is the Hispanic Cultural Event downtown, which I'm sure you're unaware of."

Alden smirks, hands on her hips, as they square off. "On the contrary," she says, all business. "I am aware. I have been briefed on your public appearances. As well as any private events." She lifts her head a hair, puffs her chest a little, and finishes with, "As far as tonight is concerned, we are leaving at six o'clock sharp."

Evelyn deflates a tiny bit and starts to fidget with the clasp on her watch. "Oh. Well. Then. I guess that's what I needed. I wasn't sure if you were going or not."

Alden rolls her eyes again. *I swear to God.* She glances at Talon, then focuses her attention on Evelyn. She licks her lips and fights the urge to be an arrogant asshole. "I know you're not happy about this, but since it's my job to protect you, Ms. Glass, I plan on being at every event."

"Well, I guess this meeting is over," Evelyn responds, her voice sharp and dripping with disdain, before turning swiftly and walking back to the house.

Alden lets out a long, exasperated breath, followed by, "Holy shit, Talon. Why does she hate me so much?"

Talon takes a step closer, looking after Evelyn. "From my somewhat limited knowledge of Ms. Glass, I can tell you that she hates needing anyone."

"That doesn't mix well if you need someone to save your life."

Talon chuckles, swipes a hand over her short hair, and shrugs. "I mean, you've got a point there."

"Be ready at a quarter till five, okay?" Alden pats Talon on the arm, then squeezes. "Big night tonight. Look sharp."

Alden takes a final look in the mirror. She decided to wear her best black suit. She looks good, skinny black pants, fitted black suit jacket, black button-down tucked in. Black heeled booties that are easy to move in, just in case anything crazy happens. She debated pulling her hair up or leaving it down. Secret Service demanded it to be pulled up and away from her face. But now? She no longer needs to play by government rules. She leaves it how she used to wear it: down with large, loopy curls, and she looks pretty fucking good.

She quickly does the combination on the gun safe and pulls out her gun. She ejects the magazine, checks it, and then slides it back. She slides the gun into her shoulder holster, then takes a deep breath. "You can do this, Alden. You can do this."

And the pep talk is over.

She turns and heads downstairs to wait and hopefully not sweat right out of her suit. The weather has taken a turn toward very warm in the last few days. The only respite is the lake breeze in the evenings. She has been looking forward to the night hours, when she can sit on her small veranda and watch Lake Michigan grow darker and darker. She slides on her sunglasses when she gets to the front door and heads outside, nervousness coursing through her veins.

It doesn't help that this situation is entirely different from what she's used to, sure, but it's also because it's *this* woman. Evelyn is so against her in every way, and it's exasperating. Alden knows what she's doing, for Christ's sake. She hasn't been given the opportunity to prove herself, which is part of the problem. It's a double-edged sword. As the bodyguard, she shouldn't want there to be a situation that calls for action because that means she's not really doing her job. But at the same time, in order to prove herself, she needs something to happen. Maybe something small. Something that proves she isn't an idiot. And also proves that she's necessary.

She never had to prove her worth when she was protecting the president. Well, except for the few times the men didn't think she was good enough. And even then, it was a lot easier than proving her worth to Evelyn Glass. Not only is she intimidating as hell, she's also almost too beautiful to look at without getting weak in the knees. There's only so much eye contact Alden can survive without needing to look away and catch her breath. She hopes this passes. There's no way she'll be able to stay if every time she looks at Evelyn, she gets a lump in her throat.

Talon is standing outside the Land Rover dressed in black, including her pants this time. She looks good. Professional. Like a driver with her black-framed sunglasses. "Talon," Alden says as she approaches. "You good?"

"Yes, sir." Talon clears her throat quickly. "I mean, ma'am."

She smiles. "It's okay. Not the first time it's happened."

"You, uh, you look good. Like, not a bodyguard at all."

Alden slides her sunglasses down her nose and eyes Talon over the top. Her cheeks are a couple shades of red, and it makes Alden chuckle inside. "And what does a bodyguard look like?"

"Like, a big man with, like, big bulging muscles and no neck."

A laugh bubbles from Alden, and she pushes her glasses back up. "Good. That's what I'm going for. Hoping I blend in…" Her words are cut short when the front door opens, and out glides Evelyn Glass wearing a long, form-hugging red dress that should be illegal.

The whole scene is moving in slow motion: the breeze blowing through her dark hair, the way it's ruffling the dress. Alden forces herself to swallow the all-too-annoying yet familiar lump that has started to accompany anything to do with Evelyn and waits for her to approach. Talon is on her game, opening the back door gracefully.

Evelyn stops, pulls her sunglasses off, and looks Alden up and down slowly, calculatingly, as if Alden's a bug that needs to be squashed. She's never felt so insecure in her life. Not even just her career, her entire friggin' life. She has no idea how to keep her mouth shut when she's nervous, and now is no different.

Nerves make her ask, "Is there a problem?" Not her brain, obviously, because her brain is still trying to figure out how to function properly after watching Evelyn look her up and down like that.

Evelyn slides her sunglasses back on, a smirk on her red, red lips. "Nope. No problem at all."

Connor sighs. "Evelyn, get in the car, and please try to cooperate." He rubs his temple, looking exhausted. He taps his dark brown shoes on the ground. Evelyn has been testing him daily. His irritation is starting to show.

"Daddy, I'm just playing." Evelyn's voice is so sweet, it makes Alden's teeth ache. From behind the safety of her aviators, she rolls her eyes while also clamping her now-aching teeth. When Evelyn climbs into the vehicle, Alden zeroes in on the gold zipper of her dress. She has never hated someone so much and also wanted to fuck them, but dammit, this relationship is really skirting the territory, and that gold zipper on that damn red dress is doing nothing for her overloaded senses.

Connor waits until the door is closed before he looks at Alden, swipes his own sunglasses from his face, and says, "She's gonna be the death of me."

Alden forces a fake chuckle because, *yeah, buddy, same.* "Everything will be fine." She's not sure if she's reassuring him or herself. Probably a bit of both, more the latter than the former. "Connor?" She places a hand on his bicep as they walk around to the door on the opposite side. "Have you had a chance to relay the severity of this entire situation?"

"The severity?"

If his dumbfounded look doesn't answer her question, his tone definitely does. He hasn't said a word. "Connor," she says, pauses, and sighs before she gathers her words. She's not only hot from the weather and turned on by the sight of Evelyn's breasts and ass in that dress, but now she's bothered, and this conversation, even though it's of her own doing, is provoking some anger she thought she had a decent handle on. "Look, I can't protect her if she doesn't understand what's going on." She manages to keep her voice down. These emotions coursing through her veins are confusing, so she's sure she's going to come unglued. It's only a matter of time, which scares her because she's never struggled like this before. She has always been able to keep her head on straight—*well, somewhat*—keep her anger managed—*eh, most of the time*—and keep her voice level and cool—*ugh, almost always.*

"I know, Alden. I know." Connor's breathing is short, shallow, and it's clear he's struggling with something as much as she is. If she didn't know any better, she'd think he was on the verge of a heart attack. His face is pale, and he seems beyond stressed.

"What's going on with you?"

"I didn't want to tell you this."

"Connor, what the *hell* is going on?"

"Robert—"

"Who I said needs to either get in line or fucking get out."

Connor scoffs. "If only it were that easy."

"Where is he, anyway?"

"He will meet us there."

"Not anymore. He either travels with us or he doesn't go. You hear me?"

"Yes, Alden, I hear you. He has her set to do a meet and greet during this event. I told him to cancel it, and he said he couldn't. Now we have a change of plans."

"How many people will be at the meet and greet?"

"At least two hundred. Possibly more. She's very popular these days."

"Okay."

"Okay? That's it?"

"Yes. *Okay.* But dammit, you and Robert have to tell me these things. I'm not going to fight you on events she needs to participate in." She turns, but as she places her hand on the door handle, she says softly, "And also?" She looks over her shoulder. "I will have the conversation about the severity with her if you and Robert, a man I am disliking more and more by the second, don't. Is that clear?"

Connor gulps and places a hand on the side of the SUV as if to steady himself. She feels slightly better about putting her foot down. And he had better listen. After opening the door for him, she rushes to hers and hops in, eager to get inside the cool cabin of the Land Rover. She smooths her sweaty palms over her slacks. She cannot stand how this whole situation makes her feel. She has to find a happy medium here, or even if Evelyn does finally cooperate, she'll never be able to focus enough to be an asset. "Let's go."

"Fast?" Talon asks, a smile on her face.

Alden laughs. "No, Talon. Just normal. Thank you."

She groans, a joking tone blanketing the low noise. "Fine."

When the vehicle advances, Alden takes a deep, deep breath. She lets it fill her lungs, holds on to the oxygen so she can remind herself that she's alive and she can breathe, and she decided to take this job because she wants to be okay again. She holds the breath, focusing on the things she can control, which unfortunately, isn't Evelyn Glass. When she releases the air, the fact that she may never be able to control everything regarding Evelyn sets in. It's not necessarily a bad thing. She can't control every move the woman makes. The only benefit is, if she can't control her every move, she can watch her every move.

And watching Evelyn's every move is going to do two things.

One, she's going to be able to memorize Evelyn's body language, every expression in almost every situation.

And two?

Alden sighs, looks out the passenger window at the side mirror. She can see herself, her pained facial expression, her clenched jaw. She's going to possibly fall for her the same way she fell for Jennifer Simmons.

The only reason that realization doesn't freak her out is because as beautiful as Evelyn Glass is, her curvaceous body, her shiny hair, her glowing skin, her dark eyes, are a mask. Evelyn is not someone Alden would ever be attracted to on the inside. Superficial beauty and women who think they're better than other people are not her cup of tea.

As she stares at herself, she finds herself smiling. Smiling because a tiny weight has lifted. Smiling because she is able to breathe a little easier now. And smiling because mask or not, Evelyn Glass is really fucking fun to look at.

CHAPTER NINE

The Hispanic Cultural Event is going very smoothly. Alden has been to numerous venues throughout Chicago, but she's never attended anything located at the Winter Garden on the ninth floor of the Harold Washington Library. A grand atrium with a glass-paneled ceiling, the space is absolutely breathtaking. The marble floors glimmer from the ambient lighting. There is a stage on the left side, windows looking out onto State Street.

So far, the security has been top-notch, which makes Alden's job ten times easier. She was told, once again, what her place was when they arrived. Evelyn's stern voice and eye contact as she said, "Please don't follow me around like a lost dog this entire event," was heard loud and clear. "This isn't a national security matter."

It took everything in Alden to not retort with, "No shit, lady," but she refrained. Thankfully. But oh, how she wanted to put Evelyn in her place. She did manage to get her to agree to occasional eye contact from across the room.

Either way, Alden takes it as a win as she distances herself most of the evening. She posts herself near one of the exits. She can see everything well, so she could have eyes on Evelyn. She also finds watching from afar the best way to get a visual of everything going on. Also, it makes it a hell of a lot easier to take in and digest Evelyn's every move, which, so far, has been very intriguing. Of the hundreds of videos Alden has watched on YouTube, she never realized how charismatic Evelyn is. She is a pro at mingling, that's for damn sure. She talks and laughs with industry people, news anchors, reporters, politicians, and she does it with poise and dignity.

Robert has been on her arm the entire time. Alden both hates that fact and enjoys it. Hates it because she cannot stand him; enjoys it because it gives her a chance to watch *his* every move, as well. Connor has explained a little about him but not enough for Alden to feel any sort of comfort regarding him. He seems sleazy, in a greasy, coat-tail-riding kind of way. Apparently, he's been Evelyn's friend for years. And has been her publicist for ten of those. Her child acting stint was cut short when she was seventeen. No one knows the reason, but after meeting Stella, Alden sort of wonders if maybe—

"Alden Ryan."

Her head snaps to the sound. "Tobias, what the hell are you doing here?" She stands a little straighter, smoothing her black tie and then running her tongue over her teeth. After reapplying lipstick, the idea that she could have it on her teeth in front of him causes her skin to crawl. She wishes she could stop fearing his judgment for one second because she really does love him. Their relationship is the epitome of a thin line between love and hate. He's been in her life for longer than some of her family. And they have so much in common. Including protecting famous people for money, now.

His smile is beautiful, too, which makes her feel even worse for wanting to slug him. "Well, I'm a donor." He turns, pointing to a woman standing over by the stage. "And I'm here on assignment. That's Felicia Jimenez. Actress turning politician."

"Ah," Alden says with a smile. He raises his glass. "You drink during these things?"

"Uh, no, it's soda water and lime."

"Oh, nice. Makes it look like you're mingling."

"Exactly." He places a hand on her arm. "Speaking of, let me give you a little tip. You're no longer in the Secret Service. You need to look less like a bodyguard."

She looks at her outfit. "Excuse me? This is a black tie event."

"Come on. You look like the president is right around the corner. Dress nice. But stop sticking out like a sore thumb." He crudely reaches over and pulls the earpiece from her ear. "And is this really necessary?"

She smacks him on the arm. "Stop distracting me." She chuckles as she fixes her earpiece. "And, yes, it's necessary. Mr. Glass didn't hire me to do a half-ass job."

"True." Tobias also chuckles. "And I get fifteen percent of what he's paying you, so really, I guess the better you do, the longer you have the job."

She looks at him, her mouth hanging open. "Because if I don't succeed, she dies?"

"Whoa, whoa, Alden, that is not what I said."

"Okay, then." She straightens her jacket and tilts her head to the left, right, cracking her neck. She smiles when she looks at him. "You're too easy."

"You're a jerk. Still."

They both laugh together and continue a semi-easy conversation about the Cubbies and their new manager. It's easier to talk about random things with Tobias than the deep stuff. And by deep stuff, she means anything having to do with her being better at the job they were both hired to do. She made it to the Secret Service, and he couldn't cut it. He couldn't pass the test, written or physical. Any mention of work seems to get him riled up. Keep it casual and light, and they're fine. And since she's working for him now, technically, she decides to not poke the bear, which makes it a little easier to try to relax. The only bad part is, her brain has been trained to be alert and on edge when she's on the job. Staying vigilant is how she stayed alive and how the president didn't get shot. Since Tobias is always looking for a way to top her, she wonders if he's purposely trying to distract her.

She laughs to herself. *You really are a hot mess, aren't you, Ryan?*

It's not until she sees Evelyn start toward an exit, not making eye contact with her, that Alden's protective mode shifts into overdrive. "Tobias, I hate to cut you off, but we're on the move." She pats him on the arm, then takes off. She slips through the crowd easily, bypassing numerous people by sticking to the outer perimeter. When she gets closer to Evelyn, she sees that she's not leaving but making her way to the ladies' room. Alden follows without making her presence known. She is sure to give Evelyn as much space as possible. If Evelyn knew Alden was standing outside, she'd be furious. But Alden doesn't care. She really should have gone in first and done a sweep, but Evelyn would have never allowed that.

She checks her watch. *Twenty fifteen.*

She waits for a couple more minutes, scanning the room. She clenches her teeth again. She's going to crack a tooth one day because of this fucking woman. Maybe she should just go in and check things out. She would in any other situation. Why not now? Then she chuckles because the honest answer is, she fears Evelyn's anger, which is unlike her.

After making herself wait for fifteen minutes, her heart rate increasing the entire time, she says, "Fuck it," takes the risk, turns, and pushes through the door. "Ms. Glass?" Alden calls from the small sitting room inside the door. She doesn't get an answer, so she takes a couple steps, then turns a corner. There are a few sinks, a restroom attendant, and three or four stalls. "Evelyn?"

Finally, she hears an exasperated sigh, a lot of material shuffling, and then a toilet flushing. When the stall door opens, Evelyn is standing there, quite flustered and completely irritated, and she looks as if she's having issues with her dress.

"I thought I specifically told you that I don't want you following me around everywhere I go?" Evelyn asks, still standing in the stall, her hand on the top of the swinging door, her other hand holding the top of her dress near her breasts.

Alden takes a deep breath, adjusts her stance, and gathers herself. "Look," she says after breathing out slowly. "I realize you don't think you need me to follow you, but it's my job. It's also my job to know certain things, and one of them is understanding how long it should take for a woman who is dressed to the nines to go to the bathroom. I wouldn't be in here if you hadn't taken much, much, *much* longer than normal." Evelyn's face shifts, so Alden softens her tone. "I came in here to check on you. I'm sorry if that upsets you, but you're going to have to take it up with your father. I'm not going to let you get murdered because you feel weird about having me follow you to the bathroom."

Evelyn takes a deep breath, and the dress shifts. Alden can tell what the issue is. She can't zip it up. And she's too stubborn to ask for help. The pleading she is doing with her eyes is so out of character. The benefit and the hindrance of having near-perfect eyesight is sometimes seeing things she isn't meant to see.

"Of course it took me longer," Evelyn finally says, her voice cracking. "I don't typically wear a goddamn ball gown to the bathroom. And now..." She takes another deep breath and lets it out; this time her lips are pursed, and her nostrils flare as the air exits. "You know what, never mind. Can you please just leave?"

"Do you need help?"

"No."

Alden's ears have heat radiating from them. "Fine," she says, dropping her hands to her side. She heads to the door, making eye contact with the restroom attendant on the way out. She shoves a twenty into the tip jar. "If she's as nice to you as she is me, you're going to need that tip." The attendant, a short older woman who probably volunteers her time for these events, offers a gracious smile.

She has her hand on the door handle and is just getting ready to pull it open when she hears, "Wait."

"What do you need?" Alden doesn't move, doesn't turn, doesn't even breathe.

"I think," Evelyn starts, then lets out an exasperated groan. "I need help...with my dress."

Alden wants to shout, "Too fucking bad," over her shoulder and keep on walking. But she can't. And even though she could have the bathroom attendant help—since the last thing she should do is see Evelyn's bare back and have to be that close to her—she decides to suck it up. She walks back to where Evelyn is standing out of the stall. "What's going on with it?" She knows damn well what's going on with it, but she wants Evelyn to say it, if for no other reason than to admit defeat.

"Well, I tried to pull it up to go to the bathroom, but it didn't work because it's so fucking tight, so I unzipped it, but when I tried to zip it up, I couldn't get it to lie right. And now..." She won't make eye contact, and Alden can hear the frustration in her voice. She seems a lot closer to having a breakdown than she'd like to admit. "Now the zipper is stuck, and I'm half-naked, and I just need help. Okay? I didn't want to ask the attendant, a complete stranger, to help. I'm asking you, but I can assure you, Ms. Ryan, I will not beg."

A couple things happen when Evelyn stops rambling. The first is small, but the bathroom attendant clears her throat and says softly that she'll take a step out and guard the door. Alden thanks her, never taking her eyes from Evelyn's bent head and embarrassed stance. The extra amount of privacy is something she can tell Evelyn is grateful for by the way her neck and shoulders relax.

The other thing is, when Alden lets out a deep breath, Evelyn glances up, and for the first time, Alden sees a tiny crack in the icy facade. "Okay, come here," she says calmly, walking Evelyn a couple steps away from the stalls over to a more lit area in the restroom. She turns Evelyn so she can focus on the problem at hand.

The gold zipper Alden spent the better part of the drive imagining unzipping is now almost fully unzipped, and Evelyn's entire back is exposed. For the first time maybe ever, Alden is seeing a very human side of Evelyn, and it's very stimulating. But she keeps the unexpected happiness of the moment to herself.

"I'm going to unzip you to get it unstuck first." Evelyn sighs, and Alden takes that as an okay. She bends down, working at the zipper, flashing back to seeing Evelyn climbing into the SUV. *Focus, Alden. Focus.* She shakes the memory from her head and kneels. The teeth are stuck on some of the material, so she works at it slowly until it finally breaks free. "Got it."

"Thank God."

"No, thank *me.*"

Evelyn laughs. It's small, but it's a laugh, and Alden takes it for what it's worth. "Fine," Evelyn says as she looks at the mirror. Alden does the same, and their gaze meets momentarily. "Thank *you.*"

Alden breaks first and looks at Evelyn's bare back, at a small beauty mark near her spine. Then, as if on command, a smattering of goose bumps appears. She gulps and refuses to take that as anything other than Evelyn is cold. That's what it has to mean. Period. "Okay, I can zip you back up now." She stands, finds the hook stitched into the top, next to the gold zipper and the eye on the other. She slips the two together, being as delicate as possible, trying to not touch Evelyn's skin.

"Ever have to do this for the president?"

Alden glances at Evelyn in the mirror again, to the smile playing on her deep red lips. "I've helped with my fair share of wardrobe malfunctions." She lets herself return the gesture before she looks back at the zipper and starts to zip it up. She does it slowly, so she doesn't re-snag the material, but dammit if she isn't thinking once more about doing the opposite, about finding another beauty mark, or seeing just how far those goose bumps traveled. "Okay. You're good."

Evelyn turns to look at the zipper in the mirror as if checking Alden's work. Then she faces her reflection. She bends down, reaches into the top of her dress, and readjusts each breast. She bounces a little after the adjustment, and Alden, mouth hanging slightly open, realizes she has been staring. She snaps her mouth closed, pulls her gaze away, and looks at the linoleum. "Is that all?" She needs to exit. *Now.*

"Yes, Ms. Ryan, that will be all."

Alden moves, her jacket-covered arm brushing Evelyn's on the way past, and jets out the door. She leans against the wall outside the restroom, eyes clamped shut, and takes deep breath after deep breath, calming herself from the onslaught of soft skin and goose bumps and eye contact and smiles. When she opens her eyes, she notices the bathroom attendant is staring. "Oh, sorry, you can go back in now."

"You okay, honey?" The woman places her hand on Alden's shoulder. "You look like you've seen a ghost."

"Yes, thank you, I'm fine."

"You handled her perfectly," the attendant says with a wink. "Don't be so hard on yourself." And she opens the door and leaves.

Alden wishes that was the case. If being too hard on herself was the reason for the erratic heartbeat and clammy palms, it'd be fine. But it's not the case. Evelyn Glass is the case, and dammit, she's far too much for Alden's still healing psyche.

"I'm ready," Evelyn says as she approaches. "Please get me out of here."

"Is everything okay?" Alden is standing guard right inside the meet and greet area. She hasn't noticed anything happen, so she wonders what prompted this change. She notices Connor and Robert having words, then Connor pulling Robert by the arm to the edge of the crowd.

"Just very ready." For the first time this evening, aside from the zipper fiasco, Evelyn's frustration is showing. Alden follows her to the elevator, and they board, leaving Connor and Robert behind. The descent is silent. Alden prefers silence, but something about the way Evelyn is acting causes this silence to be far tenser than usual.

"What happened?"

"I don't want to talk about it."

"Evelyn…" Alden is cut off when the doors open, and Evelyn exits without hesitation. Alden quickly catches up, moving in front of her and stopping her in her tracks. The look on Evelyn's face would stop traffic and not in a good way. "One second, I need to get the car." She brings her wrist where her microphone is clipped up to her mouth and says softly, "Talon, please be ready. ETA three minutes."

"Okay, boss, they wouldn't let me park close, so I am in the parking garage a block away. Give me two minutes." Talon's reply comes across her earpiece.

"Copy." Alden continues her stare off with Evelyn. "We need two minutes for Talon to get here." But Evelyn either doesn't care or doesn't hear because she takes off in the direction of the exit. Alden is hot on her trail. "Wait," she says in a hushed tone.

"No, Ms. Ryan, I need some air. Now." She tosses the words over her shoulder. How is she so fast in heels? Alden is right behind her as Evelyn pushes through the people standing around the door and out into the night. There are people everywhere. *Everywhere.* When they arrived earlier, there were a few people milling around, but now, the entryway is so crowded, it is ridiculous. And the crowd fucking erupts when they see Evelyn.

Erupts.

The sound is so loud, it almost takes Alden's breath away.

And the smile plastered on Evelyn's face?

That almost takes her breath away, as well.

Alden stands as close as possible, watching as black and white headshots are shoved in Evelyn's direction with black Sharpies wagged at her like disapproving fingers, and it doesn't faze her one bit. She takes her time, talks to her fans, smiles, laughs, poses for selfies, even goes so far as to hug one teenage girl in tears. Alden is shocked. Why the hell is the girl crying? Is this the kind of following

Evelyn Glass really has? They move down the line, Evelyn talking to as many people as possible, Alden making sure people aren't grabbing her as she passes. When they get to an older man, Alden's senses start tingling due to the fact that he's wearing a long trench coat. He is also wearing an all-black ball cap.

She leans into Evelyn's space and whispers, "Skip this guy." Evelyn looks up casually, noticing the man and tensing up.

Alden slides a hand in between her and the fans. "Ms. Glass, your car is here now," Alden says, loud and forceful. The fans whine and groan, and all of a sudden, the older man lunges at them.

Alden shields Evelyn from his grasp and grabs the back of his head. She pulls him down and knees him right in the nose. "No way, buddy." Alden pulls the guy away by the arms. "Security! Get this guy out of here."

The security officers swarm the guy, and before anything else can happen, Alden has maneuvered Evelyn into the car with Connor and Robert jumping in after them. "Drive, Talon," Alden directs, and Talon does exactly as she's told, rubber squealing on the asphalt as she pulls away from the now unruly crowd.

CHAPTER TEN

Alden leans back in one of the chairs on the veranda, propping her feet on a small table. She has a cold Goose Island 312 in one hand, and the other is rubbing her head; a dull headache has been haunting her ever since they got back. She leans her head back and forth, letting the snap, crackle, and pop of her neck release some of her stress. Overall, the event went really well. Not to mention the bathroom incident, which she cannot stop thinking about.

One of the aspects of protection she excels at is reading body language. She recognized what it meant when Evelyn's shoulders pulled back. She comprehends what nervous laughter means. She can notice a spine stiffening from fifty paces and fully understand what that move indicates.

But those goose bumps that appeared on Evelyn's bare back?

She is very familiar with what goose bumps typically mean, but *those*? Those could mean something else altogether. Something Alden isn't sure she should even want to comprehend.

She drinks, soothing the heat that begins to rise at the thought of Evelyn's skin.

The fact that Evelyn wasn't wearing a bra doesn't escape her, either.

"You have got to get a grip, Alden." Her voice sounds loud against the quiet backdrop of the night. She lets her eyes slide closed, taking in the gentle breeze, the lake smells, and the warmer than normal air.

"Ms. Ryan?"

The voice startles Alden so badly that she jumps up and spills her beer all over herself. She takes a few deep breaths as her eyes focus on the figure standing in the doorway leading to the veranda. "Jesus Christ, Evelyn. You cannot fucking sneak up on me like that."

"I'm sorry."

Alden lets out the final deep breath and laughs as it releases. "You're lucky I don't have a gun on me. And an itchy trigger finger."

"Well, that seems dramatic." Evelyn smiles, and it could be genuine, but Alden doesn't trust it. Not after the playacting Evelyn pulled earlier with the fans. "Do you mind if I join you?"

"No, yeah, um…have a seat. I'm going to um…" Alden motions to her wet shirt. "I'm going to change." She slips past a very low-key Evelyn. She isn't sure what she expected Evelyn to sleep in, but a pair of gray sweats and a ratty navy New York Yankees sweatshirt is not it. "Do you want a beer?"

"Sure," comes her answer as she sits.

Alden listens for the creak of the chair before she pulls her wet T-shirt over her head and changes into a dry one. She shakes her head, softly laughing as she moves to the small refrigerator and pulls out two beers. "Here you go," she says as she hands one to Evelyn, whose hair is swept up messily into a tortoiseshell clip. Alden's eyes are drawn to the line of Evelyn's neck where a few stray curls have snuck out of her mass of hair.

After Evelyn takes a long drink of the 312, she says, so very softly, "Thank you."

"You're welcome." Alden sits, her chair creaking. These small distinct noises are the only thing linking her to reality right now. If they weren't happening, this whole scene would feel like a dream.

"No, thank you, for…" Evelyn's voice seems to have snagged on something. Alden can't help but notice this change in demeanor. Evelyn messes with the label on the neck of the beer bottle, and she looks small, unsure of herself, which, as Alden can tell so far, is not normal for her.

"You don't have to thank me for doing what you hired me to do." She is uncomfortable with this shift in attitude, even though it's what she wanted. Now that it's actually happening, she wishes Evelyn would go back to her old ways. If for no other reason than to alleviate the uneasiness of this mood.

Evelyn blinks once after their eyes connect, the smile so small on her lips it could almost go unnoticed. Except Alden notices everything. Always. But especially about the person she's been hired to protect. Noticing everything certainly has its advantages, but the disadvantage happens when a heart gets involved where a head should be making the decisions. "I know I don't have to, but I wanted to. You should probably take it and not question it."

"That seems fair." They both drink in unison. "Is something else...going on?"

"My dad just told me everything."

The air, as if on command, stills. There's a half second when Alden wishes Connor would have waited. She doesn't know why because he did as she asked so she should be thrilled. Maybe it's the tone of Evelyn's voice. And how she shifted in her seat when she said it. Or maybe it's that Alden can only imagine how it feels finding out someone tried to kill her with a homemade bomb. She doesn't know how to respond, so she settles on a soft, "Oh."

Evelyn continues to stare into the moonlit darkness, looking very lost and bewildered. Alden has seen this face before on Jennifer Simmons, and she understands exactly what it means. Evelyn Glass is finally aware, and she is frightened.

"Do you want to talk about it?"

Evelyn's gaze focuses on her now. She looks as if she might start crying.

"Hey," Alden starts. "You're safe here with me. Okay?"

"I know." Evelyn's voice is so quiet, Alden barely hears it. "That's why I came up here."

The admission shocks Alden, but she hopes she hides it well. She never thought she'd hear Evelyn admit Alden knows what she's doing. She leans back, takes a drink, then sets the bottle on the table. "What did he tell you?"

Evelyn takes a breath. "Everything."

"The bedroom?"

Evelyn nods.

"The explosive?"

Another nod.

"The letter?"

A final nod before Evelyn looks at her. "He said you wanted to tell me as soon as he briefed you."

"Connor and I talked, yes. I wanted you to know. I feel you need to know, otherwise, well…" She tries to find the right words but realizes she needs to be completely honest. "You act like you did tonight. Without a care in the world." Alden tries to smile, but clearly, it's too soon. "I'm sorry they didn't tell you right away. But there are no secrets now."

"Do you promise?"

"Yes. I promise."

"Because I cannot stand secrets. I don't need any more in my life."

What does that mean? "I swear, if I find anything out, you will be the first to know."

"Good."

"But…" Alden leans forward and places a hand on Evelyn's knee. "You have to make the same promise to me."

"Okay," she whispers, as if she's having a hard time breathing.

Alden moves her hand, leaning back again. They sit once more in silence, and the desire to ask questions percolates inside Alden's brain. She wants to unearth what makes this woman tick. Maybe if she can do that, she can understand why this is happening, why Evelyn is being stalked. Alden can see plain as day why fans love her, why the press adores her, and why she's so popular. But what happened in her past that made someone think the only revenge is to stalk, to harm, and to threaten? It had to have been big, right? "Do you think…" Alden pauses because maybe she shouldn't push her luck right now.

"What, Ms. Ryan?"

Call me Alden, please…if for no other reason than I want so badly to hear you say my name. "Maybe you wouldn't mind sharing part of your past? So I can understand where you come from. Might make it easier to know where you're headed."

The corner of Evelyn's mouth ticks upward. "You think so, hmm?"

"I mean, it couldn't hurt." *Smooth, Alden, real fucking smooth, you asshole.*

"I will on one condition."

"And what's that?" she asks, watching as Evelyn puts the beer to her lips and drains the rest of the liquid. Alden widens her eyes at the sight. *That was...unexpected.* "Jesus."

Evelyn chuckles as she hands over her empty. "Get me another beer."

❖

"I grew up in New York City."

"I know that." Alden smiles. "I need more than that."

"Like what?"

"Who was your first boyfriend? Whose heart did you break first?"

Evelyn lets out a laugh. "Why do you need to know that?"

Uh... "To start building a suspect list." *Nice cover, Alden.*

"Hmm," Evelyn says, her eyes narrowed. "You're assuming I'm a heartbreaker."

"Let's be real," she says with a shrug. "The chances are high that you were the one breaking hearts and not the other way around."

Evelyn leans against the railing of the porch. She moved to the planked veranda floor on a blanket after her third beer. So far, she's answered every question. Her favorite food is Mexican. Her favorite food to cook is Italian. And she really loves Chicago deep-dish, but Alden had to swear to never utter a word to anyone because of Evelyn's New York connections. But this current question causes Evelyn to falter. And Alden is on high alert as to why.

"Okay, fine. His name was Joel. Joel Somers."

"Wait. Wasn't he—"

"My on-screen love interest in every movie during my Disney Channel days?" She smiles. "Yeah, that's him."

"Okay, I'm all ears."

"Oh, no, no way. I'm not telling you the whole story."

"Excuse me? Why not?"

"That's too much for tonight. It's getting really late."

Alden shakes her head. "You're being sneaky...I'll get to the bottom of this."

"Oh, will you?" Evelyn points at her with the neck of her bottle. "Don't be so sure of yourself, Ms. Ryan."

"Me being sure of myself is the reason I'm still alive. I think I'll continue the trend." She laughs before she takes a drink. They've gone through the bottles in her fridge, so she's prepared for the evening to come to an end. There's a part of her that is sad about how this night unfolded because against her better judgment, she's finding it a little too pleasurable getting to know this miserable woman, who, as it turns out, isn't miserable at all. In fact, she's fascinating in the best ways. And that? A fascinating woman who isn't as miserable as she lets on? Not to mention elegant and talented with a hint of underlying sadness...None of that is good for Alden. Not in the slightest.

"Are you going to tell me anything?" Evelyn asks. "Or do I have to stay on the outside of this *tough lady* routine you've perfected?"

Alden can't fight the furrowing of her eyebrows and the look of shock she's sure is plastered on her face. "Tough lady routine? You think this is just an act?" She's disappointed in herself. She is usually so much more composed than this. Maybe it's the beer? *Or maybe it's the fucking breathtaking woman sitting across from me?*

The small, yet amused chuckle that Evelyn lets escape reminds Alden of being young again, riding her bike in downtown Chicago with not a care in the world, summers at Navy Pier, hanging out with friends until it was way too late to escape getting yelled at by her overprotective parents for barely missing curfew. "There's no way that this is your constant state?"

"And how's that, pray tell?"

"Oh, I don't know." Evelyn pulls her legs into her body and wraps her arms around them, propping her chin on her left knee as she stares. "Buttoned up." She sighs. "Strict." Another lovely sigh. "Wounded."

The word, regardless of the truth it holds, causes Alden's heart to clench as if it had jaws and finally realized everything that's happening is far from okay when it comes to being the protector. *Rule number one: You protect. You catch. You don't fall.* It seems to be the hardest rule for her to follow.

"Hmm." Evelyn's left eyebrow rises, and the left side of her mouth also pulls upward, as if there's an invisible string that connects them. "Have I struck a chord?"

For half a second, she wonders if standing and leaving would work. She could ignore the question and kick Evelyn out, all at the same time. This precipice they're standing on is so fragile. One side has Evelyn acting like a jerk again, making moves without understanding the repercussions, and living like a vigilante with no cares in the world. The other side has Alden slip, slip, *slipping* until she's drowning in a pool of sloppy emotions and forbidden feelings. Neither sounds like a great way to go. But a tiny crack, minuscule really, has started to appear in her "tough lady routine," and she chooses to respond with, "Ask me anything."

Evelyn's dark eyes go so wide, Alden can see the whites perfectly. "All righty, then." She rubs her hands together and purses her lips. "When we were running the other day, you mentioned you were shot six months ago."

She shrugs. What more is there to say?

"Like, with a gun?"

"Well, it wasn't with an arrow." Alden leans forward, a wink happening without her being able to stop it. *Great. Now you're flirting?*

"How did it happen? Can I ask?"

She laughs. Not because it's funny, but, "Do you not watch the news?"

"Do you think I have time to watch the news?"

"Do you even read the news?"

"Unless it's about me? No." She lifts her head from her knees, shrugs, then rests it again. "I read books. I like to escape. Not be thrust back into the life I'm living every second of the day."

"Perfect career you've chosen."

Evelyn smiles. "The Oscar sort of helped me understand that."

"Maybe one day, you can explain how an Oscar winner at sixteen took the path you took."

"I will if, and only if, you ever freaking tell me why you were freaking shot. So. Please go on." She spreads a hand before her as if offering the floor.

Alden's insides are running a marathon. Her blood is coursing at a rate that cannot be healthy. She shouldn't be doing this. She can feel it deep down inside where her conscience lives, but for some reason, that tiny voice is either asleep, tipsy, or getting a midnight snack. She relies heavily on that tiny voice, and to find herself abandoned right now is both unsettling, and dare she admit it, slightly exciting. She has always listened, always obeyed, always ended up making the right moves and doing the right things. The moment she needs that tiny voice the most, the moment she needs to be shouted at to fucking apply the brakes, abort this mission, and get the fuck out of there, is the exact moment it's nowhere to be found. "I don't know if I should—"

"Why? Who am I going to tell?"

"It was on the news. I am not exactly worried you'll tell anyone." She shrugs. "It just shouldn't have happened."

"Were you protecting..." Evelyn's words, the way they trail off, are both knowing and coated with worry.

"Yes."

"Tell me."

"I have never told anyone every single one of the details." Alden swallows, trying to dislodge the lump that, for the first time, isn't caused by Evelyn. The cause is because the details are why she couldn't truly recover, why she was asked to take a leave of absence, why she's sitting on this fucking veranda instead of wearing a black suit and black tie, being completely vigilant outside the president's bedroom.

"Can you tell me any of it?"

She looks at the night sky, at the small amount of stars. They should be comforting because the ones that shine the brightest, that can be seen in the most light polluted of skies, are the most resilient. But for some reason, the thought makes her feel unimportant because what it really means is the dimmer stars have to take a back seat when it comes time to shine. Not everyone can shine at the same time. And that thought makes her want to cry.

She bites her cheek to stop the grief bubbling way too close to the surface. *You're alive, and that's what matters. Remember that. You are still shining, even if it's faintly. You didn't burn out completely.*

"Have you ever felt a pain that hurt so badly, it was almost impossible to describe?" She breathes in, realizing what she's doing, but keeps on going, not waiting for an answer. "And the sound? Flesh tearing, *ripping*, is not something I ever thought I'd hear happening to myself. And the way I could almost see the bullet, in the slowest of motions, traveling, entering my side, and exiting…There was a moment, as it was happening, where I thought maybe it was a dream." She finally pulls her gaze from the vast endlessness of the sky so she can look at Evelyn, at her sad but gorgeous eyes, and the way her chin is so gently cradled by the dip between her knees. "Or I guess a nightmare." She's loved women for most of her life, but in this second, looking at Evelyn in this vulnerable moment, is the first time she has ever fully understood why. Why she prefers women over men, why she can connect easier, why she can find a way to open up even when she doesn't want to, or in this case, shouldn't. Why she can feel the longing aching in her hands and the back of her throat. She opens her mouth to speak, and her voice snags. She clamps her jaws, groans softly because deep inside, next to where her conscience lives, is the pool of sloppy emotions she just careened into. "I can tell you that it hurt like a son of a bitch. And I can tell you that not being there now hurts even more than that."

"Were…" Evelyn's voice cracks, and the rest of the sentence comes out as a whisper, "Were you scared?"

"Yes."

Evelyn gasps, and Alden can tell she's trying to lighten the mood. "*You?* I refuse to believe it."

"Very funny."

"I'm only teasing." Evelyn smiles again, but this time, it seems even more genuine than every single smile before. Alden can't seem to look away. She finally moves, stretching her legs out, then maneuvering to stand. "I better…"

"Get going."

Evelyn's soft, "Yeah," causes a chill to zip through Alden's body. "Thank you, y'know, for the beers, and the conversation."

Alden doesn't stand. She is afraid she'll be too wobbly, and it will give her and her stupid heart away. "You remember where the exit is?"

Evelyn laughs. "Yeah, I think I can figure it out."

She watches as Evelyn leaves, moving through the attic bedroom gracefully. It's not until Alden hears the door to the attic close that she releases her breath. She stands and rakes her hands through her hair, pulling at the scalp, trying to remind herself to calm down.

Apply the brakes.

Stop careening out of control.

Focus.

You have a job to do.

She places her hands on the railing, looks out at the lake, at the dark and ever so quiet night. The beer got to her tonight. That's what it is. Alcohol plays a big part of weakening her inhibitions. She shouldn't have had drinks with Evelyn, regardless of how much she enjoyed it. In fact, that is the very reason she shouldn't have done it. Because she enjoyed it. Too much.

A decision which she should have made earlier, much, much earlier, is forming in her head as she turns and heads into the house. She is no longer going to let her guard down. This is a job. A very well-paying job. And that's it.

Evelyn Glass is a job.

A very sexy, very dazzling job.

But a job nonetheless.

CHAPTER ELEVEN

The Chicago Comic and Entertainment Expo was supposed to be in March, but they rescheduled it to this weekend."

Alden looks over at Talon from her position on her hands and knees in front of the Land Rover. She is holding a mirror on an extendable stick, checking for anything out of the ordinary. "I know."

"It's a big event."

"Yes, that's what I've heard." Alden continues to point with the mirror, showing certain things to Talon so she can keep an eye on them and explaining what foreign objects she should be looking for.

"Do you really think someone would put a bomb on Ms. Glass's car? That seems like overkill."

Alden repositions to her knees. "I have learned that it's better to be safe than sorry."

"My mom used to say that when she thought I was having sex with boys."

A laugh spills from Alden. "You are a trip, Talon."

After shrugging and laughing herself, Talon sits upright. "I knew I liked chicks when I was five. And when I came out, my mom kept pushing boys at me. Even though I told her I didn't want them. She'd be like, 'Hillary, honey, don't you want someone to take care of you?'"

"Hillary?"

"Yeah, fuck that name."

"She didn't think you could take care of yourself, hmm?"

"Isn't that fucked up?"

"I mean," Alden starts, then pauses, a memory flashing into her mind. Her ma never accepting; her pops entirely too closed up about it. "I guess it's better than her never wanting to discuss it."

"I guess." Talon stands when she does, and she can feel the question coming before Talon opens her mouth. "Was it hard for you to come out of the closet?"

"What makes you think I needed to come out?" She takes a step back, displaying as much mock shock as she can muster.

"Oh shit." Talon's hands shoot up. "I mean, shoot. I just…Oh, man, Ms. Ryan, I am so sorry. I just assumed—"

She lets out a laugh. "I'm kidding, Talon. I'm totally a lesbian."

Talon slaps her hand to her heart and lets out a breath that is dripping with her embarrassment. "Son of a bitch. You *jerk*."

After another laugh, Alden leans against the Land Rover and says, "My parents hated it at first, too. They're better now. My ma at least gets it. And my pops? He's retired Chicago PD, so it's not shocking that he doesn't like talking about it. Things changed a little after I, uh, I came home."

"That's good, right?"

It is good, yes, but knowing her parents' demeanor had changed because they were worried about losing her seems like the most drastic and dramatic of reasons. She'd like to think maybe things were changing before that, but the likelihood is far-fetched. *Some people are blessed with understanding parents, and others just aren't.*

Talon clears her throat, pushing the sleeves of her button-down up her tattooed arms. "So about tonight. Are you like, worried, or whatever because of last time?"

"Not really."

"Alden," Talon starts, looking very grim.

"What?"

"They didn't tell you, did they?"

"Didn't tell me what?" she asks, anger lacing her words.

Talon presses her fists together, popping each knuckle with a single flex. "Well, I mean, it's not really my place to tell you. I just overheard it when I was in the kitchen earlier, and I don't even know what happened, so maybe it was old news."

"Talon, tell me right now."

"Evelyn got another threatening letter last night."

Alden pushes from the car in an instant. "What are you talking about?"

"Connor and Robert intercepted it and—" Her words are cut short as Alden takes off toward the house.

She flies inside, rushing down the hallway to Connor's office. The door is open a crack, so she pushes through, her anger near boiling point. Connor is sitting at the desk, his eyes wide.

Robert turns, a greasy smile on his face. "Oh, great, the bodyguard has arrived."

She ignores him as she slams the door, marches around the desk, and wheels the chair Connor's sitting in toward her. She puts a hand on his shoulder, points at him with her other hand, and gets right in his face. "Why didn't you tell me about the letter?"

"Look, Alden—" Robert starts, but when she snaps her glare to him, he stops in an instant.

"It's very important for you to not finish that sentence. I don't give a shit what you have to say, you leather-pants-wearing asshole." She turns her attention back to Connor and, trying to not punch him in the face, asks as calmly as possible, "Why didn't you tell me?"

He places a hand on hers, and she allows him to move it. She stands upright, waiting for an explanation, and it better be fucking fantastic, or she's walking. "Alden, listen, we didn't tell you because the other night was such a disaster. Evelyn was so worked up, and she confronted me after the event and the scuffle outside and demanded to know everything. So I told her."

"I know that part." She swallows. "Why haven't you told *me* everything? You never mentioned letters, plural. You told me one letter. On the bed. That's it."

"There have been multiple letters."

"Yeah, I got that now." She rolls her eyes. "Thank you."

He moves slowly, turning to open the left drawer of his desk. He pulls out a lockbox and sets it on the desk with a clunk. The sound of his keys clinking causes her skin to crawl. She focuses on her breathing as he unlocks it. He pulls out a stack of letters and hands them over.

She glances at the stack. "Did you turn these in to the police?"

"No. Why would we do that?"

"Are you kidding me?" She glances around and sees a small garbage pail. She flips it over, trash falling onto the floor, and pulls out the liner. She flips it inside out and holds it out. "Have you ever heard of fingerprints?"

"Seriously?"

"Goddammit, Connor, put them in here now." As soon as he does, she spins the bag to close it. "How did you find the latest one?"

He licks his lips, beads of sweat dotting the expanse of his forehead. "The letter came after the event. We found it on the front door."

"And why didn't you tell me?"

"You were in your lovely little attic apartment," Robert says, his voice low, his eyebrows raised in a way that screams jealousy. "With Evelyn."

"I came upstairs to see you but heard voices and realized Evelyn was up there with you." Connor raises his hand. "I swear, I didn't come in. I just…I thought it was best that you have that time with her."

Alden folds her arms across her chest. She glares at Robert first, then looks back to Connor. "This never happens again. You tell me immediately, or I walk. You and this asshole cannot keep things from me. This isn't a fucking movie. It's real life, and Evelyn is a real person. You can't withhold this stuff and then act like it's not a big fucking deal. I told you no more secrets. And I promised *her* that there would be no more secrets."

"Evelyn doesn't know about this other letter."

Alden looks at Robert. "You are on my last fucking nerve."

"Alden," Connor starts, but she doesn't want to hear it. She turns, walks to the door and leaves before he can get another word in. He's following, his footsteps quick behind her. "Listen to me, please."

"What, Connor? What?"

"The letter was the same as the one from the bed."

She stops in her tracks, and he almost runs into her. She looks over her shoulder. "Don't do this again. You hear me?"

"I won't," he says calmly before she starts walking again, leaving him in her wake.

❖

"Serena, I need your help." Alden looks around as she walks to the edge of the property, her cell phone pressed to her ear.

"Well, well, well, imagine my surprise when I heard you were working for Tobias."

"Serena, seriously, you're going to give me shit?"

"I'm sorry," she says softly. "I just find it very funny that you hate him but want to work for him."

"I don't hate him. I just can't stand him."

Serena laughs. "Oh, okay, I see exactly what you mean."

"I need your help."

"Is everything okay?" Her voice is calm, but Alden can hear the worry behind the calmness.

"I'm coming into the city tonight for an event for this actress I'm stupidly protecting, and I have some letters."

"Need me to run tests?"

"Yes."

"What kind of letters?"

"They're…not very nice. She's got a very interesting stalker."

Serena sighs. "I thought he gave you a nice and easy job to ease you back into things?"

"Is that what he told you?"

"Yeah, he said you'd appreciate him after this. Or something like that." Serena sighs. "I don't want to get in the middle of your quarrel. You both need to let it go."

"Serena, please."

"I'll do whatever you need me to do. You know that. But I won't run messages between you guys. He's been too volatile lately. I just want to stay out of it."

Alden gets to the newly installed gate and punches the code for it to open. As it swings, she sneaks around it and heads to the end of the driveway. "This whole thing is getting out of hand. I just want to figure out who's sending this crap."

"Where will you be? I'll meet you."

"McCormick Place. C2E2. Evelyn has a panel to attend and an autograph session."

"You want me to go to that nerd fest?"

Alden sighs, switches her phone to her other ear, then laughs. "Yeah, yeah. I know. I promise, it won't take long. You're about the only person I trust, aside from Mel."

"Okay, okay," Serena says with a small chuckle. She clears her throat and asks, "You good otherwise?"

She looks up and down the road twice before turning and heading back to the house. "Yeah, just…this is far more stressful than I imagined."

"I completely understand. I'll meet you tonight. I'll have forensics look at the letters, and we'll see what we can find as far as prints. Just shoot me a text when you get there."

"Thanks. And Serena?"

"Yeah?"

"Can you keep this as hush-hush as possible? I don't want the press getting wind of this. They had a heyday with the commotion from the event the other night. I don't need the paparazzi being even crazier than normal."

"I gotcha. No worries there. Text me."

Alden disconnects without another word and slips the phone into the back pocket of her jeans. As she walks, she recalls the letters, the way everything was written, the intricate handwriting, everything. Nothing irrational or threatening, but each letter seems to get more and more intense. As if the person has been studying Evelyn's every move. It's not hard to do. She is everywhere. This comeback has been impeccably timed and is working very well. Not every child actor can do what she did: fade away only to come back better than before. She's done it, and everyone is paying attention. Including, it seems, a lunatic fan who is stopping at nothing, not even increased security measures.

And not only herself. The entire property is a compound now. She must be missing something…some way in she hasn't thought of.

When she walks to the back of the property, she sees Evelyn sitting on a blanket on the grass with Ethan. They're laughing, and it's really nice to see. Evelyn snatches his ball cap, putting it on her head, and they crack up again. Stella comes outside, bends down and hugs her mom, and sits next to Ethan.

They look very similar when sitting together. Alden leans against the side of the house, knowing if she gets too close, Evelyn won't be happy. She isn't sure if Evelyn even notices her at first, but when she looks over her shoulder and waves, Alden knows she's been spotted. She lifts her head, offering a simple nod in return. She wants to smile because Evelyn is, but she remembers the promise she made to herself.

This is just a job. Evelyn is just a job.

She only hopes her heart gets the message eventually.

CHAPTER TWELVE

Evelyn takes the time and actually speaks with each fan who approaches her table in the McCormick Place convention center. The room where the autograph tables are located is gigantic. There must be three hundred other pop culture stars in attendance, each seated behind a long table with lines stretched out before them. If Alden was at all interested in pop culture, this would be a dream come true. To be this up close and personal with so many different stars could be very exciting, but she has spent most of her life avoiding anything to do with celebrities. Maybe because the police life and then politics took up so much of her life that it was almost impossible to focus on anything else.

Maybe also because Jennifer Simmons was the only person she thought about for three years straight. *Yeah, that's probably it.*

She sighs as she refocuses her attention. She's standing to Evelyn's left, far enough back to not be a burden and close enough to make a move if need be. Shockingly, Evelyn okayed her presence. When they first arrived, and even on the way to the venue, Evelyn was very standoffish. Alden didn't take it personally.

And when she saw Evelyn in her black skinny jeans and kelly-green halter-top with matching heels, she definitely felt it in the pit of her stomach. How can a woman wear clothes like that but also look so completely comfortable and at peace in them? Evelyn, though, *damn.* She can fucking *wear* clothes. As if every single piece she puts on was made exactly for her, for her curves, her hips, her ass that Alden hopes to God she can stop checking out one day. The attraction is too much.

Even after numerous pep talks and re-centering herself while looking in the mirror and even occasionally yelling at herself in her head, she still finds her gaze drifting down, down, down as Evelyn walks.

When they arrived, and Evelyn was ushered into the venue through a back hallway, her attitude shifted. Alden noticed it right away. Her stride slowed, her posture shifted, her poise faltered. As if there was some sort of impending doom waiting on the other side of the green room. Maybe everything was finally starting to affect her in ways only Alden could sense, which isn't necessarily a bad thing. It's good because seeing Evelyn stutter-step as the time to be on got closer, seeing the way her breathing picked up pace, seeing the perspiration along her hairline, means Evelyn is taking it seriously. Maybe not as serious as she should be but serious enough to show in her body language.

"Everything okay?" Alden stopped her with a gentle touch to her forearm before they pushed through the back doors of the exhibition hall. She wasn't going to point out that she could tell Evelyn was uncomfortable, but she's being paid to protect this woman. And when Evelyn's dark eyes—makeup perfectly applied, eyeliner and eye shadow expertly done by her makeup artist—connected with hers, she was very glad she decided to ask. "Evelyn?"

"I'm okay."

"You sure?" Alden watched her chest rise and fall with a deep breath.

"Yeah, I'm good."

"As long as you're sure. We don't have to do this if you aren't okay."

A look flashed across Evelyn's features. It was as if no one in her entire life had given her the option of bailing, of not showing up, of not doing something she wasn't comfortable with. Maybe the look meant she was grateful? Or moved by the idea? Or maybe she was simply irritated? Whatever the flash meant, Alden will never forget the way Evelyn's gaze softened, and her cheeks relaxed, and she looked relieved. She leaned in, and the scent of her perfume came with her. Alden breathed deep and made sure to not close her eyes and revel in the smell of this gorgeous woman whom she should not be thinking about.

"Maybe," Evelyn had started, eyes moving from Alden's mouth, then back up, "you can stay closer tonight?"

Alden had felt the gaze in every part of her body but especially in her core, and she wanted to smack herself for allowing anything inside to respond to this woman. "I'll be wherever you need me."

"Thank you," Evelyn said, a small smile on her bright red lips. She pushed a lock of hair behind her ear and adjusted her posture so she no longer looked frightened.

Alden didn't return the smile. At least, not on the outside. But she did exactly as Evelyn asked.

Her vantage point is good at this angle. She can see everything going on at either side of the table, as well as ten or twelve deep in the exceptionally long line. Every fan who approaches is gracious and kind. Evelyn asks about their days, their lives, wondering how they found the show. A few older women have approached, gushing about how they remember her on *High School is for Winners* on the Disney Channel and have posed for pictures with their hands in the shape of a W on their foreheads. Evelyn laughs and smiles the entire time. Alden imagines how tiring that must be to constantly be on, be smiling, be presentable and approachable. It isn't so very different from what President Simmons had to go through.

The longer she does this for Evelyn, and it hasn't been that long—*has it really been only three weeks*—she starts to realize how the spotlight and everything that goes along with it is very similar, regardless of who the person is. The light is bright and warm, and even though it's meant to be exciting, it can sometimes be exhausting and cold. But the people who can do it well are the ones who shine the brightest.

Jennifer Simmons was an expert at handling the spotlight. She was perfect in a crowd, never faltered, never said anything wrong, never smiled out of place, never cried when not appropriate. She was poised, almost too perfect, but she had to be. The first female president was definitely nitpicked, and it didn't matter what she did or how she acted, she would be criticized.

Alden wondered how she learned to handle things so well. "Time, practice, and sometimes not giving a shit," Jennifer said one night, two months before the incident, after a particularly grueling reelection rally. Alden smiled, Jennifer said softly, "Your smile is lovely."

Alden pinches the bridge of her nose, hoping to get the memory out of her head. She needs to stay present.

Present with Evelyn, who, like Jennifer Simmons, is one of those people who can handle the spotlight with a shocking amount of ease. Evelyn is an actress, and a good one at that. Maybe this is an act? Maybe her skin is crawling. Maybe she's ready to get the hell out of here. Maybe she's sick and tired of having to smile all the time.

Either way, no one will ever be able to tell. And Evelyn's smile? Now that's lovely.

She's had to have braces, right? I mean, look at those teeth. Straight, white, and she drinks coffee and red wine and Diet Coke.

Alden tries to hide the grin tugging on her lips. Why the fuck is she thinking about what Evelyn Glass drinks throughout the day? She bites her lip, scolding herself for becoming less composed. She's supposed to be keeping a distance, not keeping a list of Evelyn's likes, dislikes, and eccentricities.

She's been working hard to avoid one-on-one's at the house. There is no need to be as close as the other night again. She learned what she needs to know. Evelyn's not as mean as she likes to make herself look, and she's vulnerable, and even when she doesn't have makeup on, she's still breathtaking.

Dammit. Get your head in the game, Alden.

She scans the crowd again. She has seen the same couple of people a few times, but she chalks that up to people meandering around the venue, which seems more and more packed. The crowd control is impressive, and she reminds herself that she can't control everything like they used to do in the Secret Service.

"Ma'am?"

Alden snaps her attention to the tall security officer standing next to her.

"Ms. Glass is done now. If you'd like to escort her to the next area?"

"Okay, thank you." Alden takes two steps and puts a hand on Evelyn's bare shoulder. She leans next to her ear. "It's time to go to the panel, Ms. Glass."

Evelyn places her hands on the table and stands. "I'm so sorry, everyone, but I have to go. Hopefully I'll see you all at the *Between the Covers* cast panel which starts in fifteen minutes."

Evelyn moves in the direction Alden indicates, waving good-bye to her fans, who are shouting *we love you*, and *you're so beautiful, please don't go.* As she's walking, she adjusts the bottom of her halter-top, then moves to pull the top part up a bit. Every move seems planned, as if she thinks about it minutes in advance and rehearses until it's perfect. Her movements are graceful, and that takes thought and practice. Even the way she fixes a wardrobe issue is lovely, smoothing along her stomach, her sides, down over her hips, across the back waistband of her jeans.

Don't look down, Alden. Don't do it.

When they enter a behind-the-scenes hallway, Evelyn slows and places a hand on the wall as if to steady herself. "It was hot in there."

Alden nods for no other reason than she can't form a coherent sentence.

"I just need a minute. To catch my breath."

"They sure love you." She clears her throat after forcing herself to acknowledge the obvious out loud.

Evelyn turns, leans against the wall, and heaves a heavy sigh. "They love the idea of me." She rests her head on the concrete, her eyes closed. She takes another deep breath, but this time, she holds it.

Alden waits for the release. *One-one-thousand, two-one-thousand, three-one...*and Evelyn releases.

"I love the fans, though," Evelyn says, a hint of sadness layered with the words meant to uphold her reputation. Will she ever realize she doesn't have to keep that mask on around Alden? "None of this would be possible without them, would it, Ms. Ryan?"

Alden shrugs. "I guess you're right."

"We should go, shouldn't we?"

"Yes. We have six minutes."

"Did you even check your watch?"

"I keep track in my head," Alden says. Evelyn grins, and Alden fights the smile begging to come out and play. She loses the fight and gives in to temptation. "Let's go."

As they're walking, Evelyn's heels clicking on the cement, she lets out a tiny puff of air that barely morphs into a laugh. "Like, you keep *count* in your head? You count to sixty over and over? Or do you multiply sixty by the number of minutes and then count to the bigger number? I'm so intrigued."

"That's what you're laughing about?"

Evelyn laughs again. "Yes. That's so strange. How do you even do that?"

"Evelyn," she says as they approach the stage entrance.

Evelyn stops, turns, a look on her face that has Alden wondering how she'll ever stop this ache in her throat. "Hmm?"

"You really don't think I keep count in my head, do you?"

Evelyn scans her face. For what? She isn't sure, but Evelyn purses her lips before she says, "You were just pulling my leg, weren't you?"

Alden raises her eyebrows and smiles. "Go." She opens the door and motions toward the security officers. "Knock 'em dead. I'll be right here the whole time."

And a grinning Evelyn is immediately escorted by security to her seat onstage.

❖

Alden turns when the stage door opens. Serena pokes her head in, and a security officer puts a stop to her entering. She flashes the badge hanging around her neck, then points at Alden, who feels even better about the security. "About time."

"Tell me about it. I always forget this place is like a fucking labyrinth," Serena says in a low voice after she closes the door and tiptoes over. She looks adorable, her dark hair a complete mess of frizzy waves. "I must have looked in three different backstage areas before I found you." She is wearing street clothes, which is not normal, and her badge is hanging on a chain around her neck.

"No uniform?"

"Shit, I've been wearing street clothes since my promotion to detective. You should have visited more often." Serena smacks her arm before they embrace. She pulls away, both hands on Alden's arms. "Look at you. I thought you were supposed to be buttoned up and bodyguard looking."

"That's what I thought, too. But Tobias told me I looked too much like a Secret Service agent." Alden shrugs. "Do I not look okay?"

"Are you kidding? You look phenomenal. I love this black jacket. Where'd you get it?" Serena is keeping her voice low, but she sort of squeals at the end, and it makes Alden laugh.

"I don't know. The Loft, I think? Check the tag."

She spins, and Serena is messing with the collar for a couple seconds before she says, "Oh, it'll fit me. When you're done with it, I got dibs."

"Okay, deal." Alden pulls a Ziplock from her messenger bag and hands it over. "Here are the letters."

There's some heft to the package, so Serena bounces it up and down as if weighing it. "Jesus. How the hell many are in here?"

"Fifteen."

"*Fifteen?*"

"Yes. I was told there was one letter, and now I find out there are fifteen. I was livid."

"Well, I mean, you aren't a detective." She slips the package into her bag. "You're just hired to protect her. Do you really need every detail? They're the ones who should have called the police." Serena stops speaking when she finally looks at Alden, who is boring holes into her with a stare. "Uh, I mean, good thing they told you?"

"Look, if I'm not told exactly what I'm protecting her from, don't you think it's going to make my job a little harder? I mean, I never flew blind when it came to Simmons."

"Just that once, hmm?"

Serena's tone seems sincere; aside from Mel, she's the only other civilian who knows every single detail of the incident.

A lump jumps into Alden's throat. Speaking about what happened is not something she likes doing. In fact, she loathes speaking about it, but sometimes, it does come up, and it is relevant. "Yeah, just that one time," she whispers.

"I know." Serena squeezes Alden's bicep. She waits a few beats before she says, "You're right. I'm glad you got me involved. I promise, I will do whatever I need to do to get this resolved."

Alden pulls her gaze away and looks onstage. She has a clear view of Evelyn, which helps to calm her. As much as she likes to think she's healing, she's still a fucking mess. And maybe it wasn't a good idea to thrust herself back into the fray, but she did it, she made the decision, and now she cannot fail. Even if that means she's pushing an investigation into these letters. She has no idea who's sending them and no idea where it'll lead.

"So how has she been?"

Alden shrugs. "She's been okay."

"Mel said she was a hard-ass."

"Mel can't keep her mouth shut."

Serena chuckles. "Telegraph, telephone, tell Mel."

"For real, though." She shakes her head. "I've dealt with enough asshole cops, asshole perps, and asshole politicians to know how to handle Evelyn Glass."

"Ain't that the truth." Serena puts her arm around Alden's shoulders and squeezes. "Don't let yourself get too deep. Okay?"

Her first inclination is to get pissed and shrug off Serena's touch because fuck anyone who thinks they know her well enough to give advice. But Serena does know her well enough to give advice and, *sigh*, she is right. "Okay."

"I'm going to head out. I'll get these to forensics tonight. Let me know if you need anything else."

Alden turns and hugs her. "I love you. Thank you for this."

"You're welcome. Text me. Let me know how things are going." Serena pulls away, places a hand on Alden's cheek, then exits as quietly as she entered.

Alden looks back out at Evelyn, who is speaking excitedly and gesturing wildly, answering a fan's question about the latest season of *Between the Covers*. She looks radiant up there, the way her hair is shining as the lights hit it, her smile as she listens to questions, her eyes when she focuses on her castmates. Alden bites her cheek, scolding herself yet again because it seems that as hard as she tries to not let this get out of control, she is just as taken by Evelyn as the fans.

When she hears a young woman clear her throat into the microphone, Alden takes a step forward. The woman's hair is long, hanging in her face, and she looks mortified to have been chosen to ask a question.

"Hi, um, my question is for Evelyn…um, so it's been rumored there will be a love triangle on the show this season between, um, Jake, you, and a newcomer who hasn't been named yet, but the rumors say it might be a woman. Is there any way you can confirm that?"

Alden's ears perk. *Excuse me?*

Evelyn leans to the microphone. "Thank you so much for the question. I cannot confirm or deny those reports about who the character will be." She glances down the table to one of the writers, and when he gives her a nod, she smiles. "But I'm excited for you to meet her."

Alden's mouth drops open. And so does half the audience's.

She lets out a small huff and shakes her head. *Well, son of a bitch. Evelyn Glass has been cast as bisexual? Maybe I need to tune in.*

She keeps her eyes on Evelyn as the crowd settles. When Evelyn licks her lips and looks stage right, she makes eye contact with Alden, her left eyebrow arched. This entire evening has been one interesting moment after another.

Alden Ryan, you need to calm down. And she needs to check the brakes of the runaway car she's driving down a dangerous road. But all of her self-scolding and refocusing of attention is little to no use when the reality of the situation hits her: she is developing feelings for Evelyn Glass.

Now it's not a matter of if she can stop. It's a matter of if she wants to.

"Okay, look, you can't have fans blocking the walkway like this." Alden's irritation is beginning to grow. She has been lecturing the security officers for the better part of an hour. She's starting to regret thinking they had it under control. "Clear the way so when the actors exit, no one storms them."

"Lookie here, little lady, we know how to do our jobs." The officer crosses his arms, resting them on his large belly, and glares over his glasses. "We'll get the fans to move."

"If you knew how to do your job, you wouldn't have let these people crowd the area." She takes two steps closer, hands on her hips, and says again, "Clear the way." He finally does as she says and radios to another guard to clear the path.

Alden rolls her eyes and waits, but before anything can happen, the doors open, and out steps Evelyn with the rest of the cast. The crowd of fans goes nuts, and smiles pop on the cast's faces. Alden has her eyes glued to Evelyn, and when their gazes meet, Alden lifts her chin and starts to move through the crowd.

"Come this way," she shouts. She's surprised when Evelyn cuts through to her. The rest of the cast takes off in one direction, and the fans start begging Evelyn to come to them.

Evelyn turns to Alden, her hands clasped together. "Can I go, please?"

"Not yet." She waves at the unruly crowd. "You need to let the guards get the crowd controlled first."

"I think it's fine," one of the cast members shouts.

"Come on, Evelyn, come with. The fans want you."

"Evelyn, please wait." Alden places her hand on Evelyn's forearm. She watches as Evelyn looks at the crowd, the cast, and then back to Alden.

"I'm going. I'll be fine. Come with me."

"Evelyn, no," Alden shouts, but it's too late. Evelyn is hurrying through the people to the front of the line, the rest of the cast chanting her name, when the metal barricade the security officers were working to secure gives way and topples over.

And like a waterfall, the fans rush the cast. And Evelyn. Everyone is pushing and shoving. The whole scene is chaos.

Alden springs forward and calls Talon on their intercom. "Talon, listen up, I need you ready. Loading dock, four minutes." Her eyes are on Evelyn being pushed back and forth. She squeezes through an opening and starts to force her way in. She elbows two rowdy men in the side, knees one guy in the stomach, and kicks one dickhead who won't listen in the ass. She stops another fan—this time an all-too-eager girl—from attacking one of the other cast members. When she finally makes it to Evelyn, there's a creepy looking guy way too close. She attacks without thinking, kicking him square in the balls. She grabs Evelyn by the waist, holding her as tightly as possible when she starts to go limp.

In a moment of pure adrenaline, Alden scoops Evelyn up in her arms. She's pushing through the crowd, carrying Evelyn, who is surprisingly light, shouting at people to get out of the way. When she gets through the sea of people, she rushes down a hall and finds the exit to the loading dock so easily that she's almost positive she made a wrong turn. She bursts through the door, and Talon is waiting. She helps get Evelyn into the back seat before Alden slides in beside her. Talon hops in and peels away from the loading dock and out of the parking garage.

Alden takes a few deep breaths before she looks up and finds Talon's eyes staring in the rearview mirror. "That was close."

Talon maneuvers through the streets with ease before she merges onto Lake Shore Drive, heading north. "What happened?"

"Nothing."

"Didn't seem like nothing to me." Her voice is calm, and Alden appreciates it way more than she could ever articulate.

"I didn't listen," Evelyn answers out of nowhere.

Her eyes are open now, and Alden places a hand on her forehead. "Are you okay?"

She doesn't answer, just stares out the window as they fly north.

"Just get us home, Talon." Alden sits a little straighter, torn between being pissed off and worried sick. She wants to scold, tell Evelyn how stupid she was, tell her she's too important and wonderful to take her life into her hands like that. It's not Alden's place to scold. It's her place to protect. And she did what she was supposed to do. She saved Evelyn. And she'll continue to do so.

"I can't believe you saved me."

Alden checks the final window sensor in Evelyn's bedroom, then crosses to the bed where she sits on the edge, listening to it creak softly. When they arrived, it wasn't hard to talk Evelyn into lying down. And since the security system is in place, she felt safe enough to sleep in her own bedroom.

She's barely said three words. Stella came out as soon as they arrived, asked a thousand questions, and Talon—bless her heart—answered as much as she could so Alden could help Evelyn.

"Again," Evelyn adds, her voice so quiet from the bed. She rolls over to face Alden.

"Thankfully, you don't get an up charge every time I risk my life."

Evelyn sighs, a small chuckle layered beneath the sound, and says, "Yeah, well, at this rate, I think I'd pay whatever you asked."

"Maybe, and this is just a thought, you could try not to be so stubborn?"

"I'm so sorry," Evelyn whispers, her voice shaking. "I should have listened to you."

"Yeah, you should have," Alden whispers back. She does what she's been telling herself not to and smooths Evelyn's hair away from her face. "You could have been trampled. And hurt. Or killed."

"I know." Evelyn closes her eyes. "I really am sorry."

"Don't be sorry." She places her hand back in her lap and pinches the area between her forefinger and thumb. "Just listen next time. I'm trying to make sure you don't get hurt out there, not hinder your lifestyle or your reputation."

"I know."

"Yeah, you keep saying you know, but do you really?"

Evelyn breathes out a small, "Yes." Alden takes the response as her cue to leave. She stands, but Evelyn grabs her wrist. "Will you stay here until I fall asleep?"

No. No, no, no. Absolutely not. I will not stay until you fall asleep because I am not supposed to do things like that, and I do not need this kind of confusion in my fucking life right now. "Sure." Alden stands, rolling her eyes at herself and her inability to say no the entire way to the other side of the bed. She sits on top of the comforter and props herself against the headboard. She listens as Evelyn's breathing deepens and slows, a steady pattern occurring.

Okay, get up. Go upstairs to your own room. Get the fuck out of here, Alden.

She looks at Evelyn's back, at the contrast of her dark hair on the snow-white pillowcase. She's not going to leave. So why keep berating herself? Within seconds, she's allowing herself to close her eyes. Sleep happens quickly, and when she dreams, she dreams of kelly-green, of red lips, and black pants. She dreams of hands. And she dreams of a low voice saying her name.

Ms. Ryan...Alden Ryan.

CHAPTER THIRTEEN

After the past few weeks of making sure every aspect of the outside security system is installed correctly, including the new gate, monitored fence, and state of the art intercom system, Alden starts to feel more at ease. She can't let her guard down too much, but at least while they're at the house, she'll know it's secure. Maybe it'll offer her a couple of seconds of breathing room. After all, taking a moment to breathe isn't such a bad thing.

And there aren't many of those, even with the new security system. Her days have become repetitive.

Mornings, she checks the perimeter while getting her morning jog in. She's been trying to run farther and harder, just in case. She's pushing herself. Sometimes too much, but it's the idea of not being prepared that makes her dig a little deeper. After the last two situations, she found herself very winded and extremely tired. The constant ache from the gunshot wound is always there, reminding her of her failures. Sure, she may not have failed protecting the president, but the fact that they had been in that position in the first place?

Yeah, she failed.

"You used poor judgment, and you let this get in the way," Director Stevens said while jabbing his fore and middle finger into her chest where her heart lay, beating like a bass drum. "You know better than that, Agent Ryan."

And he was right. She knew better.

Hell, she still knows better, yet...

Her mind floods with the memory of Evelyn's bare back and soft skin, and then she trips over a tree root and stumbles. She hits the ground with an *umph*. "Jesus," she whispers as she stands, brushing herself off. She has scraped her forearm, and blood bubbles to the surface. She sighs. *Great*. She turns back to the house when she notices someone about a hundred yards away, standing in the brush.

She drops her arms to her sides, creeps as quietly as possible to a line of trees, and inches closer. When she's twenty yards away, she can see that it's Stella, Ethan, and *is that Talon? What are they doing?*

She continues to creep, carefully getting closer, and she finally sees what they're up to. Stella is holding a pistol, pointing at a target strapped to a tree thirty yards away. Alden wants to stop her but she can't startle a person holding a gun. She waits and hopes to God Stella doesn't shoot. She holds her breath, counts every second that passes, and when Stella finally lowers her arm and looks at Talon, an apologetic expression displayed, Alden calls out.

"Stella? Talon?" They both spin around. Stella drops the weapon and bursts into tears. "What are you doing?"

Talon has her hands up as she takes a step. "I told her not to do this. I promise."

"And I had nothing to do with this, either," Ethan says, shoving his hands into the pockets of his shorts.

"I'm so sorry, Alden." Stella's face is streaked with wetness, and the resemblance to her mother is disconcerting. The last thing Alden wants to do is have a talk with Evelyn's children about guns and gun safety. Both are subjects she understands, but to teach them to kids? She so wishes she was a kid person.

Stella runs the back of her hand under her chin and takes a deep breath. "I just keep hearing things, and Tal said the events have been getting bad. And I thought about Mom, and I just...I just..." Her expression falls again as she puts her hands on her face and cries into them. "I'm scared," she finishes, her words muffled between breaths.

"Ethan?" His head snaps toward Alden. She takes a step toward him. "Are you okay?"

He shrugs. "Yeah, I'm okay. I wasn't going to touch the gun."

Alden bends and picks up the Glock. She clicks the release, and the magazine slides out. She pulls the slide and unloads the bullet from the chamber. Once the gun has been safely unloaded, she slips it behind her, into the waistband of her pants. "Where the fuck did you get a goddamn Glock, Stella?"

Her eyes are wide now, eyelashes soaked, her face wet. "I b... bought it."

"Where?"

"Off this weird white guy with no teeth and I knew it was a bad idea. But I was downtown, and he said..." She stops, takes a breath, and looks as if she's trying to calm herself. "I could have it for a hundred dollars, so I did it. I was on the green line, and I missed my stop on purpose, and I just did it. I don't know why. B...because I'm stupid, I guess."

Alden sighs. "You're not stupid." *Yes, yes, you are.* "You need to use your head. Promise me you won't do anything like this again." Stella twists her hands and looks scared and embarrassed. "I'm not mad at you. Okay?"

"You probably should be."

Alden shakes her head. "I'm just glad I found you before you hurt yourself. If you really want to learn, I can teach you, but in a controlled environment and with your mother's permission and"— Alden gestures around them—"not here. You realize firing a gun here is not wise, right?"

"I mean, I didn't know where else to go."

Alden groans. "You go to a *shooting* range. With someone who knows what the fuck they're doing." She glances at Ethan. "Sorry, buddy. I mean, with someone who knows what they're doing."

He chuckles and so does Stella as she says, "Okay."

"And you, Talon—"

"Alden, I swear to God, this was Stella's idea. I tried to talk her out of it."

"She did, Alden. I promise." Stella moves in front of her. "She literally found me out here when she was walking with Ethan."

"Ethan? Is that true?"

"Yes, I promise. Stella was being her same stubborn self, so she wasn't listening." He glances at the glare she's shooting at him. "What? You are. Just like Mom."

"Thanks," she says, sarcasm dripping thick and slow off the word.

"Please call me next time," Alden says after she pulls Talon off to the side. "This is not okay. None of this."

"I know. I froze. I don't know why."

"I get that you're probably a little smitten with Stella, but"—Alden places a hand on Talon's shoulder and squeezes—"you cannot tell her what we encounter out there. You have to keep that between us. Okay?" Talon's spine straightens, and she lifts her head a little higher. "Oh no, what else have you told her?"

"I may have mentioned—"

"The letters," Stella says from behind them. "She mentioned the letters."

Alden sighs, looks at the moss and leaf covered ground, and wonders how she even begins damage control with this. "Oh, Talon." She keeps her voice low and glances up. Talon seems to know she's made a mistake. It's clear as day on her face. "No more. You hear me?"

"I promise." The only thing missing is a salute. She looks exactly how Alden felt years ago when she was new and wet behind the ears and made her first mistake.

"Stella? You and Talon head back to the house, please." Talon moves past, and Alden listens to them walking away. She sighs, one hand on a hip, the other gripping the magazine and solitary bullet from the Glock. So much for the run helping to calm her nerves. Her shoulders are tighter now than when she started.

"Are you mad at me?" Ethan's voice is small, and it softens her resolve.

She now feels horrible for how she's handled this. "Oh, Ethan, no. Why would you think that?"

"You just seem mad."

"I'm not. I promise." But even though she's not mad, she is one-hundred-percent worried because how much does *he* know? She doesn't want him to know the gritty details of everything going on with his mom and her very skilled stalker. And sometimes, worry is worse than anger in a case like this. She closes the distance and puts her empty hand on his shoulder. "Let's walk to the house."

He does as she says. She can tell that he's thinking about something. He's nibbling on his lip, a trait she's seen from Evelyn numerous times. "I don't think I want to learn to shoot a gun."

"No?"

He shakes his head. "I know it's not like Nintendo or Xbox, and chasing real life bad guys doesn't sound like my kind of thing."

She smiles down at him. "You are right about it not being a video game. But..." She pauses, shrugs. "Sometimes, chasing bad guys is fun."

"Yeah, well, I'll let you do that part." He chuckles. "I mean, you're the one getting paid."

"Very true." As they approach the front gate, he stops, so she pauses, too. "You okay?"

"Promise you'll protect Mom?"

The sound of his small voice and the way it wraps around the words *promise* and *Mom*, as if they are the most important words he has ever said, shakes her to the core. She clears her throat. She wants to answer because his plea deserves a damn response, but her voice is stuck, her words mush, and she finds herself staring into his dark eyes, the same as his mother's. She forces herself to nod. He needs more, even though the gesture is anything but simple. She promises herself to respond one day, when she isn't as lost between what's right and what feels right.

Alden's mind has been racing since the incident that morning with the gun. She's waiting to tell Evelyn. Not because she doesn't want to, even though she really doesn't want to, but because she hasn't been able to get a word in edgewise with her. Evelyn has been nonstop at the house, doing photoshoot after photoshoot for *Entertainment Weekly* and *People*. Alden has stayed in the background. She doesn't want to call attention to herself, and Evelyn doesn't want that, either.

The sun is getting lower, which is apparently the best lighting for outdoor pics, and since they're right on the water, the *People* photographer requested beach shots.

Because that's exactly what the people want to see: Evelyn Glass on a beach.

Alden chuckles. That is why she'd pick the magazine up, so maybe the photographer knows what she's doing after all.

The set goes quickly, with Evelyn walking along the water barefoot, splashing and kicking around in a couple shots, and ending with a few shots of her sitting in the sand looking out across the water. Alden would love to say she hasn't been watching Evelyn's every single move in that white linen shirt, those dark skinny jeans, and that wide-brimmed sunhat, her hair swept into a messy braid, pulled over her shoulder, but she would be lying. Completely and unequivocally lying.

When Evelyn stands and says her good-byes, the photographer takes her leave after her assistant loads up the cameras and lighting equipment. She's a tiny little thing, but her personality seemed to mix well with Evelyn's because the shots look like they're going to turn out amazing.

Evelyn lifts her hand to shield her eyes from the sun. She smiles and waves at Alden, motioning for her to come closer. "Thanks for, y'know, letting me do that."

"Letting you?" Alden tilts her head. "You make the rules, lady. Not me."

Evelyn shifts her stance and digs her toes into the sand. "I mean…" She pauses, looking at her bare feet. "I don't know. For being okay with it or whatever."

"For not interfering."

"Yeah, I guess that." Evelyn's smile is so relaxed, and this is the first time Alden has experienced this side of her, so prepping to un-relax her is causing Alden to rethink the whole "honesty is the best policy" viewpoint.

"Evelyn, I need to tell you something."

"Is it about the gun?"

Every muscle in Alden's body tenses. "How did you know?"

Evelyn is still smiling, now looking into the distance when she shrugs. "Ethan cannot keep anything to himself."

"Good to know." She takes a deep breath and lets it out as slow as possible before adding, "Are you upset?"

"Upset? No." She takes a step closer to the water, then another, before she has her feet in the coolness of the lake. "I'm disappointed more than anything."

"I'm very sorry I didn't tell you sooner." Alden doesn't move any closer for fear of getting her shoes wet. And also for fear of getting her heart any more involved than it already is.

"Alden," Evelyn says as she looks over her shoulder. "I'm not disappointed in you." She smiles. "In my children. Disappointed in my children."

"Oh." Alden laughs a fake laugh, praying it covers up her nerves. "*Whew.*"

"I have a question for you." Her voice is soft and full, like a new pillow.

There's a split-second when Alden wants to run. She wants to about-face and sprint away as fast as her legs can carry her because whatever the hell Evelyn wants to ask cannot be something she's either A, prepared for, or B, has any desire to actually answer. Her heart seems to have stopped beating, too, which is making it hard to respond with anything other than blinking. And even blinking is difficult.

"I'm assuming your lack of a response means you're okay with me asking." Her crooked smile acts like a defibrillator to Alden's heart, and the shock ripples through her body. She offers a tiny nod, hopes it's enough, and watches Evelyn take a very deliberate breath before she says, "I guess I want to apologize more than ask something."

This, an actual apology, is like a second shock to her system and spurs her to ask, "For what?"

Evelyn's very understanding and knowing look, the arched eyebrow, the tilt of her head, the pursing of her lips, is enough of an explanation. But Alden is thrilled, deep down, when Evelyn says, "Very funny. I think you know what I mean."

"Oh, do I?"

"Yes." Evelyn starts to walk, her feet still in the water, her pace slow, but it's clear she wants to move from whatever prying eyes might be on them from the house. Connor, Robert, Ethan, Stella...someone is always watching. "Y'know, when you first got here, I really didn't want to be fussed over. Not because I don't like the attention because believe me, I do."

Alden laughs as she follows. "I had no idea."

"I'm sure. I hide it very well."

"Oh, yes, so well."

Evelyn glances back, an expression on her face that has never been there before. One that has Alden wondering if the brakes in the vehicle they're driving are intact or if they should just drive right over the cliff, *Thelma and Louise* style. "You have a sense of humor?"

"You'd be surprised."

The silence is not nearly as uncomfortable as it should be. The momentary pause lets Alden gather her own thoughts, pull oxygen into her lungs and blood stream, and remember that sometimes, listening to her heart over her head isn't always a bad thing.

"This makes me feel so awkward. Maybe it's the threat or the threat of the unknown. I'm not sure. But I didn't want this or need it." Evelyn stops and turns in one fluid motion, crosses her arms, and looks into Alden's eyes. "Things have changed, and I feel it's important to tell you that...and to thank you, or whatever."

"You're welcome." It's the appropriate response, but it comes out as a whisper, and she's embarrassed by her inability to control the tone of her voice. She clears her throat and says it again, deeper, more forceful, more in control.

"I heard you the first time," Evelyn says.

Oh, Alden, you're really getting too deep.

"I have another question for you...or rather, I want to ask for your help."

Disappointment floods her because it means this whole conversation had an ulterior motive.

"Yes." Evelyn licks her full lips, which are still stained a lovely shade of pink from the photoshoot. She adjusts her hat, pulling it farther onto her head. "I want to..." She stops, her lips still parted, and then laughs. "I don't know why this is so hard."

"Unless it's killing someone, I'll help you do anything." She smiles, and Evelyn lets out another laugh.

"I definitely do not want to kill someone."

"Well, then, tell me."

"Okay, so," Evelyn starts again, lets out a very shaky breath. "I want to go out. Go eat dinner. Y'know, like, a date."

Alden's throat constricts. "Oh."

"Yeah, and I know it's a lot to ask, but I didn't want to—"

"Do anything without running it by me? Thank you for that." She pulls her shoulders back because this whole conversation has deflated her. "I can stay at a very safe distance, leave you and your date alone, make sure the perimeter is good. It's not a problem. And I can make sure you're not bothered and be ready when you're finished."

Evelyn's scoff is hard to read. "Thanks, *Agent* Ryan, but that is not what I was going to say." She chuckles, shaking her head. "I was going to say, I didn't want to ask you to do something you're not comfortable with."

Um, what? "I don't follow."

"I want you to take me out."

Um, what?

"Like, on a date."

Alden stares at Evelyn's face, at the look of determination. "You. Me. Dinner. A *date*."

"Evelyn, that's not something I can do."

"Oh, come on, I'm not the president," Evelyn says as she smacks Alden on the arm. Even though her tone is light and playful, and she wants to lunge forward and capture Evelyn's lips and kiss that smile off her face, push that hat off her head, rip that shirt off her body, there's also a small part of her that has been wounded by the words. "You know if I go anywhere with anyone, you're going to be there, and no offense, that's going to cramp my style."

"Um, none taken?"

Another laugh spills from Evelyn's mouth. "It doesn't have to be a romantic date. I'm not saying that. I just want to get the fuck out of this house, and I don't want it to be to an event, and I really don't want my father and Robert to come along, and honestly, I am going slightly stir-crazy, and I want to go get a beer and some pizza and not be stared at and fawned over." She takes a breath. "Woo. I don't think I took a breath during that." She's not smiling now, and her expression has gone from asking to pleading. "Please, Alden, let's go hang out. I want to not be me for an evening. Just one evening."

She's going to say yes. She actually wants to scream yes. But the part of her that knows she should say no is begging her to be careful, to think about this, and why the hell is it a bad idea to test the waters first before jumping in? Even sticking a pinky toe in would be a fine idea. "Okay."

"Seriously?"

"Seriously."

Evelyn squeals. "Oh my God, thank you." She has her hands on Alden's biceps, and she squeezes tightly before she starts to run toward the house. "I'm going to get ready."

"Wait, you meant now?" Alden shouts after her.

"Yes. Come on. Go get ready."

"Jesus Christ," she says quietly. What has she gotten herself into?

❖

"You're taking my mom out?" Ethan is reflected in the floor to ceiling mirror in Alden's apartment. He stands at the steps, a basketball in one hand, his ball cap pulled down. He's smiling, which calms Alden's nerves, but being questioned by him, or by anyone, about what she's doing is not something she wants to endure right now. She turns and looks at the twinkle in his eyes. He's so much tanner than he was when Alden first met him, and his hair is getting long.

"I mean, it's not really a date, kid. Your mom wants to get out of the house. It'll be easier if I take her instead of tagging along on an actual date."

"So her smiling and giggling like a dork downstairs is because she is getting out of the house? Okay," he replies with a wry smile. He pushes his hat up and moves his bangs out of his face. "It's totally okay either way. I think it's cool. You're the coolest person she has brought into my life."

Against her better judgment, she lets that comment hit her square in the heart. It brings a smile to her face. A genuine smile and it feels really, really good. "Yeah, well, you're one of the coolest people, too."

"Duh," he says. "You know, she hasn't had a lot of men in her life."

Alden gulps. She hopes it isn't audible. "Well, I'm sure it's hard to find the right person when you're a movie star."

"Yeah, or maybe she's not into guys."

"She's into guys."

"Name the last guy she brought home."

"How would I know that?"

"The paparazzi?"

"True."

"But see? You can't."

"How'd you get so smart?"

"I have eyes, Alden," he says and laughs. "I just see stuff. I dunno."

She crosses the room. "How do I look?"

He eyes her up and down before he says, "I like that shirt. Navy is a good color on you."

"The jeans look okay?"

"Yeah, for sure." He eyes her. "Are you leaving your hair up? I think you should wear it down."

She laughs as she pulls the ponytail holder from her hair and fluffs it. "I can't believe I'm taking a thirteen-year-old's fashion advice."

"Hey, I am good with this stuff. I've been reading *Vanity Fair* since I was three."

"Oh, well, I didn't realize you were a regular Tim Gunn."

"Hey, don't diss *Project Runway*. I never miss an episode."

"Ethan, you're a trip."

He giggles, and it instantly warms her heart. "Where are you taking her?"

"Pizano's."

"Oh, good choice. She likes their pizzas a lot."

"Anything else I need to know?"

"Don't get Miller Lite. She hates it."

"Good advice." She watches his gaze shift downward. "Hey, look at me. Are you okay?"

He bites his lip before he finally asks, very quietly, "Is Mom always in danger?"

Alden sighs as she moves even closer. She sits on the top step so she's eye level with him. "Not at the moment, no."

"Was she, though?"

"Not when I'm with her."

"What if you're not with her?"

She shrugs. "That's not going to happen, so I can't answer that."

"Stella scared me. A lot. I shouldn't have asked questions, but I just want to know what's going on. I'm old enough to know."

"You really are a smart kid, you know that?"

He smiles, blushes a little, and then looks at the basketball again. "I guess."

"No, you are. But listen to me. Being thirteen is great, and I get why you think you're old enough to know what's going on. I do. But I think you're trying to be too much of an adult right now, and that's not your job. Your job is to be happy and have fun. Knowing things isn't all it's cracked up to be, y'know?"

"I guess."

"Ethan, buddy, I promise, if something happens that you need to know about, I will tell you." She squeezes his shoulder. "Until then, let's work on that basketball game. We can start tomorrow. I saw you shooting, and I feel like you could be pretty good with some practice."

The smile that spreads across his face causes Alden's heart to flutter. "Okay."

"And don't worry about your mom. I promised you, and I don't plan on breaking that."

A look washes over his face. Alden isn't sure what it means, but she wonders if he's struggling with something deeper. "Mom was, like, super mean all the time when we first moved here. She was being so uncool. Yelling at me and stuff, and I don't know *why*. I mean, I guess moving and the new job was hard for her. But man, she was getting so mean." He pauses, stares into her eyes, and for a moment, she is very self-conscious. "But she's happier since you got here. She never used to smile. And now..." He rubs the basketball before he pushes away from the wall with his shoulder. "Now she smiles a lot."

"Maybe she's just feeling better about the house and the security system?"

He lets out a laugh. "Alden, I'm thirteen. Not five. The only difference is you."

"You need to stop growing up so fast."

He laughs and playfully punches her arm. "Have fun on your *date*." And he takes off down the stairs, giggling the entire time, and disappears before she can say anything else. She is not going to let his words affect her or her feelings at all. No way.

Except that's impossible, isn't it? Because the instant those words were out of his mouth—*the only difference is you*—she was ready to combust and filled with hope. Stupid, ignorant hope. And she isn't naive to the fact that every single thing she does from here on out is going to do nothing but fuck her up even more than she already is.

At least she's prepared this time because being blindsided is not something she can handle again.

CHAPTER FOURTEEN

"Wait, so you don't want me to drive you?" Talon asks.

Alden laughs. "I can drive just fine."

"But for an event, don't you need to be, like, ready to flee the scene?"

"This isn't an event."

"Hold up. It isn't?"

Another chuckle. "Didn't I just say that?"

"I'm confused. Where are you going?"

Alden moves around the Land Rover and places a hand on her shoulder. "Are you concerned because you care about the car or about Evelyn? Either, I assure you, are acceptable answers."

Talon scrunches her face, then tilts her head. "Probably the Rover more than anything. I mean, it's a fantastic ride."

"That's what I assumed."

"If you aren't going to an event, where are you going? Why are you taking her?" Talon stops in her tracks. "Wait a second. Are you taking Evelyn *out* out?"

"What do you mean?"

"Like, a date. Like a, what the hell, I didn't even know she liked women, kind of date?"

"Talon, keep your voice down." Alden waves. "Stop. Right now."

Talon's goofy grin is almost enough to calm Alden's nerves. She bounces on her toes a couple times. "This is so exciting. I mean, also kind of forbidden, right? You aren't supposed to fall in love with the woman you're protecting." She releases an excited squeal. "Except I don't care. I'm so excited about this."

"Jesus, please stop. You have got to pull yourself together. This is not a date. It's simply a woman needing a break and me being the only one who can take her."

"Meh. I don't believe that, but whatever." She shrugs. "And besides, I can freaking see the way you look at her."

The sigh is involuntary. Alden pulls her sunglasses off, wishing she could take the sigh back for the simple fact that she is giving herself away. "Can we please come to an understanding here?"

"Yes, ma'am."

"I, in no way, shape, or form, have feelings for Evelyn Glass. I was hired to protect her. That is all."

"Mm-hmm."

"Talon, seriously."

"*Okay.*" It's clear by her tone that she is not convinced.

"I'm being serious."

"So am I."

"Talon, listen—"

"No, Alden, you listen." She puffs her chest a bit, stands taller, and lifts her chin. Whatever she's about to say is taking more courage than normal, and a strange mixture of overwhelming pride and slight irritation weaves within Alden. "I've known Stella for a long time, so I've been in Evelyn and Ethan's lives, for just as long. Evelyn took me in when my family refused to accept me, and for that, I will forever be grateful. And I will always be protective of them all but especially Evelyn. She's like a mom to me. To be honest, I didn't trust you at first. But y'know what?" Talon breathes deep, her hard-ass facade shifting the tiniest of amounts. "I do now. I trust you. I don't care what you have for Evelyn. But the fact that you risk your life to make sure she doesn't get hurt?" Another deep breath before she shrugs and tries to work past the emotion clearly bubbling beneath the surface. "Just don't think I take any of this lightly or that I'm teasing you because I don't care. I care. Okay?"

Alden needs to respond, but she's bowled over by Talon's rawness. She was privy to some of her backstory. She had no idea how deep Talon's feelings ran for the Glasses, though, and she is definitely glad she decided to keep Talon on as the driver. As much as being emotional in a protection role can have devastating effects, being connected and on top of things also means certain feelings will always be involved. Talon's emotions run deep, but she keeps herself intact and that is exactly what Alden needs on her team. There are few people she can trust, but after that outburst, she will one-hundred-percent hand over her life for Talon. And Talon may feel the same way.

That sort of trust is hard to come by and cannot be bought, regardless of the amount of money. Alden smiles. "Okay. I get it. And listen, I've been meaning to talk to you about the gun incident some more."

Talon's shoulders slump. "I'm still so sorry about all of that."

"I know you are. I was thinking, though, maybe we need to get you enrolled in a weapons' class. You can get your license to carry a concealed weapon. It might come in handy."

"Seriously?"

"Yes, seriously. I trust you, and I know the Glasses do, so it makes sense."

"I definitely want to do it then." She smiles. "Thanks, Alden."

As she starts to respond, the front door opens, and out walks Evelyn, followed by Robert. "Oh, great."

Talon chuckles, and it makes Alden feel better about not acknowledging her confession. "Take care of that goon. I expect an update later, and if you need help, please let me know. I'll find a way to get wherever you are."

Alden watches Talon walk away before she turns to confront the very annoying look on Robert's face. Evelyn has never looked more relaxed. She has a Cubs ball cap on and her hair pulled to the side, still in the loose braid. Her *I Love NY* sweatshirt looks comfortable, and her skinny jeans have holes in the knees. She's even wearing white running shoes. Alden is grateful her jeans and navy shirt aren't too casual. Pizza and beer is all this is, after all. Not a gala at the Met. She expected Evelyn to look as classy as always, so this is a surprise. Not a bad one, just a surprise. Evelyn Glass looking like a normal, everyday person is a very welcome surprise. The most hilarious part is that even looking normal, she still looks absolutely incredible.

"Are you ready?" Alden asks as Evelyn removes her sunglasses. Her eye roll gives Alden life, as well as the courage to say to Robert, "What has your panties in a twist?"

He huffs loudly and clicks his tongue. "I do not approve of any movement that I haven't scheduled."

"Now you know how it feels." Alden reaches for the handle on the Land Rover and opens it wide so Evelyn can get in. "We'll be available by cell if you need us."

He huffs yet again, and Alden wants to record the sound and replay it over and over because it is everything she loves about finally being the one in charge. "You are breaking your own rules." He laughs. "If something happens tonight, it'll be on your head."

Alden freezes. She clenches her jaw on the shitty fucking blame he's throwing at her and wishes she could clock him in the face. She lets herself glance at Evelyn, a silent conversation held between them, and then she closes the door to the SUV. "Robert," she starts before turning, "I hope you realize what will happen if you continue to dig your heels in against me."

"Ha," he yells unconvincingly.

Alden takes a step closer. She watches him swallow. "What?"

"Nothing."

"That's what I thought." She slips her sunglasses on and moves to the driver's side. She opens the door, glances at the house, and notices Connor in the doorway. He is smiling and giving Alden a thumbs-up. As she hops in and slams the door, a sense of belonging she hasn't felt in a long time fills her up. And it feels really fucking good. Almost as good as putting Robert in his place.

There are numerous Pizano's Pizza and Pasta around Chicago, but Alden's favorite is the one on State Street just past the River North neighborhood. It's small and intimate and has the most amazing old-school Chicago feel. The bar is long and green. In the past, she and her friends would sit there for hours watching the Blackhawks or Cubs and end up catching a cab home. Now she's at a corner table, her back to the wall, Evelyn's back to the restaurant, and as much as she might miss the bar, the view is remarkable.

How is it that Evelyn looks even more beautiful with hardly any makeup, looking like a tourist who stumbled off the River Boat Architecture Tour? Alden needs to stop questioning these things. Her infatuation is getting worse and worse, but at the same time, easier and easier to handle, so she should take it as a win.

"One day, you're going to go with the flow, and it's going to be wonderful," Jennifer Simmons said to her once, which started a chain reaction Alden ended up regretting. She has been trying not to blame the fact that she got shot on going with the flow, but it's hard not to. Even if she had been as buttoned up and strict as she always was, there was no way to anticipate what had happened.

"So Ethan confronted me," Alden says before she drinks from her pint glass. Evelyn Glass ordering a pitcher of Old Style beer was the cherry on top of the entire evening thus far. She has a feeling more might happen that will blow that out of the water, so she's keeping her options open.

"I kind of thought he might." Evelyn pulls a piece of cheese garlic bread from the plate, the mozzarella string snapping, and takes a generous bite. She chews and chews, a low moan humming from deep inside her. "This is exactly what I needed."

Alden finds herself chuckling. "That good, hmm?"

"Yes. God, yes. And I'm on my period, so I just needed it. Y'know what I mean?"

"I know exactly what you mean."

"What do you crave?"

"McDonald's french fries." Alden props her elbow on the table, her chin in the palm of her hand, and sighs dreamily. "I could eat them every single day of mine."

Evelyn lets out a small laugh around her next bite. She washes the first piece down and smacks her lips together. "Thank you so much for doing this with me. I know it was completely out of left field, but I needed it."

"You don't have to thank me for eating pizza and drinking beer with you. Both are things I really love doing."

Evelyn looks like she wants to respond, but she waits, eyeing Alden before she says, "I get a weird impression you'd do anything for me."

The comment, the accuracy, as well as how Evelyn delivered it in that smooth voice, an octave lower than normal, has Alden feeling a little light-headed.

"I get the same impression that you did whatever the president asked, as well."

Alden has her hand around her glass; the condensation is rolling over her fingers. She uncrosses her legs and makes sure her feet are firmly planted on the ground, steadying herself because of the inevitability of this conversation.

"I researched what happened." Evelyn's fingers drum on the red and white checkered tablecloth. The noise isn't loud, but it's enough for Alden to focus on, and it's giving her a moment to breathe. This conversation shouldn't be as difficult as she makes it. But the idea of letting go, of going with the flow, has a way of making her freeze up.

"I can't wait to see you let loose and relax," Jennifer Simmons said to her.

"You were the only one injured...is that right?" Evelyn says now. "That seems...odd."

Yeah, no shit. It is odd. Alden wouldn't have been the only one hurt on a normal outing, but it wasn't. It was a lot like this one. Unplanned. Spur of the moment. But instead of pizza and beer at six o'clock in the evening on a Friday, it was ice cream at eleven o'clock at night on a Tuesday. "Standard operating procedure."

"That's interesting."

"Mm-hmm."

Evelyn leans forward, a concerned expression on her face. "You don't have to tell me what happened."

"You've done the research."

"I think it's pretty obvious I don't believe what I read." Evelyn smiles. "Don't you think?"

"Can we please change the subject?"

"Oh? Uncomfortable talking about yourself again?"

Alden shakes her head and chuckles. "Shocked?"

"Not at all." She licks her lips. "Tell me, then, what did Ethan say to you?"

Alden thanks God that the conversation about her, her wound, her inability to not fall for the president of the United States, is done and forces herself to relax. "Oh, the usual. Take care of my mom, please don't let anything bad happen to her, don't order Miller Lite because she hates it. That sort of thing."

Evelyn leans her head back and laughs. A chill zips through Alden's body, goose bumps erupting on her forearms. She rubs them quickly to ease them. "He is the most protective of the kids."

"Oh, I don't know. Stella was attempting to pack heat to protect you."

"Don't remind me," Evelyn says after a groan. "What the hell was she thinking?"

Alden laughs. "I have no friggin' idea. She's yet to talk to me since I found her with it."

"Thank you for stopping her. I can't even imagine what would have happened."

"I'm sure she would have shot it, scared the shit out of herself, and stopped. The kick on that Glock isn't awful, but it'll mess you up if you aren't prepared for it."

"No," Evelyn says as she reaches across the table and places her hand on Alden's clenched fist. "*Thank* you."

Alden looks into Evelyn's eyes, then at her hand, mesmerized by the way Evelyn's skin looks against her own. She's stared at hands before, at how fingers wrap around the grip of a gun, at the twitch a hand can make before it reaches for a weapon. But staring at Evelyn's hands has morphed into studying them. The veins beneath her light brown skin, the way her nails are perfectly manicured, the almost undetectable follicles between her knuckles. Alden never thought she'd actually touch this woman's hand. Or have Evelyn touch her. Not like this. And the weight of Evelyn's hand is much lighter than the thoughts in Alden's mind. She pulls her gaze back to Evelyn's eyes. "You're welcome." When Evelyn moves her hand, Alden can't help but wonder what this means. She wishes she could shut her brain off, but these touches and lingering gazes and intense conversations are hard to work around. "Can I ask you something?"

"Sure."

"This may seem like a weird question, but I think it's super important."

Evelyn tilts her head.

"What is your favorite cartoon from your childhood?"

The smile that spreads across Evelyn's face almost makes Alden regret asking because sweet Jesus, is it gorgeous. She leans back in her chair, chuckles, and says, *"Tom and Jerry."*

"Perfect answer."

"And yours?"

"He-Man."

Evelyn laughs, the same wonderful laugh she did moments earlier. "What about sitcoms?"

"Oh, come on? Seriously? *The Golden Girls.* Hands down."

"Favorite character?"

"Dorothy Zbornak. She was witty and hilarious and larger than life. She is goals, most definitely."

"I loved Blanche. I always wanted to be that confident."

"You don't think that you are?"

"Oh my God, Alden," Evelyn says while laughing. "You really know nothing about me." She stops talking as the pizza comes, and her eyes go as big as saucers. "That looks so good."

Alden laughs as the server dishes them each a slice.

"Can I get you anything else?" the server asks with a smile. She seems to know who Evelyn is, but she's been exactly how she should be. Nice, without an ounce of sucking up. Alden is thrilled because it means no one else has been alerted.

"Not right now, but I might need to take a pizza home." Evelyn grins, dissolving into laughter. "Not for the family, for me." She cuts the pizza with a fork and blows on it before placing it into her mouth.

As she chews, Alden watches, smiling the entire time. For a New Yorker, Evelyn sure doesn't know how to eat thin crust pizza.

But damn, she sure is striking when she's relaxed and not *on.*

The ride home is uneventful, especially since Evelyn is pretty tipsy. "You're so much more girly than I expected from a bodyguard," she slurs as Alden drives. "I was expecting a big manly man, and then you showed up in your skinny jeans and white shirt and what even is that outfit? Is that acceptable interview attire?" Evelyn laughs. "I thought you were going to be the worst thing that happened to me."

"Oh yeah?" Alden asks because she can't stop herself. "The worst thing, hmm?" The stalker isn't the worst thing that happened to Evelyn Glass. Oh, no. It's Alden Ryan. She chuckles as she hangs on every word because she wants to know more and more.

"Yeah," Evelyn says, hiccups, then lets out a small burp. "Excuse me." She hiccups again. "You were all, 'I'm in charge,' and I was like, 'yeah, no, that's not gonna happen.'" She mimics Alden's tone perfectly, which isn't surprising since she really is a good actress, but damn. Alden feels attacked but in a good way, which is so confusing. "And then, and then"—another hiccup—"and then you saved me." Evelyn lets out a dreamy sigh, and when Alden looks, her expression has Alden's stomach tying itself into a knot. "I'm glad you're girly," she says softly. "And you're pretty." She sighs. "And you have really nice hair and…" She pauses, a lazy smile forming on her lips. "You're not manly."

And then she passes out, leaving Alden completely flustered and even more enamored.

Evelyn can really put away the beer. It's impressive, considering how reserved she always seems. Never judge a book by its cover, or a woman by the way she seems. One day, Alden will learn that.

She stopped drinking after her first beer. It would have been nice to let loose and go down the tipsy road, but the last thing she needs is to get pulled over, get a DUI, and also have the famous, and now inebriated, Evelyn Glass riding shotgun.

When they get home, she is able to get Evelyn into the house and up the stairs to her bedroom. Evelyn comes to life just enough to pull the covers down and plop onto the bed face first.

"Do you want to brush your teeth?" Alden chuckles when Evelyn waves her off, then snores softly. "She's gone," she whispers with a small smile before leaving the room far more quietly than she entered and heading up to hers, where she sits on the veranda and thinks about every second of the night.

When her cell phone vibrates, she flips it over and looks at the name. "Tobias. What the hell does he want?" She slides her finger across the message, opening it to see, *I heard things are going well. Connor is very happy. Nice job, slick.*

I told you I could handle this, she types and hits send.

Don't get cocky.

She rolls her eyes and sets her phone on the table again, facedown. She doesn't want to keep texting him. He's only trying to get her goat, and because he's so good at it, he will. When her phone starts vibrating and ringing, she groans. The last thing she wants is to *speak* to Tobias. She picks it up and without looking, answers it with, "What do you want?"

"Well, geez, that's not very nice."

"Serena, I am so sorry. I thought it was Tobias."

"Caller ID. Ever hear of it?" Serena lets out a small chuckle. "I have some good and bad news. I'm sure you want the bad news first."

"You know me so well." Alden leans forward, elbows on her knees. "Hit me."

"No fingerprints on the letters."

"Not surprising."

"But the good news is that the glue on a couple of them is the same, so you can assume it was the same person. And…" She pauses. "We found a hair."

"Wait, that's great news, isn't it?"

"It's not human."

"Like, pet hair? A dog or a cat?"

"Yes, it's a canine. I know this sounds crazy, but it's a wolf hair."

Alden lets out a laugh. "A wolf? Like a *ahwoo*?" She imitates a long howl.

Serena joins in the laughter. "Yes, like a *ahwoo*. Our forensic scientist thought for sure that the letters were tampered with. Evelyn doesn't have a dog, right?"

"Nope."

"You're sure?"

"Don't you think I would have noticed a giant fucking wolf roaming the compound?"

Another laugh comes from Serena's end of the line. "Yeah, I hope so. I mean, not much of a protector or a tracker if you can't even notice a wolf. Who even owns wolves?"

"I have no idea."

Serena sighs. "I'm looking into that first to see what the rules and regs are for owning a wolf. I swore they were protected." Her voice trails off, and Alden can hear clacking on a keyboard.

"Are you still at the office?"

"Yeah. I'm, uh, not much fun these days, so Howard asked to... take a break."

"Oh, Serena, I'm so sorry."

"Don't worry about it. I'll be fine. And you know"—she chuckles—"having this crazy case to focus on is definitely helping."

"Let me know if it gets too much for you."

"It won't. I promise." And she hangs up before Alden can even say good-bye.

A wolf. What the hell? That doesn't make sense. It must be a fluke because why, oh why would someone who takes the time to be so meticulous with a note do something as careless as leaving a piece of pretty remarkable evidence behind?

Unless it really is a clue.

And since every single letter has seemed thought-out and perfect, Alden imagines the wolf hair was just as planned. Just as well thought-out. And those two things mean the hairs mean something.

But what?

CHAPTER FIFTEEN

It's been a week since the date that wasn't a date.

A week.

And Alden has done nothing of importance except obsess about every single thing that happened that night. And every night since.

She accompanies Evelyn to the sets for filming. She's more accepted now, and it's really nice not fighting with Evelyn at every turn. In fact, no altercations have happened at all, and Alden doesn't know whether to thank God or wait for the other shoe to drop. She's positive if the shoe drops, it'll be more like an Acme anvil, and it'll smash right onto her.

The on-set discussion about who she is and why she's always with Evelyn has petered out as well. Everyone knows her now, and no one asks Evelyn, "Who is the hot blonde always trailing behind you?"

Alden was pissed the first time. But now? She's okay with it. After all, it's sort of nice being referred to as the hot blonde. Even if she always hated the idea of being the only woman in her profession. Respect has never been easy to come by, and sometimes being "hot" means respect is even harder to earn. In this case, she suspects her looks have garnered her respect a lot easier and faster. She finds it sad, to a certain extent, because her appearance should not matter.

But this is showbiz, kid, and, good or bad, looks for sure matter.

The next event is a week and a half away. Another comic convention. Evelyn hasn't wanted to talk about it much, which worries Alden to a certain extent. Evelyn is probably still gun-shy after the last event. *It's easy to let those moments freak you out, and it's hard to come back from them.* It's easier to stay away from them all together, but Evelyn can't, and she said that on more than one occasion.

"I'll pull myself together and be fine," Evelyn says as she sits on the rock ledge at the house, looking across the lake. She is stiff, uncomfortable, and Alden is well aware of the change in her posture. Evelyn keeps her eyes glued forward. The day is perfect, with hardly any clouds, and the temperature is just right.

"We can discuss logistics beforehand if you'd like," Alden explains. "Maybe it will take some stress away if you know the details."

"No." Her response is quick. Almost too quick.

Alden can guess the reasoning. "Evelyn?"

"What?"

Again, her response is too fast, and Alden can tell this conversation is not going to go well. "You need to talk to me about this stuff."

"You're my bodyguard. Not my fucking therapist."

"Well, maybe you need a fucking therapist."

Evelyn turns her head so fast, Alden wonders if she hurt her neck. "Excuse me?"

"Listen, what you're going through is not normal. These things are not *normal*. Being sent letters by an anonymous stalker is not normal. It's supposed to freak you out. That's *why* this person is doing it." She sits on the ledge but faces the house. She likes to make sure she is always watching Evelyn's back. Hell, she likes to always watch her own back. She stretches her legs and crosses them at the ankles. "Admitting you're freaked out, that this person is succeeding, is not a weakness. I hope you know that." She glances at Evelyn's profile. She is listening, which is a surprise. "You're one of the strongest women I've ever met."

Evelyn scoffs, then lets out a small laugh that seems hardly impressed. "You don't really hang out with many women, do you?"

Alden looks down and sighs. "Yeah, you're probably right." She shrugs. "I only fucking protected the first female president of the United States of America." She can feel Evelyn looking, and when their eyes meet, she lets herself smile. "No biggie, right?"

Finally, Evelyn lets out a, "Ha," and follows it with a deep belly laugh Alden has only ever heard once before. And that pizza night laugh is something she has replayed about a million times.

Alden leans into Evelyn's side, nudges her ever so lightly, and says with the most caring voice she can summon, "I will always be here to talk to if you need me. Okay?"

And Evelyn only nods before Alden stands and walks fifteen paces away, keeping her distance but not wanting to go far.

Just in case.

❖

Alden is not surprised later that afternoon by Evelyn's plea to get out of the house again. Her, *I need to feel like a normal human*, argument is hard to debate because of all the amazing opportunities Evelyn has had in life, acting like a normal human being was usually not one of them.

"What do you want to do?"

"I do not care." Evelyn smiles as she leans against the wall at the bottom of the stairs. "I just…" She looks over each shoulder. "I've been thinking a lot about what you said earlier, and maybe you're right."

"That you need to talk this stuff out?"

"Unfortunately, yes." Evelyn shrugs. "I don't know how to talk about myself without it being on the record."

Alden chuckles. "You mean in an interview? Do I seem like the interviewing type?"

"Yes, that's what I mean and don't laugh." She smiles shyly, tilting her head as if to hide the blush filling her cheeks, and in that moment, Alden will do whatever Evelyn asks.

"I have a place I could take you. But it's around other people."

"Really?" Her eyes light up, and she looks as if Alden has given her the world in one small statement.

"Calm down. It's nothing crazy. Secluded but it'll get you out of the house."

Evelyn bounces on her toes. "Okay. What do I wear?"

"Jeans. Bring a sweatshirt. And normal shoes."

"Like?"

"No heels."

"Oh," Evelyn squeals. "I love you for doing this for me."

And everything in the room skids to a stop. The air, the breathing, the ticking of the clock above the mantle of the fireplace. Alden's mouth is slick with saliva, and she wonders, if they both turn and leave, can they escape what has been said? They don't need to discuss it. It's not important. It's not true at all. It was said in a playful way, so it means nothing. Nothing at all. That much is obvious. Evelyn was simply saying it in that valley-girl, *oh my God, I love you so much*, way, and that's it.

As if on cue, Evelyn skips over the impending embarrassment and bounces again. "I'll go get ready." She rushes through the loft and down the hallway toward her wing of the second floor.

Alden braces herself with a hand on the wall as she sits on the steps. "You're so fucked," she whispers. And she is, but there's no use trying to stop it now.

In a moment of pure stupidity, Alden purchased a fully-restored, 1967 International Harvester Scout when she was sixteen. She worked her ass off to make the money, and she bought it from the neighbor. Zigzag used to be a big foreboding man with a gruff voice who rode Harleys and was never seen out of his "uniform," a black Harley Davidson T-shirt and jeans. He was a big fan of marijuana and back in the day, when it was far from being legalized, her pops would warn her to, "Stay the hell away from Zigzag."

She didn't really listen because Zigzag was a lot of fun to talk to. He was an old Chicago boy with Hell's Angels ties, and really, what better person to have in her back pocket than a Hell's Angel? The day she found her father toking on a joint with Zigzag, things changed. Drastically. That was the day she learned that her Chicago police officer dad was far from perfect. And it was also the day she decided she was going to purchase that Scout if it was the last thing she did.

People always say she has a lot of gumption, especially when she was a teenager.

"She was low on oil. And she needed coolant." Pops runs his hand over the hood of the Scout. As what he calls a "solid favor," he pulled it out of storage and drove it up to her at the house. She was sick of needing to borrow his Oldsmobile, and this time, she didn't want to roll up in a Land Rover.

"Did you help a girl out and do that for me?"

"You know I did."

"Thanks, Pops."

"Listen, Alden, I gotta talk to you about this…" He motions to the mansion. "Do you really think you're doin' the right thing here? I mean, look at this place. This ain't you."

Alden laughs. "Pops. Seriously? This is nothing compared to the White House."

His cheeks puff as he lets out a huff. "Hmph. I guess you're right."

"I'm okay here. I promise."

"Your ma misses you."

"I was only home for a couple weeks."

"Yeah, well, she does. You know how overbearing she can be."

"Oh, I know."

"She keeps moping around the house. It's driving me nuts."

"Go golfing."

"I have."

"Go for a drink with the guys."

"Done that, too."

"Take out Zigzag's motorcycle he gave you since he can't ride anymore."

Pops sighs. "I've done that, too." He crosses his arms and leans against the dark gray matte of the Scout. "Now you know why I smoked pot."

Alden can't help but laugh. "Well, you sure had me fooled for a while."

"Had the whole force fooled. Not sure how I escaped those drug tests." He shakes his head, a faraway expression on his face. "I'm glad you bought this. I thought you were half a bubble off when you said you were gonna."

She steps back and admires the old SUV. Her pops has taken care of the little things she asked him to—Armor All the tires, don't forget to keep the rims shining, if you drive it in the snow, wash it immediately because I don't want the salt to eat the dark gray paint off—before she left for the Secret Service. She took great care of it, and besides the awful gas mileage, she loves everything about it, including, and especially, how rugged it is. "Thanks for loving her for me."

"Well, Dorothy here has given me no trouble at all. And truth be told"—he sniffles and wipes at his nose—"I'm gonna miss her."

"Pops, are you crying?"

He sniffles again. "No, not at all."

"You're lying."

"You shush," he says with a wave and a sweet, low chuckle. "Okay, my ride's here. O'Connor's making me hit the pub on the way in. It's boneless wing night."

"Good. Tell him I said to not drink and drive."

"Who's the parent? You or me?" His brow is furrowed, and he's pointing, a half-smile displayed. "We can get a ride if we need it. You be good, Alden."

"The best."

"Always." He leans in and kisses her on the cheek before he shuffles toward the gate. Alden's love for him knows no bounds, even when he used to struggle with her sexuality. Even now, he may not bring it up, but he's more open to at least acknowledging her happiness. It took a long time for her to understand him, understand why he was so locked up and unable to talk about himself. For the longest time, it frustrated the shit out of her. Until recently, when she realized she's exactly the same way. The thought carries with it a warmth and a smile she hasn't experienced in a long time. And for that, she's grateful.

Alden checks her mirrors as she merges onto the Dan Ryan Expressway headed toward New Buffalo, Michigan. She finds a good speed to keep up with traffic before relaxing into the driver's seat. She drums her fingers on the steering wheel along with Stevie Nicks on the only station that comes in worth a damn on the old radio in the Scout. The benefit is WXRT is a fantastic station, and so far, the music has been perfect. One of the only things she hopes she can change about the Scout is the radio. Or maybe say fuck it and get a new sound system. She'll be able to afford it after this job. She can even get one with Bluetooth.

She chuckles to herself. She's so nervous that she's thinking about Bluetooth. *What the hell, Alden?*

And why is she so nervous? Oh, because, y'know, she has managed to fly through every single stop sign her brain tried to install along the way when it came to Evelyn Glass. She's starting to think maybe her heart doesn't know how to accept any sort of direction from her brain. Except for, of course, beating, which it does too rapidly at times and barely at all during other moments. Even the simple task of *beating regularly* is something her heart has a hard time accomplishing.

At this point, a part of her wonders if maybe she should throw caution to the wind and see what happens. Under Evelyn's hard exterior is a woman who is lost and scared and needs saving, and those things are Alden's specialty. In fact, every single woman in her past was every bit of those things.

Lost.

Scared.

In need of saving.

And how the fuck did that work out for you, Alden? Hmm?

"This is a great ride," Evelyn shouts, interrupting her overthinking.

"Thank you." She relaxes for half a second. "She's my baby."

"I can see why." Evelyn's voice fades away but Alden can feel the stare. She wants to freeze, as if not moving will make her disappear. "You sure are deep in thought over there."

She glances over while continuing to grip the steering wheel like a lifeline. She shrugs. "Just focusing on the road and the other horrible drivers."

"Oh, is that it?"

She forces her attention to not wander again. "Yep."

"I don't believe you at all. I hope you know that."

Do not look at her again, Alden. Don't do it.

"I find it odd that you want me to talk to you, but you don't want to talk to me."

"I don't mind talking to you."

"Let me rephrase: you want me to open up to you, but you don't want to open up to me."

Alden rolls her lips inward, then pushes out a breath through her nose. She allows herself to glance, *but quickly*, at Evelyn. "I guess you're right."

Evelyn's laugh is loud but not irritatingly so. The roar of the V8 isn't exactly easy to communicate over.

"No, no laughing." Alden shakes her head. "I don't open up with anyone. So don't take offense."

"I'm not offended."

"Good." She pauses. "Then what are you, if not offended?" She checks her rearview and side mirrors before looking to Evelyn, seeming comfortable in the copilot's chair. She has her legs crossed and her flipflop-clad foot is bobbing lightly. Her toes are painted dark red, and Alden wishes she could say it wasn't something she noticed, but she did, almost before she noticed anything else as Evelyn walked outside to leave.

"I'm intrigued."

It's Alden's turn to laugh as she turns her gaze back to the road. "You are going to be very disappointed."

"Somehow, I doubt that."

The sound of her voice when she utters those words causes Alden's stomach to flip and her heart to flop, and she's positive that if she wasn't trained in how to focus when under immense pressure, she'd have driven them right off the expressway into a pussy-willow-filled ditch. "I promise you," Alden responds.

"Mm-hmm." Evelyn clears her throat. "Where are you taking me, anyway?"

"My friend Melissa's beach house. She and her husband Patrick always throw a party on the beach with live music and a fire. I didn't think I'd get to go this year because…"

"Because of me."

"Because of this job, yes."

"You're allowed to take days off, y'know." She sounds irritated. Or hurt. As if she believes the only reason she's along for the ride is so Alden can attend.

"I know," Alden answers. "But I haven't needed a day off." She looks at Evelyn, at the sadness in her eyes. "I haven't wanted one, either." Then the sadness is replaced by sparkle. "Anyway, Mel and Pat bought this old house on the coast in New Buffalo, and they spent a few years fixing it up. Pat isn't super handy, but Mel is, so they did the renovations a little at a time. Now it's just gorgeous. They really put a lot of time and effort into it. I think you'll like it. It's no mansion, but it really is lovely."

Evelyn is chuckling when she says, "Excuse me? If it's not a mansion, I refuse to go."

"Sorry, lady, it's too late now. We're almost there."

"Lucky for you, I don't enjoy jumping out of a car while it's moving, so I guess you're stuck with me. And besides..." She takes a deep breath. "I'm excited to meet your friends. Maybe I'll be able to pump them for some inside info about who Alden Ryan really is."

"I guess I should feel honored that the great Evelyn Glass wants to know more about me."

"Yeah, you should. It may sound conceited, but I don't really like many people."

"Whoa, whoa, whoa. You're saying you like me?" Alden clutches her chest. "You might need to take the wheel. I feel like I am going to pass out. Am I having a heart attack?"

Evelyn starts laughing and smacks her on the arm. "You are hysterical."

"I never thought I'd see the day where you admit that I'm likeable."

"I didn't say you're likeable." She laughs again. "I said I don't like many people. Big difference."

"Oh, okay. Whew. I'd hate to think I won you over with my charming personality."

"Hardly."

Alden smiles, keeping her eyes glued to the road when she hears Evelyn clear her throat again.

"I've always wondered, did you ever research me? Or Google me or whatever?"

Alden sees the tail end of Evelyn's erratic hand movements as she speaks. Is she the nervous one now? "Yes. Google was helpful, but the real winner here? Tumblr. There were a lot of posts dedicated to you. There were entire blogs dedicated to you. It was, uh, eye-opening."

"That doesn't sound good," Evelyn says softly, and thankfully, they stop at the sign off the New Buffalo exit so Alden hears her.

Otherwise, her response of, "No, it was good," would have never seen the light of day. "There are a lot of pictures. Really nice pictures."

Evelyn's cheeks have turned that lovely shade of pink Alden is starting to love seeing and maybe being the cause of. "I do have a lot of fans," she says as their eyes meet.

"Yeah, you do." Alden can barely feel her hands as a horn blasts behind her. She snaps her attention back to the road and heads in the direction of the shoreline. "For good reason," she adds and doesn't really expect to be heard.

"Oh, really?"

"I guess I can admit that I've watched some of your movies." She slows as they get to the quaint downtown area. The sidewalks are full of people going from bars to restaurants. It's a gorgeous evening.

"And?"

Alden takes a deep breath, keeping her eyes on the road when she says, her voice shaky, "I think you're breathtaking." She can hear the inhale, the exact reaction she hoped for. It's when she feels Evelyn's hand on her arm for one, two, three, four, five seconds before it's gone, does she think maybe she should go with the flow and have some fun. After all, it never hurts to relax, especially when it's been so long since she's been able to.

Mel and Pat have spared no expense for this party. The food is out of this world, live music is on a small stage to the right of the large firepit, and there are twinkle lights in every tree and along the boardwalk that leads to their private beach. The fire is roaring, and the party-goers are roasting marshmallows and hot dogs while they jam to the awesome cover band, Nawty. The setup is perfect, especially the Adirondack chairs and large outdoor pillows surrounding the fire pit.

For the first time in a while, Alden is relaxed. And she's enjoying herself, which hasn't happened without alcohol or sex in quite some time. Maybe because no one knows where they are. Not Connor. Especially not Robert. She did give Talon a head's up, but she only knows they're going somewhere together. Talon isn't comfortable knowing too many details.

She has had a hard time not watching every movement Evelyn makes. Not for the reasons she's been obsessing over but because even when she's off-duty, she's never really off. Evelyn is sitting, her jean-clad legs crossed, her black leather flip-flops sitting next to her in the sand, and she's talking to Serena. Alden isn't sure if that's a good or a bad thing. And as she stands on the opposite side of the fire, watching every move, trying to listen to what Mel is rambling about, she finds it so strange that the song is a cover of Bob Marley's "Is This Love."

Seriously?

She takes a long drink from her water.

"Have you heard a word I've said?"

Alden glares at Mel. "Of course I have."

"What did I say?"

"You were going on and on about that last project you had."

"Wrong." She rolls her eyes before she drinks her rosé. "You're ridiculous."

"Excuse me?"

"That didn't take long, did it?" Her tone is accusatory, and Alden's immediate reaction is to laugh her off. There's no way she's that transparent. *Right?*

And without an invitation, Pat strolls up and says, "Yeah, like, what? A month? Not even, right?" He taps his koozie against Mel's wineglass and laughs. "Quick Draw McGraw over here."

"Tell us what happened to being professional, Alden?" Mel asks, her eyebrows raised to her hairline. "Was it that she's gorgeous or that she's rich?"

"Whoa. What the fuck?" She's insulted. Fully. "None of what you're thinking is accurate. She motions to Evelyn as nonchalantly as possible. "This is not what you think."

Pat leans his head back and laughs, then drapes an arm across Mel's shoulders. "You're too easy," he says, still laughing.

Mel grins, looks at Alden, and says, "I was just joking around, but damn, your response was classic. I'm thinking I hit a nerve."

"Oh my God, I hate you." Alden laughs. "I thought you were fucking serious."

Pat smiles and leans close. "Not that anyone would blame you. She's smokin' hot. I'm not going to lie, I'm a little starstruck right now."

Mel rolls her eyes again. "Are you kidding me, Patrick? Keep it in your pants, man." She smacks him on the arm. "I can't believe I married this asshole."

Alden chuckles. "You guys are seriously the worst."

"No, we are the best." Mel places a hand on Alden's shoulder. She squeezes before she asks, "Are you doing okay? I know when you were deciding to take this job, you were sort of..."

"A hot disaster of a mess?"

"Yeah, sort of."

"No, definitely, I was." Alden sighs. "I still am."

"Oh, great, perfect mind frame to be in, hmm?" Mel chuckles, and thankfully, the conversation has bored Pat enough that he dissolves into another group of people.

"Can I be honest with you?"

"Um, yes. I'm not friends with you for the lies."

"True." Alden takes a long drink of water. She glances around before finally saying, "I have been struggling with...not falling for her."

"Oh, Alden."

"I know."

"Honey, you can't do that again."

"I know."

"Why do you keep doing this to yourself?"

"I have no idea." Her throat is on fire. Is that bile or reality? She wants to escape this conversation, and she's the one who brought it up. She does not want to get into this, whatever this is. Not now. Hopefully, not ever. *But please not now.* Yet, here she goes. Opening up and regretting it. "Thrill of the chase?"

"Helping people?"

"I like that answer better."

Mel laughs. "Yeah, well, both are sort of fucked up."

"I hate when you're right."

"I love it when I'm right, which is so often, you'd think it would get old. Alas, it does not. I never tire of the thrill of victory."

"You're kind of a dick." Alden laughs as she bumps Mel with her shoulder. "I love you, but you really are."

"Yeah, takes one to know one." She drinks again, this time finishing in two gulps. "I do have to say, you have some phenomenal luck."

"What do you mean?"

"She's fucking gorgeous. Her skin is flawless. What the hell? She's older than both of us."

"Tell me about it." Alden's face fills with heat. "I wish I could say this is just another notch in my belt. But this time? I don't know. This whole experience is different."

"That's good," Mel says before leaning again into her. "Don't jump into anything. See where it goes. Stay professional but test the waters. Who knows what might happen?"

"Oh, wait, no, it's not going to happen. She's not into me."

Mel lets out a laugh, and numerous people look over. She covers her mouth and continues laughing. "Are you kidding me?"

"No. I'm not freaking kidding. You're going to embarrass me with that loud-ass laugh."

"Listen to me right this second." She grips Alden's forearm tightly. "That woman is as taken with you as you are with her, and if you don't fucking see that, you're an idiot."

"An idiot? Really?"

"Yes, really." She loosens her grip and rolls her shoulders back, composing herself. "You need to stop selling yourself short. People fall for you, whether they want to or not. And I truly believe sexuality has nothing to do with it."

"Aw, Mel, that's the sweetest thing you've ever said to me."

"Yeah, well, you're still an idiot."

"I know," Alden replies, her eyes tearing up slightly. "And you're a dick."

Mel laughs and pushes her on the shoulder. "Go. Sit by her."

Alden waits a couple seconds and composes herself before she moves around the fire to where Evelyn is seated next to Serena. "What are you two talking about?" She pulls up a pillow and sits between their chairs. She leans against Evelyn's leg, and is elated when Evelyn presses back against her. Nawty's rendition of Oasis's "Wonderwall" on the night air is the perfect complement to this moment.

"I'm just fangirling like a total and complete jerk." Serena laughs. "I'm sorry."

"Don't be," Evelyn says softly. "You're adorable."

"Well, thank you. I still feel like a jerk. Alden, I've been watching her since I was a kid. Oh, wow, that sounds creepy. You know what I mean." She laughs again, her chuckle laced with nerves. "So anyway. Enough about me."

Alden can't help but laugh, too. "You are supposed to be the calm and collected detective. Get your shit together, Serena."

"I know, I know." She takes a couple deep dramatic breaths. "Okay, I'm better."

"Good." Alden releases a sigh as she looks at the last lingering effects of the sunset on the water. "This is a beautiful night."

"*Ope*, I'm being summoned." Serena jumps up. "Harold came with me tonight. Guess the separation is over." She shrugs before she says, "Evelyn, it was lovely to meet you and fangirl over you. Alden, I'll call you." And she takes off in the direction of a very impatient Harold, who waves good-bye from across the party. He's such a weirdo.

"I apologize about that." Alden goes to stand but stops when Evelyn leans forward and places a hand on her shoulder. She glances at the hand for what feels like a whole minute before she relaxes again.

"Thank you."

Alden hears the words but is unsure why a thank you is necessary. "For?"

"Putting in a little time and effort to get to know me." She is still leaning forward, so the laugh that seems to slip from her mouth is shaky, and Alden can smell the wine on her breath. "For bringing me here. I'm sure most of the people are going to question you for the next however many months."

"Oh, yes. I already received, 'How the hell do you know Evelyn Glass?' at least ten times tonight." Not to mention the amount of times the guys felt the need to tell her how hot Evelyn is. *No shit, boys. No fucking shit.*

"Did you tell them the truth?"

"Actually, no." She grins. "I said I was the babysitter."

Evelyn lets out a low laugh. She pushes gently, instructing Alden to scoot over. Then she gently moves Alden's hair to the side and guides her back to the chair. "You wish," Evelyn says before she starts running her fingers through Alden's hair.

"What are you doing?"

"I'm thanking you." Evelyn's nails scrape lightly over her head, and chills erupt over her entire body. She is going to melt right into the sand. She's sure of it. "Your hair is so gorgeous."

"This is…" The words are caught. They're right there, locked and loaded. *This is not what should be happening. You shouldn't be touching me like this, Evelyn. I don't need this kind of a thanks. The paycheck is enough.*

"Every time I ask you to bend the rules, you've done it for me. I don't know if you understand how nice it is being normal."

Yes, I do understand it. It's why she got shot. It's why she broke the rules and snuck Jennifer out of the White House. It's why…

"And you keep giving me alcohol, so honestly? I'm the most relaxed I've been in months."

She smiles, tries to hide any nerves that are surfacing, and says, "My evil plan is working then."

"Yeah, well." She presses the soft pads of her fingertips along Alden's neck and shoulders. "Evil plan or not, I feel like I might have the upper hand right now." She pulls gently, making Alden lean her head back even farther. "You are right where I want you."

The heat rises from Alden's center toward the pit of her stomach. She gathers her self-confidence. "Maybe *you're* right where *I* want you. Ever think about that?"

A low laugh spills from Evelyn's mouth as she leans forward, pressing her lips against Alden's ear. "You," she says, her breath rushing against Alden's skin, "have no idea what I'm capable of."

Sweet Jesus. Her brain has short-circuited. "Am I having a stroke?"

The laugh that bubbles from Evelyn is so adorable. "You are definitely putty in my hands."

"Oh, I know." Alden is positive her legs are numb. They sit in silence for a few moments, listening to the fire, Alden trying to decide if her heart is beating or if she has flatlined. Her friends are laughing and talking on the opposite side of the fire.

Evelyn sighs. "I never knew the Midwest was so *beautiful.*"

Alden lets out a laugh. "There's more than corn in the Midwest," she says before drinking the last of her water. "Except for Indiana. Indiana only has corn."

"I hope this night never ends."

"I know what you mean." Her reply comes out as a whisper, and she wonders if Evelyn really does know how stupid this is. Does she know how this is not okay? Does she even know what the fuck she's doing? Does she have any idea how this could mess up the effort Alden has put into her mental health, her emotional health?

"I love this song."

Evelyn's voice breaks through her thoughts, and she listens to Nawty as their lead singer, a woman who has one hell of a voice, brings down the house with a rendition of "I Will Always Love You." She also loves the song, and now this entire evening has done nothing but solidify every thought Alden has had considering Evelyn Glass:

She's a complicated woman.

Who has no idea how she comes across.

She is full of herself but also insecure, a strange mixture that somehow works.

She is damaged.

And wants to be protected.

She is afraid of everything. Including and especially falling in love.

She is interesting.

And interested.

And Evelyn Glass clearly has every intention of going somewhere with Alden that neither of them should want.

"Alden?" Evelyn's hands have stopped, and she's sitting completely still.

Something has gone through Evelyn's mind, and Alden is struggling between desperation and indignation. She's had this same feeling once before, seconds prior to being shot. She was staring at Jennifer, who was smiling as she licked her ice cream cone, and she was falling so in love that it both excited and angered her. "Yes?" *Oh no, did my voice just crack?*

"Are you really willing to die for me?"

She can't help the small laugh. That was not what she thought Evelyn was going to say. She really had no idea what was going to come out, but that? Yeah, that was not it. She leans forward and looks over her shoulder. Evelyn has a look of confusion plastered on her delicate features. "Why are you asking me that?"

"Why did you laugh?"

"You shocked me." She looks at the pillow, at her jeans, how the sand has found a way to cover almost everything. As annoying as sand is, she wishes she could be half as resilient. "Protecting people is my job. I'm willing to do whatever necessary, no matter the sacrifice, including dying." She sighs. "And this case is no different."

"Do you think your life means less than mine?"

If a group of words strung together so elegantly could have the power to both destroy a person and also heal her, those were them. "That's…that's not it."

"Then? Why are you willing to risk your life to protect *me?*" She sounds troubled, as if she's trying to wrap her brain around the entire idea of a stranger sacrificing something so fragile as life. "And don't say it's the money because even if I barely know you, I know without a shadow of a doubt that is not the reason."

"Why did you start acting?"

"No, this isn't about me for once."

She moves so she's facing Evelyn, her legs folded, her hands on her knees. "Answer the question. I'm trying to explain it to you."

Evelyn sighs. "Well, I can't sing."

"That's not the reason."

"At first, it was my dad pushing me to do it. I was a cute kid, and it was everything I wanted to do, so he supported me and pushed me."

She runs both hands through her hair. The lake breeze has been kind to her and has only made her natural wave more beautiful. "But now I do it because I love it. It makes me feel alive."

"Exactly."

"You love protecting people?"

And before Alden can stop herself, she answers with, "I love protecting you." She wants to take it back. She wants to rewind and take every part of this conversation back.

"Alden," Evelyn says, quietly, and *oh no, are those tears?*

If there's one thing Alden simply cannot handle, it's seeing a beautiful woman cry. "That's it. No more questions about me."

"But—"

"No, we should go. It's getting late, you have an event tomorrow, and we really should be going." She stands and heads away from the conversation, from Evelyn, and from the feelings she shouldn't be having. She only hopes she left them right there in the resilient sand.

CHAPTER SIXTEEN

The ride home was horrific. Alden was thankful for the Scout's loud rumble because it helped with the lack of communicating. Silence has never bothered her before. She enjoys it most of the time. But when Evelyn is silent, it means she's trying to work things out in her head. And the only thing Evelyn seems to be working out these days is how to crack the code for Alden to start talking.

Why is it so important? Why can't she just take what Alden can give, which isn't much, but it should be enough. There's no need for details. There's no need for backstory. None of that should matter. Once this crazy fan is caught, Alden can leave, and another bodyguard can step into her position. At least, she hopes that's the case.

She wants to be back at the White House one day. She wants to be back serving her country. And even though it's a long shot, she really wants to go back to serving President Simmons.

If Jennifer wins the reelection, maybe it's possible.

Even though they will never be able to have what Alden wanted. Hell, what Jennifer said *she* wanted. And being back at the White House will take her mind off Evelyn Glass and the entire family.

Alden finishes her perimeter walk at midnight, sharp. Walking around at night isn't the safest thing to do, but these night dates— *they're not dates, Alden*—okay, *outings*, have really cramped her routine. The perimeter check seems like overkill, but it's the first place where she can see if something has been tampered with.

She can't see shit tonight, so this was a stupid idea. As she heads back to the house, she continues to berate herself. She wants to quit and run back to the Secret Service and beg for reinstatement. Maybe that is what she'll do. Maybe that will help her get back to a good spot. Or maybe it'll just fuck her up even more.

"Hey, Ryan?"

She stops in the large hallway that leads to the back staircase, the one that won't take her past Evelyn's room. "What do you need, Robert?" She doesn't turn. He is the last person she wants to see tonight. His voice sets her teeth on edge, and if he says one wrong thing, she's afraid she might clean his clock.

"I think these late-night outings need to stop. Evelyn needs her sleep. She can't be galivanting around and expect to wake up refreshed for shooting."

"Fine by me."

"And if she needs to go out, I'll take her."

"And I would go with, to protect her. Do you really want that?" She tosses the question over her shoulder.

"She got another letter tonight."

"What?" She turns, and he's manhandling a piece of pink paper. "What the hell?" She rips it from his hands.

Wouldn't it be lovely if you were outed to the public?

She turns it over and inspects the back. "Where was this?"

"You don't want to know."

"Yes, I do."

"It was on her bed again."

"How? How is that possible?"

He shrugs. "You know when you're not here, locked in this house, anyone can get in at any time."

"The alarm was set."

He shrugs again. "I don't know what to tell you."

"How did you find this? Why were you in her bedroom?"

"I walked past, and her door was open. That's not normal." He sounds so fucking guilty that she wants to rip him to shreds.

She takes a step closer, completely in his face. "Are you the motherfucker doing this, Robert?"

His face falls. She is either right or very, very wrong. "How dare you?"

Shit. She's wrong. "I'm sorry. I'm sorry, Robert. I just...I'm under a lot of stress right now. I know you love her."

"I would do anything for her. I would never..." His voice cracks, and he stops talking. He places his hand over his mouth.

"Look, I'm sorry. I shouldn't have snapped."

He steps away, removes his hand from his mouth, and pulls his shoulders back. "It's fine. I get it. Everyone is on edge."

"Thank you."

He lifts his chin, then struts away. It was awful to accuse him, but things aren't adding up. One second she had the upper hand, and like that, he came out on top. That's exactly why getting emotional never works out well. She knows it, and honestly, he probably does, too.

Alden has always held herself together. She was trained to, "Keep your fucking shit together, Ryan!" She's been yelled at, cursed at, and slammed into more times than she can count. Years and years of training—physical and mental—have gone into conditioning herself to be a hard-ass, to protect and serve, to put someone else's life before her own. It is always business. It is never personal.

Except that's wrong, isn't it? It doesn't matter who the person is or what the person's profession is, it is damn near-impossible to turn off the part that cares. Unless the person is an asshole, and she has certainly been on detail with some major assholes.

Maybe she is out of whack right now because of being relieved from duty, or maybe it's because she is starting to like every single thing about Evelyn Glass. Either way, she's positive that her training, albeit very intense and tremendously helpful, is absolutely wrong this time.

The knock on her door at one thirty in the morning startles her. She wonders if it's Connor. Or maybe Robert again. Or even Talon. They have an event tomorrow, and maybe she wants to go over the game plan.

She hopes it's Evelyn, and that's when she realizes there is nothing that could stop her from having feelings. Including her training.

And when she opens the door, sees Evelyn standing there, she fears where this could lead. Two things can happen: one, she asks Alden to take her away from all this; or two…

"May I come in?"

Tell her no. Tell her no, you idiot. Alden steps to the side and holds the door open. She latches it behind her and turns to watch Evelyn walk through her living area. She is barefoot and nervous. Everything about her stance is screaming it.

"I know the media painted me to be some sort of lover scorned because Joel left me for another woman. A younger, more attractive woman." Her shoulders rise and fall.

Alden doesn't move. She can make a quick exit if need be. Leave Evelyn standing there and get the fuck out of this situation.

"I wasn't mad or upset about it."

"Why not?"

She turns, her arms hanging at her side, and shrugs. "Because I wasn't in love with him. I don't think I ever was."

"Is that the only reason?"

She purses her lips, shakes her head.

"Are you going to tell me?"

"He left because I…" She pushes the wavy curls behind her ear. "We had an agreement that I was allowed to do what I needed to do as long as he was the man on my arm."

"And what did you need to do?"

"Dammit." Her voice cracks. "I could have sex with women whenever I wanted."

The revelation doesn't shock Alden as much as she assumed it would. Instead, it fills her with questions and fear and excitement. The idea that she hasn't misread what has happened is a welcome respite. Nothing makes it okay to go where they are headed, though, even if the confession does make it less jarring.

"At the time, I was the darling of the Disney Channel. I was sixteen. He was eighteen. We were stupid and young, and he rode my coattails. And then a year later, I got pregnant. And we married, and it was so wrong, and the only thing I don't regret is my children." She's breathing harder, and tears are starting to flow, and it's definitely time for Alden to spring into action, but she can't. "I haven't been in a relationship since he left. I don't have that luxury. And I can't keep paying people to be quiet. I'm done with that."

"Aren't you paying me...to be quiet?"

Evelyn wipes at her face and lets out a tear-stained laugh. "You don't have to be quiet. You can go to the press tomorrow if you want. I don't care who knows anymore. Robert cares. My father cares. I needed you to know, though. I needed you to understand. I'm not who everyone says I am. I was a lost kid when I married Joel, and I found myself, even in the darkness of the last few years. We were ready to go our separate ways. So he found someone and left, and I was fine." Her shoulders slump a tiny amount, and she sits on the edge of the bed. "I needed to lose those years to find myself again. And I have. I'm so much happier now. And I'm acting again, and he's not jealous or holding me back any longer. And he's happy now, too, which is the only thing I have ever wanted for him."

"Can I ask one thing?"

"Anything."

"Don't you think it's a bad idea to mix business with pleasure?"

"It's the worst idea ever." The answer is breathless, and Alden's abdomen tightens.

"Then?"

"I can't stop thinking about you."

"Evelyn—"

"No, wait." She rushes the distance between them and lays her hands on Alden's arms. "You make me feel alive again after so many years of feeling like I have wasted my entire life. The awards didn't matter. The accolades didn't matter. I was hiding who I am, and when Joel and I split, I thought that was it. Then *Between the Covers* happened. And unwanted attention notwithstanding, you ended up happening."

"What exactly are you saying?"

Evelyn drops her hands and stands straight. "I'll stop paying you if it means you'll stop being my bodyguard and start being my girlfriend."

Alden laughs. She can't help it. This is nuts. "Evelyn, that's not how this works."

"Then tell me how it works because I can't keep living like this."

"Like what?"

"With this constant desire to touch you, undress you, kiss you, map out every single square inch of your body with my hands, my mouth, my tongue." Her voice is low and sultry, her expression so determined yet pained, Alden is having a hard time standing without her knees buckling. "You're the first person who has cared enough to get to know the real me. Yeah, maybe it's because you're paid to kiss my ass, but it has to also be because you sort of like me back."

"It has nothing to do with the money," Alden whispers.

"So you like me?"

"More than I should."

"Do you want to kiss me?"

"Way more than I should."

"Then? Why haven't you?"

"The president was almost shot because I was in love with her, and I completely lost sight of who I was and what my position was. I was relieved of duty, and a massive coverup happened because of my irresponsibility." She sighs after her confession, which is way more freeing than she imagined. "Wow. That felt good to say."

Evelyn closes her mouth, then opens it, then closes it again.

"Shocked?"

"Sorta, yeah."

"All of that is why I'm the way I am now."

Evelyn places her hands on either side of Alden's face, smooths a thumb over her cheek, and smiles. "I really like the way you are, though."

Remorse rises in her throat. "Do you think you'd still like me if I lost sight of the mission, and you got shot?"

"Alden, that's not going to happen."

"You don't know that."

"Well, you don't know that you're going to lose sight of me." She smiles. "I'm the mission, right?"

"Yes," Alden answers with a laugh. "You're the mission. Keeping you safe is the mission."

"Keep me safe then." Her eyebrow is arched as she adds, "Lock the door and keep me safe all night."

A sound clatters around Alden's skull as she finally captures Evelyn's full lips with her own, and not once does regret enter her mind. Her lips feel like waking up after passing out. She tastes amazing. Wintergreen toothpaste and MAC lip gloss make a lovely combination. Alden grabs her ass and pulls her closer until she wraps her arms around Alden's neck. Alden walks her backward to the bed. When Evelyn sits and their kiss never breaks, Alden realizes what the sound was clattering around her skull.

She threw caution right out the window.

The minute Alden rips the first button off Evelyn's shirt, it doesn't matter that they shouldn't be doing this. She can't stop it even if she really wants to.

And she definitely doesn't want to. She's wanted Evelyn since the first moment she saw her.

She needs to stop. It isn't right. *Yet…*

It's the way Evelyn arches her back and whispers Alden's name like a prayer.

And the way she smiles when Alden easily removes her black lace panties.

And her voice when she says very softly how much she loves this.

And it's the way she giggles, honest-to-God giggles, when Alden says maybe she should blog about this on Tumblr later.

All of it makes Alden feel like everything in her life may have been leading up to this very moment.

The words, *this is a job*, only fly through her mind once. And the same for, *Evelyn Glass is my boss*. And, *you shouldn't be mixing business with pleasure*. And, *if this backfires, you're so fucked. And not in a good way.*

But how can this backfire? How can this feeling in her heart and soul backfire?

With Evelyn's naked body underneath her, their bare legs intertwined, Alden's thigh pressed against Evelyn's wet center, she decides it's time to stop thinking so fucking much and focus on Evelyn's curves. On the plumpness of her lips. On the taste of her saliva. On the scent of her breath. On the sharpness of her jaw line. Evelyn is so perfect that she can't quite think straight. And as she latches on to Evelyn's neck, sucking on her pulse point, running her tongue down to her collarbone to place tiny kisses along the soft skin there, she realizes the only thing that matters right now is that Evelyn trusts her, and Evelyn wants to feel loved. And safe.

And if Alden is the only one who can do that?

So fucking be it.

Alden stops kissing so she can gauge Evelyn's reaction. She drags her thigh up across Evelyn's center, and is thrilled at how wet she is. She seems okay, but what if this is just an act, like everything else in her life has been? What if Alden is only helping to relieve stress and release pressure? While it might be fun to be the woman Evelyn chooses to sleep with, her heart would never be able to handle another situation where she doesn't get the girl in the end. And as Alden kisses her, delights in the softness of her tongue pressed against her own, she realizes how damaged she will be if this doesn't go the way she wants.

Evelyn presses a knee into Alden now, drags her nails down Alden's back, and her heart can barely handle how amazing every single sensation is. An awareness inside her causes her to pull away. The feeling of jumping too soon and realizing she forgot a parachute floods her mind.

She looks into Evelyn's eyes, "Is this okay?"

"Oh, Alden," Evelyn's voice is low, and her touch runs up Alden's back and then to her sides, where she holds on tight. "This is so okay. So, so, *so* okay." She smiles, genuine, beautiful, heartbreaking.

The words go straight to her heart, wrap it in a heated blanket, and warm it to the point of defrost. "*So* okay, hmm?"

A laugh bubbles from Evelyn's throat; it's deep like her voice, and Alden loves everything about it. She sounds happy. Legitimately happy. "Yes, so very okay. The most okay I've ever been. Oddly enough."

And that's enough for Alden to be okay as well. "Well, then." She places a gentle kiss on Evelyn's nose, then her lips, then her chin. She allows Evelyn's words to calm her. "Let's not waste any more time." She cocks an eyebrow before she pushes herself up and straddles Evelyn's leg. She pulls her hair over her shoulder, out of her way.

"Jesus." Evelyn sighs. "You're gorgeous."

Alden's entire body flushes, and she tries to hide her embarrassment by leaning down to Evelyn's chest, smiling against her soft skin, right at her amazing cleavage. She should take the compliment. She should allow herself to feel good that Evelyn Glass thinks she's gorgeous. Instead, she says quietly, "You have horrible eyesight."

Evelyn's fingers thread through her hair. "No, I really don't."

Alden uses her forefinger and thumb to lightly tease one of Evelyn's nipples. *Deflection*. It's a tactic she's been using for as long as she can remember. And thankfully, it still works. She places her mouth on the other nipple, sucks, flicks, and bites and hears a soft gasp, followed by a sexy-as-fuck moan. She does it again. And again. And each time, the moan is just as exhilarating as the first.

Evelyn's head arches, her neck exposed. "Kiss me. I want your lips on mine," she says, pulling Alden's hair.

Alden giggles as she gives in, her lips crashing into Evelyn's with more passion than she thought could exist. "Holy shit," she says as she breaks, breathless. "What the hell are you doing to me?"

Evelyn smiles and places a tiny kiss on her lips. "Y'know, I didn't win the MTV Movie Award for Best Kiss for nothing."

"Oh my God." Alden pulls away and laughs. "You're ridiculous."

"What?" Evelyn is also laughing, and with every move, her full breasts move.

Alden is drenched. "By all means, continue to hone your skills with me because you're good at this."

"I won't want to kiss another person after you. You're pretty damn good yourself." She places a hand on Alden's face. "I had a feeling about you."

"Oh, you did, hmm?" She settles beside Evelyn and lightly runs her fingertips over the smooth stomach, across the faint stretch marks from two pregnancies.

"Yes." Evelyn is studying her. That look in her eyes Alden has seen before. And it's causing her heart to thump wildly. "I knew you'd be just as passionate in the bedroom as you are on duty."

"I don't half-ass anything." She chuckles. "Ever." She dances her fingertips down Evelyn's side to her hip bones.

"Good to know."

Down, down, down.

Evelyn breathes in. "It's been"—their gaze connects—"a while since…"

Alden licks her lips, stills her hand, and takes a deep breath. "I promise I'll be gentle," she says, her voice as soft and smooth as possible.

"You don't have to be gentle," she whispers, and Alden almost passes out.

"Jesus *Christ*."

Her smile and small giggle shows how pleased she is at causing Alden to falter. "I trust you to not hurt me. I just wanted you to know how much this means to me."

Those words.

Fuck, those words.

Because they mean Evelyn could be in the same spot Alden is. Scared, excited, hesitant, not just about having sex, but because of the feelings involved. And if both of them have feelings…

Fuck, those words.

"You mean more to me than you ever should have."

"I know." Her voice is filled with understanding. Two simple words, and Alden is sure she has been given Evelyn's world.

She moves her hand lower, following the dip of Evelyn's muscles, up and over the soft patch of short dark hair, until she finds what she's been searching for. She gently slides through Evelyn's wetness and hears a soft moan. "You're so wet," she breathes when she bends her head down, places her lips on Evelyn's, and pushes a finger inside. "God."

"Yes, Ms. Ryan, I'm *definitely* wet," she responds in between kisses and breaths. And then as Alden slips another finger inside, she moans and says, "Dammit," through clenched teeth.

"Am I hurting you?" Alden asks.

Evelyn chuckles, digs her nails into Alden's back, and opens her legs wider. "Alden, no, God. Don't stop."

Alden complies, finding a rhythm again, sliding gently in and out, her thumb brushing Evelyn's clit on every pass. She adjusts herself so she is hovering over Evelyn, pumping, her forearm starting to burn, when Evelyn's knee slides between her own thighs. She groans, finding another rhythm against Evelyn's soft skin.

"Alden?" Evelyn breathes before biting on her lip.

"Yes?"

"I could fall in love with you," she says, breathy and raspy, right before she leans her head back and moans, clamping her thighs and shuddering.

Alden's heart leaps into her chest as her own orgasm approaches from riding Evelyn's thigh and just as a second orgasm seems to hit Evelyn, Alden's cascades through her body. She stills her fingers as she collapses, her forehead resting against Evelyn's. "Holy shit." She breathes deeply as Evelyn holds her face. What the hell did she say? "Evelyn?"

"Yes?" Her voice is still shaky.

"What...did...you...say?"

Evelyn smiles, wrapping Alden in her arms. "Stop. Don't think. Just kiss me, please. And then, let's do it again."

"You're the boss," she replies. She's stuck between wanting to push, to make sure she heard correctly, but she also wants so badly to fuck Evelyn again, to hear her moan again, to taste her, and make her rip the sheets, especially after how incredible they are together. These are the moments when she wishes she could just shut her brain off because doing this is way more important than the warning flags her brain keeps throwing up. *Fuck the flags, Alden. You are too far gone to stop now.* She adjusts her position and starts to slide down Evelyn's body.

"Where are you going?" Evelyn asks, propping herself on her elbows.

"Oh, I'm doing it again, but this time with my mouth."

Evelyn lets out a laugh that quickly changes to a gasp and then a moan when Alden finds her clit and begins again.

CHAPTER SEVENTEEN

Alden leans over the sink in her tiny bathroom, swishes mouthwash, spits, then looks in the mirror. She can see Evelyn sleeping under the white sheets. She stares at her own reflection. "What are you doing?" she whispers. In the warm, bright light of day, her actions from last night are coming back to haunt her. Her stomach is in knots, she can barely breathe, and she's a hot fucking mess.

I could fall in love with you.

"Dammit." *You are such a fucking idiot.* Because she could fall in love with Evelyn, too, and that is so not what should be happening.

She has done everything wrong the past four years of her life. She let herself get too close to Jennifer and fucked that up. And now she's gone and done it again. She let herself get way too deep. Definitely deeper than before. And Evelyn saying exactly what Alden has been thinking? Falling in love? Jesus. This cannot happen. What the fuck is she thinking and doing? Clearly, she's *not* thinking. Her brain has been urging her to not go here, and she waved it off every time. And now, after ignoring every warning, she is terrified about what has happened. She knew better, yet she fell right into those eyes and those arms and those legs and that laugh and smile and *fuck.*

She has fucked up.

Royally.

She bites her cheek hard enough to almost draw blood before whipping around and leaving the bathroom.

Her stomach drops to her knees when Evelyn stirs, opens her eyes, and props herself up with an elbow. Oh man, and the sheet falls and *Jesus*...Her resolve is teetering on a precipice. How can this woman look so amazing and so fuckable at seven thirty in the morning after a night of some of the hottest sex she has ever had? Her mind flashes quickly to Evelyn on her knees, to Evelyn on top, fingers deep inside her. Then to Evelyn riding her face. And then to Evelyn between her legs. And then...*Alden, you have got to be strong.* "You need to get going," Alden says, her voice strained but her words short, to the point. They taste like bile in her mouth.

"Is everything all right?"

"Yep. Everything is fine. Just get up, get dressed. You have a full day today with a photoshoot at noon and an interview at four. Don't want to be late."

"Alden," Evelyn says as she reaches out.

Alden takes a step back, shoves her hands in her pockets, and turns to the door. "Come on. You need to get up."

"What's going on?"

She stops moving and looks over her shoulder. Evelyn's sad eyes are too much. It's taking everything to not crumble under that intense gaze. "We shouldn't have done what we did last night."

Evelyn's face completely falls. Alden's heart almost squeezes itself to death in her chest.

"I don't want to get confused. This is still a job and I just...I feel like it will confuse me. Confuse you."

Evelyn blinks, her face going from hurt to pissed off in a matter of seconds, and she pulls the sheet up to cover herself. "I'm not confused."

"Well, *I* am."

"Did I do something wrong?"

"No," Alden says quickly. She's messing things up even more. She can feel it in her heart. "You did nothing wrong."

"Then tell me what happened."

"I need to take a step back from this. I'm really sorry."

"Don't apologize," she says, her voice deep. "Tell me what I did wrong."

"You didn't do anything wrong," Alden snaps. "I should have never done this. I shouldn't be fucking my boss."

"Your boss?" Evelyn asks, her voice breaking.

Alden walks toward the door and stops. "Get up and go get ready. I'll meet you in the car at eleven."

It's been a day and a half since Alden's massive mess up. The photoshoot was canceled, and Evelyn rescheduled the interview. After that, Alden received an earful from Robert about the importance of keeping Evelyn happy. Little did he know that she had kept her very, very happy...until she hadn't.

Evelyn hasn't spoken a word to her. For good reason. Alden deserves the silent treatment. Shit, she deserves a hell of a lot more than that. And it nauseates her to think about how badly she hurt Evelyn. But she can't go back. She can't forget what her job is. She can't let this get in the way. Right? *Right*?

Oh, who is she kidding? She has no idea if she's right or not.

Alden places a paddleboard in the water next to Ethan. He's standing in his swim trunks and white Cubs T-shirt, sunscreen smeared on his face, wearing an unzipped life vest. A pair of goggles hangs around his neck. "Just in case we see some cool fish," he said, excitedly when he begged her to come with him. And now with the early sun barely in the sky, she's regretting her decision. The idea of not being able to see the bottom of the lake is freaking her out. And Lake Michigan is more like an ocean. There are currents and an undertow and *ugh, what am I doing*? "What?"

"What happened between you and my mom?" he asks.

Alden trips over her feet as she's pulling the paddleboard farther into the water. She huffs as she rights herself. "What are you talking about?"

He laughs as they walk deeper. He zips his vest, hops onto the board, sitting upright, the board between his legs. He sure has come a long way since the first time she saw him. "She said you took her to a nice beach party the other night." He steadies himself and stands, holding the paddle. "Is something really happening, or are you two just, like, hanging out or whatever?"

"Ethan," she starts but stops herself so she can focus. The vest is scratching her back. Maybe she should have worn a T-shirt under it like Ethan did. Or not worn her two-piece because why does a suntan even matter right now? And the last time she was on a paddleboard, she was twenty-two, and this is almost as nerve-racking as shooting a gun for the first time. When she finally situates herself, she takes a deep breath, paddle in hand. He's smiling, but the smile doesn't last when she says, "This is not something we should discuss."

"Why not? Come on. No one ever wants to talk to me about stuff. I'm so *bored*."

She laughs. "I understand that. I do. But this? This is different."

"Ugh, whatever. You suck." He laughs when she splashes him with her paddle.

"I do not."

"Yeah, well, I'm going to win this competition."

"Wait? We're competing? That isn't fair."

He takes off, expertly moving his paddle from one side to the next. She flounders as she tries to keep up. It's impossible. She stops and breathes, maneuvering the paddle until she finally gets the hang of it.

He turns and laughs, paddle in the air.

When she gets near him, he sits and faces her. "Lemme guess," he says, and waits for her to sit. "Are you being weird because this is supposed to be you protecting her, and you went and started to like her like in some horrible movie?"

Alden almost flips over off her board. She steadies herself and shakes her head. "What? No, that's not it at all."

He lets out a puff of air and splashes her. "I know you think I'm a dumb kid, but I'm the most observant person, like, ever. I mean, come on."

She takes a deep breath and looks away, over one shoulder and then the other, as if someone in the middle of Lake Michigan might hear. "You know, I have been around a lot of people in my life. I know how to handle most of them, which is definitely a good power to have."

"Like a superpower?"

She laughs. "Yeah, sure." She kicks lightly in the water. "But your mom?" She looks across the vast space between them and the shore. "I don't know how to handle her at all. And it really scares me."

"Can I give you some advice?" he asks. "You gotta stop acting like she's anyone you've ever met before."

Her heart leaps into her throat. How can a thirteen-year-old be so wise? "You think so?"

"I know so," he says, smiling before pushing his hair away from his forehead. He looks toward the shore. "Is that Robert?"

"How the heck can you see that far? You should be in the Secret Service with eyesight like that."

He chuckles. "You won't even let me shoot a gun. How good of an agent would I be if I didn't have a weapon?"

As Alden stands, she places one end of the paddle in the water. "Kill 'em with your smart mouth, you little shit." She takes off toward the shore, hearing him laugh. She glances back to make sure he's following and lets him catch up. "You think you can beat me again?"

"You know it."

And just for good measure, she lets him.

When they get to the shore, she waits for him to be far enough away before she pays any attention to Robert strutting up to her. "What?" she asks before he can open his mouth.

He tosses a magazine at her. *Entertainment Weekly* slaps against her wet life vest. She pulls the wet paper from her body. On the cover is Evelyn from one of the many photoshoots. The headline reads, "Emmy Bound Evelyn Glass: Welcome Back." She looks up at Robert. "Is this a problem?"

"No. She's a sure thing. You already knew that, though, didn't you, Ryan?"

She glances to where Ethan is waiting, then gets closer to Robert. She shoves the magazine into his chest. "You'd better walk away right this instant, you sorry excuse for a human being." She watches him retreat, hands on her hips, when she feels Ethan standing beside her. "If you heard that, I'm really sorry, Ethan."

He looks up and shrugs. "Robert's a jerk. I don't listen to him most of the time." He chuckles. "But, Alden?"

"Yeah?"

"Fix whatever happened with Mom. She likes you a lot," he says with so much sincerity.

"Okay," she whispers. "Okay."

❖

"Alden Ryan."

The sound of Robert bellowing her name is enough to make her skin crawl right off her body. Her coffee mug is frozen between her mouth and the countertop, and she makes eye contact with Talon, who, seconds earlier, was munching away on Lucky Charms. "What the hell did I do now?" she mumbles before she finally takes a drink.

"Ryan! Are you hearing me?"

"Jesus Christ, Robert, yes, I can fucking hear you." She spits the words as he's entering the kitchen. He's dressed in a very nice suit, and for half a second, Alden wonders if she forgot an event.

As if reading her mind, Talon says, "Nope, this wasn't on the calendar."

"Evelyn canceled a photoshoot and an interview, and I'm just finding out about it?" He's panting with anger, and she is enjoying it far too much.

She smirks. "Yep. She didn't tell you?"

"Do you think I'd be this upset if she had?"

"I have no idea, Robert. I thought if the wind blew in the wrong direction you'd get your panties in a twist, so..."

"Very funny. You do know I can fire you."

She rolls her eyes. "Go for it. Do you think I need this fucking job? Because I don't. At all."

"Robert, you need to stop getting in her face." Talon has moved from the countertop to Alden's side. Her arms are folded, and the look on her face? Shit, if Alden didn't know better, *she'd* be frightened. So far, though, Talon has been no bark *and* no bite. *Let's see if this bark will be enough to scare Robert away.*

"So you're *her* bodyguard, hmm? Seems fitting. One dyke protecting the other."

"Why, you sorry son of a bitch—"

"Whoa there, children," Alden says, springing into action. She stands between them, fingertips pressing into Robert's chest, her other hand up to stop Talon from pouncing. "Calm down, okay? Both of you." She looks between them. "I knew Evelyn canceled the events, but I had no idea you didn't know. I would have communicated with you."

He rolls his shoulders and straightens his spine. "Okay, then." He clears his throat and turns to leave as if he's escaping from something.

"Why are you dressed up?"

"She's making a surprise appearance at the Cadillac Palace."

"Excuse me?"

"Oh, you didn't know? Hmm." He smirks. "We leave in a half hour."

As he saunters away, head held entirely too high, Alden lets out a heavy sigh. "What the fuck, Talon? Why didn't we know about this?"

"Surprise appearance. Sounds like he scheduled it and didn't tell us on purpose."

"Well, go get the Rover ready. We leave at six on the dot."

Chapter Eighteen

Tensions have been running very high since the surprise appearance at the Cadillac Palace. Nothing out of the ordinary. In fact, it went down exactly how past events had, with Evelyn ignoring Alden completely. They're back to how things used to be. It was what Alden ultimately wanted when she freaked out after their night together.

But now she has regrets. This arrangement was easier when Evelyn would look at her.

"Yeah, I know," Alden says into her cell phone. She decided to call Stella and check in as she breezes through the lobby of the Peninsula, an upscale Beverly Hills hotel where Robert has taken care of the reservations—against her advice—and heads to the bar. Everything about the hotel is gorgeous. Intricately designed marble floors, ornate sculptures in perfectly placed areas, beautiful floral arrangements on every table, and a staff that kisses your ass the second you enter. It's the perfect place for someone like Evelyn Glass and the perfect place to set Alden's nerves on edge.

She leans against the bar, flags down the bartender, orders a bourbon, neat, and sighs. This trip, unlike the Cadillac Palace, wasn't a surprise. The press junket around the corner at the Waldorf Astoria has been on the books for a while, and it has been the most nerve-racking event Alden has prepared for. A lot goes into securing a venue for any sort of appearance. But lately? The Evelyn Glass appearances have been very well attended, and with the buzz surrounding the possible Emmy nomination, this event will be huge. Securing an entire hotel is impossible, so she's been on the horn with the security detail for the junket and is literally praying they are as good as they say they are.

"Everything will be fine while you're gone," Stella says. "I know you're worried. But Ethan listens to me."

"I'm sorry you were left to deal with this by yourself. I would feel better if Talon was there to help you." Alden accepts the drink, narrows her eyes at the bartender's wink and crooked grin, and shakes her head before she takes a sip. It's smooth and burns, but these days, she welcomes anything that reminds her why she's alive and working for Evelyn.

Stella laughs, low and light, just like her mother. "It's probably better that Talon isn't here."

"Oh geez," Alden whispers. "You're incorrigible."

"Hey. You know how it goes when you're young and in love, don't you?"

Alden chuckles. "Sure, whatever." She wishes she could say that, without a doubt, she understands young love, but the only time she's ever experienced feelings that made her do something stupid has been in the last three years. Well, make that the last four years.

"Don't tell me you've never been in love." Stella laughs again. "I know someone had your heart at one point, or you wouldn't be such a jerk most of the time."

"Whoa, ouch," Alden says with a laugh.

"I'm sure you've been called worse."

She isn't wrong. "Okay, go over the game plan again with me. Just to make sure you know what to do if something happens."

"Alarm on at all times, especially if we leave the house, but we shouldn't leave the house because that is inviting trouble, and you guys will only be gone for two days, and there's no need to leave, so just stay put." Stella recites everything perfectly and tries to mimic Alden's tone and delivery. "And no parties."

"You're a smartass."

"That's fair."

"Promise me that you'll call if anything seems weird. My friend Serena will be coming by to check in, so only answer the door for her."

"What about pizza delivery?"

"Talon bought you frozen Home Run Inn pizzas, so nice try."

"Ice cream?"

"There's a gallon in the freezer."

"Doritos?"

"Fully stocked." She chuckles. "Just take care of Ethan. And yourself. Okay?"

"Ethan is my top priority. I promise. I'm just, like, second or whatever." She chuckles into the phone and then says, "Alden?"

"Hmm?" She drinks again and closes her eyes, taking in the one minute of peace she's had since arriving.

"Take care of Mom. Something happened between you guys, and I just..." She breathes in, and the phone goes silent for a beat or two. "She's different these days, and I don't hate this new version, so just take care of her."

"Stella—"

"Just promise me."

Alden stares at the tumbler, at the final swig of bourbon. "I promise."

"And whatever happened, fucking fix it." And the line goes dead.

She pulls the phone from her ear and sets it on the bar. The screen has her makeup mixed with sweat smeared across it, so she wipes it with the napkin. She has never sweated as much in her entire career as she has in the last couple of months. Her nerves can't handle this for much longer, so she's going to have to do one of two things: fix things with Evelyn or quit.

She picks the glass up and downs the rest, slaps a twenty on the bar, and starts her loop around the interior of the hotel. *Casing the joint*, her father would say when she was young, and he was trying to teach her police lingo. More and more these days, she longs for the safety of her childhood. Her overbearing parents, her nagging mother, her stubborn father. She'd give anything to turn back time and be back on her bicycle, eight at night, racing to get home before the streetlights came on. Things were so much simpler then, and all she wanted was to escape. If only she had known how crazy her life would get.

"I so wish things were different between us," Jennifer Simmons whispered as she pressed Alden against the wall of the Oval Office, nylon-covered knee sliding between Alden's legs. "I wish I could be out. I wish I could fire you and turn around and marry you." Jennifer kissed her as if the only thing standing between them and happiness was, y'know, the fucking United States of America. It was everything she loved about Jennifer, but it was ultimately what wrecked her.

She walks around the restaurant, the kitchen, the lounge area, the pool, and the fitness area. Everything looks secure. Business as usual, which is good to know. She finds her way through the back halls to the door that leads outside to the Peninsula Villa. Robert sure knows how to spend Evelyn's money. Two floors, a gorgeous stairway, multiple bedrooms, a fantastic private courtyard with a hot tub.

A hot tub Evelyn already commented on. And Alden already imagined her in.

A jolt of need and desire races through her veins and settles as an ache in her hands. Things have been so tense and uncomfortable that it really would be easier to cut ties and run. It's easier and *safer*, and no one gets hurt.

Except in this case…everyone could get hurt.

Evelyn.

Ethan.

Stella.

Talon would be crushed.

And Alden…she's already hurting. And hates herself more and more every single day.

She slides the card key into the lock and enters the villa. The foyer is ridiculous. It's bigger than Alden's first apartment. It opens into a huge seating area, with steps leading up to a living area with floor to ceiling windows. The decorations are tasteful yet ornate, everything Evelyn loves, and the flooring has a modern design. The kitchen—as if any of the people who can afford this place cook—is just as enormous. And the bedrooms? Well, one person doesn't really need that much space.

There is much more commotion than when she left because the other fight she lost with Robert was his idea to host a party.

"A pre-Emmy nomination party," he explained, "to remind Evelyn of her importance."

Apparently, he's never heard of jinxing something. Since the incident, Evelyn won't look at Alden, won't speak to her, and will absolutely not acknowledge her. Instead, she has taken to siding with everything Robert suggests:

The Peninsula, which is way too freaking close to the junket.

The villa, which is too big and too easy to lose track of people in.

The party, after Evelyn confided that she can't stand parties that are for her and her alone.

Yet, here they are.

Evelyn has done everything in her power to ignore Alden's suggestions, and sometimes pleas, at almost every turn.

And it is *maddening.*

"Alden," Talon says as she trots down the steps from the living area. She looks good in her black Member's Only jacket, fuchsia colored button-down, and dark-blue jeans. She's super proud of her new black and white wing-tips, too, so whenever she gets the chance to wear them, she struts around like a millionaire. As close as they've gotten over the past couple of months, Alden can't help but have a soft spot for her. "Everything check out?"

Alden bites her lip. She looks over Talon's shoulder to where Evelyn is perched on a chair, her hair down, straight, and full of body and her makeup person applying finishing touches. They make eye contact for a half second longer than normal, and her heart clenches. "Everything's fine. The hotel is secure. The fans know she's here, though, so we need to be careful."

"Okay. We will be." Talon puts a hand on her arm and squeezes. "Are you all right?"

"Yeah."

"Are you sure?" Talon has her eyes on Alden's. "Because you seem sorta on edge."

She scoffs. "I'm the bodyguard. I'm paid to be *fine*, right?"

"You're allowed to not be fine after everything that has gone on."

"I know. Thank you for the reminder." She shrugs. "Do me a favor and stay vigilant out there tonight. Keep your eyes peeled."

"Will do, boss," Talon responds, nodding and rolling her shoulders back so she's standing straighter.

"Connor," Alden half shouts, lifting her hand and signaling that it's time.

"Evelyn," Connor says. "Let's go."

"Is the perimeter secure? The crevices checked?" Evelyn asks loudly enough for Alden to hear. Her tone is dripping with sarcasm, and when Alden sees her perfectly sculpted eyebrows rise to her hairline, she wants to tell her to stick it where the sun doesn't shine.

Instead, she rolls her eyes and places her hands on her hips. "If you'd like to be safe while you're here, Glass, you'll let me do my job."

"Oh, I know. Your precious little *job*. I remember what *your* job is, Ms. Ryan. No need to remind *me*."

Alden slowly shakes her head, her mouth open in an attempt to form a comeback. But she turns and walks away. "Five minutes."

The junket is successful, and thankfully, nothing crazy goes down. As they're walking toward the exit, Robert jockeys for position. Alden really hates how she can't trust a thing he does, including anything he might say to Evelyn. Whatever he whispers in her ear has a smile spread across her red lips in an instant, too, which is unsettling.

"Robert, what the hell are you doing?" She wraps a firm hand around his bicep, gripping him so hard that if he wasn't wearing long sleeves, her nails would pierce his skin.

He tries to jerk away, unsuccessfully at first, then does it again, and she releases him. "Unhand me, Ryan. We need to get Evelyn to her fans."

"No, we do not. I have lost every battle with you, but not this one."

"You know nothing about stardom, do you?" He is practically shouting over the crowd. "*I* brought her back from the dead. *I* resurrected her. If she doesn't do this, if she doesn't kiss some fucking ass, her career dies."

"Robert," Alden shouts, grabbing his arm again. "If she does this she could die. What don't you understand about that?"

"Look." He spins around, pushing Evelyn slightly out of the way. He pulls Alden closer so his face is only an inch away. "This woman is my everything, and if you don't like how I deal with her fame, you can get yourself another job. She will make these appearances, and she will listen to every last word I say. Do you hear me?"

She clenches her teeth, narrows her eyes, and places a firm hand on his chest before she makes a fist with his shirt in it. "Let go of me, you asshole, or I will put a fucking bullet in your head." His grip loosens as he takes a step back. "And for your information, she is my client, too, and I give a shit about what happens to her. Unlike you, who only cares about a goddamn paycheck."

"Are we doing this or what?" Evelyn asks, standing as regal as ever, her black form-fitting dress hugging every single curve perfectly.

"No," Alden says forcefully.

"Yes," Robert says. "We are."

"Calm down, Ms. Ryan, and protect me. Isn't this what I'm paying you to do?" Evelyn's voice is salted with anger and peppered with hurt.

Alden tilts her head. "Evelyn," she starts, placing a hand on her arm. "This isn't a good idea."

"No. None of it was a good idea, was it? Yet it happened. And this is going to happen, too." She swaggers toward the exit.

Alden rushes to her, places a hand at the small of her back, does everything in her power to quiet the butterflies in her stomach, and looks her square in the eyes. "You have a death wish, don't you?"

"No," Evelyn answers. "It's just really nice when people aren't ashamed to love me."

The words sting like a slap as Alden squeezes between the fans and Evelyn. They keep glancing at each other and, finally, Alden puts two and two together. This display isn't about Evelyn wanting to be famous.

It's about getting back at Alden, and that thought makes her want to vomit.

Watching Evelyn's every move at the party is a lot to handle. She's mixing and mingling and not giving a damn about checking in. Stressful isn't a strong enough word to describe her actions. And it's a lot for Alden's heart to handle. Having to keep dibs on a person at all times is fine when her heart isn't involved. But since Alden's is fully involved, it's as if she's witnessing the love of her life move on from what they had together. The worst part? Evelyn moving on, if that's what she's really doing, is Alden's fault. She's the one who put the fire out before it raged out of control. The damage is already done, and the scorch marks are difficult to ignore.

If she wasn't on duty and could get insanely drunk, she would, but she can't, which makes her want to drink even more.

Instead, she sips Perrier and tries to pretend it has enough vodka in it to kill a small horse. Unfortunately, and unsurprisingly, it's not working. At all.

"Alden Ryan."

She turns. "Tobias? Holy shit, what are you doing here?" She lunges, embracing him in his matching vest and pants, a loose tie around his neck. She's excited to see him for once. And it looks as if it shocks him as much as her. "You look great. Your hair is shorter."

He lets out a laugh and pulls away. "Yeah, I was looking scruffy. You look good, too." His smile fades as he leans against the wall. He is much stiffer than normal. It causes the hairs on the back of her neck to stand at attention, but she's on high alert because of other factors. She mimics his position so the entire party is in view. "How are things going with Evelyn?"

Fuck. If he finds out, she's done. She plasters the most intense not-guilty look onto her face. "Things are fine."

"Fine, hmm?"

"Yes."

"She giving you any more trouble? Connor said she is a live wire most of the time."

Any *more* trouble? How much has he heard? She lets her gaze move from the party to him. He's not looking at her, thankfully, so she looks away quickly. "It's nothing I can't handle."

"Is that what those years in the almighty Secret Service taught you?"

It's not like him to be so loose-lipped, especially when essentially in uniform. "You didn't answer me," she says quietly. "Who are you here with?" When she looks away, she sees Evelyn approaching, a mischievous smile plastered on her lips. Alden stands a little straighter and clears her throat.

"God," Evelyn says as she glides up to them, followed by a huff. She smooths her hands down her sides, over her hips and thighs, then heaves a heavy sigh. She looks at Alden, then at Tobias. Her eyes widen, and a tiny smile appears. She's perspiring along her hairline, but otherwise, she looks as good as she did when they left. "This party is going to be the death of me." She snatches Alden's glass and raises it to her lips. "I need a drink." She takes a long swallow, then shakes her head. "Jesus, there's nothing in this." The slight slur of her words signals that she doesn't need a drink because she's already intoxicated. Her eyelids are heavy, and even her movements are indicating she's very close to being three sheets to the wind.

Alden looks at the ground. "I think you've had enough," she says as softly as possible after she leans into Evelyn's space. In return, she gets a glare that could give Medusa a run for her money.

Evelyn shoves the glass back at her and motions gracefully at Tobias. "And who is this handsome devil?"

"Tobias Markham," he says, taking Evelyn's long fingers and placing a kiss on the top of her hand.

She slides an arm around Alden's shoulders, keeping her eyes on Tobias. "I see you've had the pleasure of meeting my bodyguard." She laughs sarcastically.

"Oh yes." Tobias grins. "We used to work together. Chicago PD."

She raises an eyebrow at Alden, and then looks back at Tobias. "Oh, I *see*."

"He is the one who found me for this position." Alden removes her arm and tries to get her to follow. "Come on, let's get you some water."

"Wait." She pulls her hand away and faces Tobias. "Are you working now?" Her voice is low, sexy, and it is driving Alden absolutely nuts.

He glances between them. "Not right now." He waggles his eyebrows, and Alden wants to punch him in the face.

"Well, then, why don't you come get me a drink instead of that Shirley Temple bullshit Alden Ryan is drinking?" She leads him away, glancing over her shoulder as they retreat.

Alden looks away, her heart in her throat, her knees wanting to give out. She finds them in the crowd, her with a fresh drink, him whispering in her ear. She laughs, leans her head back, exposes her neck, and it makes Alden want to head to the Hollywood sign and pull a Peg Entwistle. She's being dramatic. These are the moments a drink would probably do her good, but being inebriated while trying to remain vigilant is damn near-impossible.

She tries to pull her eyes away from the public display of flirtation but can't. They get closer and closer and closer. As if the clock has a rope around them and as every minute passes, the rope gets tighter and tighter. And just when Alden is about one-million-percent sure she's going to combust if she witnesses any more heavy petting, Evelyn pulls Tobias up the two or three steps to the master bedroom. Alden clenches her fist, her teeth, every muscle in her body.

"Fuck it." She pushes off the wall and walks in the direction of the open bar. The bartender asks her what she'd like as soon as she slides up to the counter.

"That bottle of Absolut, please." She points casually but also keeps her voice firm because there's no way she's leaving the bar without that fucking bottle.

"The *whole bottle*, miss?"

"Yes, the bottle. *Now.*"

He looks a little closer this time, and he must be able to see the sadness in her eyes because he hands over an unopened bottle and smiles. "Promise me you won't drive anywhere?"

Alden shrugs. "No worries, boss," she replies as she heads toward the private courtyard.

CHAPTER NINETEEN

It's a beautiful morning in Beverly Hills. And as Alden sits on the couch, reading *USA Today*, she wonders what kind of mood Evelyn will be in when she finally emerges. Just as that thought finishes, Evelyn's door opens. Alden peers over the top of the paper, trying to look as inconspicuous as possible. Evelyn stumbles out, her hair pulled into a ponytail, and her face completely clear of makeup. That is the look of a hangover if Alden has ever seen one.

The housekeeping staff is finishing the clean-up from the party and aren't exactly being quiet about it. Evelyn's look says that she's not thrilled, and she's most definitely annoyed.

She walks very slowly to the bar, where there is a carafe of coffee, and pours herself a cup before sitting on one of the stools. She takes a sip, her hand slowly moving to her forehead and rubbing. Alden, fortunately, was able to head her headache off at the pass with ibuprofen at four in the morning, which is the only reason she's able to smile while she pretends to read.

Evelyn opens her eyes, a glare plastered on her face. "What are you smiling about, Ms. Ryan?" Her voice is only half as harsh as she probably wanted.

Alden wipes the smile from her face and lowers the paper. "I wasn't."

"I could see it in your eyes."

She hates that Evelyn knowing her "eye smile" along with her lips makes her feel good. "I wasn't smiling." She snaps the paper back upright. "Just enjoying the news."

"Yeah, well." Evelyn grabs a bagel from the pastry tray and goes to take a bite. She points at Alden first, though. "Find something else to smile about. My life isn't amusing."

"You're right." Alden stands, grabs her coffee, and starts out of the room. She stops when Evelyn latches on to her wrist, pulling her back. "What?" She is not in the mood after seeing Evelyn with Tobias last night.

"I *didn't*," Evelyn says, her voice barely above a breath. "Not that you wanted to know."

"You didn't what?" She's pissed off, and she doesn't want to talk right now.

"I didn't sleep with him." Evelyn stares into her eyes. "I wouldn't...I couldn't. I didn't want to. Not when I feel this way about you."

Alden's stomach drops to her knees, and even though she wants to grab Evelyn, pull her into an embrace, and thank her and God for not fucking Tobias, she fights the urge. But Evelyn's eyes are full of sadness, regret, and it's hard for Alden to stay strong. She places a hand on Evelyn's face. Evelyn's eyes slide shut as she leans into the touch. "I'm really happy to hear that," she whispers, heartfelt and sincere, before walking away.

❖

"So you have a lead?" Alden asks into her phone as she leans against the wall of the lobby, keeping her eyes moving, sweeping the surroundings.

"Possibly. This whole wolf hair thing has been such a waste of time. I don't even know what to think."

Alden shakes her head. "Maybe it was a red herring."

"We ran DNA testing, and it came back saying it was wolf mixed with German Shepherd. There's no wolf registry or anything, so we have to leave it." Serena clears her throat as if trying to keep her voice down. "Either way, these letters? They had to have been placed by someone close to her. You realize that, right?"

Alden lets out a deep sigh and pushes off the wall with her foot. "I'm starting to think the same thing."

"Just keep your eyes peeled. I don't trust anything about this situation. And some of these letters are so ambiguous. Are they even aimed at her?"

"What do you mean?"

"Like, this one in particular, 'You have taken everything from me.' Who did she take what from? You told me her ex-husband is happy and living overseas? And this one, 'The time has come for you to be punished.' What the fuck kind of crazy fan doesn't want the actress he or she is after to not get ahead? It doesn't make sense."

Alden lets out a soft, "Hmph." She pauses as she thinks. It doesn't seem feasible that these aren't aimed at Evelyn because why go through someone to get to someone else? "I never considered that maybe they aren't aimed at her. Wouldn't that be overkill?"

"I don't know if you should use that word." Serena sighs. "I don't know for sure. I'm trying to think outside the box because this entire plot seems lazy and not planned very well. And it's driving me nuts. It's just a crazy theory I had while showering this morning, like, maybe this nutjob is trying to be messy?" She pauses and groans. "But who knows? I also have ideas like battery-powered Crock-Pots and salt spritz for popcorn." Serena laughs. "I tried the salt spritz one time."

"And?"

"It was awful. The popcorn got soggy, and it was way too salty. It was stupid."

Alden laughs along. Taking a breath and not thinking about Evelyn for half a minute causes her shoulders to relax. "God, Serena, what the hell have I gotten myself into over here?"

She chuckles again, this time a little harder. "You really know how to pick 'em."

"Tell me about it. I'm fucking batting zero over here." She pulls in a deep breath and lets it out slowly. "Did you check on Stella and Ethan?"

"I did. They're both good. I was instructed to bring pizza."

"There was pizza in the freezer."

"Ethan doesn't like the crust. I don't know, Alden, I just do what I'm asked. Stella made me hang out for a while and play Mario Kart. They're really cut-throat."

Alden laughs. "Um, yeah, Ethan is a maniac. He'll run you right off the road."

"For real."

"Hey, listen, I gotta go. Give me a call when you find something."

"Will do. Keep your chin up," Serena says before Alden disconnects. She heads back to the villa, thinking about the conversation.

Maybe it's someone close to Evelyn? Who? There is no motive from anyone.

Maybe the letters aren't to her? Connor or Robert? And if it's one of them, why?

A wolf mixed with a German Shepherd? Talk about a big fucking dog.

When she gets to the villa door and lets herself inside, it seems eerily quiet. She looks around the entryway. "Evelyn?" She moves into the living area. "Evelyn?" She hops up the steps to the master bedroom and pushes the door open. Empty. Her heart starts to beat harder. "Connor?" Harder. "Robert?" Harder. "Oh, fuck." She lets out a groan and takes off for the exit. Talon comes downstairs from the second bedroom. "Where is she?"

"I have no idea," Talon replies, her voice scared. "I thought you were with her."

She pulls her phone from her pocket and dials Connor. It rings and rings. No answer. "Shit," she shouts and dials Robert's number. Same thing. She calls Evelyn's phone, hoping she'll answer…ringing and ringing and no fucking answer.

"Where the hell is she?" Alden rakes a frantic hand through her hair.

Just as she's about to freak out and dial 9-1-1, the door to the villa opens, and in walks Evelyn, followed by Robert and Connor.

"Where were you?" Alden shouts, and Evelyn stops in her tracks. She doesn't look happy, either. Her eyes are red, her nose is pink, and if Alden didn't know better, she would swear Evelyn Glass has been crying.

"We took her shopping without you." Robert gets in Alden's face. "She needed to be away from you. You hold her back. And make her feel bad about herself."

She doesn't look at him, just keeps her eyes on Evelyn the entire time, and thankfully, she can tell by the way Evelyn's gaze is cast downward, how her hands are clasped in front of her, how she's standing, shoulders slumped, that it's not how she really feels. Everything about her is pleading, as if she is not only not okay with the decision to leave without letting Alden know, but she probably fought it and lost.

Alden takes a step around Robert. "Evelyn?" She waits for her to look up, their eyes finally connecting. Her expression causes Alden's hands to ache. "Are you okay?"

She looks away, at Robert, then Connor, then back to Alden. "Yes, I'm...I'm okay," she whispers, her voice shaking. "They said...I mean, *I* needed this. I needed to get away." She licks her lips, and it's clear she's only saying what she's been told to say. She may be a great actress, but she is not happy about being wrangled. Alden was the one she didn't want to be wrangled by before, so this body language is very easy to comprehend.

Connor's body language also says loud and clear that he wasn't comfortable with this plan, either.

"What the hell?" Alden places her hands on her hips. "How am I supposed to protect her if you don't let me know what you're doing?"

Connor doesn't get a chance to answer before Robert steps in. "Look here, Ryan. I don't know how many times I have to tell you that *I* run the show here. Evelyn does what I want, when I want. And if you don't like that, then you might as well walk."

"Don't."

"Don't what?"

"Get in my face like that," she whispers. "I swear to Christ, Robert."

"What are ya gonna do?"

"Listen to me," she starts, breathing in deep, then finishing with, "if you don't want Evelyn to survive, then fine, get rid of me. But don't you dare act like I don't have her best interests at heart because you damn well know I do." She steps around him once more.

"Is that so? Is that why you've turned her into a raging dyke?"

Alden's fists clench, and she can't process stopping herself before barreling one fist into Robert's face. But even if she could have stopped, she wouldn't have.

He grabs his bleeding nose while shouting and cursing. Alden's heart swells. She shakes her hand out, pleased she didn't break any bones, and then looks at Connor. "I'll get you back to Chicago, and then I'm done."

"Alden," Evelyn whispers, one hand covering her mouth.

"I'll find you a decent replacement." And with that, she stomps outside, slamming the door behind her. She's holding back anger. Anger she does not want to release. Anger she has no right to have. She did this to herself, so being hurt about how it's taken a hard left without using a blinker is her own damn fault. *Do not cry, Alden. Don't do it.* Only when the elevator doors slide closed does she let herself fall apart.

CHAPTER TWENTY

A lden runs a finger around the rim of her tumbler full of ice and vodka and lets out a deep sigh. "I can't keep doing this, Talon," she says, softly.

Talon, like the good right-hand-woman that she is, chased her after the blowup in the villa and tried to calm her down, tried to make her see that it wasn't like Evelyn to be this way.

"I know you can't. I know." Talon pushes her hand through her short hair and swivels on the barstool. "You know it's okay that you fell in love with her, right?"

Alden lets out a laugh and shakes her head. She wants to protest. She wants to tell Talon that she's nuts, that she has no idea what she's talking about, that she's clearly blind as a bat and needs to get her eyes checked. But when she looks over, her resolve fades, and her shoulders fall, and she's a fucking coward. "It's not okay," she whispers. "I was supposed to stay professional. I was supposed to…"

"Supposed to what?" Talon sighs. "Look, I don't blame you for falling for her. No one blames you. Well, maybe Robert, but he's a douchebag. I wish you would stop blaming yourself."

"It's not that easy." She takes a sip. The ice has melted too fast, and it's watered down now. The potency has worn off. She looks at the ceiling of the bar. "I fell so hard for her." She can't hide the exasperation in her voice as she finally breathes in and out, in…and… out.

"You can't walk away now."

"I have to," Alden responds without thinking. "I can't do this anymore. Mentally, emotionally, I just can't."

Talon's phone starts vibrating on the bar top just as Alden's does the same thing. She looks at Talon and picks up her phone. "Ryan," she says firmly.

"Alden, it's Connor. You have to get up here right now."

"What's wrong?"

"It's Ethan and Stella. They're fine, but you need to get up here."

Alden disconnects. "The kids," she says softly. "Let's go." They arrive in record time and rush inside the villa. Alden flies through the entryway into the living room, where Connor is sitting in an armchair, his head in his hands. "What is going on?"

He stands. "Evelyn got a phone call from Stella. She heard someone shouting for her, maybe Ethan, and then the alarm went off as someone tried to break in. When the cops got there, they found a letter taped to the door that said, 'The kids are next.' And Ethan said he was asleep in his room, so it wasn't him shouting."

Alden dials Stella. When she picks up, she says, "Alden, Ethan is fine. I'm fine. We are both fine."

"No one got in?"

"No."

"Are you sure you're okay?"

Stella is sobbing, her breathing erratic.

"Stella, listen to me, you need to breathe. Breathe."

"I...I can't." She's working hard to talk, and it's only a matter of time before she starts to hyperventilate.

"Stella, please, listen to my voice. You need to breathe. In through your nose, out through your mouth. Do you hear me?" She waits, hearing only the deep breathing as a response. After a few rounds of deep breaths, she asks, "Are you okay?"

"Yes," Stella answers, then coughs. "I'm sorry, Alden. I'm so sorry."

"This is not your fault. Okay?"

"O...okay." She's still hiccupping through sobs.

"Did you tell Serena about the letter?"

"Yes, yes, she h...has it now. I...I just got off the phone with her. I'm sorry, Alden. I am." She can barely communicate and the worst part is Alden can completely understand. "Alden?"

"It's okay, Stella, you don't have to explain."

"No, I n…need to tell you…Ethan has been my number one priority. I swear."

Alden runs a hand through her hair and sighs. Talk about an experience Stella will likely take a while to get past. It shouldn't be something she needs to deal with. Neither of them. Hatred has been growing inside her for this stalker, and up until now, she's been able to keep it at bay. But now? With the kids in danger, her hatred has fully blossomed. "I know. I don't want anything to happen to either of you."

Stella pulls in another deep breath, lets it out slowly. "Have you talked to Mom?"

She walks out to the courtyard. "No, not yet."

"She's a mess." Stella coughs again. "You need to talk to her."

"Okay, be safe," she says before they both hang up. She turns and is startled to see Evelyn sitting on a bench near the wall. Her eyes are red, her hair is a mess, and she seems very shaken. She has a thick cardigan pulled over her shoulders, a blanket over her lap.

Alden takes a step in her direction, then stops, not really sure how to approach her right now.

"I'll do whatever you say," Evelyn finally says after they have a few moments of silence.

Alden sighs. "No, you won't."

"Yes. I will." She pulls the cardigan tighter around herself and closes her eyes. "I thought, this is it, my children are gone." She pauses and opens her eyes. "My children, who I've fought so hard for, who I've loved through every one of my ups and downs. My children, who are both so much more important than anything I could ever do. Nothing means more to me than them. Period. I cannot let anything happen to them. I will die if something happens to them."

Alden kneels in front of her. "Okay. But I want to take you away from this." She watches Evelyn's reaction and wonders if she really knows what that means. "Away from filming, away from Chicago, the show, being a celebrity, away from everything."

Evelyn doesn't hesitate. "Whatever you say."

"No questions. You won't know where we're going until we get there."

"Okay."

"And you fire Robert."

"Already done," Evelyn answers firmly.

"What?" Alden eyes her. "You did?"

"I would never keep him after what he said to you." She stares off into the distance.

"Wow."

"He was not happy." She shrugs. "He actually lunged at me, and my dad thankfully grabbed him like a wet rag and threw him out of the villa."

"Sort of sad I missed that."

She lets out a very, very small chuckle before she pulls her shoulders back and sits a little straighter. "I have always been ashamed of this part of me. This part that loves women. This part that needs validation from other people. This part that can't just be okay with who I am. And now?" She closes her eyes, and her chin trembles. "I don't want anyone around me who wants me to be ashamed of who I am. I need people who have my children and my best interests in mind. Period." She breathes in, but her nose is plugged from crying, and for some dumb fucking reason, it is so endearing. "He's out," she says succinctly as she opens her eyes and looks back at Alden. "And you're in."

"If that's what you want."

"It is."

Alden moves and sits next to her on the bench. They sit in silence for a few moments, Evelyn breathing, her clogged nose whistling with each intake of air, Alden struggling with wanting to wrap Evelyn in her arms and also feeling so incredibly helpless and lost. "So you'll go with me?"

"I'll do whatever you say."

"You can't bring your dad."

This demand causes her to falter. She finally turns and makes eye contact. "Why not?"

"He's not the one in danger, Evelyn. You are. And the kids are. And if push came to shove, he could take care of himself. I want to be able to focus on you and the kids. I will explain it to him, though. Okay?"

Evelyn blinks. She looks like she's chewing the words and isn't sure she likes the way they taste.

But Alden doesn't care if she likes it. It's the meal being served, and she can eat it or starve. "The only people you take are Ethan and Stella, and I take Talon and Mel."

"Why Mel?"

"She has protection training, and I want her to be there. I trust her. You can trust her, too." She watches everything washing over Evelyn. She's seconds from drowning, and Alden can sense it loud and clear. "And Evelyn? You have to listen to me." She takes a deep breath. "I mean really listen. Because dammit, if you don't, I swear, I don't know how much longer I can go without wanting to kill you myself."

The corner of Evelyn's mouth pulls slightly upward. Alden is thankful she understood the semi-joking tone. "Alden," she whispers, her gaze never faltering. "I'll listen. I promise."

If she continues to look at Evelyn like this, she's going to pull her into her arms and never let go. It might be the best idea she's ever had, but it could also be the worst. Against her heart's encouragement, she breaks eye contact and goes to stand but stops when Evelyn's hand lands on hers. "Yes?"

"I'm sorry…for what Robert said."

"For which part? Where he said I hold you back or the part where he told me I'm the reason you're a dyke?"

Her face twists, and she looks down before glancing back up. "All of it. I never have felt like that. Ever."

She squeezes her hand and smiles. "I know. We're leaving in the morning, so you'd better get ready."

"So," Evelyn says from the passenger seat of the rental Jeep Wrangler. "This is a nice area."

"It sure is," Talon shouts from the back. Her eyes catch Alden's in the mirror, and she raises her eyebrows. She knows where they are. Being Alden's right-hand woman has its perks. But she's been sworn to secrecy. The less Evelyn knows, the better.

"Are you ever going to tell me exactly where we're going?" Evelyn is still looking out the window at the scenery flying by. Lush green fields, forests, and rolling hill after rolling hill. "It's not like I'm going to tell anyone."

"Why don't you practice some patience, hmm?" Alden asks. "You know what state we're in. Isn't that enough?"

"Michigan is a big state," Evelyn replies, her voice coated with worry. "How are the kids going to find us? I feel like that is something I should be allowed to know."

"Ethan and Stella are with Mel, and they are meeting us there." She glances at Evelyn as she tries to relay as much calmness as possible. "And yes, you're allowed to know that."

"Thank you," Evelyn says before crossing her arms and leaning her head back. "Am I allowed to say how beautiful it is?"

Alden laughs as she flips on her blinker and turns down an old country road. "Yes, you're always allowed to say that." They wind back and forth on the dirt road, pulling over a couple times to let people pass. Northern Michigan really is a gorgeous area. The state has its moments, and the drive north is indeed one of them. Tim Allen wasn't wrong when he said take a deep breath of pure Michigan. Her ma's parents' cabin in Beulah, a quaint town that borders Crystal Lake—where Alden spent every summer as a kid—is where she's taking them. Not only is it off the beaten path, but it's also a great space to gather oneself if need be. *And lately, the if need be is very, very strong.* And not just for Alden, but for every one of them.

Her grandmother, Edith—Edie to her friends—and grandfather, Herbert—Herb only to Edie—at eighty-five apiece, are both still going strong. Alden always teases her grandmother about her age. "You have to be younger than that, Grandma. Let me see your ID." And Grandma laughs and waves her off. "It's that country livin'. Keeps me young."

Her grandparents are the only people she trusts who live as off-the-grid as possible, so it really is a perfect spot. That and they love having family visit, so they were tickled pink when Alden asked.

"Golly, Aldie, you know I love me some company. Bring those two young'uns, and I'll make sure to teach them to fish if they ain't learned already," her grandfather said over the old, static-filled, rotary phone line. She laughed and promised they would be thrilled to learn whatever he wanted to teach them. And hearing him so excited about the house bustling with activity for a few days was a real treat.

When they finally reach the driveway, Alden takes a deep breath. "Smell that fresh air?" she asks, sticking her head out the window.

Talon chuckles. "And here we thought you were a city girl," she says with a laugh.

Evelyn smiles. "You do seem to be in your element right now."

Alden can't fight her grin. "Just wait." She slows as she pulls into a clearing in the tall pines and maples. "We're here." She parks next to an old, beat-up Jeep and a Lexus SUV. When she hops out, she stretches, reaching for the clear blue sky, and breathes in. Some of her favorite memories take place with this cabin as the backdrop.

The last time she was here, her grandmother wouldn't stop feeding her. If there was one stereotype that her grandmother lived up to, it was the constant spoiling of her grandchildren. Alden is the favorite, and when she made it onto the Secret Service, no one was more proud than her grandmother. An old-school democrat, she was almost more excited about the election of a woman president than anyone else.

"I never thought this would happen in my lifetime," she said after the winner was announced. "A woman in office. Hot dog." Her excited giggle only made Alden happier that she was going to be a part of such a trailblazing administration.

She only hopes her grandmother isn't as disappointed in her release from the Secret Service as she is in herself.

The cabin is absolutely picturesque: log exterior, A-frame structure, brick and stone accents, a giant wrap-around porch, beautiful windows, and an outdoor firepit and seating area. The house is surrounded by woods, and in the winter, the amount of snow they get is unreal. And they do not want to be snowbirds.

When Alden approaches the front door, the screen door comes flying open, and Ethan bounds out, followed closely by Thelma and Louise, her grandparents' black cocker spaniels. Unsurprisingly, the dogs sprint to Alden. Thelma jumps into her arms, and Louise whines like crazy until she kneels to accept their affections.

"Mom, you made it." Ethan jumps into Evelyn's arms. She buries her head in his neck. The scene is right out of a movie, and Alden's pride bubbles beneath her chest as she watches with both dogs in her lap. She has turned so soft in the past year.

"I missed you so much." Heartache stains Evelyn's voice.

He lets out a chuckle. "I missed you, too, Mom." He tries to pull out of the hug, but when he almost escapes, she grabs his face and places numerous mom kisses on him, from the forehead to the cheeks, before he finally pushes away with a joke about how he's not going anywhere. He kneels by Alden so he can pet the dogs. "Hey, Alden."

She smiles and squeezes his shoulder. "Hey, buddy. You doin' okay?"

"Heck yeah, this place is awesome. Herb has shown me around. It's been so frigging cool."

"Whoa. Herb?"

"Oh yeah, he said, 'All my friends call me Herb.'"

She knew her grandfather was going to love him. "Well, I'm glad you're settling in."

Stella walks out of the house, Mel close behind. Stella's expression is painted with worry. She's staring at Evelyn as if she thinks she's going to be in trouble for everything that happened.

"Evelyn?" Alden asks as she lifts her chin toward Stella.

"Hmm?" She turns to look. She's crying again as she walks over. "Come here."

Stella does as she's told, a relieved expression on her face.

"Girls," Ethan whispers and lets out a heavy sigh.

Alden laughs and nudges him. "Right? Too many feelings. Blech." She stands and helps him up, both dogs quickly running up the steps and into the house through the dog door.

Mel has made her way down. "You good?" Her tone is not her normal happy-go-lucky. She's worried, with a crease in her forehead and nerves glazing her voice.

"Thank you for getting them here safely."

Mel nods and wraps both arms around Alden, pulling her into a very tight hug. "You are driving me crazy with all this fucking worrying," she whispers before placing a kiss on Alden's cheek.

"I know, I know." She sighs and pulls back. "We're safe now."

"Yes, you certainly are," a voice from the cabin says.

"Grandma," she says softly, her heart filling up. She moves swiftly to her grandmother's outstretched arms. When they hug, she can smell her childhood, and for the first time in almost a year, she thinks maybe she's going to be okay.

"Oh, Aldie, honey, you gotta stop giving us a fright like that. We're old. Our hearts can't take it."

She chuckles. "I'm sorry. I really am. I just didn't have anywhere else to take them."

"And you wanted waffles and crepes. Right?"

Another laugh and Alden pulls away. "You know me so well."

Grandma places both hands on Alden's arms and squeezes her. "You are going to be okay. You hear me?"

Alden wants to respond but she can only force herself to blink.

"Now," Edie says loudly. "Who's hungry?"

CHAPTER TWENTY-ONE

Alden strolls along a trail with Evelyn. She pushes some pine branches aside, lets Evelyn walk past, then falls in line behind her. She clears her throat and points to a trail off to the west. "Through there is one of the best views." She pushes her braid over her shoulder. "Or we can go that way and find the clearing where we used to camp. It's up to you."

Evelyn looks back and forth. "Let's go with the best view. You can show me the camping area tomorrow."

Alden nods and heads west. She's nervous about being alone with Evelyn, but they need this time to talk. Maybe they can yell at each other, too, work through some of this pent-up tension. Maybe Evelyn can cry and scream about how Alden has handled their relationship or whatever it should be called. Maybe Alden can cry and say why everything between them has her questioning herself. Or maybe they can make up and make out and leave the awkward bullshit behind them. Either way, the signs are pointing toward *whatever happens, it is necessary.* She just hopes the necessity doesn't end in more heartache. She isn't sure she can handle that.

"How are you not getting turned around?"

"Years of practice." Alden climbs over a fallen tree and holds out her hand to help Evelyn over. "I used to spend every summer here with my grandparents. We'd hike almost every day. I love being one with nature, as stupid as that might sound."

"That doesn't sound stupid at all." Evelyn lets out a small laugh. "I have never been much of a nature girl. Did a lot of growing up on both coasts and not much in between."

Alden can hear something scratching the surface of the speech. Regret, yes, but something deeper. A revelation. Or a confession.

"Then I filmed *Two Rivers, One Spirit*, and we were on location for a month in central California." She pauses again. Not just in her words.

Alden is taken aback by how beautiful Evelyn looks in the afternoon sunlight. Her forehead is covered in perspiration, she has dirt smeared across her cheek, and her shorts are not protecting her legs from the brush, so she has tiny scratches along her shins.

"The High Sierra at dawn is like nothing I have ever seen. I fell in love with that feeling of newness and rebirth. I guess you could say I found myself." She shrugs. "Joel and I split right after I filmed that movie." She starts walking again, leaving Alden standing there.

"Wait," she says as she jogs up. "You just came home and what? Broke the news?"

Evelyn laughs and glances over her shoulder. "I mean, yeah. He kind of already knew. I told him we needed to divorce. He agreed. A week later, we had papers. Two weeks later, it was final. Three weeks later, the tabloids started painting me as the bad guy even though it was mutual..." She pulls her shoulders back, clears her throat, and looks at the sky. "We are both happier, and that's all that matters."

"True, very true. Still must have hurt, though."

"Yeah, ain't no business like show business, kid."

"I guess so."

Evelyn stops at a fork in the path. "Left or right?"

"Whichever. Both are great views."

"Left."

The path is a lot clearer than normal, and Alden figures her grandfather has cleared it so he can get to his fishing area easier. She hopes she's half as active as her grandparents when she's their age. "Follow me," she instructs as she starts to climb a large sand dune. She gets to the top, reaches for Evelyn, and helps her up the rest of the way.

When Evelyn gets to the top, she stumbles, and Alden catches her. "Goodness, I'm sorry. I'm such a klutz," Evelyn says with a laugh.

"Is that why you don't do action movies?"

"Honestly? Yes."

They both laugh, and Alden nudges Evelyn lightly, prodding her to look up. The dune is on the edge of Crystal Lake, and she can see for what seems like forever. The afternoon sun is hitting the crystal clear water just right, sparkling and dancing, and the green trees are almost iridescent. Alden shrugs and smiles. "It's no Pacific Crest Trail, but it's something."

Evelyn brings a hand to her mouth. "Alden," she whispers. "This is…"

"I know." She pulls her gaze from Evelyn's and breathes deep. "It's moments like these that make me really happy I survived that gunshot." She sits in the sand, patting the spot next to her. After Evelyn sits, Alden breathes the fresh air and sighs deeply.

"Alden?"

"Hmm?"

"Have there really been times when you wished you didn't survive?"

The question is said with such a soft voice, but it still seems to echo off what, for months and months, used to be a hollow area inside Alden's chest. A space where her heart should be. A space she closed off because she did what she was never supposed to. She should have never kissed Jennifer. She should have never ever slept with Jennifer. She should have stayed strong when she was asked, ever so gently and lovingly, to go get ice cream. She should have never allowed Jennifer to make it an order. Because then it was impossible to say no.

She closes her eyes. The sound of flesh being torn by a bullet echoes through her head.

"Alden?"

Evelyn's hand is on her thigh. Her palm is warm, yet it causes a chill to zip through Alden's body. "In the beginning? When I was being reprimanded because I broke every protocol known to the Secret Service?" She stares at the hand. "Yes. I wished I had bled out. Because I would have never been asked to leave. Jennifer wouldn't have signed off on my dismissal."

"You are even more dramatic than I am."

Alden snaps her attention to Evelyn's face, and when she sees the smile, she lets out a laugh. "Touché."

"Is that why you have been so against…" She motions between the two of them.

Alden nods.

"That makes sense." She looks out over the water, another smile on her face. "I could just fire you."

After she laughs, Alden says, "I tried to quit. You didn't want me to."

"I don't know if I would trust anyone else to protect me."

"Oh, please, bodyguards are a dime a dozen."

Evelyn sighs. "Yeah, well, you're not, and I am attached to you."

"Seems like you're stuck with me then."

"I could quit acting. Then I wouldn't need to be protected."

"You'd miss acting. The spotlight, the hustle and bustle, the fans."

"I don't know," Evelyn whispers. "I've never loved it."

"You haven't?"

Evelyn shakes her head, a very sad expression on her face. She looks at the lake in front of them, the sun dipping farther.

"That's the way you *act*, Evelyn. You *act* like you love it."

"That's how it is for anyone who's halfway decent at it. The awards are nice. Don't get me wrong. And, let's face it, I look damn good in Versace." They laugh, Evelyn leaning into Alden's shoulder. "It's not something I need to be complete. It's just something I'm good at. Something that happened to me." For the first time, she seems to be allowing herself to open up without anxiety. It's lovely to witness, and Alden is focused on every word, every move. She wants to remember this Evelyn for as long as possible. "You know, the first time I auditioned…" She pauses, her tone melancholy. Gone is the Evelyn who puts on the smile for the fans. In her place is the Evelyn who is struggling between the push and pull of the desire for fame and the desire to simply fade into the background. "My dad made me. And when I got the job, my parents split, and my mom left. I never heard from her again. I did it in spite of her after that. Then Joel happened. Then the kids."

"What are you saying?"

She shrugs. "Who knows? I'm just rambling now."

"It's nice."

"What is? Hearing me ramble?"

"Hearing you admit you struggle with fame."

Her spine stiffens. As if being called out isn't normal. And it's not. At least ten seconds pass between her being insulted and her acceptance. "This role was written for me. Did you know that?"

Alden nods.

"And the Emmy buzz..." Her voice fades, and she pushes the strands of hair that have fallen out of her ponytail behind her ear. "I never wanted to be pushed this hard. I never wanted every aspect of this life."

"The money has to be nice, though."

"Oh, Alden," Evelyn says, and breathes out a shaky laugh. "You know money doesn't buy happiness."

She can't help placing her hand on the side of Evelyn's face and gently tugging so their eyes can meet. She runs a finger along Evelyn's jawline, then leans forward carefully, as if she fears moving too fast will scare them both away. Evelyn leans in to meet her, and when their lips touch after what has been the longest and most excruciating dry spell in history, Alden's heart explodes, and her hands start to ache. Evelyn's lips are so soft, her tongue is so warm. She tastes of salt and lip gloss, and Alden never wants to stop. She was around Evelyn every single day, but she had still missed her so much. And finally kissing her again is incredible, as if it's a dream, and any moment she'll wake up.

"You make my heart hurt," Evelyn whispers as she pulls away. "I can't survive that again. You hear me?"

Hearing Evelyn say that shrinks Alden in a way she never knew could happen. It's so easy to forget that her actions can affect more than only herself. "I know."

"I want this...I want *you*."

"Evelyn, I want you, too." She slides her hand down Evelyn's neck and rests it there before she finally says, "I am so sorry for pulling away."

"I understand why you did." She places another kiss on Alden's lips. "But I'm really glad you came back to me."

"I am so mad at myself for ever leaving." Alden places small, intimate kisses on Evelyn's lips and along her cheeks and jawline.

She's sorry for everything. For Jennifer. For breaking the rules. For falling. For being released. For not understanding those things meant she desperately wanted to love someone and to be loved in return.

Now here Evelyn is, wanting to be loved and wanting to love in return.

Alden is sorry it took her so long to realize that falling for the person she is protecting isn't the problem. Loneliness is the problem. And rejection is the problem.

She isn't lonely with Evelyn.

And she isn't being rejected.

It feels really amazing. And for that? She is definitely not sorry.

CHAPTER TWENTY-TWO

Alden leans against a tree and gazes through the window and into the kitchen. Her grandmother and Evelyn are cooking dinner. Everything is lighter since their hike in the hills. So much calmer, more at ease. She'd never be able to relax into what this place means to her if she and Evelyn were at each other's throats. Knowing that everything is okay for now, well, she feels like a million dollars.

"Hey, catch!"

A basketball comes whizzing toward her, and she catches it before it slams her in the face. "Jesus, Talon," she shouts while laughing. "What the hell?"

"Come on. Play with Ethan and me."

"Yeah, Alden, show us what you got."

She bounces the basketball twice and walks toward the make-shift three-point line. "You know this is dangerous, right?"

Ethan laughs and says, "Oh, sure. Like when you tried to beat me at chess that one night?"

She laughs, shakes her head, and raises her arms, her form perfect as she shoots the ball. It swishes through the net and bounces off to the side. "You were saying?" she asks, smug. She picks up the ball and bounces it to Ethan; he shoots it from the free-throw line. It swishes through the hoop, and he cheers.

"Don't get too cocky." Talon laughs as she rebounds the ball. "You know Alden here never misses a shot, right?"

"Hardly," she replies as she dribbles to the three-point line, spins, and shoots. It also swishes through the hoop, and she smiles. "I do have a killer shot from behind the line."

"Whatever. Ever hear of 'check mate'?" Ethan teases as he runs up and steals the ball.

"Hey, poor sport," Stella shouts from her position on one of the wooden chairs around the makeshift court. Both Thelma and Louise have made themselves comfortable in her lap, and she seems the happiest she's been in weeks.

"Shut up, Stella," Ethan shouts.

"Hey, none of that." She puts her hand up. "Apologize."

He rolls his eyes. "Sorry, Stella."

"It's fine. I deserved it," she says before laughing as Thelma licks her face.

"Your grandfather said you know how to shoot a bow," Talon says.

Alden shakes her head. "Seriously?"

"Show us, please?"

She looks at Ethan's pleading stare and relents.

He follows her to a shed on the side of the house, giddy. "This is so fun," he says through a giggle. "I thought paddleboarding on Lake Michigan was fun. I was wrong. This is way more fun."

She chuckles as she does the combination on the lock. There are two bows and two quivers with arrows on the wall. She hands a set to him. "You think you can learn?"

"I can try." Another laugh as he slings the quiver over his shoulder. He starts to walk away, then stops. "Hey, I keep meaning to ask…are you and Mom okay?"

She steps out of the shed, quiver over her shoulder. "I guess you could say that."

"Good. You guys fighting was the worst. Not that I love that lovey-dovey stuff," he scoffs, his nose wrinkled.

"What lovey-dovey stuff?"

"Oh, please, you guys are so dumb. How blind do you think I am? Seriously?"

She laughs as they stroll to where Talon and Stella have set up a target on a pine tree about fifty feet away. "I guess you're right."

"You realize she asked me every day if I had, like, talked to you or if we had gone paddleboarding or whatever. Like, come on."

"She used to ask me the same stuff," Stella says loudly.

"Well," Alden says, "She's definitely the most stubborn woman I've ever met." The image of Evelyn fighting her at every turn and resisting help are still so raw. Relief fills her chest now because finally, that part of their relationship is over.

"You mean besides yourself?" Talon's voice cracks, and she slaps a hand over her mouth, a chuckle sounding from behind it.

"Zip your lips. I am not stubborn."

"Uh," Talon starts. "Aren't ya, though?"

"You realize I could shoot you, right?"

Ethan laughs. "Don't worry, guys, she can't hit you if you get far enough away."

Everyone descends into a fit of laughter as Alden stands with her hands at her side. "What the hell?" she asks, trying not to laugh with them all. "What did I do to deserve this?"

"You beat her, huh?" Evelyn asks.

"Yeah, but I think she let me win."

"No way, kid. That was all you." Alden puts her hands in the air. "I swear."

He slides an arm around Evelyn's waist as she stands at the kitchen counter. She looks far more relaxed than she has in quite some time.

"She's not lying," Grandma says as she stirs the sauce on the stove. "She was never a good shot with a bow. She was more of a knife and gun girl."

"See?" Alden laughs. "Knives and guns. Total mountain man material."

"You always had a good eye with that old rifle. That's for sure." Grandma smiles as she slides a loaf of bread toward Alden. "Use those knife skills and slice this," she says, winking.

Alden slices the Italian loaf lengthways and then spreads homemade garlic butter over the soft inside. "I haven't hunted in years," she says, walking the bread to the oven. After she slides it in, she sets the timer. "I've been away from this place for too long."

"Now that's something I certainly agree with," Grandma says with a smile. She gently lays a hand on Alden's shoulder. "It's been a while for me, too. Hunting, I mean. But my aim is still good."

"Oh man, I want to go," Ethan says from one of the stools. The kitchen is the one room in the old house that has evolved through the years. Walls were taken down, and the space was opened up so it was easier for everyone to congregate. Especially Alden because she wanted to be glued to her grandmother's hip at all times.

"Ethan," Evelyn says softly. "You were told once no guns. I'd hate to have to say it again."

"Geesh, Mom. I'm not a child, ya know." He sighs, a full-on pout on his face.

She points a finger at him and raises an eyebrow. "Watch it, mister. I can still ground you, regardless of where we're calling home."

Grandma and Alden exchange glances.

Home.

Alden's heart is in her chest. "Yeah, kid, don't sass your mother." She nudges him gently to drive it home. "Why don't you go clean up for dinner?"

He laughs before he stands. "Oh, I know what that means. Time for some adult talk." He strides out of the kitchen, but Talon runs up and throws him over her shoulder like a sack of potatoes.

Alden shakes her head and smiles. "It's kinda weird being here… all of us."

"It reminds me of when we had everyone up for the holidays. Remember? You and your cousins would sleep in the living room in front of the fireplace so you could—"

"Catch Santa. Oh yes, I remember." She kneels onto the soft leather cushion of a stool. "It was more fun when I got older."

Grandma laughs. "Especially when you had your own room and your grandpa and me to yourself."

"It sounds like you three are very close," Evelyn says as she finishes scooping vegetables into the salad bowl.

"You want to tell her, or do you want me to?" Grandma's voice is smooth, her eyes twinkling.

"Tell me what?"

"Oh, nothing," Alden says with a wave. "I just…I, um…hated my parents for a couple years."

"She ran away once when it was time for her to go home, and it took us twenty-four hours to find her. She was sopping wet, hunkered down in a cave about three miles from here. She gave us a real fright."

Evelyn smiles, wineglass now in hand. "You mean to tell me she's always been stubborn?"

"Oh, honey, you have no idea." A smile spreads across her thin lips, her weathered face lighting. "Thank goodness she held on to that. Didn't let those men push her around in the Secret Service."

Alden can feel the heat in her cheeks. "Yeah, well."

Grandma wraps a strong arm around her waist and kisses her on the cheek. "Mule."

"Nag," Alden replies, her voice almost cracking. She glances at Evelyn and is surprised by the look of love on her face and the slight shine in her eyes.

CHAPTER TWENTY-THREE

Dinner at the grandparents' hasn't been this well-attended for as long as Alden can remember. And, holy cow, the spaghetti is absolutely delicious. Paired with the homemade garlic bread? She could eat a third helping, but she's trying not to look like a pig. After all, she hasn't had many meals in front of Evelyn. A couple slices of pizza. A hot dog at the party. And beyond that? She's kept her eating habits to herself. There's something about eating in front of someone she's falling for that intimidates her. It's irrational, but what if Evelyn doesn't like the way she chews? Or something ridiculous like that?

She rolls her eyes at herself. Good to know she's at the irrational fear stage of a new relationship.

Oh, fuck, she just referred to it as a relationship.

You're so fucked, Alden. No way out now. Not even if you wanted to.

"Evelyn, this salad is perfect," Grandpa says, his mouth full of lettuce.

The smile on her face is absolutely breathtaking, and Alden has to force herself not to sigh dreamily. "All I did was cut it up."

"Yeah, but the dressing. That was really great," Talon says around a mouthful.

Stella lets out a laugh and whispers loudly, "Close your mouth when you chew, you barbarian."

"Everything was just delicious." Mel raises her glass from the opposite side of the table. "Thank you so much for everything. Especially Edie and Herb, maybe the best hosts ever."

"Maybe?" Grandpa laughs. "I think you should strike that, my dear Melissa."

She chuckles. "You're right, you're right. No maybe. They're the best."

"Hear, hear," everyone says, holding their drinks in the air.

"How long have you had this place?" Talon asks. "Looking to sell? I could get used to it out here." She pushes her sleeves up, goes to lean on the table, then stops and places her hands in her lap. She makes eye contact with Alden, a small smile on her face. It's interesting to see how far Talon and Stella have come. Stella seemed very standoffish about her relationship with Talon at first, a clear indication that she thought her mom wasn't okay with it.

But the more Evelyn seems to be comfortable in her new skin, the more relaxed Stella seems. Hell, the more relaxed Ethan seems as well, and it's really lovely to witness. Alden wishes Connor could see this level of calm. Maybe he would decide that pushing Evelyn isn't good for anyone. Not Stella. Certainly not Ethan. But most importantly, not Evelyn.

It was surprising to hear acting isn't everything to her. Alden thought it was the only realm she could survive in. It's interesting how peeling back her layers has revealed much more than Alden ever expected. The spoiled celebrity routine is really just another role. But this time, the only award she's receiving is being afraid for her kids and her life.

Grandma smiles as she leans back, her short curly hair slightly frizzy from the day's activities. She lets her glasses dangle around her neck from a homemade bejeweled chain. "This house has been in my family for over a hundred years. It was my grandfather's and then my parents', and when Herb and I married, my parents gifted it to us. And while I'm not looking to sell, you can always move in, Talon. I do love the company."

Talon's cheeks turn a deep red, and everyone laughs. "Well, I appreciate the offer," she replies with a shy grin.

"Ethan, honey?" Evelyn asks softly with a smile. "Have you taken a breath during this meal?" She smooths a hand over his hair, and he beams.

He wipes his mouth with his napkin and takes a gulp of milk. "I've been conserving my energy by taking as little breaths as possible," he finally answers.

Grandma laughs as she gathers the plates. "I'm glad to see he has a healthy appetite. Ethan, honey, I have homemade ice cream for dessert."

Alden laughs when Ethan's eyes light up, and his mouth drops open. "I'm never leaving," he says as he looks at his mom. "Sorry."

"Whoa, there, little lady. You cook, I clean." Grandpa holds his hand out, and Grandma shrugs as she sits down. "And then it's time for a fire. And beer."

Alden heads into the kitchen, carrying as many plates as she can to the sink. Evelyn pushes her lightly out of the way. "I'll do the dishes."

"No, I can do them." Alden's protest seems to fall on deaf ears, though.

"I'll wash, you dry."

"Fine."

"And then we go have beers around the fire." Her smile makes Alden feel lightheaded. "Right?"

"Yes. Is that okay?" Alden fights the urge to apologize for thrusting her family and their traditions on Evelyn. She's used to her grandparents. Her grandfather's crass comebacks and her grandmother's inability to not call people "honey." None of it is something to be embarrassed about, but she's straddling a line and has been for quite some time. The one side is complete and total privacy. And it was the side she was stuck on for the past couple of months because that was where she thought she needed to be to do her job. The other side of the line is where complete familiarity resides. In the past fifteen hours, she has jumped right back over the line into a relationship with Evelyn. Was it too fast? Probably. But Alden can't help these feelings she has for her.

"Of course it's okay." Evelyn hands over a clean plate. "I'm enjoying myself."

"You sure? I mean, I can see how it might be uncomfortable."

Evelyn chuckles. "You need to start trusting me."

She's right. She's so right. "I'm sorry."

"Don't. Don't apologize. Just try to remember that I am not going to hurt you." She hands over another plate but as Alden goes to take it, their eyes meet. "You wanted me to trust you. And I do."

"Even though two weeks ago, I told you I couldn't do this and that it was a mistake?"

"And now you've swept me away to Michigan and are making me and my children have drinks around a firepit with your grandparents?"

Alden laughs. "I mean, yeah. Doesn't it seem fast? Like, should we slow down? How can you trust me after I was such a jerk?"

Her face softens as she reaches forward with a sopping wet hand. She places it on Alden's face, smearing bubbles from the dish soap all over her cheek. Now grinning, she says, "I am loving every second of this with you."

Alden can't fight a laugh. "You have no idea how much that means to me." And for the first time in a really long time, she decides to stop questioning every aspect of this relationship. She decides to not just act like she's breathing but to actually let the oxygen she's pulling into her lungs help calm her.

She's going to breathe.

She's going to heal.

She's going to survive.

She's going to *live*.

And she's going to do it all with Evelyn.

"Here are the Bell's," Grandma says as she passes along a string of Two Hearted Ale IPAs from a tray she's carried to the firepit. It's Grandpa's favorite beer. Hoppy, a light fruit taste, and it gets him just tipsy enough that he only needs two. "And hot cocoa for Ethan."

"Is this cinnamon?" Ethan asks after he sniffs the whipped cream.

"It sure is," she answers before she whisks back into the house.

"Mom, she does cinnamon, too," he says with a smile. "Just like you."

Alden nudges Evelyn, who is sitting next to her on the outdoor blanket, leaning against one of the giant logs at the perimeter of the pit. Thelma is sitting next to her, face propped on Evelyn's lap. "You do cinnamon?"

"Always have." She smooths her hand over the dog's head and down her back. The cocker spaniel sighs, and Evelyn chuckles.

"So do I," Alden says quietly. She smiles when Evelyn looks at her.

When Grandma reappears, she is holding a bottle of whiskey and a glass tumbler. "And a nice little nip for me."

"Grandma, what is that?"

"Journeyman Last Feather Rye, and it is delicious." Grandma smiles and passes the glass to Alden. "Take a sip."

"What if I want a glass?" She smells it, and boy, does it smell nice. She sips it, savoring the smokey notes. "Holy cow."

"You're going to have to buy your own," Grandma says with a laugh, then pulls another tumbler from her fleece jacket and hands it over. "Here."

"Whiskey, hmm? I had no idea, Grandma." The joy inside Alden's chest is so unfamiliar. She wants to bottle it because what happens when this joy, this happiness, leaves? It always does.

"It's the real reason why I've lived so long."

Evelyn laughs. "I am going to have to get on that bandwagon."

"Feel free, sweetheart." Grandma chuckles.

"Alden, honey, it's time." Grandpa is carrying out an ornate chessboard, the pieces still standing.

"Oh, man," Alden whispers. "And it begins." She scoots closer to the board on a small table, and excitement layers over the flood of memories.

"This again?" Mel whines from her Adirondack chair.

"Always." Grandpa takes a sip of his beer. He slaps Alden's hand as she tries to pick the white side. "Hey, that's my side. You're the black."

She chuckles and rubs her hand. "Geesh, are you sure?"

"My last move, I took your rook with my bishop right there," he says, pointing.

"Goodness." Stella leans forward, running a finger along the dust on the chessboard. "How long has this been going on?"

Alden clears her throat. "Uh…three years."

"She almost beat me the first year," Grandpa says softly.

Ethan clears his throat from behind Alden, and she smiles. "See something?"

"Queen to rook five."

Alden shakes her head. "You're crazy," she says with a smile, until Grandpa leans forward to get a closer look at the board. "Well, *shit.*" And with a fluid move, she moves the queen and topples a rook.

Grandpa's eyes go wide. "Ethan, my boy, I'll give you some ice cream if you help me and not her." Everyone starts laughing. And it is so damn nice to feel this light, this stress-free.

"He has beaten me at chess before." She looks back at Evelyn, who seems to be fading fast. Alden places a hand on her knee. "You tired? I can take you up to bed."

"No, no. I'm okay."

"Evelyn, you're allowed to be tired."

"You sure are. After the week you've had?" Grandma smiles as she places a hand on Evelyn's knee, too. The sight causes Alden's heart to swell.

Evelyn returns the smile. "Yeah, I guess you're right. Thank you, Edie."

Alden stands, holding out a hand. Thelma and Louise stir and get to their feet, wagging their butts and nub tails, waiting to head inside. "Looks like you have a couple new best friends."

Evelyn slips her hand into Alden's and looks at the rest of the company. "Good night, everyone," she says with a wave as Alden walks her toward the house. "You're about the only friend I've ever had." Her voice is covered with a blanket of sleep.

"I understand that." There's so much that is similar about their lives, and the more she gets to know Evelyn, the more she realizes that everything was supposed to happen to her in the exact way it did. Maybe she was supposed to feel perplexed about her place in this world and frightened of what the future holds. Because now she can see everything with more precision and is at peace far more than she ever was before. She is at ease, finally, even though the other shoe will have to drop at some point. But for now? She's going to enjoy the clarity.

❖

Alden lies next to Evelyn, both dogs curled up next to them, and smiles as she props her head up with her hand, elbow on the bed. "You comfortable?" She brushes a lock of hair from Evelyn's face.

Evelyn lets out a deep breath and closes her eyes. "I'm so happy here."

"You have no idea how much that means to me," Alden whispers before placing a kiss on Evelyn's temple.

"Alden?"

"Yes?"

Evelyn's eyes are still closed, and Alden lets her gaze wander over her features, her flawless skin, the slight wrinkles at the corners of her eyes, her perfectly shaped eyebrows, the slope of her nose, her chiseled cheekbones, the fullness of her so pink lips. *She is so gorgeous.* "Would you do me a favor?"

"Anything." Her answer comes out as a whisper, soft and light in the quiet of the bedroom she used to sleep in as a child.

"Would you kiss me again?" The sincerity is almost too much to handle. Her eyes slide open. "Please?"

Before Alden has another second to think about it, she captures Evelyn's lips. The kiss is light at first, as if they haven't shared something this intimate before, which is an interesting phenomenon considering the moments they have shared. She wants to remember everything about *this* moment, though, as if this is the first time.

Is it because she's finally open to what is happening?

Is it because she is ready and willing to dive into a relationship?

For the first time in forever, she is no longer swimming against the current of her past mistakes. And it is the most at peace she has felt.

She's going to let every second burn into her memory as if it's the first time all over again.

The way Evelyn tastes—toothpaste and a hint of whiskey—and the way her lips feel—silky and smooth but firm, encouraging. The way her tongue slips into Alden's mouth, tentatively, then desperate.

Alden deepens the kiss, their lips fitting as if they were meant to find each other, perfect puzzle pieces put in different boxes, separated by stupidity and force, and finally reunited.

"I've missed your lips so much," Evelyn says, breathless, then pulls Alden back, deepening the kiss again. She isn't holding back. She was just as ready to cross this line the first time.

If Alden doesn't stop this right now, they're going to have sex in her childhood bedroom, in her grandparents' home, and she simply cannot imagine doing that. At least, not with everyone still wide awake. She breaks from the kiss, panting, her panties damp, her heart racing. "I'm going to devour you if I don't leave."

"And that's a bad thing?"

Alden chuckles as she kisses Evelyn again. And again. And again. "No. Fuck, no, it's not a bad thing."

Evelyn bites her lower lip, pulls gently, and then releases it as she says, "Please...I need you."

"Evelyn." Alden groans as she caresses her body, her breasts, the flat stomach, and slips a hand under the waistband of her yoga pants and panties. *Christ, is she ever wet.* She bites her lip as she pushes a finger into Evelyn, and the moan is way too loud.

"Shh," Alden whispers as she kisses Evelyn again, pushes another finger inside, and catches Evelyn's moan in her mouth. She continues the kiss as she slides her fingers over Evelyn's clit, back and forth, soft at first, then gaining speed and intensity. Evelyn breaks apart, leans her head back, exposing her neck, and pulls a pillow over her face. She moans through her orgasm, shaking the entire time, and Alden keeps moving as much as Evelyn's clamped thighs will allow.

Finally, her tense body relaxes. She takes a deep breath, the pillow still over her face, and Alden can hear her laughing. "Jesus. That was...yeah. I needed that."

"Yeah? Well, I'm happy I could oblige."

She places her hands on either side of Alden's face and kisses her deeply. "Goddamn you," she whispers against Alden's lips. "You have ruined me."

"Well, you made me ruin this pair of panties, so I feel like we're even."

"Come to bed. Please." She smiles, and the shockwave inside Alden's body is so intense.

"I'll be here shortly. Gotta start out separately, okay?" Alden explains as she starts to get up.

Evelyn sighs and closes her eyes. "I feel like a high schooler again. You sneaking into my bedroom, not wanting to wake anyone up, hoping we won't get caught. It's very exciting."

Alden walks to the door. "As long as you're quiet and have that pillow nearby, I'm sure we won't get caught." She laughs when Evelyn flings the pillow at her. "I'll see you soon."

CHAPTER TWENTY-FOUR

Alden wakes up the next morning with an arm draped across her torso, Thelma lying between her legs, Louise wedged between the headboard and her pillow, and the smell of coffee seeping in underneath the door. She moves to check the clock on the bedside table, and the arm tightens, which causes her to laugh softly and kiss the top of Evelyn's head.

"No, not yet," Evelyn murmurs against Alden's chest. "I'm not ready to let go."

"You must have been super tired." She runs her fingers along Evelyn's bare arm.

"Why's that?"

"Because when the dogs and I snuck back in here, you didn't even move." She smiles. "And you snored a little bit, too."

Evelyn picks her head up. "I beg your pardon. I certainly do not snore."

"Eh, you kinda do."

"Sorry, no. You're mistaken." Evelyn lies back down and goes back to holding her.

"Next time, I'm going to record you." Alden waits for a response. "Because you, Evelyn Glass, were totally snoring last night. You even woke Thelma at one point." Alden motions to the dog between her legs, and Thelma picks her head up, clearly annoyed at the racket.

"I refuse to believe it," Evelyn replies, a laugh vibrating her body. "Why don't you kiss me and stop this arguing?"

"Oh, yeah? You want me to stop insisting that you snore?"

"Yes," Evelyn whispers, a smile playing on her lips. "Kiss me, Alden, please?" Her words and breath brush against Alden's lips, but there's a knock on the door. They scramble, both dogs jumping to the floor. Evelyn clears her throat while Alden tries to stifle her laughter. "Yes?"

"Breakfast is almost ready," Mel says. "Did you hear me, Alden?"

She lets out a laugh, and Evelyn falls back into the pillow, throwing her arm over her eyes. "Yeah, yeah, yeah. I heard you, you jerk. We'll be right down."

"You'd better hurry. Ethan's patience is wearing thin. He's ready to devour these pancakes."

"We're hurrying," Alden shouts a second before Evelyn snakes an arm around her neck and pulls her into a very passionate kiss. With one fluid movement, Alden straddles one of Evelyn's legs and presses her arms above her head, kissing her way over Evelyn's white tank top. "We can't do this now," she says, panting against Evelyn's neck as she slips a hand underneath the yoga pants and panties, just like the night before. She slides a finger through the wetness and teases before gently slipping two fingers inside. "We really need to get up."

"Alden, for Christ's sake, stop talking," Evelyn rasps, a moan following when Alden pulls her fingers out and slides them back in with ease.

"You're *so* demanding," Alden says, making sure that her thumb is now hitting Evelyn's clit on each pass. "So, so, *so*..." She breathes against Evelyn's lips. "Demanding." Evelyn tightens around her fingers as she moves her thumb in tight circles. When she pulls back, there are tears welling in the corners of Evelyn's eyes. "Oh my God," Alden whispers. "Are you okay?"

"Shut up, I'm fine, but don't you dare stop," Evelyn threatens through clenched teeth. She clamps her eyes shut, leans her head back, exposing her neck, her breasts thrusting forward, and a low moan comes out as her orgasm hits. Alden chuckles a little when Evelyn muffles the sounds with a pillow again. When her body goes limp, and she moves the pillow, Alden leans down and kisses her.

"Good morning," she whispers through the kiss. She slowly slides her fingers from their spot and receives Evelyn's moan into her mouth.

"God," Evelyn breathes. "That was…"

"Yes?"

"Incredible," she finishes, pulling Alden down for another kiss.

"I have bad news," Alden says softly.

Evelyn's face falls. "What?"

"We have to get up now." Alden smiles and places three soft kisses on Evelyn's lips. "What's wrong?" she asks when Evelyn doesn't move. "Are you okay?"

Evelyn runs two fingers down the side of Alden's face, along her jawline, down her neck. "I just"—she takes a breath—"I really just… I think…"

Alden lets a small laugh escape as she sits back, pulls her hair over her shoulder, and tilts her head. "I've never seen you so tongue-tied," she teases, smiling.

Evelyn sits up and pushes her fingers through her hair, and wipes her eyes. "Things haven't been easy for me since Joel and I split."

Alden nods and wants to reach for her but decides to let her speak.

"And even though it was mutual and we don't hate each other, there has always been this idea in people's minds that I'm the bad guy. That I was the reason he left, which…" Her cheeks expand, and she sighs. "I guess I kind of was the bad guy. I mean, maybe we both were? I don't know." She licks her lips, then smiles. "But you…" She draws a deep breath and lets it out slowly. "You came along when I didn't think I needed anyone. I wanted to re-carve this space in entertainment, and I took this role, never thinking I'd be unlucky enough to attract negative attention…yet I have."

This isn't her fault. She can't possibly believe this is her fault. Alden opens her mouth to tell her to stop.

"No, let me finish, please. I have to say this. I have to tell you that…that…I've fallen in love with you."

Alden blinks rapidly, not really knowing what to say, but as she goes to take a breath to speak, Evelyn follows up with, "Please, don't say anything right now. I don't want you to say it just because I said it. It's not about that. It's that for years, I never thought I could love again and truly never thought I wanted to. And then you came along and changed everything."

She does love Evelyn, and she wants to say it back so badly. "Evelyn—"

"Alden, Evelyn, come on," comes Mel's voice from the other side of the door while she knocks on it feverishly.

Evelyn scoots closer and leans her forehead on Alden's. "Go downstairs. I'll be right there."

Alden pushes her hands into Evelyn's hair before she kisses her so deeply, it takes her own breath away. "Hurry."

"I will," Evelyn says, placing one more kiss on Alden's lips before she pushes her out of the bed.

Alden rolls over onto her stomach and props herself up on the large picnic blanket. The whole group took a hike so Grandpa and Grandma could show off Alden's favorite camping spot. It's around the back side of the lake, complete with a dock, a small boat, and plenty of open space to run around. Ethan is keeping busy with Grandpa, who has taught him all there is to know about baiting a hook and casting a line. They're standing on the dock, and Alden isn't sure she's seen her grandpa as content as he is right now. Mel is sitting next to Grandma on the dock, their feet dangling over the edge while Talon and Stella are playing cards, and it's so picture perfect and serene. A wave of guilt washes over Alden. Not being constantly on edge and ready to jump into action feels very weird, especially since the threat is still very much alive.

Evelyn clears her throat as she sits and stretches her legs, crossing them at the ankles. "This is so peaceful."

"It's no downtown Chicago at rush hour, is it?"

Ethan comes running up to them, panting like one of the dogs. "This is...so..." He takes a few more breaths. "Much...fun." He plops down on the blanket. "Herb says that I am really picking this fishing thing up. But he also said I ask a lot of questions."

Alden chuckles. "Yeah, he's sort of a quiet guy when he's fishing. You don't want to scare the fish."

Evelyn laughs and pushes his hair away from his sweaty forehead. "You are really enjoying this, aren't you?"

"Yeah, Mom, this is so awesome." He launches into a story about how Grandpa showed him deer prints. "Herb even said he's seen bears up here."

Alden can't help but chuckle at how adorable he is.

"Well, I hope you don't go looking for bears," Evelyn says. "I don't think that's something our bodyguard can protect you from."

"You are very right about that." Alden laughs again.

"Well, you have saved Mom a whole bunch of times, right?" Ethan asks, a lopsided grin on his face.

Evelyn shrugs. "Just a few times."

"More than a few." Alden sits straighter, her spine stiff. The memory of Evelyn crying in the courtyard in California is still fresh in her mind. "If only you weren't so stubborn."

"Me? Stubborn?"

"Yeah, Mom, *you*." Ethan runs both hands through his hair, making it stand straight up. "You're, like, crazy stubborn."

"I cannot believe you have my son on your side."

Alden holds up a hand, and Ethan high fives it. "Thanks, kid." They exchange smiles, and Evelyn rolls her eyes, a grin playing at the corners of her mouth "There ya go." She laughs, pushing Evelyn's leg.

"Alden, can you teach me how to drive the boat?"

She looks over at Evelyn, who nods. "Yeah, let's do it."

They head to the dock, Evelyn shouting, "Be careful," after them.

She climbs in first, helping him in after she gets stabilized. "Whoa, easy there," she says when he almost slips. "You sit there, and I'll teach you how to start the motor, okay?" He smiles, but his eyes are as big as saucers as she dictates the different steps to start the motor on the old johnboat. "You want to give it a try?"

He almost flips them with his enthusiasm. She gets them both situated before she lets him pull the cord two or three times, finally helping him to get the motor running.

His smile is almost too much to handle as he shouts, "Can I drive it?"

She nods, instructing him on how to steer with the handle that attaches to the rudder. She leans back as he gets the hang of it, lets him tool around the lake while they wave to the crew on shore. They're in the middle of the lake when the motor stalls.

"I just filled the tank," Alden mutters. "That's weird."

"What happened?" Ethan asks as if afraid he did something wrong. He goes to stand, and she grabs him.

"You can't stand," she says but notices the fear on his face. "You're okay. You didn't do anything wrong. Okay?" He nods, and she carefully switches sides with him. "This happens sometimes. This boat is old. I mean, it has been around way longer than me."

"Whoa. That is old."

She laughs, mock shock coating her tone as she says, "Excuse me?"

He shrugs. "You asked for it."

"That's fair." She reaches around to the control panel and fiddles with a few spots where there could be issues. Sometimes the spark plug wiggles loose, or a wire rumbles off the contact point.

"Is everything okay?"

She situates herself on the floor and quickly loosens a panel on the motor. "Shout to them that we're okay."

"We're okay," he shouts. "We are, right?" The tone of his voice says he is starting to worry.

"Yes, we—" Something strange is attached to the underside of the wiring harness, and worry instantly fills her brain. "Ethan, hand me that flashlight in the tackle box under your bench." He slaps a small flashlight into her hand after rummaging around a few seconds. She clicks it a couple of times before it comes to life, then holds it between her teeth. A wire goes from the strange device to the gas tank. A small blinking light flashes consistently...until it starts to flash faster.

Her stomach becomes so heavy so fast, as if it's full of lead. Any heavier, and it could sink the boat.

She knows what that is. And the worry is replaced with dread. Terrifying dread.

Oh, shit. Oh, shit.

"Ethan," she says calmly.

"What? What'd I do?"

"Nothing at all, kid. But we're gonna play a game. Because, well, we ran out of gas." She's a horrible actress, and he doesn't believe her. The expression on his face makes it very clear. "Seriously, listen to me."

"Alden, what is going on?" He's one second away from freaking out.

She sits upright and takes his hand. "I need you to jump out of this boat right now and swim to the dock. As fast as you can."

"Alden…"

"Now," she says, her gaze not wavering. "You can do this." She squeezes his hand. "Ethan. Go. Now."

He dives into the water and starts swimming as fast as he can. It's a blessing that he has been practicing back at the mansion. Alden drops to her knees so she can unscrew the mounting bracket to the motor. "Fuck." The handle breaks off in her hand. "Fuck, fuck, fuck." She can't drop the motor into the water. "What the hell do I do?" The johnboat will not flip over easily. She bails into the water. The beeping from the bomb is faster now. It's going to kill her if she doesn't get out of there. She grabs the edge of the boat and with all her strength pushes it farther away from the dock. She dives underwater and starts to swim as fast as possible. When she swims far enough away, she comes up for air. Ethan makes it to the dock and out of the water, Evelyn rushing up to him. Him being safe makes her feel a million times better. It's only a matter of time…

"Everyone, get away from the dock," Alden shouts. "Get back!"

"What's going on?" Talon shouts as she stands next to Stella, Mel, and her grandparents.

"Get back now!" And just as she finishes, the bomb explodes.

The blast throws everyone down, including her grandparents, and as Alden struggles to swim against the choppy water, anger mixes with fear and flares inside her chest. Seconds later, heat from the explosion slams into her, bringing with it the stench of burning gasoline. Not only is her heart racing, but she can barely feel her limbs as she tries to get to safety. Adrenaline coursing through her is the only reason she's able to swim at all. As she treads water, she looks back to see flames and smoke and the remnants of the boat.

She finally grabs a rung of the dock ladder and is yanked upward, Talon on one side, and Mel on the other. She kneels, panting and holding back hysterics after they set her on the dock.

"Jesus Christ, Alden, are you okay?" Mel asks, grabbing her face. "Alden? Honey? Can you hear me?"

"Fuck," she says quietly as her anger begins to morph into panic. "That son of a bitch found us. How?" She stands and turns away from everyone because letting them see this side of her isn't what anyone needs. It shows weakness, and she cannot be weak right now. She needs to be strong, be the savior they all think she is.

After a few deep breaths, she kneels in front of her grandparents. "I'm so sorry," she whispers as she places two fingers under her grandma's chin and lifts so she can see the cut on her forehead. "Are you okay? Did you hurt anything?" She lifts her grandma's arms, one at a time, inspecting her. "And you?" She moves to her grandpa. "Are you hurt?" She searches his face for scrapes, cuts, anything.

"Honey, it's okay. We're okay. You didn't do anything wrong. You saved that boy." Grandpa's tone is filled with sincerity as he presses a white handkerchief against Grandma's forehead.

Her heart sinks. "But you got hurt, Grandma. I'll never forgive myself."

"Oh, please, I've had worse scrapes than this. You look worse than I do. Like a drowned rat."

Alden chuckles and wipes her nose with the back of her hand. "Thanks a lot." She looks up at Mel and Talon. "How did this guy find us? I was so careful. No one knew. No one."

"I have no idea," Talon answers, her voice calm.

"Alden!" Evelyn rushes over, Ethan and Stella in tow. "Are you okay? Please be okay." She pushes between Talon and Mel. "Are you hurt?" she asks, cradling Alden's face in her hands.

"I'm so sorry, Evelyn." Her voice is a whisper. "I am so sorry. I almost...goddammit, what if that had gone off while Ethan—"

"Stop it right this instant. Stop." Evelyn pushes Alden's damp hair behind her ears, then pulls her into a hug.

Alden grabs both Ethan and Stella, pulling them into the hug. "Thank you for saving me." Ethan's voice is muffled, but she can hear the worry and fear. This is the moment she feared from the beginning. Getting so close to this family that the very idea of not having them in her life causes genuine sadness. She tried to stop it, but clearly, she failed. And she almost failed at protecting Ethan. This isn't going to stop until this stalker is caught. And goddammit, she's going to be the one to catch him.

❖

Alden walks up to the front porch where Talon is standing by Mel. "The batteries on the cars are dead," she says, wiping her hands on an old towel she found in the shed. "And the brake lines have been severed."

"Why cut the brake lines and kill the batteries?" Mel's face twists. "Isn't the whole point of cutting a brake line to make sure you drive it, and then you're fucked when you can't stop?"

"I have no idea."

"Someone who doesn't know what they're doing would do that," Talon says. "Or at least, that's what they want us to think."

Alden folds her arms across her chest. "Which one of you opened your mouth?"

Mel lets out a laugh. "Are you serious? Why the hell would I tell anyone? I didn't even tell Patrick where I was going."

"Talon? Was it you?"

"I didn't say a word to anyone. You know I wouldn't do that to you," Talon says, her hands up in defense. "I would never do that to them."

Alden softens. "I know. God, I know. I'm sorry." She pushes her hands through her hair and sighs. "I just don't get it."

"Maybe someone else told?" Mel says, her arms crossed.

"Like who?"

Talon's face falls, and she looks like she's seen a ghost. "Oh no."

"What?"

"Stella."

"What about her?" Alden asks through clenched teeth.

"She can never keep a secret. The other night, I saw her texting with Serena." Talon reaches for Alden's arm. "Wait. What are you going to do?"

"Yeah," Mel says, "Stella wouldn't hurt her own family intentionally."

Alden pulls her arm away. "You told me you spoke with her about how important it is to keep her mouth shut." Talon looks as if she might cry, and Alden wants to kick herself. Talon is young. And Stella is even younger. And expecting them to handle the situation without cracking is almost impossible. "I just, what was she thinking?" And as those words leave her mouth, the door to the house opens, and out walks Stella, followed by Evelyn, stoic as ever, and Grandma, who should look as if she has regrets about opening her home but instead looks worried and concerned for a family she barely knows.

"Stella has something she'd like to confess," Evelyn says softly.

Stella takes a deep breath and starts crying, her big brown eyes shedding tears like it's their job. "I am so sorry. I let it slip to Serena—"

"Why did Serena want to know?" Alden asks. "Why were you telling her anything?"

"She texted asking if everything was okay. I told her we were fine and that you had taken us somewhere safe. With people you trusted. And that's all I said." Stella takes a deep breath. "But then she kept pushing, so I finally broke down and told her."

"Wait. Why would she even want to know? I told her we were leaving." Alden shakes her head. "That doesn't make sense."

"I thought it was weird, too, but she said she had to talk to you about something super important. I kept telling her no, but then she was getting really pushy, and her texts made it seem like she was irritated with me." Stella is spilling the story now, and she is a hot mess. "Then she said it was urgent and that she needed to know where we were."

"That does not sound like her at all." Mel pulls her phone from her back pocket. "I have three voice mails from our precinct mainline. Shit." She quickly taps through the notifications and plays the first message.

"Melissa, what the hell, call me right away. I need to speak with you and Alden now."

She taps to the next message.

"Oh for fuck's sake, why the hell are you up in fucking Michigan with no fucking cell service, you dumbasses."

Mel rolls her eyes before she plays the final message.

"You dicks. It's Robert. Call me right now."

Mel's eyes widen. "What the hell?"

"Call her back right now." Alden watches impatiently as Mel taps the phone number to call Serena's cell. It rings and rings, then connects to voice mail. "Call the office." Mel does as instructed.

The line rings, and Serena picks up. "What the hell took you so long?"

Alden grabs Mel's phone and puts her on speaker. "Serena, what is going on?"

"Goddamn, you both are too hard to get a hold of, by the way. I have tried to call a million times. Is there no service up there or what?"

"Serena, seriously?"

"It's Robert. It's been Robert this whole time."

"How did you—"

"He came down to the station last night, well, I mean, early this morning...like four in the morning, and was being belligerent. Sandy at the front desk buzzed me and said there was a pushy guy asking for a detective, and she needed help with him. I took him to my office. He said he was looking for Evelyn Glass. That someone kidnapped her, then listed your name, and I was very confused, and I kept asking questions, which he did not like. I asked him if he wanted a water, and he said yes. But by the time I got back, he was gone."

"Okay, but he's always like that whenever he doesn't know where I'm at." Evelyn's voice is low. "That doesn't prove he's the one who did this."

"I know... But listen, after he left, I took my chair down to forensics, and they found a dog hair on it. The same DNA as the other hair."

"Holy shit."

"I *know.*"

"Holy *shit.*"

"*I* know. But the real kicker is," Serena pauses. "You're gonna kill me. This is such a rookie move."

"What did you do?"

"When I left to get the water..." She takes a deep breath. "He stole my cell phone."

"Fuck."

"Yeah."

"Why the hell don't you have it locked?"

"I don't know. I never thought...I'm sorry. I really am."

"He used that phone and your relationship with Stella to drag the information from her." Alden clenches her fist.

Evelyn's face changes from disbelief to anger in the blink of an eye. "I swear to Christ, I'm going to murder him myself."

"Serena," Alden says as she places her hand on Evelyn's arm and rubs lightly. "Get on the horn to the local police here in Crystal Lake. Let them know what's happening."

"Okay."

"And can you please put a fucking lock on your next phone?"

"I know, I know."

"Call if you need me."

"Take care of yourself, please. And don't be mad at Stella."

Alden says good-bye and hangs up. "We can't stay here."

"I know," Evelyn says. "I already told Ethan."

"What do we do?" Stella asks, falling into Talon's shoulder as she wraps an arm around her.

"Well, for one, we need to teach you 'what keep your mouth shut' means," Alden comments, her voice laced with irritation.

"Alden," Evelyn says, her voice quiet. "She didn't mean for this to happen."

"I didn't," Stella says. "I never would have…Ethan is my best friend. I love him, and I would have never…" She collapses into Talon.

Alden glances at Mel before she hangs her head, takes a deep breath, and tries to formulate a plan. "We can't leave right now. The cars are dead, and it'll be dark soon. Talon, can you fix the cars?"

Talon nods. "Yes, sir. I mean, ma'am."

"We'll hunker down in the cabin for now. Wait for first light." She walks to the opposite end of the porch. Footsteps follow her, and she hopes it's not Stella, even though she needs to apologize for being so harsh. But she needs to calm down first. She's got this. She can handle anything. She needs to remind herself of that a lot more often but right now, especially. A hand falls on the small of her back. She knows that touch now. She glances over her shoulder at Evelyn and looks into those eyes that have captured her heart and soul.

"We'll be okay." Evelyn's voice is calm. "We'll be okay."

"I'm the one who's supposed to be telling you that," Alden says. She props her elbows on the railing, looks out toward the forest, and takes a deep breath.

"It just means you're doing your job."

"Does it?"

"Yes. I'm alive. Ethan's alive. Stella's alive, even if you'd like to kill her for opening her mouth." She rubs Alden's back. "Maybe I can take care of you a little bit now."

Alden lowers her head. "I cannot fucking believe that asshole is involved in this."

A small laugh leaves Evelyn, and she mimics Alden's position against the railing. "Are you really surprised?" Her profile is beautiful against the backdrop of the green trees, and if this wasn't such a shitty conversation, it'd be a perfect moment.

"What do you mean?"

"He never really cared about me or our friendship. Just about my fame." Evelyn breathes deep and holds it for a beat. "I should have fired him years ago when he got mad at me over the breakup with Joel."

"What do you mean?"

"He was always jealous of Joel. Plain, old-fashioned jealousy. I think he always had a thing for Joel, and then when Joel wasn't around any longer, he started pushing me more and more to get back into show business."

Alden breathes deep. "I'm not going to let him hurt you, Evelyn," she says before standing upright. "I promise you that."

Evelyn wraps an arm around her shoulders and pulls her closer so their bodies are pressed together. "I know. I trust you." The best part about that trust is Alden feels the same way. She trusts Evelyn implicitly, which she never thought she'd let happen. And now that she has, she can't lose it. Not again.

CHAPTER TWENTY-FIVE

Alden leans back in the leather armchair in the living room. The house is completely dark, no noise. Mel and Talon are at the back of the house, standing guard with shotguns, courtesy of Grandpa, who, along with Thelma, is sitting across the room from Alden, shotgun across his lap.

Evelyn is on the couch, Ethan fast asleep under one of her arms. Stella is leaning against her other side, and Louise is lying half on Evelyn's lap and half on Ethan.

Grandma is pacing the kitchen, quiet as a mouse.

Everyone is trying to stay calm, to not cause drama. And overall, it's working. *Thank God.*

Alden has gone over the details of every event in her head. It was Robert's idea to have the fans lining up at the culture event. It was Robert's idea to book Evelyn solid at the comic conference in Chicago. And it was Robert's idea to hold the party after the press junket. He orchestrated these incidents. But still…it seems too easy. And even though he's connected, the whole idea of him being the mastermind seems flawed.

And why would he want to harm Evelyn? He always speaks so highly of her. Maybe he really is jealous. But why?

Evelyn's eyes are closed, Louise's head resting on her knee, and it makes Alden's stomach hurt to realize what a close call the boat incident was. Ethan could have…they both could have…died…and then what? That would have killed Evelyn without actually killing her. And maybe that's what the asshole wants to do.

Maybe he wants to hurt Evelyn so badly that she never recovers.

Her eyes slide open. Alden forces a smile, small but there.

Louise picks her head up, ears perked.

Alden jumps from the chair and picks up her gun. Grandpa flips the shotgun into his hands and stands in one fluid motion. Alden raises her hand, two fingers to her eyes, signals toward the left, then looks over her shoulder at her grandma, who must have heard something from the kitchen.

Louise's lips curl, a low growl coming from her. Alden takes two steps toward the hallway toward the back of the house. She slides along the wall, quietly making her way to the back, when a floorboard creaks. She stops, safety off her gun, and takes two more steps.

"Alden?" comes a hushed whisper.

"Mel, *Christ*, what the hell are you doing?"

"He's on the west side of the house."

"Are you sure?"

Mel lowers her shotgun and looks at her with an expression that screams, *seriously*?

"I'm just checking, Mel."

She looks over her shoulder. "You need to go. Now. He just rounded the trees. I'll watch Evelyn."

"Mel—"

"Now!"

Alden turns on her heels and runs to the bedroom on the west side of the house. When she gets to the window, she quietly slides it open, then climbs out and lands in a crouch. She freezes, gun at the ready, and listens. The moonlight is just bright enough to see by.

She holds a breath so she can hear. Nothing.

Until *snap*, a branch cracks to her left. She pops to her feet and takes off, running through the forest with little effort, ducking branches and sliding around a tree before stopping to listen. She can hear breathing. She can almost feel it.

She closes her eyes, sees the forest in her mind, the trees, the way the branches hang, the clearing to the left that she has walked through a hundred times, the tree she used to climb.

The wind blows. A branch snaps, feet shuffle, then dry leaves crunch. She opens her eyes. Something is out there. It's not an animal. The sounds of deer and of critters scurrying around at night are noises she comprehends. Wind blows through the branches, causing the old oaks and maples to creak and moan. She smells leather on the breeze, mixed with the scents of the earth. Her eyes have adjusted, and the moonlight is sharper. Her instincts are screaming: some*one* is out there. She grabs a rock, flings it, hoping to cause movement. She is positive a person is about fifty yards away to the right. She focuses, waits for the rock to hit, and when it does, she squeezes the trigger. The bullet zings off a tree, and the person takes off. She shoots two more times and hears the final bullet hit her mark.

Alden turns around a tree and reaches the dirt road. Someone is limping ahead, climbing into a vehicle. The tires peel out, and the taillights begin to retreat.

"No, no," she yells as she takes off. Her feet are flying as she sprints. She's so close. And then the entire time, she's cursing herself. She cannot let this guy get away. She hit him. *Goddammit, I know I hit him.* She will never forget the sound of a bullet striking flesh.

When she gets to the road, she hears the tires squeal and fires off five more shots, shooting out a taillight and striking the rear of the vehicle. The lights get farther and farther away, finally disappearing around a curve ahead. "Fuck." Knowing it's useless to continue the chase on foot, she stops. After waiting a few more beats, as if the person is going to turn around and come back, she decides to head back to the house.

She realizes when she's halfway back that she actually fired her gun. It's the first time since the incident. She's disappointed in herself, sure, but the realization that maybe she's finally healed causes her to smile. There was a time when she didn't think she'd ever find this part of herself again.

The part that has instincts.

That actually listens to those instincts.

And enjoys shooting a gun.

That uses adrenaline to her advantage.

The part that isn't afraid.

The mediocrity of failure is something she thought she was going to live with for the rest of her life. And she hated herself for it. But tonight, she finally recognizes why.

Failing is not the problem.

The problem is not getting back up and trying again.

While she may have failed tonight, she will not stay down. She will get back up. And she will not fail again. There isn't a bone in her body that will allow it. And there isn't a bone in her body that isn't completely relieved about that.

❖

When Mel and Talon walk into the dark kitchen, Mel's face looks like she's seen a ghost and Talon, well, she's not looking so hot, either.

"What now?" Alden asks, Evelyn's hand on her back as she leans over the center island.

Mel clears her throat. "I alerted the local authorities. Just so you know."

"Great. That's not why you look like that, though, so what's going on?"

"Well." She crosses her arms and leans against the island with her hip. "I just got off the phone with Serena. She tracked her cell phone, and it led them straight to Robert. They arrested him about two hours ago." She runs her fingers through her dark curls and sighs.

"How is that possible?" Alden stands upright, looking frantically from Mel to Talon and back.

"Well, whoever was out here today wasn't Robert, but he has confessed to delivering the letters."

"Wait." Alden waves frantically. "What are you saying?"

"Robert said he didn't write them, but he delivered them."

"Which makes no fucking sense," Talon says, palms against the countertop, her voice strained with stress.

Evelyn takes a deep breath. "What do we do?"

"What do you want to do?"

"You aren't going to like hearing this, but I am sick of hiding," Evelyn says.

"You do have one more appearance scheduled," Talon says and shrugs. "We could go. Put on a brave face."

Evelyn looks to Alden. "That's an idea."

"Evelyn, no. Use you as bait? No way."

"You'll protect me."

"But—"

"No, Alden, you'll protect me. Won't you?"

Alden's heart clenches, her throat tightens, and her palms sweat. "Always," she replies, barely above a whisper.

"That settles it," Stella says as she enters the kitchen. "We'll leave for the airport in the morning."

Grandma clears her throat, and they look over at her in the kitchen doorway. "You need to get some rest. There's no way that guy's coming back after Alden clipped him."

Grandpa lets out a low deep laugh. "I can't believe you nailed him in the dark. Great shot, my little hunter."

Alden senses a smile tugging at her lips as her cheeks fill with heat. "Well, I have always been a sure shot." She just wishes tonight, she'd have dropped him instead of clipped him.

❖

"Alden?"

She turns from her seat in the dark living room. "Ethan? What are you doing up?"

He takes a couple steps and sits carefully next to her, his hair sticking up in all directions, and his Star Wars T-shirt wrinkled from bed. "I couldn't sleep."

"Is your mom asleep?"

"Yeah." He looks up at her, his eyes big. "Are you scared?"

She tries to force herself to sound brave, but the flimsy smile and the way her eyes are tingling is no doubt giving her away. "No, I'm not." She's lying and thankful for the cover of night. His bottom lip trembles. She hasn't protected him enough to make sure he has nothing to be scared of. "You don't have to be scared."

"I am, though," he whispers.

"Oh, man." She breathes out as she puts an arm around his shoulders. "You have nothing to worry about. I promise."

"But the boat...I keep seeing it in my mind, over and over again."

Her heart skips, and she squeezes him. She knows all too well how that feels. Seeing the exact same scenario play out in the exact same way every single time she closes her eyes. "I know. And I'm so sorry about that."

"That was meant for my mom, wasn't it?"

"I don't know," she answers with a matter-of-fact tone. They sit in silence. She doesn't know what else to say. The boat was too much and too close, and it scared her just as much as it scared him, if not more because once again, it means she let her guard down. And this guy that's after Evelyn is good. Too good. Alden's hunted before. She has tracked people down before. But this guy…

Ethan sighs. "I don't understand what happens to people to make them bad. I wish I could understand it."

She wants to say that she knows exactly what he's talking about, that sometimes it's hard to understand why people are the way they are, but instead, she says, "You obviously like Star Wars, right?"

He lets out a breath. "Yeah, why?"

"Well, there is always a struggle between being good and being evil. It's in every person. Luke fought with himself to stay good, to stay true to the Force and to himself."

"And Darth Vader turned bad because of a girl," he adds, a chuckle following his words.

She smiles. "It's never that simple, kid." They sit in silence for a while before Ethan opens his mouth as if he's going to say something and then closes it again. "What?"

"So good people can turn into bad people."

"Exactly." She leans her head back and listens to his breathing. He seems very deep in thought. She hopes he is because learning that some people are inherently evil is probably a lot easier than figuring out some people actually choose to be hurtful and hateful.

"I don't want her to die," he whispers. "I love her so much."

"I won't let her die."

"Because you love her, too?"

She smiles against his hair. "Yeah, kid, because I love her, too."

CHAPTER TWENTY-SIX

Alden pulls her hair into a half-hearted ponytail; it's messy and bumpy, but she doesn't care. She looks around her small apartment, the bed with Evelyn still sleeping beneath the sheet and her half-unpacked luggage. They arrived home yesterday afternoon. and after a security sweep, Alden deemed it safe to enter. And now? Life seems to be slightly back to normal, which is what everyone kind of needed.

She steps out onto her veranda and looks out to the lake, breathing deep before she takes a drink of coffee. Even though everyone seems to be settling back into their normal lives, she can't quite find the mental space to relax. She's on edge, constantly waiting for the stalker's next move. It's good to be vigilant, but damn. She won't even allow herself to enjoy her one true love: her first cup of coffee in the morning. Talon keeps telling her it'll be fine, but she can feel that something bad is going to happen. *You can take the girl out of the secret service, but you can't take the secret service out of the girl.*

And tonight...*Shit.*

The Chicago Celebrity Auction is tonight. Alden is one-hundred-percent against going. But the look on Evelyn's face when she said she was sick of hiding has been playing over and over in her head. Evelyn is right. She can't hide forever, even if it would make Alden's job a hell of a lot easier.

A throat clears gently before an arm wraps around her from behind. "Good morning," comes the whisper against the back of her neck.

"Good morning to you." Alden turns. "How'd you sleep?"

"Surprisingly well, considering."

"No worries. This place is a compound. Ain't no one breaking in here." She raises her mug and motions to the perimeter of the property.

"If you say so." Evelyn heads back in toward the coffeepot. She's dressed in an oversized white T-shirt and white cotton panties, so uncharacteristically Evelyn, and pours herself a mug as if she's been living with Alden since day one. Evelyn looks at her over the rim and raises her eyebrows. "What?"

"You look good," Alden smiles. "I could get used to this."

"Yeah, well, this apartment is too small and super-hot. I don't know how you've survived the poor air circulation."

Alden steps closer, places a hand on Evelyn's cheek, and looks into her eyes. "Well, I wasn't having insanely hot sex in here, so I never noticed." She smiles when Evelyn's cheeks flush deep red. "Not that I minded any of it."

Evelyn kisses her while wrapping a free arm around her neck. "You certainly know your way around my body," she says against Alden's lips.

"Yeah, well." Alden sets their cups on the small countertop. She backs Evelyn to the counter, runs a hand down her side, up under the soft T-shirt and along her smooth stomach to her bare breasts. Evelyn's nipples are erect in an instant, and Alden delights in the fact that she has that kind of power. When she pinches each nipple lightly, Evelyn's deep moan weakens her knees. "I have definitely loved getting to know the lay of the land," she whispers as she caresses Evelyn's sides to her panties. Her skin is like silk, soft and cool from the early morning air. She begins to pull the panties over her hips, thighs, until they go slack and fall to the floor. She kneels, pushes Evelyn's T-shirt up so she can kiss each hip, kiss her soft stomach. Every fiber of her being loves being able to do this, loves being able to love every inch of Evelyn. As she leans forward and places her mouth on the soft hair at the apex of Evelyn's thighs, she hears a soft sigh before she guides Evelyn's leg onto her shoulder. She starts to lick Evelyn's glistening wetness, and finds her clit with ease. She is thrilled at how Evelyn is responding, a hand on her head, Alden's name moaned along with *yes*, and *don't stop*. She flicks Evelyn's clit lightly, then harder and faster.

"Jesus," Evelyn breathes, bracing herself against the countertop, one hand on Alden and the other wrapped tightly around the edge of the granite.

Evelyn is getting closer; Alden can tell. So she slips a finger inside and feels her tighten. When she slips a second finger inside, Evelyn opens a little wider, so Alden stands and wraps an arm around Evelyn's waist. Evelyn holds on a little tighter, and as Alden starts to thrust ever so slowly, she is rewarded with the softest, lowest, sexiest moan she has yet to hear from those beautiful bruised lips.

"Fuck," Alden whispers as she slides in and out of Evelyn's wetness. And she knows Evelyn is close when she leans her head back, and she exposes that fucking gorgeous neck. Alden places her tongue at the base and licks her way up to Evelyn's chin, over it to her mouth. "Kiss me," she says against Evelyn's lips. "Kiss me while you come."

"God, Alden," Evelyn pushes her words out into Alden's mouth as they kiss, deeper and deeper.

Evelyn tightens around Alden's fingers and releases a deep moan into her mouth as she comes. Her nails dig into Alden's shoulders as she goes slightly limp while she pants against Alden's lips.

"What the hell?" Evelyn says between breaths, a small chuckle escaping her at the end. "That's…yeah…wow."

Alden smiles as she pulls her hand away and sees it glistening in the daylight. "Someone was very wet." She pulls Evelyn close and places a gentle kiss on her lips.

"Yeah, well, you made me that way," Evelyn responds, bringing her hands up to push her dark hair away from her face. "You are incredible, Alden."

"No," Alden whispers. "You are."

Evelyn kisses her once and then twice before pulling away. "Are you okay about tonight?"

She shakes her head and looks away. "But I know it means a lot to you to not hide."

"Alden," Evelyn starts, softly guiding her face back. "Do you really think something bad will happen?"

Alden looks into her eyes, the way the light is hitting them just right. She should tell her that this is too soon to put on a brave face, that this is exactly what this asshole is probably expecting, but she stays silent, keeps her expression as stoic as possible.

"Alden, dear, you have to understand something about me." She pauses as if expecting a reaction, so Alden nods. "I have worked so hard to get to this point. And even if this life, this fame, isn't everything I want, it's what I have, and I can't roll over and let someone take it from me. When I walk away, I want it to be because *I said so*." She takes a deep breath and lets it out slowly.

Alden can see the determination written on her face, so she gathers her courage. She is prepared for anything, including the worst case scenario. "Okay. But no going rogue. You listen to every single thing I tell you, okay?"

"I promise."

"You're gonna drive me crazy, you know that?"

Evelyn laughs as she pulls Alden into a hug and runs a hand down her arms. "Yeah, well, I'll take care of *you* then."

When Talon comes out of the garage with a black suit on and her black shoes shined, Alden smiles and remembers the very first time they went on an outing. "You look good," she says as Talon swipes a hand through her short hair.

"I almost forgot how to put this earpiece on," she says, motioning to her sleeve. She smiles, pats Alden's shoulder, and asks, "You nervous?"

"Yes," Alden replies, matter-of-fact. She straightens her skinny black tie and looks Talon square in the face. "Is this thing straight? I haven't worn a tie in a while."

Talon straightens it. "You have to settle down." She places her hands on Alden's shoulders. "You're going to be fine. She's going to be fine. You can't lose your composure now."

"I know." Alden breathes, looking anywhere but into her eyes.

"You've trained most of your life for moments like this. All you have to do is trust your instincts. Right?"

"Right." Alden smiles. "I got this." Her voice cracks, and she's trying her hardest to not sound scared. She's not scared. Not really.

"Alden Ryan," Talon says, folding her arms across her chest. "You realize you protected the president of the United States, right?" She smiles. "The president. POTUS. You. Protected. Her."

"I know, and I got stupid, and I got fucking shot."

"But the president didn't," Talon responds with no hesitation. "Stop. Calm down. You're fine."

Stella and Ethan come strolling up. Stella smiles and slips an arm through Talon's. "Are you freaking out?"

"Nope, not at all." Talon smiles. "She just needed a reminder that she's fine."

Ethan smiles before saying, "BAMF, right?"

"I'm not sure you should be using that acronym, Ethan," Alden says with a laugh.

"What? Why? What does it mean?" His face falls. "I heard it on a video game. I just thought it meant someone who's good at their job?"

Talon chuckles. "Little man, it means badass motherfucker."

Alden joins in, laughing as she puts an arm around Ethan's shoulders. "You're adorable."

"Well, that seems fitting. You really are a badass motherfu—"

"Whoa, whoa." Stella slaps a hand over his mouth. "You're too young for that word." She starts to walk away, pulling Ethan with her. "You guys take care of each other, okay? And protect Mom."

"We will."

When Stella walks away with Ethan, Talon turns to Alden. "We're looking for a man who's limping, right? You shot the son of a bitch. And Serena and Mel will be there. We have our posts. Do not worry about this. We will not let this dick get past us."

Alden finally cracks a smile. Talon has come such a long way, and Alden can't help but feel a sense of pride. "That's true," she finally replies, letting herself relax just the tiniest of bits. "I'm just nervous. I don't know why."

"Because you love her."

"Talon," Alden says, trying to protest, but it's useless.

"It's okay. We won't let anything happen to her," Talon says with another squeeze on Alden's arm. "Now come on. We have to get this show on the road. Don't want to be late."

"Hey, I thought I was the boss here?"

Talon turns and slides her sunglasses on. "You are. I'm just the kickass assistant."

Alden chuckles. If there is one thing she's learned throughout all of this, it's that life is way too short to keep everything to herself. "You're way more than that, my friend," she says, and Talon's smile is something she will always remember.

"I'll stay at her side the entire time," Alden says as she looks at Mel and Serena, who are dressed like professional bodyguards. It made her laugh when she first saw them. They're standing at the back entrance of the Chicago Hilton. The front was too crowded to even dare, which frustrated Evelyn, but she allowed Alden to win that argument. "Mel, you'll be on my twelve o'clock, and Serena, you're on my six. Copy?"

"Roger that," Mel almost shouts.

"Jesus." Serena laughs. "Calm down, Mel. It's been a while since you've seen some action, hmm?"

"I'm just nervous." She sighs and shakes her head. "After what that prick did at the lake?"

"We got it," Serena says. "Earpiece on and active?" They check their earpieces and sleeve mics and nod.

"And remember, if you see anything out of the ordinary, speak up," Alden says as she pulls her gun, ejects the magazine, and checks it. She slides it back into place and looks at Evelyn, who is watching with wonder and a little fear. "You okay?"

"Yes," Evelyn answers, her hands clasped in front of her. "Just ready to get this over with." Alden has to stop herself from reminding Evelyn that she's the one who wanted this. Hiding probably sounds like a much better idea now.

"Talon, you good with keeping an eye on things from the back of the room?"

"For sure." Talon flips both thumbs into the air. "I can see more at a distance anyway."

Alden takes a deep breath and casually fixes her tie, checks her watch, her earpiece again, and tries her hardest to calm the fuck down. She can sense everyone watching, so she finally breathes out. "We got this. Right?"

"Yes. Everything is going to be fine." Evelyn smiles. "Let's go."

"Wait." Alden grabs Evelyn's wrist before she enters the building.

"Stop," Evelyn says as she turns. "Stop." She places a hand on Alden's face and steadies her until they're looking at each other. "I love you."

Alden swallows once. "I love you, too," she whispers, feeling every set of eyes on them but not even caring right now.

"I know," Evelyn replies, her voice low, and she places a soft kiss on Alden's lips. She trails her fingertips down Alden's cheek and neck and stops over her heart. "I trust you."

Alden nods, and Evelyn's smile is the first thing that has helped to calm her down since they arrived.

"It's time," Talon says.

Alden's heart thumps loudly as she glances over her shoulder, then back at Evelyn. "I won't let anyone hurt you."

"I know, my love. You're my bodyguard, after all," she says with a smile and a small laugh. "Let's do this."

CHAPTER TWENTY-SEVEN

"All clear backstage, Alden."

"Roger that. Mel, report?"

"All clear from the balcony. No Robert. No limping assholes. We're good."

Alden relaxes slightly before she places a hand on Evelyn's arm and guides her through the doors of the Grand Ballroom. "We're clear," she says, her eyes constantly scanning the crowd. "Talon, I need you up here with me. I'll have Serena check the back of the room."

Talon appears as if from thin air and begins walking alongside Evelyn as they approach the group of costars, who shout and hoot as Evelyn approaches. She looks at Alden as if asking permission, and Alden nods. She stands back as Evelyn rushes over to them, receiving hugs and kisses on the cheek. They were worried she wouldn't come back after the incident at the C2E2 event. And when news hit about the LA press junket, her costars started calling and asking if she was going to continue filming. At the time, Evelyn didn't know. She might be willing to risk her own safety for fame, but when it came to her kids, the promise of fame meant absolutely nothing.

But as Evelyn laughed and smiled, Alden knew acting really made her happy, even if the lifestyle wasn't all it was cracked up to be.

Alden's pocket buzzes, and she pulls out her cell, slides her finger across the screen and sees a missed call from Ethan. She holds her free hand to her ear.

He finally picks up and shouts, "Alden."

"Ethan, what's wrong?"

"I know who it is."

"Wait, what? What's going on? Are the police still out front watching the house?" She swings around and moves to a quieter area in the ballroom.

"Yes, they're still here. Are you listening to me, though? I'm telling you that I know who it is. It's the man who hired you."

"Tobias? No way. How is that even possible?" She turns and finds Evelyn in the crowd, Talon standing guard about ten paces away.

"I remember from when Robert and my grandpa talked about hiring a bodyguard. Robert suggested this guy, Tobias. And my grandpa said no because Robert was dating him."

"Whoa, whoa, whoa." A tsunami of memories slams into Alden. Tobias with women. Lots and lots of women. "I don't think that's right. Tobias isn't gay. Or bi."

"That you know of," Ethan says loudly. "Because I am telling you, my grandpa said he's dating Robert."

"Kid, I appreciate you calling," she starts, trying to not sound as exasperated as she feels by this information. "But I'm having a hard time wrapping my head around this."

"Check your phone." He hangs up.

She gasps as she pulls the phone from her ear and checks it. "That little shit just hung up on me." More memories continue to pop up as she tries to figure out why Ethan would think this. What evidence could he be sending that has him convinced? Whatever it is, it's gotta be big because she cannot remember Tobias ever being into men. Sure, he was always into his looks. He's attractive. Why wouldn't he be into himself? And he was friendly with a lot of men. But aside from her, he is friendly all the time to everyone. So that doesn't mean anything.

Then she remembers a guy in the police academy who Tobias used to hang out with. He was devastated when the guy dropped out. Like, way more devastated than he should have been. At the time, it seemed normal. But now, looking back? Maybe he is bi.

She looks at her phone as a message slides across the screen. She taps it to reveal a picture of two men and a giant German Shepherd.

She zooms in. *Holy shit. Tobias.* Another text alert pops onto the screen, and when she pulls it up, she is shocked to see Tobias standing with Evelyn and Robert. The picture mustn't be that old because they're on the patio of the mansion, but Tobias has a beard, and his hair is much longer than it is now. And honestly, if she didn't know him so well, she would not have recognized him, which has to be why Evelyn didn't know who he was at the party in LA. Alden forwards the pictures to Mel, Serena, and Talon, then drops her phone into her jacket pocket and moves as quickly as possible to Talon without looking suspicious. Her heart is racing. How could Tobias be this kind of person? How was she so naive to not realize how horrible he really is? She's so foolish for trusting him.

"Whoa, Tobias knows Robert?" comes Serena's voice from the earpiece. "What the hell?"

"Your guess is as good as mine."

"I fucking knew he was up to no good," Mel says.

"What do you mean?" Alden is on the highest of alerts now.

"He said before you came home that he was going to find you a good job. One that would change your life. One that would make him feel better for hating you for getting the Secret Service job over him." She sighs. "He fucking set this all up."

"I knew he was still mad about that but to go to these lengths?" Alden presses her earpiece harder into her ear so she can hear.

"He never got over it," Serena answers. "Oh, sweet Jesus."

"What?"

"What if, and hear me out, because this is going to sound really out there."

"Spit it out, Serena," Alden says with force.

"What if Evelyn isn't the target?"

"What?"

"What if you are, Alden? You're the target. He can kill you and make it look like the person was after Evelyn."

Alden's stomach drops to the floor. "No way. That can't be true."

"Think about it. Come on." Serena's words echo in her head as she scans the crowd. Is this really what hers and Tobias's friendship has come to? If so, it certainly isn't a friendship. She racks her brain, searching for anything that would make him guilty of something as crazy as this. He is always so jealous. He has no real sense of humor around her. He jokes, but he's never actually laughing. He is rough, abrasive, mean. "Fuck," she says as quietly as possible. She glances at her hands and expects to see them trembling. She's pleasantly surprised that they aren't. She's cool and collected but far from calm. "The event is going to start in three minutes. Let's get in place." She closes the distance between her and Evelyn and touches her elbow gently. "Evelyn, we need to get you to your seat."

Evelyn smiles, runs her hand down Alden's arm and intertwines their fingers. "Okay." Her costars exchange looks. Alden notices and tosses a weary glance over her shoulder to Talon. She escorts Evelyn to her seat, staying vigilant the entire time. Her senses are on high alert. She hates to admit that this is the most alive she's felt in a really long time because it seems to negate all the amazing times she's had with Evelyn. But this is what she was trained for. These situations are what get her adrenaline pumping.

"Alden, where are you going?" Evelyn's voice is laced with worry.

"Just taking some extra precautions," she says, trying to sound as calm, cool, and collected as possible.

"I'm not stupid, Ms. Ryan. Please don't treat me as such."

Alden glances down, the *Ms. Ryan* making it glaringly obvious that Evelyn won't be kept in the dark. Evelyn grips the armrest of her seat; her other hand wraps around Alden's wrist.

"Okay," Alden starts, squatting. "The guy at the cabin? He's not after you. He's after me."

Evelyn sits up straighter and looks around frantically. "What are you talking about?"

She passes the phone to Evelyn. "Do you recognize this man?"

Evelyn stares at the phone, enlarges the picture. "Yeah, that's Robert's boyfriend, T. I met him briefly. Seemed nice."

"Yeah."

"Yeah, what?"

"That's him."

"Hold on a second." Evelyn looks at the picture again. "This does not make sense."

"You remember the guy you almost slept with in LA?"

"How could I forget?"

Alden swipes to the first picture of Robert with Tobias, where he looks exactly how he looked that night. "Now can you see it?"

Evelyn doesn't say a word.

"Are you okay?"

"So that night, he was trying to get to you and not me?" She closes her mouth and swallows. "We need to go right now. You're not going to get shot on my watch," she says as she starts to stand.

Alden places her hand on her calf and squeezes it lightly. "Stop, Evelyn, please calm down. Everything is under control. I'm going to draw him out, and everything will be fine."

Evelyn's eyes go wide, and her mouth falls open slightly. She reaches up to cover it. "Oh, my God," comes her muffled reply. "Alden, you...cannot...leave me."

"Look at me," Alden says, taking her phone and sliding it back into her pocket. She motions for Talon to sit next to Evelyn. "We have this under control. I promise."

"Alden—"

"Trust me, okay?" Evelyn sits back a tiny bit as Talon slides into the seat next to her. "You keep her safe. You hear me?"

Talon nods and says, "Yes." She flips her jacket open to reveal her gun holstered in a shoulder harness. "I won't let anything happen to her."

Alden smiles at her. She's so glad she made her enroll in a class and get a concealed weapon license. She's also really happy she took her to target practice as often as they did. She squeezes Evelyn's leg again before she stands. "I'll be right over there."

"Okay," Evelyn whispers, still gripping Alden's hand. "Please be careful."

"I promise," Alden replies, her gaze unwavering. "No wardrobe malfunctions while I'm gone, okay?"

Evelyn cracks a small smile and gives her hand another squeeze before she walks away. She grips the weapon beneath her jacket. She thumbs open the retention strap that holds the gun in place, then brings her sleeve to her mouth. "Serena, Mel, Talon, do you copy?" When she gets three responses, she takes her post next to the stage, in the shadows. "Evelyn goes on in twenty minutes. I'll be backstage. I need your eyes out here now, Serena and Mel."

"Roger that," comes their voices. They signal to her from their opposite posts. She makes eye contact with Talon, then with Evelyn, and the lights dim, the music begins, and the start of the auction commences as the emcee takes the stage.

❖

Evelyn's fingernails dig into Alden's arm almost through her jacket. She looks over while they stand backstage, waiting for the lunch with Evelyn to be auctioned. "Breathe. It's going to be fine."

"I thought I was the one who wanted to go through with this," Evelyn says, half-accusatory and half-nervous.

"You don't have to go on." Alden smiles as the makeup people flit around Evelyn. They are making sure she looks flawless. And they are succeeding.

"I know," Evelyn starts, a very serious expression on her face. "I don't want you to get hurt while I'm gone. What if this guy—"

"Ms. Glass, you're on," says the backstage director.

"I'm right here," Alden says and then watches as Evelyn walks onstage. The crowd goes wild, fans yelling and screaming, a few of her costars also shouting that *Glass is a MILF* and other random terms that enrage Alden slightly, but only because she's so protective now.

"Good evening," Evelyn says into the microphone as the noise from the audience subsides. "Thank you so much for attending the Chicago Celebrity Auction. All proceeds tonight go to Lurie Children's Hospital, so the fact that we have already raised fifty thousand dollars is outstanding." The crowd goes wild, and Evelyn smiles and raises her hands. "Tonight, not only are we auctioning off many different items, but we're also auctioning off a couple of passes for fans to be on set during filming of the hit show, *Between the Covers*." Again, the audience goes wild.

Alden brings her sleeve to her mouth. "Any movement?"

"There is a lot of movement, Alden. The crowd is going nuts," Mel says, her voice shaking, no doubt with adrenaline.

"Everything looks like it's supposed to. Wait," Serena says, calmly. "Balcony. Two o'clock. Man with a ball cap. I'm on my way to check it."

Alden moves farther onstage and checks her two o'clock. She can see someone but can't make out the face. "Mel, can you hear me? I don't think that's him." Then, as Alden looks across the stage, she sees someone standing in the shadows. "Wait. There's someone backstage who I don't think should be there. Do you guys copy?"

When the figure moves, she makes eye contact. "It's him. I repeat. It's him. He's backstage. Do you copy?" No one is responding. Frustrated, she pulls the earpiece from her ear. She waits a half a second, mentally pumping herself up before rushing the stage, but then, as he pulls a gun, her entire body starts to shake. He aims at her, and the only thing she can think about is how getting shot led her to this exact moment. How the sound of a bullet ripping through flesh as she jumped in front of President Simmons is why she's about to get shot again. The gun shifts, and an evil grin comes across his face. That motherfucker knows if he aims at Evelyn, Alden will absolutely save her.

But what if I get shot again? It's worth it. Evelyn is worth it.

She runs onstage and pulls her gun in one clean movement. The crowd starts shouting, the sound of screaming reverbs off her eardrums, and the smell of panic floods her nostrils. While Tobias aims at Evelyn, Alden takes off as fast as she can, jumping between Evelyn and where Tobias is standing backstage.

The spotlight from the opposite side of the stage flashes onto Tobias, blinding him. He fires wildly. The shot nicks Alden's arm, knocking her to the ground. A wave of relief washes over her when she realizes she's okay.

As she goes to stand, he fires again. The bullet rips through her left side, under her shoulder. This time, the sound is exactly how she remembers. Only the pain is different. It's excruciating, and for some reason, the only thing going through her mind is how she's in the same exact position.

"Alden. Oh my God. Someone call 9-1-1!"

Someone shouts, "There's so much blood."

"Alden, I got him. I shot him. Can you hear me?" Mel's voice is strained as her face comes into view. "I got him. I got him, Alden."

She blinks twice. "I'm sorry." The familiar taste of iron fills her mouth, and she remembers the flashing of blue and red lights, the press of a hand to her face, the way the air smelled.

"Alden, oh baby, don't leave me. Please don't leave me."

All she sees are the bright white of the lights and Evelyn bending over her. She tries to speak. She wants to tell Evelyn it was worth it. She was worth it. But no words come out, and she's surrounded by darkness.

CHAPTER TWENTY-EIGHT

Two Weeks Later

"Do you need help with that?"

Alden looks up from trying to get the shoulder sling attached correctly. Her ma is standing in the doorway of her bedroom. She's been great so far and hasn't annoyed Alden once with her overbearing tendencies, which makes Alden's heart swell. "Yeah, that'd be nice," she says, her voice cracking a bit.

Ma places a hand on Alden's shoulder and smiles. "You know I don't mind helping...whenever you need it."

"I know."

Ma tightens a couple straps, then adjusts the Velcro belt that goes around her ribcage. The first bullet ended up nicking the outside of her arm, but the second one was a direct hit right through her left shoulder. The bullet went clean through, a centimeter away from striking the brachial artery. If the bullet would have hit that...things would have been a lot different. She's not as upset about this round of wounds as she was about the last, which makes no sense because this was as much her fault as the last set. Maybe it's because she was the intended target, yet she did her job perfectly. And that felt really fucking good. She hated admitting that, but she can't help it.

"How's that feel? Too tight?"

"It's fine." Alden tries to pull down on the V-neck T-shirt she has on under the brace. She shrugs, and pain shoots down her arm. She breathes in sharply and glances up at Ma, hoping she doesn't notice.

"Alden, you need to take those pain pills."

"I'm fine, Ma," she replies, never looking directly at her mother, who is trying to not be overbearing, but it still finds a way to slip out. "I'm fine."

"Are you?" Ma asks when Alden tries to escape. "Because you've been home for a week, and you don't seem fine at all."

Alden stops, not looking back, and takes a deep breath. Sadness and heartache sting the backs of her eyes. She reaches to the bridge of her nose and squeezes her eyes shut. "I got shot, Ma. Again. I'll be okay eventually."

"You know, I spoke with Mel the other day, and she had a lot to say."

"What are you talking about?"

"Apparently." Ma places a hand on her back and rubs back and forth gently. "This Evelyn woman really misses you. You can go back. She wants you to—"

"Ma," Alden says, cutting her off. "I know, okay?"

"Then what are you waiting for? She was at the hospital every day while you were unconscious. Every single day. And now you're not even going to go see her? That's, if you'll pardon my French, fucking bullshit." Ma folds her arms and shakes her head as Alden turns to stare. "I am disappointed in you, Alden."

"I'm scared, Ma."

"Of what?"

"Of losing her."

"You make no sense. You know that, right?" Ma says softly as she pulls Alden into a hug. "You're gonna lose her if you don't go see her, you stubborn ass. You're worse than your father. You know that?"

Alden sniffles against her shoulder and lets out a small laugh. "I know," she whispers.

Ma pulls back, her hands on Alden's shoulders, and looks her in the eyes. "I will drive you. I don't mind."

"You hate driving."

"Yeah, well, I hate seeing you upset more." She walks to the closet and opens the door, revealing a packed duffle bag. She slings it over her shoulder. "Let's go."

"Ma, what the hell? You packed a bag already?"

"Yes. Let's go. I asked Mel to let them know you'll be arriving."

"Wait," Alden says as she follows. "Why are you doing this? You don't even like...that part of me."

Ma stops and turns. "I love every part of you, sweetheart. And if this will make you happy and you'll stop moping around here like, well, a wounded puppy—"

"Very funny."

"You know what I mean. I just want you to be happy. You're not happy here with your father and me and..." She pauses, adjusts the duffle, and takes a few steps while pulling on Alden's free hand. "Come on, let's go."

"No, what were you going to say?"

"Alden, this woman loves you. She's in love with you." Ma pulls a final time and then smiles. "And I know you're in love with her, so come on. Stop being a Secret Service agent turned bodyguard and start being a real person with a beating heart."

Alden smiles as she lets herself be pulled through the house and out the front door.

"This is Ryan," Alden says into her phone as she rides shotgun in the Scout on Lake Shore Drive toward Winnetka.

"Well, well, well, Agent Ryan."

Alden almost drops her phone. "Madame President," she says, her voice laced with shock.

"I was calling to check up on you. I heard about what happened."

"Wow. You didn't have to...wow. Thank you so much for calling." She tries to sit a little straighter, as if Jennifer can see her, and instantly regrets it as the pain shoots through her shoulder.

Jennifer takes a deep breath, and Alden can picture her in the Oval Office, fingers drumming lightly on the Resolute Desk, dressed impeccably in a pantsuit and looking as lovely as ever. "How are you holding up? I know you're no stranger to gunshot wounds," she says, the hint of a smile showing through her tone.

Alden smiles and looks out the window. "I am recovering nicely."

"That's wonderful news. Do you need anything? I've been told I apparently have some pull." A laugh follows her words, and Alden can't help but chuckle along with her.

"No, ma'am. Thank you, though."

"You're not wallowing in self-pity, are you?" Alden can hear the worry in her voice. She saw firsthand how Alden wallowed, and it was part of the reason for the dismissal. Only part. The other part was because they were in love, and it was not possible. "There's no need to be scared. You did your job. Again. And you did it well. *Again.*"

"Jennifer…"

"Alden Ryan, you listen to me. This is an order. Pull yourself together and get back on that horse. Life, my dear, is not a spectator sport."

Alden's throat tightens. *My love* has been replaced with *my dear*, and while it most definitely hurts, it also feels final. Her entire body fills with grief for the tenth time that day. "Yes, ma'am," she says, leaning on the headrest.

A few seconds pass before Jennifer says, softly, and with so much sincerity, "I still love you, you know?"

The pain caused by that confession radiates in her old wound. "And I you."

"You take care of yourself, Alden."

"I will."

The phone disconnects, but she can't move. She keeps it pressed against her ear. Then, as if a switch has been flipped, she decides once and for all that it's time. It's time to turn the page on that part of her life. She can't keep reliving those moments. Or she at least, can't continue to be upset about them. They happened. Period.

"Was that who I think it was?"

Alden smiles as she slides the phone away. "Yes."

"Wow."

"Yeah."

"More happened there than you're willing to tell your old ma, didn't it?"

Alden sighs. "Yeah."

"I figured." Ma floors it around a couple of cars, then settles back into the middle lane. "The president, eh?"

"Ma."

"That's one helluva notch in the ol' headboard."

"Jesus, Ma." Alden laughs. "That's not…no. That's not how it was."

"Mm-hmm."

Alden looks at her hands. The same hands that used to tremble at the very thought of what used to be. They're not shaking. At all. And it makes her feel the lightest she's felt in over a year.

Ma chuckles. "You're quite the ladies' lady, hmm?"

"Oh, for fuck's sake," Alden whispers as she pushes her good hand through her hair. "I am not discussing this with you." And they laugh as Alden refocuses her attention on the road and takes a deep breath. She was nervous and scared and excited, all at the same time, before the phone call. She doesn't want to say it took the wind out of her sails so much as it relaxed her. There's something to be said about closure, and maybe, just maybe, that was what she needed. The final sentence in the book about her journey to heal.

And now she should be headed back to Evelyn, a woman who not only helped her see that life could exist after heartache, but who also stayed by her side when no one was looking. Evelyn had been there for those first three days while she was unconscious, but when the doctors released her, Alden didn't know what to do. Did Evelyn really want her, or did their affection transpire out of the fear of danger and forced proximity? Did this really need to happen? Was everything going to be okay?

She should have called Evelyn immediately, but she didn't. She called her ma, and that was the end of it. She needed to get over the past wounds that the new ones uncovered. She was always so sure of herself, but it was all an act, and getting shot, not once, but twice, helped her to see it was just an act. She was definitely not sure of herself or who she was or wanted to be.

Alden was scared, and up until this all happened, she didn't scare easily. Instead of fear being something she laughed in the face of, now she'd let fear laugh in her face. And she was sick of being that way. She didn't want to be afraid anymore.

"Get out of your head," Ma says. "You gotta stop over analyzing this whole thing."

"Ma, that's, like, impossible." Alden closes her eyes and listens to the soothing sounds of Grace Potter and the Nocturnals sing and hopes her heart heals quicker than her other wounds.

GUARDING EVELYN

CHAPTER TWENTY-NINE

"Alden Ryan, as I live and breathe," Doc says from the entry gate. He's a new addition after the lake incident. "I thought you were long gone. It's good to see you again."

She smiles and waves. "Glad to see you're still standing guard," she says with a nod. "Any news?"

"Nothing new to report, ma'am." He tips his hat and buzzes the gate open. "You take care now. It's good to have you back."

"Thanks, Doc," Alden says as Ma pulls through the gate and down the driveway. The landscaping company is still making sure the bushes and shrubs are trimmed back, and she can see the security cameras. It makes her happy to know her hard work didn't fall to the wayside.

When they pull up to the front door, Ma chuckles. "You chose to come home instead of coming back here? Is there something wrong with you?"

Alden laughs. "Ma, a big house doesn't mean it's home."

Talon comes trotting up to the Scout, a dirty rag over her shoulder. She places both hands on Alden's door, her eyes bright. "Well, look what the cat dragged in," she says as she helps Alden out of the car. To Alden's surprise, Talon wraps her arms around her and gives her a very big hug, being careful the entire time. "I've missed you, boss."

She laughs. "I've missed you, too, my friend."

"Did you hear? They raided the condo where Robert and Tobias plotted everything. The place was like a shrine. Pictures of you both. It was creepy."

"I did hear. And I heard Connor has been making sure every person who comes onto the property has a thorough background check."

Talon laughs and bounces on her toes. "Even I had to go through one."

"What'd they find on you?"

"Nothing. I'm clean," Talon says, her hands in the air. "But you knew that already."

"Alden!"

She turns as Ethan races out the front door, his brown hair flopping as he runs. Happiness starts to replace worry as he slams into her good side. "Hey, buddy."

"I am so happy you're home."

Her heart tightens. "Me, too, kid. Me, too." She looks up as Stella runs toward them, too.

"Oh my God, Alden, I have never been happier to see someone before." She wraps her arms around Alden and Ethan. "Mom is going to be so happy."

"She doesn't know?"

"Nope," Ethan answers with a smile. "Mel and Serena are coming, too. They're picking up pizzas."

Alden's heartbeat starts to race. "Where is Evelyn?"

"Out back." Stella places a hand on Alden's arm. "You should go by yourself."

"Okay," she says, her mouth very dry. Nerves are coursing through her, but there's something familiar and calming about this entire chain of events. She takes a couple steps away and then looks over her shoulder. "It's good to be back."

When she gets to the steps that lead to the beach, she stands and admires the sight. Evelyn is knee-deep in the water, her capris soaked, and a sunhat on her head. Alden descends the stairs and walks up behind her. Evelyn never moves. "Excuse me, Ms. Glass?"

Evelyn spins, stumbling from the waves crashing into her. "Oh my God."

Alden can't fight back a laugh. "Evelyn, I am so sorry. I didn't mean to scare you."

"What are you doing here?" she asks, hand clutching her heart. She's breathing deep, either from being frightened or from her own nerves, Alden isn't sure.

It's not the reception she expected, even if it's exactly what she deserves for cutting off communication. "Um, I just thought..." She looks to the house and then at Evelyn, who has finally started to move toward her. "I don't know what I thought."

"Dammit," Evelyn says under her breath. "Dammit. Alden."

She takes the final two steps. "I'm sorry," she whispers.

"For?" Evelyn asks, her expression softening. She takes off her hat and lets it dangle.

"For everything. For getting shot, for leaving, for everything."

"Stop." Evelyn smiles. "Just stop." She touches Alden's shoulder softly, moves her hand from the shoulder to the arm and then down to the brace. "I'm so sorry. You could have died."

"It was my job," Alden whispers, her voice cracking.

"Not anymore," Evelyn says flatly.

Alden raises her eyebrows and tilts her head. "You're firing me for saving your life?"

"As a matter of fact, yes." She moves around Alden, heading down the beach.

Is she joking? Alden very nearly lost her life protecting this woman, and now she's going to fire her? "What the hell?"

"If you're going to be my girlfriend, I'm not going to have you—"

"Whoa, whoa, wait a second." Alden hurries and grabs her arm, stopping her in her tracks. "Your girlfriend?"

"Yes."

Alden's heart, for the first time in so very long, springs to life, beating harder and faster than it ever has before. "You want me to be your girlfriend?"

Evelyn's eyes fill with happiness, and she looks down, wiggling her toes in the sand. "Well, yeah," she says softly before looking up. "If you're going to go to these events on my arm, you can't be protecting me, too."

"That makes sense," Alden replies, smiling. "Is this really what you want?"

"I've never stopped wanting it, wanting you." She closes her eyes and takes a deep breath. "You scared me, Alden Ryan."

"I know, and I'm sorry. I shouldn't have snuck up on you."

A small smile comes to Evelyn's lips when she says, "No, not now. I mean, I thought…" She pauses, her eyes glassy. "There was so much blood. And you…Then you didn't come back to me. And I didn't know…"

"Don't," Alden urges as she places her free hand on Evelyn's face. "I'm here now. I'm right here." She leans in and nudges Evelyn's nose with hers, and their lips meet. The kiss is soft at first, but it intensifies, and the passion is ready to explode. Alden has been thinking of nothing but kissing her for the past two weeks. She breaks the kiss, pulling away breathless to say, "It's your turn to take care of me now."

Evelyn smiles, and a laugh escapes as she leans into Alden's kiss again. "It sure is," she says between kisses. "It sure is."

The ache Alden has been living with, right where her heart resides, subsides. There were times in her life when she assumed she would never settle down; she would never find the right person to spend her days and nights with. She is hard to handle and even harder to get to know. But something about Evelyn made her realize how very wrong she was. She is okay with being wrong this time. Because this time, she finally has what her life has been missing. She has love, and she has hope. And she is never going to let any of it go.

EPILOGUE

It's been a little over a year since Alden lost her job as Evelyn Glass's bodyguard. Her life looks entirely different now that danger isn't lurking around every corner. In fact, the most dangerous thing she does now is helping Evelyn run lines. Which is way more fun when there's a kissing scene, but Alden helps with whatever scene Evelyn wants.

"It's been six months since that entire ordeal." Evelyn's voice is low, her tone determined. She plays this part perfectly. And it is so fun to watch her slip into character.

"Oh, I know." Alden sits back in the leather wing-back chair and looks up from the tattered script at Evelyn sitting across from her. "The best of my life."

"So far."

"Well, yeah, so far."

"And Peter? How's he doing?"

Alden licks her lips. Evelyn's so intense when they do this scene, and it turns Alden on more than she ever thought was possible. "Peter is fine."

"Maybe you need to remember to keep your affairs in order before you decide to butt into people's lives."

"Wait," Alden says as she lifts her hand. "Isn't the line supposed to be, 'Maybe you should keep your own life in order before you butt into other people's'?" She's been over this scene with Evelyn a couple times now, and for some reason, Evelyn keeps forgetting her line. "Yes. I'm right."

Evelyn groans. "God, I can't seem to get that stupid line right." She stands and grabs the script and reads the lines again. She whispers to herself as she walks away. She pauses, then holds the script out. "Okay, let's run it again."

"Wouldn't you rather practice the first kiss scene again?" Alden raises her eyebrows and grins as she takes the script. She thumbs through to three pages later. "I feel like this scene alone will melt televisions."

"Alden?" Evelyn's voice is soft, and Alden can sense something bothering her. "Are you worried about this? What this kiss could do… to us?"

"What are you talking about? We'll be fine. Look at what we've gone through." She waves, batting the idea of intense jealousy away. Yes, she's going to be jealous Evelyn is sharing an intimate moment with someone else onscreen, but that's what she signed up for when she decided to quit her job and shack up with an actress.

"This is going to blow up. You know that, right?" Evelyn places a hand over her chest. "This has been what the fans have wanted for over a year. This kiss. Right here. And I need to know you're going to be okay with it. Because this is going to change my life."

Alden laughs. "You're joking, right?"

"Oh my God," Evelyn says, followed by an exasperated sigh. She stalks to the windows in the conference room of the mansion. "You are not hearing me."

"Evelyn, listen to me." Alden moves to where she is standing. "You are the only one who is nervous about this. And I don't know why."

"Because I just…" She turns, her eyes sad. "I don't ever want to lose you. Especially because of something like this."

"Oh my goodness," Alden says with a small laugh. "You are not going to lose me. I am not going anywhere."

"You promise?"

"I promise. In fact…" She tosses the script on a chair. She reaches into her pocket, gathers every ounce of courage she has, and kneels. "Would my asking you to marry me calm your fears?"

Evelyn's hand is over her mouth. "Alden…"

She's been going over this exact moment in her head for the past four months. She doesn't want to ever let Evelyn go. She wants to hold on to her for as long as humanly possible. She breathes in. "I have loved you since the moment I helped you with your zipper. You are the only person my heart beats for, ever since you asked me to stay with you that night. You are my everything, and I promise, my heart will be yours forever." Alden holds up her grandmother's ring, acquired during a recent, secret trip to the lake. "Evelyn Glass, will you marry me?"

Evelyn drops to her knees and throws her arms around Alden's neck, smashing their lips together. She kisses her deeply, then pulls away and whispers, "Yes, yes, yes, I will marry you," before she starts kissing her again.

After they find their way to the floor, and this simple line runthrough becomes one of the best impromptu sexual encounters Alden's ever had, she slips the ring onto Evelyn's finger. "I am so excited to spend forever with you."

"I love you so much."

"I love you, too." And she does. Alden loves Evelyn with her entire being, more than she ever thought possible. She never would have thought a relationship like theirs could work. The trust and respect they have for each other bowls her over. Evelyn makes her so very happy. She has thanked her lucky stars every day that she decided to take this job, too, even though she was so reluctant at first. If she hadn't taken the job, she would have never figured out how to trust again, how to love again, and most importantly, how to heal. And all of it has been worth it.

Guarding Evelyn was worth everything.

About the Author

Erin Zak grew up on the Western Slope of Colorado in a town with a population of 2,500, a solitary Subway, and one stoplight. She started writing at a young age and has always had a very active imagination. Erin later transplanted to Indiana where she attended college, started writing a book, and had dreams of one day actually finding the courage to try to get it published.

Erin now resides in Florida, away from the snow and cold, near the Gulf Coast with her family. She enjoys the sun, sand, writing, and spoiling her cocker spaniel, Hanna. When she's not writing, she's obsessively collecting Star Wars memorabilia, planning the next trip to Disney World, or whipping up something delicious to eat in the kitchen.

Books Available from Bold Strokes Books

Coming to Life on South High by Lee Patton. Twenty-one-year-old gay virgin Gabe Rafferty's first adult decade unfolds as an unpredictable journey into sex, love, and livelihood. (978-1-63555-906-4)

Fleur d'Lies by MJ Williamz. For rookie cop DJ Sander, being true to what you believe is the only way to live…and one way to die. (978-1-63555-854-8)

Guarding Evelyn by Erin Zak. Can TV actress Evelyn Glass prove her love for Alden Ryan means more to her than fame before it's too late? (978-1-63555-841-8)

Love's Falling Star by B.D. Grayson. For country music megastar Lochlan Paige, can love conquer her fear of losing the one thing she's worked so hard to protect? (978-1-63555-873-9)

Love's Truth by C.A. Popovich. Can Lynette and Barb make love work when unhealed wounds of betrayed trust and a secret could change everything? (978-1-63555-755-8)

Next Exit Home by Dena Blake. Home may be where the heart is, but for Harper Sims and Addison Foster, is the journey back worth the pain? (978-1-63555-727-5)

Not Broken by Lyn Hemphill. Falling in love is hard enough—even more so for Rose who's carrying her ex's baby. (978-1-63555-869-2)

The Noble and the Nightingale by Barbara Ann Wright. Two women on opposite sides of empires at war risk all for a chance at love. (978-1-63555-812-8)

What a Tangled Web by Melissa Brayden. Clementine Monroe has the chance to buy the café she's managed for years, but Madison LeGrange swoops in and buys it first. Now Clementine is forced to work for the enemy and ignore her former crush. (978-1-63555-749-7)

A Far Better Thing by JD Wilburn. When needs of her family and wants of her heart clash, Cass Halliburton is faced with the ultimate sacrifice. (978-1-63555-834-0)

Body Language by Renee Roman. When Mika offers to provide Jen erotic tutoring, will sex drive them into a deeper relationship or tear them apart? (978-1-63555-800-5)

Carrie and Hope by Joy Argento. For Carrie and Hope loss brings them together but secrets and fear may tear them apart. (978-1-63555-827-2)

Death's Prelude by David S. Pederson. In this prequel to the Detective Heath Barrington Mystery series, Heath discovers that first love changes you forever and drives you to become the person you're destined to be. (978-1-63555-786-2)

Ice Queen by Gun Brooke. School counselor Aislin Kennedy wants to help standoffish CEO Susanna Durr and her troubled teenage daughter become closer—even if it means risking her own heart in the process. (978-1-63555-721-3)

Masquerade by Anne Shade. In 1925 Harlem, New York, a notorious gangster sets her sights on seducing Celine, and new lovers Dinah and Celine are forced to risk their hearts, and lives, for love. (978-1-63555-831-9)

Royal Family by Jenny Frame. Loss has defined both Clay's and Katya's lives, but guarding their hearts may prove to be the biggest heartbreak of all. (978-1-63555-745-9)

Share the Moon by Toni Logan. Three best friends, an inherited vineyard and a resident ghost come together for fun, romance and a touch of magic. (978-1-63555-844-9)

Spirit of the Law by Carsen Taite. Attorney Owen Lassiter will do almost anything to put a murderer behind bars, but can she get past her reluctance to rely on unconventional help from the alluring Summer Byrne and keep from falling in love in the process? (978-1-63555-766-4)

The Devil Incarnate by Ali Vali. Cain Casey has so much to live for, but enemies who lurk in the shadows threaten to unravel it all. (978-1-63555-534-9)

His Brother's Viscount by Stephanie Lake. Hector Somerville wants to rekindle his illicit love affair with Viscount Wentworth, but he must overcome one problem: Wentworth still loves Hector's brother. (978-1-63555-805-0)

Journey to Cash by Ashley Bartlett. Cash Braddock thought everything was great, but it looks like her history is about to become her right now. Which is a real bummer. (978-1-63555-464-9)

Liberty Bay by Karis Walsh. Wren Lindley's life is mired in tradition and untouched by trends until social media star Gina Strickland introduces an irresistible electricity into her off-the-grid world. (978-1-63555-816-6)

Scent by Kris Bryant. Nico Marshall has been burned by women in the past wanting her for her money. This time, she's determined to win Sophia Sweet over with her charm. (978-1-63555-780-0)

Shadows of Steel by Suzie Clarke. As their worlds collide and their choices come back to haunt them, Rachel and Claire must figure out how to stay together and most of all, stay alive. (978-1-63555-810-4)

The Clinch by Nicole Disney. Eden Bauer overcame a difficult past to become a world champion mixed martial artist, but now rising star and dreamy bad girl Brooklyn Shaw is a threat both to Eden's title and her heart. (978-1-63555-820-3)

The Last First Kiss by Julie Cannon. Kelly Newsome is so ready for a tropical island vacation, but she never expects to meet the woman who could give her her last first kiss. (978-1-63555-768-8)

The Mandolin Lunch by Missouri Vaun. Despite their immediate attraction, everything about Garet Allen says short-term, and Tess Hill refuses to consider anything less than forever. (978-1-63555-566-0)

Thor: Daughter of Asgard by Genevieve McCluer. When Hannah Olsen finds out she's the reincarnation of Thor, she's thrown into a world of magic and intrigue, unexpected attraction, and a mystery she's got to unravel. (978-1-63555-814-2)

Veterinary Technician by Nancy Wheelton. When a stable of horses is threatened Val and Ronnie must work together against the odds to save them, and maybe even themselves along the way. (978-1-63555-839-5)

16 Steps to Forever by Georgia Beers. Can Brooke Sullivan and Macy Carr find themselves by finding each other? (978-1-63555-762-6)

All I Want for Christmas by Georgia Beers, Maggie Cummings, Fiona Riley. The Christmas season sparks passion and love in these stories by award winning authors Georgia Beers, Maggie Cummings, and Fiona Riley. (978-1-63555-764-0)

From the Woods by Charlotte Greene. When Fiona goes backpacking in a protected wilderness, the last thing she expects is to be fighting for her life. (978-1-63555-793-0)

Heart of the Storm by Nicole Stiling. For Juliet Mitchell and Sienna Bennett a forbidden attraction definitely isn't worth upending the life they've worked so hard for. Is it? (978-1-63555-789-3)

If You Dare by Sandy Lowe. For Lauren West and Emma Prescott, following their passions is easy. Following their hearts, though? That's almost impossible. (978-1-63555-654-4)

Love Changes Everything by Jaime Maddox. For Samantha Brooks and Kirby Fielding, no matter how careful their plans, love will change everything. (978-1-63555-835-7)

Not This Time by MA Binfield. Flung back into each other's lives, can former bandmates Sophia and Madison have a second chance at romance? (978-1-63555-798-5)

The Dubious Gift of Dragon Blood by J. Marshall Freeman. One day Crispin is a lonely high school student—the next he is fighting a war in a land ruled by dragons, his otherworldly boyfriend at his side. (978-1-63555-725-1)

The Found Jar by Jaycie Morrison. Fear keeps Emily Harris trapped in her emotionally vacant life; can she find the courage to let Beck Reynolds guide her toward love? (978-1-63555-825-8)

Aurora by Emma L McGeown. After a traumatic accident, Elena Ricci is stricken with amnesia leaving her with no recollection of the last eight years, including her wife and son. (978-1-63555-824-1)

Avenging Avery by Sheri Lewis Wohl. Revenge against a vengeful vampire unites Isa Meyer and Jeni Denton, but it's love that heals them. (978-1-63555-622-3)

Bulletproof by Maggie Cummings. For Dylan Prescott and Briana Logan, the complicated NYC criminal justice system doesn't leave room for love, but where the heart is concerned, no one is bulletproof. (978-1-63555-771-8)

Her Lady to Love by Jane Walsh. A shy wallflower joins forces with the most popular woman in Regency London on a quest to catch a husband, only to discover a wild passion for each other that far eclipses their interest for the Marriage Mart. (978-1-63555-809-8)

No Regrets by Joy Argento. For Jodi and Beth, the possibility of losing their future will force them to decide what is really important. (978-1-63555-751-0)

The Holiday Treatment by Elle Spencer. Who doesn't want a gay Christmas movie? Holly Hudson asks herself that question and discovers that happy endings aren't only for the movies. (978-1-63555-660-5)

Too Good to be True by Leigh Hays. Can the promise of love survive the realities of life for Madison and Jen, or is it too good to be true? (978-1-63555-715-2)

Treacherous Seas by Radclyffe. When the choice comes down to the lives of her officers against the promise she made to her wife, Reese Conlon puts everything she cares about on the line. (978-1-63555-778-7)

Two to Tangle by Melissa Brayden. Ryan Jacks has been a player all her life, but the new chef at Tangle Valley Vineyard changes everything. If only she wasn't off the menu. (978-1-63555-747-3)

When Sparks Fly by Annie McDonald. Will the devastating incident that first brought Dr. Daniella Waveny and hockey coach Luca McCaffrey together on frozen ice now force them apart, or will their secrets and fears thaw enough for them to create sparks? (978-1-63555-782-4)